BEAR

MARKET

ROULETTE

LAURENCE ANTHONY

Black Cat Publishing LLC
Alexandria Virginia

To the brave Ukrainian fighters.

Bear Market Roulette

1

The blur of green pines with flashes of sunlight piercing through them was endless as the old Mercedes flew along the countryside road at more than a hundred and fifty kilometers an hour. The whine from the engine was becoming more pronounced even over the music from the CD player. Lev suspected it was the water pump and hoped they would make it to the refinery. Who knows how long they would have to wait for help if there was a breakdown. In more than two hours they had seen only one vehicle, a logging truck loaded with branchless pines. This was going to be a day trip from Moscow to the Achinsk refinery, but Kemerovo Airport had closed for reasons unknown. Novosibirsk turned out to be the next closest airport for the Gulfstream. Hundreds of kilometers now had to be covered in the 16-year-old Benz. It was that or a 21-year-old Lada.

"Arkadiy, this music is making me sleepy."

"You don't like Rachmaninoff?"

"I have something much better."

An edgy guitar rift started to blast out of the surround sound speakers followed by a methodic drumbeat. It set the tone for Brian Johnson's "Ohhh..."

Arkadiy started to sing For Those About to Rock word for word without the hint of an accent.

Lev's head turned to the back seat in shock. He always pictured his boss as a buttoned-down reserve guy. Sure, there had been some crazy drunken nights here and there but nothing of the rock star nature. Arkadiy's life had always been about work. Work, women, and the occasional vacation to a warm tropical island. At 49 he had never been married, no kids; just focused on making money and lots of it. He was part of an elite circle of extremely powerful men. Men that divided up Russia's assets through chessboard maneuvering and dodging attempts on their lives as emerging oligarchs. Oil and mining interests were the bulk of Arkadiy's multibillion-ruble fortune, but there were many investments throughout the world to insure financial stability in the event of the golden egg cracking in Russia.

Lev and Arkadiy were now singing in perfect unison at the top of their lungs as the Mercedes vibrated along at 190 kilometers per hour. In the middle of the song Arkadiy was in full air guitar mode, it was so electrifying it would have made Angus do a double take. Now with the roar of the canons firing the windows violently shook and the speakers were about to blow.

Johnson and the guys bellowed out the final word, "FIR... at that exact moment, the car blasted up into the air, the steering wheel airbag deploying instantly, as it was flipping end over end and landing on its side with a deafening thud. Glass, chrome, and bits of engine were scattered all over the road and around the car. The smell of gas and antifreeze permeated the air. Lev's ears were ringing, and blood was running into his eyes. He was coming in and out of consciousness trying to make sense of what just happened. He couldn't move his left shoulder and when he tried the pain was excruciating. The seat belt that saved his life had to be released but it wasn't going to be an easy task with his body crumpled over the release latch. He let out a guttural scream as the latch released, and his body dropped to the other side of the car. He now had glass embedded in his right shoulder.

He called out for Arkadiy. There was no response. Again, nothing.

After what seemed like hours but was just several minutes Lev kicked out the broken windshield. He rolled forward over the dashboard onto the road cutting himself more along the way. The bright side of all this he thought was that the car hadn't gone up in flames.

"Arkadiy" he called out, still nothing.

He managed to get to his feet, called for Arkadiy again and this time heard a moan. It was coming from a ditch about 15 meters behind the car. He slowly limped over; what he saw wasn't good. Arkadiy was on his back with blood oozing from the side of his mouth. His right leg was bent up behind him like something from a horror movie.

Arkadiy was trying to talk.

"Arkadiy keep your eyes open, don't talk."

"Pocket," Arkadiy was saying.

"Arkadiy, save your strength. I'll get us help."

"Pocket. Black book. Pocket."

That was his last words before the life left his eyes.

Lev reached into Arkadiy's jacket and found his phone, not much good in the wilderness. He checked the other jacket pocket and found a well-worn little black book. He put it in his pocket knowing this had to be very important if this was Arkadiy's last concern.

As Lev stood up, he saw a truck barreling down the road towards him; his knees buckled and at that moment lost consciousness.

2

"Lev, it's Tatiana. Can you hear me?"

"Lev?"

His eyes opened for a second and then slowly closed. A warmth came over his body. He was bathed in sunshine with Tatiana and her long blonde hair next to him as they lay on the grassy bank of a creek. He felt happy and free of worry. They were both eleven and enjoying the summer off from school. Tatiana lived in the house next to theirs since the age of four. It was quite rural with plenty of space and places to explore. They had been classmates from the beginning often mistaken as brother and sister.

"Come on Lev let's finish making that raft so we can float down the creek. It will be fun; we can go fishing." The best raft came together in an hour with a couple of small fallen trees and branches laying around. They were off. Dreams were great that way: think it and it happens.

There they were in the sunshine one minute and disappearing under the shade of weeping willows the next. Drifting past fields of sheep and then into open water with fishing rods magically in their hands.

"Lev, I caught something. It's big, help me pull it in."

The sky started getting cloudy: small waves started to swell on the lake they were on now.

"Tatiana, we need to get back to shore."

Rain started to pelt down; the waves were about to knock them off the raft. Bolts of lightning crackled all around them.

"Lev, can you hear me?"

Lev opened his eyes to see Tatiana inches from his face. The part of his forehead not covered with the bandage was beaded with sweat.

"Tatiana?" he gasped.

"Lev, you're okay. You were in a bad accident, you're safe in the hospital now."

"What happened?"

"Don't worry about that now. Just rest."

"Arkadiy's dead, isn't he?" he whispered.

"Yes, but let's worry about you now. I'm here to make sure you get better."

Lev felt himself starting to fade again.

Tatiana was by his side; they were on a bus. This time they were 17 and Tatiana was going to check out a university in St. Petersburg. She was interested in economics, something that made his eyes glaze over when she talked about it. They were sitting there quietly thinking about how their lives were changing. They were going to be apart for the first time since early childhood.

The silence was broken with Tatiana asking him his thoughts.

"Tatiana, I'm so happy for you. You have the pick of the best business schools. I know you're going to kill it."

"Lev, I wish you'd come with me. You're my best friend. I can't imagine not seeing you every day."

The bus pulled up in front of a diner; more people got on. Lev started thinking about some of the school trips they had taken together and the friends they made over the years. He was smiling for Tatiana, but deep down was filled with sadness. He knew he would just be a distraction in her new life and didn't want to get in the way. There was also a selfish side to him that made him feel guilty. He was going to travel, see the world, spend time with guys his age and get into the usual trouble.

"Tatiana, we'll have the summers together when you're home. We'll talk on the phone all the time. You'll have lots of fun with your new classmates."

"I know but it won't be the same without you."

"You can call me anytime day or night."

"Even when you're in London or Paris or Amsterdam?"

Lev's eyes opened again. He wasn't in Amsterdam. He was staring up at the hospital ceiling. This time he was all alone. It was dark outside, but the room was lit up by the light of a TV high up on the wall in front of him. His eyes were just starting to focus, he could make out the news anchors on the screen. Their lips were moving but there wasn't any sound. The next image that appeared was a funeral procession and the name of his friend and boss at the bottom of the screen. As the hearse slowly advanced the president appeared in the background dressed in a black overcoat surrounded by big burly bodyguards.

Grief poured over him, he turned away from the screen. He should be there, he thought. Arkadiy's only surviving family was a sister that he no longer was in touch with. They had a falling out after his mother passed. Arkadiy had many friends but family members were scarce; there may have been a cousin here or there. It was probably his assistant Katerina that handled all the funeral arrangements. She was actually more than an assistant; she was his right hand.

His mind started to race. What happened. He remembered driving down the country road on the way to the refinery. The front of the car exploding and flying through the air like he was on an amusement park ride that had gone awry. His pulse was getting quicker, and the doctor came in. He had so many questions but the doctor's only concern was

10

calming him down. After seeing him inject a clear fluid into his IV line his eyelids got heavier and heavier. He was out.

Thursday, October 3, 1996

Lev awoke to the sound of the doctor's voice. He seemed irritated.

"He's had serious trauma to the head. He's not up to your questions. I must insist you let him rest."

"It will only take a minute, came a stern reply."

"My name is Alexander Litskevich; this is my partner Igor Dryga. We are from the FSB. We need to ask you some questions."

"Okay," came a groggy reply.

"Where were you going?" Alexander asked taking the lead.

"The refinery in Achinsk."

"For what purpose?"

"I'm not exactly sure. It had something to do with the books being off. Arkadiy was going to see the CFO at the refinery."

"Why were you on that road near Topki?"

"We were going to fly into Kemerovo but were told a couple of hours before we left that it was closed. We flew into Novosibirsk instead."

"Who knew about your trip?"

"Other than the pilot just Arkadiy's assistant, Katerina."

11

"What is Katerina's last name?" Dryga asked.

"I don't remember now. What happened? Why did the car blow up like that?"

"We don't have all the details yet. We are investigating but think it was an RPG. We know Mr. Abramov had many enemies but do you know of any threats lately?" Litskevich asked.

"Nothing comes to mind but I'm not thinking too clearly. My head really hurts. I want to help but I need to sleep. Can you send in the doctor? My head is really hurting."

"Certainly. We'll be back in a couple of days. Please try and think of any details that might help. Hopefully, we'll have more information about this for you."

A minute later the doctor returned. Relief was instant as more magic formula was injected into the IV line. Back to la la land.

"Lev, where are you?" his mother was asking in his very real dream.

"I'm in London. I took the Eurostar from Paris two days ago. It's great here. I've seen Big Ben, Buckingham Palace, and the Tower of London already."

"Make sure you take lots of pictures. Your papa and I want to see all the places you've gone."

"Tomorrow me and Mikheil are going to the Greenwich Observatory. You know how he is into the stars and all that."

"Are you two getting along okay now?"

"Yes, you know we're like brothers. We get over our rows quickly."

"Mama, I can't talk too much longer, my phone card is running…" The phone connection died.

Mikheil and Lev were now getting off the tube at Tottenham Court Road station to do some boozing in Soho. They were drinking beer after beer and more beer like water and not getting drunk. Dancing with women that looked like supermodels. Bouncing from clubs to bars and bars to clubs. In real life they'd be in the bed he was in now. They stumbled down the stairs of a bar with no sign outside. Two beautiful women descended the steps moments earlier and they were in hot pursuit. When they got to the bottom of the stairs the women had vanished. It was all huge guys drinking shots of vodka and slamming the empty glasses down on the bar.

"Let's go," Lev said and quickly changed his mind when he heard two of the guys at the bar speaking Russian.

"Where are you guys from?" he asked in Russian.

The bigger of the two said Voronezh, the other Moscow.

"Where are you guys from?"

"Just outside of Nizhny. I'm Lev and this is Mikheil."

The big guy was Dmitri and the Muscovite introduced himself as Arkadiy.

This dream is so real Lev was thinking, it's almost like I'm awake, and just like that, he was. A panic set in, had his parents been contacted. Then a sinking feeling remembering his father was dead. He was killed at work in a freak accident at the shipbuilding yard. A huge piece of metal slipped from a crane and crushed him. His mother never got over it, they had been joined at the hip. There's never a day when she doesn't talk about him. The saying only the good die young was often used when talking about his father. It happened four years ago but it seems like yesterday.

He buzzed the nurse; she was there in seconds.

13

"Has someone contacted my mother?"

"Don't worry, your sister has."

"My sister?"

The nurse looked back at him with an equally puzzled look.

"Tatiana."

"Oh yes, my sister."

It clicked; the hospital probably only allowed family members to visit.

"Thank you."

The nurse left wondering about the extent of his head injury.

Friday, October 4, 1996

Tatiana was waiting at the Molodezhnaya train station to pick up Lev's mother, Olena, and take her to see her son. It had been four years since she had seen her last. It was at Iosif's, Lev's father's funeral. She felt guilty it had been so long but knew Olena would understand. Life was always hectic; she barely saw her own mother. Her mother would ask her when she was coming home after every phone call, she would just say soon to minimize her mother's disappointment.

Olena was a husky, energetic 62-year-old woman. She moved with speed and purpose; age wasn't slowing her down. Tatiana spotted her emerging from the station steps with four large shopping bags, and purse tucked under her right arm. Her colored brown hair looked a little windswept but it had been a four-plus hour trip.

Tatiana waved. "Olena, how are you?"

"I've been worried sick. How are you, Tatiana?"

"I've been worried too but I'm fine. Lev seems to be getting better each day."

"That's wonderful news. What happened? I know his boss was killed; it was all over the news."

"I really don't have any details, it's like it's a big secret. There is speculation in the papers of anything from a personal vendetta to a terrorist attack. Let me take a couple of those bags. My car is on the next street over." The two bags she carried weighed a ton.

"Olena, what is in these: gold bars?"

"I've cooked up a few of Lev's favorite dishes, you know how he loves my perogies. There is some sausages and pigs in a blanket. A couple of books and magazines as well as some candies. Do you mind if we stop, I'd like to pick up a box of chocolates?"

"Olena, I think you've done enough. Come on, let's go see your son."

The women chatted nonstop all the way to the hospital. There wasn't nearly enough time to make up for the four years.

"Lev, how are you?" Olena choked out as tears welled up in her eyes.

She was normally a strong, stoic woman but the sight of her son's puffy bruised face with his head wrapped in a thick white bandage caught her off guard. She put down her bags and gave her son a tender hug afraid of damaging him further.

"Mama, I'm fine don't worry. I'm so glad you're here."

Tatiana stood in the doorway taking it all in with tears in her eyes. She couldn't imagine losing her lifelong friend. The person she could talk to about almost anything. There were times they'd talk on the phone all night and laugh when the sun came peering through their windows at dawn.

"How was your trip?"

"You know, the usual. The trains never run on time. Son, what happened?"

"I have no idea. We were driving through the countryside and bam, the car flew into the air end over end, coming down like it had fallen from the sky. Arkadiy was in the back and wasn't wearing his seatbelt. He got thrown from the car." Lev started to choke up, his mother wrapped him in her arms.

"I'm so glad you're all right. I brought you your favorite – perogies. You look too skinny. We need to fatten you up."

Tatiana came in from the doorway and sat on the edge of the bed taking Lev's hand. "You don't have any more news on what happened?"

"No, I'm still waiting on hearing back from the FSB guys."

"How is your head feeling today?"

"It still hurts, little has changed there."

"Do you have any idea how long they're going to keep you in here? I want you back home so I can take care of you." Olena inquired.

"They're going to run a few more tests and figure a few more days."

"How did you end up here if the accident happened near Novosibirsk?"

"Apparently, a log truck driver picked me up off the road and took me to the local hospital. The police showed up a couple of hours later to ask me questions, but I was out of it. They found Arkadiy's assistant, Katerina, and she made arrangements with the refinery to airlift me here."

"I'm going to talk to the doctor and make sure they are doing everything they can. Do you need anything?"

"Ask him for something for my head. I'm so glad I have my mama looking out for me."

"Tatiana, are my things in that closet?"

"Let me check. Yes, there's a bag with your clothes, there's blood all over them. It's gross."

"Are my jeans there?"

"Yes."

"Check the pockets and see if there's a black book and a phone."

"Yes, the black book is here. Is this where all the girlfriend info is? You must be feeling better."

"It was Arkadiy's. It was the last thing on his mind before he died. It must be very important. Please take it and put it in a safe place. Is the phone there?"

"No, I'll check with the nurse before I leave."

"There should be two phones, mine and Arkadiy's."

Olena, returned saying the doctor would be in shortly to check on him, he had the okay to eat all the perogies and sausages he wanted.

Lev smiled realizing the good fortune he had having these two ladies looking after him.

"Mama, you're too much. Where are you staying tonight?"

"Tatiana is letting me stay with her for a few days so I can come and see you every day and then take you home with me."

Tatiana returned to tell Lev that they had a phone, his watch, and wallet locked up and that they needed to leave, doctor's orders.

Lev thought there should be two phones but then remembered his was probably still in the car.

Hugs and kisses were exchanged, and they were off.

Lev sat in bed watching an old movie on TV. His mind wasn't really focused. If you asked him what the movie was about, he couldn't have told you but that changed when the news came on next. He reached for the remote turning up the sound.

"More bloody violence on the streets of Moscow today." The news anchor began with. "Outspoken businessman Konstantin Berezovsky was badly burned, his driver killed in an assassination attempt. Berezovsky, who has been critical of Kremlin policy, was rushed to a nearby hospital where he remains in intensive care in the burn unit."

The next story came on about more violence and left Lev deep in thought. It was like the wild, wild east out there; he had fallen victim to it too. There had been numerous assassinations of very rich and powerful men, all in the name of money and power. He was wondering if it was time to get out of Dodge. He was also amused by the brief coverage about such a horrific story. He knew Konstantin Berezovsky from the Presidential Club. The Presidential Club was Arkadiy's favorite place to hold court. It wasn't uncommon for hundred-million-ruble deals to be made under the influence of hundred-year-old cognac. He often saw Konstantin surrounded by a large group of comrades while he loudly boasted support for Yeltsin and his free market policies. He was what Americans would refer to as a "mover and shaker." It was becoming more difficult to concentrate. Lev's headache was getting worse but despite that, he slipped into a deep sleep.

Litskevich and Dryga were at the crash scene in the middle of nowhere. The middle of nowhere was 25 kilometers west of Topki, midway between Novosibirsk and Kemerovo. The local police filed a detailed report that the two of them had thoroughly examined. There weren't any skid marks, just an indication of an explosion then gouges in the pavement that lasted only a few meters just before the car came to rest. The Mercedes had sailed more than 300 meters in the air. This car was moving at a very high rate of speed according to these findings.

Right away Litskevich suspected a rocket-propelled grenade aka an RPG. This was derived from his years of combat experience in various USSR hotspots with the latest being Chechnya. It was going to make the investigation difficult. If it was an RPG, it could have been fired from 100 meters away or as much as almost a kilometer. His gut was telling him this wasn't going to be an open-and-shut case. This had been a well thought out calculated attack.

He shared his suspicions with Dryga; the two of them split up and started searching the surrounding dense woods weaving around the pines, oaks, and maples. It was the beginning of fall and leaves were just beginning to settle on the forest floor. A couple of weeks from now they would carpet the area in yellow and red concealing potential evidence. Both men knew this would be a needle in a haystack. The launch point could have been a range of seven or eight football pitches in area coupled with the fact they were probably dealing with smart criminals unlikely to leave behind incriminating evidence. The walk in the woods would be a nice break from the office.

They walked the woods for a couple of hours, but nothing was found. It was time to move on and examine the Mercedes. The mangled mess of a car had been flat bedded to the local police station with instructions to keep it securely locked away. Litskevich left a couple of logs on the side of the road about 900 meters apart to make it easier to locate the area in need of further examination.

The pair were greeted at the Topki police station by a young cadet officer who quickly returned with his superior, Major Petrov. Gregory Petrov was a man that obviously enjoyed the good life. He had a large gut in the frame of a bear. His 55-year-old wrinkled face had a bulbous, red-veined nose supported by a thick gray walrus mustache. His dyed jet-black hair seemed out of place.

"Gentlemen, I've been expecting you," he bellowed.

"Major, it's a pleasure. We've read the report and have many questions. Is there somewhere we can talk?"

"This way."

Litskevich expressed his theory, and the Major instantly concurred. He too had combat experience in Afghanistan. Gregory had actually been involved in an RPG attack when a UAZ-469 he'd been riding in was struck. He'd been thrown clear but had a constant reminder of that day with a ringing in his ears. The driver of the vehicle, a man the Major completed basic training with, wasn't so lucky. He was killed instantly and the pieces of him were shipped home in a box. The nightmares of that day were lessening but were still happening.

"I instructed my men to place all the pieces of the car that were on the road to be bagged as evidence. There are a few bags that I'll give you before you leave."

"Can you give us any details that weren't in the report? Any suspicious people in the area? Have any interviews been done at local hotels? Passenger checks from flights at Kemerovo or Novosibirsk?" Dryga asked.

"I'm sorry gentlemen, but no. We are a very small, short-staffed unit. We just don't have the time for that here."

"Would you be able to deploy some of your men to the woods to search for evidence? It's a large area that needs to be covered. My partner has marked the side of the road."

"Again, we are too short-staffed, but I could spare a couple of cadets and request the training academy send over a dozen or so recruits."

"That would be very helpful."

"I'll personally oversee the search and report back to you."

"Thank you, Major."

"Please follow me. You can see the car or what's left of it."

The black Benz was a mess. It was amazing that the driver had walked out of it. His saving grace was probably the airbag that now lay crumpled hanging from the steering wheel. Litskevich was immediately drawn to the front of the car, most of it gone. Many of the larger pieces sitting five meters away.

"Dryga, my suspicions have been confirmed. It was an RPG, no doubt."

"Our job has just gotten tougher."

"It has."

The pair continued their examination of the wreck. Dryga managed to force the least damaged back door open and crawled around the car's interior. At 44 he wasn't as agile as he once was. It was scattered with papers, a couple of empty coffee cups, CDs, Arkadiy's briefcase, and a phone. Anything that appeared important was bagged up to be looked at later.

The Major met them at the front desk holding the remnants of what had been swept up at the scene.

"Could you please send us pictures of the wreckage and keep us updated about anything found in the woods?"

"Definitely gentlemen. Please feel free to call me with any questions you might have."

Saturday, October 5, 1996

"Doctor, I need you immediately," the nurse called out.

They were hovering over Lev. The doctor peeling back Lev's eyelids and shining a light into his pupils called out to the orderlies.

"Get him down to x-ray. We need a full skull workup."

Lev was whisked from the room. One pupil was about 5 mm, the other 2 mm. Dr. Kuznetsov knew what was really needed, a CT scan but budget cuts at the hospital made that impossible. His years of experience told him he was likely dealing with a subdural hematoma.

"Nurse, call for the neurosurgeon on duty and have the O.R. readied."

The call to Tatiana came about 10:00 that evening.

"Your brother, Lev was rushed in for emergency surgery but he's doing okay."

"What happened, what's wrong?"

"He had some bleeding from the brain, the doctor performed surgery to relieve the pressure but he's doing fine and resting now."

Olena cried out in the background, "Tatiana, what's wrong? Did something happen to Lev?"

"Lev's okay. Give me a minute and I'll explain."

"Nurse, when can we see him?"

"He is resting now, why don't you call us in the morning, we'll have a better idea then?"

"You're sure he's okay?"

"Yes, we believe the issue was caught early enough, but I'll have you speak with the doctor tomorrow, he can explain everything in detail."

"Thank you, I'll call back in the morning."

With that Tatiana hung up and gave Olena the details of the call.

Lev woke up in a different room with gadgets all around him. The first thing he noticed was the relief of pain in his head. It was still there but in another form. What had been pressure was now a sharper pain on one side. He had new bandages that were considerably thicker. What had happened. When was he moved. He let out a moan and the nurse was right there.

"You're all right, Lev. You were taken into surgery last night. You had some bleeding in your brain, but Dr. Kuznetsov caught it early, you're going to be fine. How are you feeling?"

"My head is hurting."

"That's to be expected. Let me get the doctor, we'll get you something for the pain."

The doctor ordered a magical elixir, Demerol, and Lev fell into another dream-filled sleep.

"Another shot for my friends."

"Lev that girl over there has been looking at you since we got here, go over there."

"Which one?"

"The brunette."

"The one with the huge tits?"

"Ya, get over there."

"I'll be back after I complete my mission."

"Bring back only the pretty prisoners."

Super Freak was Lev's song of the month, and it was cranking, he was tearing up the dance floor with the brunette. She already had her arms around his neck pulling him in against her big chest. Lev looked over toward Mikheil with a shit-eating grin.

"Ingrid, this is Mikheil, and this is Hans and Daan our newfound friends."

"What are your friends' names?"

The blonde's name was Ava, and her attractive friends were Marie and Helena. Amsterdam was like heaven with all the beautiful girls. They were everywhere.

Before Lev could call for another shot Mikheil was dancing with Ava. Human League was blasting from the speakers. Seconds later Lev found himself in an alley looking for a place to piss. Every time he pulled it out people would appear from nowhere and he had to look for another spot. This occurred a few times until he stumbled into another bar. He looked around finding Mikheil and Ava kissing at a booth in the corner.

"Where's Ingrid?"

"She is freshening up for you loverboy," Ava said over the music.

This time it was You Light Up My Life. Even in his dream, Lev was wondering where the fuck did that come from.

Ingrid slipped into the booth next to Lev, Mikheil and Ava were going at it even more passionately. Ingrid looked even hotter and now with a vanilla, jasmine, musky scent about her. He slid back the hair from her neck giving it a gentle kiss. She turned to him, and soft kisses and tongues were exchanged. Within minutes Ingrid had taken him by the hand, and they were leaving Mikheil and Ava behind.

24

"Where are we going?"

"Shut up prisoner," Ingrid said with a provocative smile.

Next thing he knew Ingrid was providing him with a stunning view as they ascended a steep narrow staircase to her third floor apartment. She was wearing a plaid schoolgirl skirt that revealed sheer white panties underneath. The apartment was small with the bed being the centerpiece. The scent of her perfume floated in the air.

"Get on the bed prisoner," she ordered.

He complied.

She took off her white blouse revealing the most perfect pair of tits he had ever seen. She pulled off his pants, they came off like a silk tablecloth in a magic act. Her short skirt slid to the floor; the sexy panties came next. His shirt was pulled over his head and she was riding his hard cock like she was on a bucking bronco.

"Lev, Lev."

Oh, shit mama was his very first thought. The bulge in the covers was his next.

"How are you feeling? You had us so scared."

"I feel better mama. You don't have to worry; they're taking good care of me here."

"The doctor said they had to drill holes into your skull. Are you sure you're okay?"

"Yes, the pain medication has me feeling like superman."

It was Tatiana's turn to give Lev a hug. She whispered in his ear, "it looks like you were having sweet dreams, big boy."

Sunday, October 6, 1996

"Litskevich, Dryga. Get in here," shouted their commanding officer, Kovalyov, from across the vast office usually filled with FSB officers and their assistants. It was Sunday, sometimes a day of rest.

"Yes, chief."

"We've received a call from Katerina Grigoryev, Arkadiy Abramov's assistant. She went to Arkadiy's primary residence in Kuntsevo just now and found it trashed."

"I guess it can't wait until tomorrow. We'll head right over and have her meet us there. We wanted to speak with her anyway. We'll be killing two birds."

Litskevich pulled up to an aging stone house discreetly tucked away in a scenic wooded setting. The only thing that seemed out of place was the barbed wire-topped chain-link fence.

"It's beautiful here if it wasn't for the prison-like fence," remarked Dryga from the passenger seat.

Katerina pulled up behind them in a new shiny white 5 series BMW. "I was waiting down the street for you. Which one of you is Litskevich?" She said in a manner that gave the impression she didn't suffer fools.

"That's me, Miss Grigoryev."

"You must be Lieutenant Dryga. Follow me."

She walked like a model with her long dark hair swaying back and forth, wearing super tight Jordache jeans and an equally tight T-shirt. Casual and well put together would be an understatement. "I'll open the gate for you."

She opened the gate got into the officer's car and headed down the driveway; it was about a 75-meter drive. The front upper portion of the house jutted out over the driveway giving the front entrance protection from the elements.

"When did you arrive here this morning?" Litskevich inquired.

"It was a little more than an hour ago, about 9:00."

"Did you hear any noises in the house?"

"No, nothing."

"Please wait in the car until we come for you."

The pair approached the front door, that was slightly ajar with their weapons drawn. Katerina thought to herself they've done this many times before. Dryga made a quick dart to the right, his gun straight out in front of him. Litskevich followed behind making a mirror move but to the left. They cleared the first floor after several minutes. It took a little longer than normal due to the fact the house had been thoroughly trashed. Not only was furniture overturned, books and papers strewn all around, but many walls had massive holes in them. It must have been a team of somebodies not finding what they were looking for. They proceeded upstairs to find a similar scene. Mattresses were thrown from beds and cut open. Holes were in many of the upstairs walls too, the master suite the biggest in the huge walk-in closet. They both agreed that was probably where a safe had been. At least two men the size of bears would be needed if they had some kind of dolly with them.

Dryga escorted Katerina into the front vestibule where tears began welling up in her eyes. The emotions of the week coupled with the destruction of her boss's beautiful home were becoming too much. Dryga fetched an overturned chair placing it beside Katerina. She slowly sat down while dabbing at her eyes attempting to keep her massacre intact.

"Miss Grigoryev, do you have any idea who would do this? What they would be looking for?"

"Your guess is as good as mine. Arkadiy, as you know, was very powerful and that alone brought many dangers. Every time you turn on the news a rich man is being killed. I don't need to tell you guys that."

"Were there any recent threats? Any suspicious people seen around him?"

"Not really. Nothing that comes to mind. You might want to talk to Lev. Oh, poor Lev."

"Yes, we've spoken to Lev."

"How is he? I hope he's doing better than the day of the accident."

"He was in rough shape when we saw him and had a horrible spell. He was rushed into emergency surgery yesterday."

With that news, Katerina lost it. The mascara was beyond repair now.

"But he seems to be doing well now," Dryga quickly interjected. "His mother and sister have visited; he apparently is well enough to answer some questions for us."

"Please tell him I'll be along to visit him very soon. I've tried to see him, but the hospital hasn't permitted it since I'm not family. Talking about family, Lev doesn't have a sister."

"Tatiana?" Dryga asked.

"Tatiana is a longtime friend. Tatiana Belov, I spoke to her a few days ago. Ahh, I see the family policy," Katerina said now with a bit of a smile.

"I'll definitely pass along your well wishes. Can you please lead us around the house and assist us by telling us if there are any notable things missing and then we can get you on your way?"

The only things that Katerina could point out were Arkadiy's collection of valuable watches, there were about a dozen of them. Rolexes, Cartiers, and a favorite of his a Breguet. There were a few prized masterpieces that hung on various walls tied to the alarm system which had been masterfully disarmed. The Melting Watches by Dali that hung in the living room, a Jackson Pollock in the main hall, and a Water Lilies brushed by Monet in the bedroom all had fallen victim to these thugs. Katerina also noticed a prized jeweled Faberge egg, something she admired for years was gone. Litskevich was very pleased to hear this, although it saddened him to think about the potential damage to these treasures. Cases were often solved when criminals get too anxious to unload their loot.

As they were about to exit the house Katerina noticed all the file drawers laying on the floor of Arkadiy's office.

"It looks like they've taken all of his personal files too."

3

Lev's eyes shifted from the TV to the doorway to see a welcomed sight, Tatiana.

"I see you have new digs, one without all of the wires, tubes, and gadgets. How are you feeling?"

"Tatiana, it's so nice to see you. I'm feeling so much better. The doctor said I should be out of here in a couple of days. They just want to run a couple of tests first."

"That's great news. Your mama is dying to get you home and stuff you with perogies and sausages."

"Is my mama coming?"

"She's down in the gift shop buying up their entire supply of chocolate for you."

"She's too much. I'm going to gain 10 kilos a week under her care."

"Before your mama gets here, I wanted to talk to you about something. It's probably nothing but it's raising my cat senses. I noticed two big men parked on the street across from my apartment yesterday and saw one of them outside the gift shop just now. I'm sure it's just a coincidence."

Lev thought for a second before he spoke, "Tatiana, have you looked in the black book that I gave you?"

"Yes, the front part was full of names and phone numbers, the back names of businesses and banks with what appears to be account numbers. I have it in my purse."

She handed it to Lev; he went straight to the back of the book.

"These are, I mean were, Arkadiy's businesses in several countries and these do look like bank accounts."

At that moment Lev's mother came in with a bag full of candy and chocolate bars. There were several of each, Mishka Kosolapy, Rot Front, Kara-Kum, and his childhood favorite Rulada. Scattered among these were Zolotoy Klyuchiks. He would have been in heaven, but his mind was now on more serious matters. Olena placed the bag on the bed and gave her son a big hug, this time she wasn't worried about hurting him.

"Mama, how is Tatiana treating you?"

"We're having a lot of fun but we're still worried about you. You've given us quite a scare."

"I was just telling Tatiana I should be out of here in a couple of days. You have nothing to worry about."

Lev was starting to worry though; he knew that things could go south very quickly. He knew the power vacuum Arkadiy's death created would endanger anyone with access to Arkadiy's assets. He didn't want to worry his mother by rushing them out but knew each minute was of utmost importance. The next five minutes seemed like five hours as niceties were exchanged. When Olena excused herself to use the bathroom he waved Tatiana over to him. He sternly whispered to her.

"Get my mother to Mikheil's place and you need to leave the country now. I'll have the nurse give you my stuff. There are credit cards in my wallet. Get as much cash from them as possible, do the same with yours then throw them away. You must destroy anything that can lead them to you."

"Who are the *them*?"

"I don't know, that's the scary thing. The *them* are probably the same people that killed Arkadiy."

Lev buzzed for the nurse.

"Can you please give my things to my sister? She'll need them to take care of some things."

While they were waiting for the nurse to return Lev called his mother over giving her a big hug. He told her he loved her. Olena was happy by this but also a little concerned. There was an intensity that set off alarm bells.

Lev said to his mother while embracing her, "Mama, you need to listen to Tatiana. She's going to take you to Mikheil's."

"Why? What's going on?"

"Mama, please listen to me. I don't know. I want to make sure you're safe. I'm probably being paranoid but please just trust me."

"Lev, are you in danger?"

"No, mama, I'll make a couple of calls. I'll be fine."

The nurse returned with Lev's bag that contained his wallet, keys, and Arkadiy's phone.

"You need to leave now. Just go straight to Mikheil's."

"We need to go back to my place get a few things and get Jacques. What am I going to do about Jacques?"

Jacques was Tatiana's black cat, also known as Squeaky. She took him in after he turned up at the front door of her apartment every day after school for three weeks. He got the nickname Squeaky because of his vocalness. She treated Squeaky like a child, the two of them were inseparable.

"Okay, get Jacques and a few things but do it quickly. Mikheil loves cats, I'm sure he'll take good care of your buddy. You really need to make yourself a ghost. Let's meet in London two weeks from today at the clock in Waterloo Station at noon. I love you."

Olena gave her son a big bear hug. "I love you."

The two of them cautiously left the hospital from a side exit.

"Tatiana, I'm very worried. What's going to happen to Lev?" Olena said as they approach Tatiana's apartment.

"Don't worry, Lev is well connected. He'll be fine."

"Oh no! Tatiana cried out as she opened the door. Jacques, Jacques."

The apartment had been ransacked. All her books and drawers were laying on the floor with the contents strewn everywhere. Olena stood in the doorway with her hand on her mouth, speechless.

"Olena, quickly get your stuff together. Just take what you really need. Jacques, Jacques!" she was crying out in a panic.

She looked under the bed; he wasn't there. He emerged from the closet in the bedroom squeaking with a scared look.

"Squeaky, Squeaky it's okay," she cried as she squeezed him so tightly almost crushing him.

Within minutes the trio were at the back door of the apartment.

"Wait here I'll go get the car."

They quickly piled in and were off. Jacques in the back seat emitting worried cries. He knew something was wrong.

"Olena, can you let Jacques out of the carrier? He really hates that thing."

As Olena leaned back to free Squeaky she was jerked over against Tatiana's shoulder.

"I think we're being followed. Olena, put on your seatbelt."

Olena complied and Tatiana floored the British racing green Mini Cooper. They were in her neighborhood; she knew it like the back of her hand. Flying down Moscow streets three times over the speed limit and then she slammed on the brakes to take corners at speeds that would roll most cars. Jacques was hunkered down on the floor of the backseat. He was quiet now as was Olena, both afraid of distracting a highly stressed Tatiana. The silver Mercedes was still about 100 meters behind them, but Tatiana was slowly getting the advantage. After another five kilometers and with the help of a slow-moving Moscow bus, they finally lost the pursuers. The panic had left Olena's face and was replaced with relief. Even Jacques seemed to sense that the danger had subsided for now.

About 45 minutes later they arrived at Mikheil's place. He was outside waiting for them; Lev had filled him in.

"Shit," he slammed the cards down on the table, walked over to the bar, and poured himself a triple from a half-finished bottle of Stoli. Beside the bottle was one of the night's other losing poker players sleeping with his head on the bar. He swallowed back the drink thinking to himself I got to get home. His shift with Litskevich started in three hours.

Litskevich pulled up in front of Dryga's drab, concrete apartment.

"Rough night?"

"Let's not talk about it. Coffee."

"Yes, sir comrade Dryga."

Over coffee, Litskevich laid out their day. First on the agenda was to look into the whereabouts of a hedge fund attorney. The details were sketchy at best as to why they were tracking him down. His years of experience told him it wasn't always a good idea to ask a lot of questions. He had spent more than his fair share of time organizing the evidence room and other menial tasks. Next, they would contact the hospital and follow up with Arkadiy's employee, Lev.

So far, the investigation was going painfully slow. Major Petrov's team in Topki found nothing in the woods, not a trace of evidence. The changing of the season was putting an end to any chance there. Other agents from their office had been dispatched to find any leads at area hotels and airports. Nothing. Feelers were put out all over Moscow for any activity involving the works of art, watches, and Faberge egg, but nothing on that front either.

"He's releasing himself?" Dryga repeated back to the nurse on duty.

"Is he still there?"

"Yes, the doctor is checking on him before he leaves."

"Thank you, nurse."

Dryga quickly made another phone call. "You have to get over there now, he's about to leave the hospital."

"We're just around the corner, we were just grabbing some lunch. We'll grab him now," came the reply.

Lev stepped out of the front door of the hospital with the bag of bloody clothes in his hand and started to look around for Elisei. Where is he, he thought getting frustrated with the delay.

Thirty seconds later a gray van pulled up, and two huge burly men emerged. One of them had a Taser in his hand that was utilized on their approach. The back doors of the van opened at the same moment Lev's muscles froze and his knees buckled. The burly men caught him under his arms and hurled him like a rag doll into the back along with Lev's bag. A third burly guy jammed his knee against Lev's throat. The guy with the Taser jumped into the back, slammed the doors, and started duct-taping Lev's mouth. He was then rolled over and his hands were taped behind his back, the feet were next. As the van sped off a black hood was draped over his head. Panic streamed through his body. Fucking Elisei, he thought.

Litskevich, a former KGB intelligence officer, thought he knew his partner, Igor, well. That couldn't be further from the truth. Igor had a dark past that involved illegal gambling, smuggling, and blackmail. The once very fit bodybuilder had often used his badge instead of his fists to obtain outcomes in his favor. Initially, these activities were done to cover family obligations. His mother had been chronically ill for years, then there was a wife and four kids to clothe and feed. Not one to manage stress well vodka became a close friend, but this close friend didn't help the decision-making process at the poker table. When the occasional score would pay off some crumbs would be thrown to the family he now abandoned. Things were getting worse by the day, and it wasn't just his beer gut and receding hairline. The gambling debts were mounting, his badge would go only so far in saving his ass. To say he was desperate was an understatement.

Elisei waited in his car for about five minutes. His blood pressure increased with each minute that passed, and he was well aware of the lurking dangers. Finally, he found a parking spot for the car and went to the hospital reception.

"Our records show Mr. Drozdov is on the fourth floor," an attractive young receptionist told him.

Elisei proceeded to the fourth floor where he was told Lev had just left about ten minutes ago.

"Shit!"

The nurse gave him a shocked look. He wasn't there. Elisei bolted back down to the front door with hopes Lev had just gone to use the bathroom or something like that. No such luck.

He called their work colleague, Katerina, "have you heard from Lev?"

"No, weren't you going to pick him up about noon?"

"I'm here at the hospital, he's not. This is not good."

"I'll call Vlad from security and get him on it. Elisei, meet me at the office."

Lev's side was still burning on the spot where the Taser made contact, but he couldn't rub it to relieve the pain, his hands were still taped behind his back. He could sense they were moving at a fairly high rate of speed; he assumed they were on a highway. The smooth ride lasted, as best as Lev could judge, about half an hour before they made some turns on a somewhat bumpier road. The final minute of the journey had him jostled about on a pothole-filled gravel road. The van came to a stop, the driver got out and he heard the clutter of a large garage door opening. He quickly became aware of his two travel companions that were in the back with him as they opened the van doors and dragged him along a concrete floor. The smell in the air was of heated metal and oil. Was he in some kind of metal or machine shop he thought.

His companions stopped; he heard clunking and then a high-pitched squeal as the door to his new home was opening. He was dragged a few more meters, his feet pulled over a small step. The air was several degrees cooler here. He was dropped on a metal floor, and the tape that bound his hands and feet was removed. The hood over his head remained as the door quickly closed behind his exiting kidnappers. He quickly removed the hood; it took several seconds for his eyes to adjust to his new surroundings. It was a brightly lit metal storage container with a cot, blanket, large plastic bucket, and a few one-liter bottles of water. He was fortunately provided with a roll of toilet paper also. The first thought that went through his mind was that he wasn't the first tenant of these luxury digs. His second thought was how the fuck am I going to get out of here.

He sat on the cot and drank one of the bottles of water. He could hear the three talking outside the container. The next sound was the garage door closing, the van being fired up and tires on gravel gradually fading as the goons left.

Lev's mind started racing, and beads of sweat broke out on his forehead and under his arms. If they killed Arkadiy and kidnapped him, who was next. His concern went straight to Tatiana. He hoped she was out of Moscow with his mother in tow and had made it safely to Mikheil's. He walked over to the container door and drop-kicked it as hard as he could. Again and again, nothing. He threw the weight of his body against it; it didn't budge an inch.

Litskevich knocked rapidly on Lev's apartment door on Marshala Koneva Street in the trendy Shchukino District. It wasn't as posh as Arkadiy's Kuntsevo neighborhood but was considered upscale. Arkadiy took care of his close employees and liked them nearby in case he needed them for unexpected duties. Lev lived only about 10 minutes north of Arkadiy.

Litskevich was surprised, unlike his partner, that Lev wasn't there. Where would someone that had head surgery just several days ago go.

"We should go to the hospital and see who came to pick him up," Dryga added, trying to appear puzzled.

"Let's stop for lunch on the way, I'm starved."

The fourth floor nurse that had fielded Elisei's queries described Elisei to the investigators. She also told them about the visit by his mother and sister. The pair decided to head back to the office and get some information about Lev's relatives.

As they got off the elevator they were greeted by their boss, "Litskevich, Dryga, come in here."

They dreaded that greeting as it usually meant another assignment on an already full docket.

"What have you found out about that attorney, Sergei Magnitsky?" Major Kovalyov asked.

"Not very much. We've been all over the place on the Abramov case. We just got back from the hospital where his driver had been. He's not there anymore and we're trying to track him down."

"I want you to prioritize finding the attorney, start at his office. His home address is also in here," he said handing Dryga a file folder.

"It must be important; it seems this is coming down from the top. I'm being kept in the dark as to why we need to locate him. I want immediate updates."

"Yes, sir," the pair said in unison as they exited.

"It must be very important if it takes precedent over an RPG attack," Litskevich remarked to Dryga as they got back on the elevator.

They arrived at the law offices of Firestone Duncan, located in a recently built stainless steel and glass skyscraper. They took the super-fast elevator to the 32nd floor to be told that there wasn't an attorney named Magnitsky.

"There's no Sergei Magnitsky here, Miss?" Dryga questioned.

"Oh, Sergei Magnitsky is a tax advisor here. The receptionist informed them. Let me try his office."

When there was no reply she ushered them to his boss's office; it was vast with a stunning view of Moscow. "Hello, I am Sergei's boss and the owner, Jamison Firestone. Please call me Jamie."

"We haven't heard from Sergei in several days. Has someone from our office called you gentlemen about this?" Jamie cautiously asked.

"No, we are here on a confidential matter," Litskevich added, trying to sound like he knew why they were there flashing his credentials while staring at Jamie's yellow power tie.

"When was the last time he was in the office?"

"I'm not exactly sure, but roughly about four days ago. I was going to call his wife, Natasha, but things kept cropping up around here."

"Would you please try her now?"

"Certainly. Miss Malkin, would you please get ahold of Sergei's wife, Natasha for me?"

"Yes, Mr. Firestone," came the reply over the speakerphone.

Jamie fielded questions about the nature of Sergei's work until Miss Malkin interrupted them with news there was no answer. This was actually a relief to Jamie. Litskevich and Dryga left with assurances they would be given any news that came in about the auditor's whereabouts.

Jamison's act was very convincing. He knew damn well why they were there; he was on the next plane to London Heathrow.

Tuesday, October 8, 1996

Tatiana was safe and thinking of Lev. She had no idea that her worse dreams had just come true, and Lev was held prisoner by dangerous thugs. After a restless night Mikheil was taking her from his home in Kubinka to Smolensk, this would get her close to the border of Belarus.

Like Lev, she had no idea who was behind Arkadiy's death or who was in the silver Mercedes. What she did know was they were looking for the black book or some kind of record of Arkadiy's treasure. Why else would her apartment have been destroyed.

Mikheil was worried sick by Tatiana's and Olena's encounter with the silver Benz. "Are you okay?" Mikheil had left Tatiana alone with her thoughts for the past 15 kilometers.

"Yes, I'm very worried about Lev. I'm trying to make sense of this. I'm trying to lay out a game plan in my head. I need to find out who trashed my place and was following us."

"I'll check on Lev as soon as I get home. He told me yesterday that he contacted Katerina, Arkadiy's assistant, she was making sure he was being looked after." He really hoped Katerina was on it, things were getting crazy. Lev also told Mikheil about the black book, but other than Tatiana no one else knew of its existence.

"I'll get you to the bus station in Smolensk, from there you shouldn't have a problem getting to Minsk. You have your passport?"

Tatiana nodded and tapped on her purse which also contained about 20,000 rubles that she had pulled together from Mikheil, her bank account, and a couple of Lev's credit cards. This would get her a couple of flights; a week of hotel stays, and the basics covered for a little while. She was curious about what the black book would reveal.

"Where are you going from Minsk?"

"Zurich. I recognized a couple of the banks in the black book." Her work as an economist at Menatep was starting to pay dividends. "I'll start there and then go to London. The plan is to meet up with Lev there in two weeks."

The thought of her job popped into her mind. "Shit, I haven't called into work. They're going to fire me. I'm just going to tell them I have a family emergency I'm dealing with."

"It's really not a lie. Just think of what you've gone through with Lev and his poor mother. It's been a week of insanity. Your best friend and his boss are blown up, Lev has brain surgery, your apartment has been trashed, and you and Olena chased through the streets of Moscow. If all that isn't an emergency, I don't know what is."

"I am really worried about Lev. Anyone can get to him at the hospital."

"I wasn't going to tell you this because I didn't want you to worry but Lev was checking himself out of the hospital yesterday. He called Katerina, she sent someone over to pick him up. You know Katerina is on top of things. She's been looking out for Lev this entire time. He's in good hands."

"Mikheil, why didn't you tell me this earlier? No more secrets. This news puts me at ease in one way but now I'm worried he might not have been well enough to leave."

"The doctor checked on him before he left and gave him his home phone number if he has any problems. I'm sure he's going to be all right."

The highway in the wilderness was becoming one with the occasional building on its sides. They were approaching Smolensk; Tatiana was beginning to realize that she would be on her own. For the past week, she had Olena's ear and Mikheil to rely on but now she was going off the grid.

They reached the city bus station. Mikheil opened the trunk and pulled out a medium-sized suitcase and Tatiana's carry-on bag. They both hugged with tears in their eyes. The tears were a combination of worry and sadness, but both were determined to keep it together.

"I'll call you when I get to Minsk," Tatiana said as she turned toward the bus station entrance.

Mikheil just waved. A lump in his throat prevented words from coming out. He was having a tough time with all this, and he hadn't gone through a fraction of what Tatiana had.

After half an hour on the road, the drone of the bus was making Tatiana's eyes heavy. She drifted off a couple of times only to wake with a sudden jolt as her body fell forward. She leaned against the window, any adrenaline that was there had left her body. She was out.

"Passports please, passports!"

Tatiana bolted upright in her seat, wiping away a bit of drool from the side of her mouth. The adrenaline was back and streaming through her entire body. Calm down she said to herself a few times. You're just going to Minsk to visit a friend.

The border guard dressed in a gray uniform with the new Belarus flag emblazoned on both shoulders had the passport of the man in front of her in his hand. "Purpose of your trip?" he said in a no-nonsense tone.

"I am going to visit my mother," was the reply. His passport was returned.

"Miss, your passport."

Tatiana handed it to her left in a smooth steady motion slowly bringing her hand back to her lap trying to remain as relaxed as possible. She wasn't shaking on the outside but her whole body felt like it was going to go into convulsions on the inside.

"Thank you," he said as the passport was handed back without any query.

She slowly exhaled through her nose keeping her eyes straight ahead. She deliberately tried not to think about this crossing so as not to freak herself out. This was probably the most stressful part of her journey. If the FSB had been looking for her this is where it would all go down.

The bus pulled out of the compact border inspection station at Zaol'sha without incident. In a little more than two hours she'd be in Minsk. Despite her efforts to remain awake a good part of the journey was spent comatose.

Lev awoke from a shallow sleep to the sound of the squeaky container door. He bolted upright and considered charging the door until he saw the hooded bear men blocking the light in its opening. The first guy filled the door frame, the second guy was back up. There was no way he could make it past one of them on a good day let alone both in his present condition. The first bear man dropped a McDonald's bag of food on the floor and said they'd be back soon. It contained a bottle of water and three blini rolls that were filled with cottage cheese, raisins, and dried apricot. They vanished in less than two minutes. It was then he realized just how hungry he was and pondered how long he'd been locked up.

He heard murmured talking with bursts of laughter, then the sound of a vehicle on the gravel outside. The garage door must have been open. The engine of the vehicle died, two doors slammed, and the laughter abruptly halted. There was more murmured talk, the container door swung open.

A medium-sized man, also with a hood over his head and wearing a black Members Only jacket, entered the container with the bear men behind him. The last man in closing the door behind him. The container seemed quite small at this moment. The Members Only guy stood over Lev while he sat on the cot.
"Are they treating you well?" was his opening question.

Lev just shrugged. "Why am I here?"

"To answer my questions. What is your name?"

"Lev."

"Lev what?" came a stern reply.

"Who are you? What do you want from me?"

"Again, you are here to answer my questions. It will benefit you greatly if you do. First off, I know who you are, Lev Drozdov. Your mother's name is Olena, you have a *sister* named Tatiana. You are from Nizhny, and you worked for the now-deceased Arkadiy Abramov."

Lev just sat there silently with even more questions bouncing around in his head. One thought was relief that the men were wearing hoods. It indicated they didn't want to be recognized and was a sign he might make it out of this alive. Were these the men responsible for Arkadiy's death, extremely likely. Would they harm Tatiana and his mother, also very likely. The strategy he came up with was to drag this out as long as possible. He knew the wheels would be set in motion, and Vlad and his guys would be searching for him. It would also get Tatiana further away from this mess.

"Why were you going Achinsk?" asked Members Only guy.

"I'm not going to answer any of your questions."

"Well, maybe not today but you will."

The three thugs left; Lev sat there wondering what was next. They didn't go through all this trouble to walk away empty-handed. He heard some shuffling going on outside the container and then loud music blasted into the container. Familiar fiddle music started to play. The Devil Went Down to Georgia filled the air. What the fuck is going on, are they having a hoedown. It wasn't a hoedown it was a mindfuck beatdown. This went on and on and on and on. It was on a never-ending loop. Sleep was impossible. He ripped off bits of his T-shirt to make earplugs but that didn't help. It was loud and wouldn't stop. Lev was kicking at the door and ramming the cot against it, nothing.

He laid down on the cot with his fingers in his ears and trained his mind on thoughts of pleasant times. There was the time when he and Mikheil journeyed up to St. Petersburg to visit Tatiana at school. They started doing shots of vodka with her friends Marina and Lily before they went out for dinner. Dinner that evening consisted of pirozhki grabbed from a street vendor as they exited the Gostiny Dvor metro. The plan was to hit student bars, cheap dives up and down Lomonsova and Dumskaya streets. Loud DJ or live music usually blared out of their open doors inviting drunken students inside.

It was strange times for Lev and Tatiana. Both were moving on in life, not always in the same direction. Tatiana never spoke to him about boys and his exploits were never shared either. They had teased each other about crushes they'd had but that was the extent of it. There were times in their early teens when there had been awkward moments, but their level of friendship would have made it seem unnatural to act on these desires.

It quickly became clear that Marina had taken a liking to Mikheil and was hanging from his arm. Lily, a foreign exchange student from London, was showing her interest in Lev. In near-perfect Russian, she told him about her family that was of Russian descent and living in Chelsea. Her father thought it would be a good idea to study abroad in Russia to stay in touch with her heritage. Lev picked up on her privileged upbringing despite Lily's attempts to downplay it.

"Let's dance," Lev said taking Lily and Tatiana by the hands and pushing through the crowd to join Mikheil and Marina. He needed to lighten up the mood; he didn't want to have Tatiana feel left out.

It was a great night with them drinking liters of beer and shots of fuzzy navels in between. The fuzzy navel shots were not Lev's or Mikheil's idea. They staggered crisscrossing the busy streets grabbing more street food as the drunken munchies set in and the number of new bars to visit diminished. The evening drew to a close with them all piling into a taxi and the driver repeatedly yelling there wasn't enough room for all of them in his car. Eventually, he gave up knowing he wasn't going to be able to reason with these drunks. With four of them squished into the back seat, they made it back to the dorm. Mikheil and Marina crashed on one bed and Tatiana, Lev, and Lily in the other. Events like this took place every few months when Tatiana started school but lessened as she got deeper into her studies. By Tatiana's fourth year, they had only gotten together once.

Lev had no idea how much time had passed with his mind travel. This music was driving him to the brink now. He banged on the door a dozen times before laying back down.

"Make it stop! Make it stop! Make it stop!" he cried out at the top of his lungs.

It did. The door opened, and the meeting reconvened.

Ex-KGB officer Vlad Sokolov summoned his security team. It consisted of three colleagues from across the country, men that were in charge of securing Arkadiy's various business assets and the safety of key management personnel. Vlad had already talked to Elisei, the fourth floor nurse and the head of hospital security. The only possible lead was going to be hospital security and access to their security camera footage. It was going to take days to get word on access to that footage from the head of hospital administration and could be denied since they weren't a government agency.

Katerina contacted Major Kovalyov about Lev's disappearance early that morning and was told he would have Litskevich and Dryga on it first thing in the morning. They were out on assignment and not expected back in the office that day. He requested a recent photo of Lev and a list of friends and acquaintances that might be of assistance that she could give his investigators.

Katerina had just arrived home, kicked off her black Christian Louboutin's, and put the kettle on the stove when the phone rang. It was Mikheil.

"Hi, Katerina. How are you? Olena told me you called this morning. I just got back from dropping Tatiana off at the bus station. Do you know how our mate Lev is doing? He's not answering his phone."

"Oh, Mikheil! I should have called you yesterday but with all the craziness I forgot."

"What craziness? Is Lev, okay?"

"No. We believe he's been taken. Elisei went to pick him up at the hospital today, but he wasn't there."

"How could that have happened? You knew that he wasn't safe. How could he be taken from the hospital?"

"Mikheil, I'm so sorry but we still don't know what happened. Vlad and the security team are looking for him. I've informed the FSB, we're doing everything we can. Apparently, he left the fourth floor and hasn't been seen since. Elisei went in looking for him, but hc wasn't there."

"Katerina, have Vlad call me as soon as possible. Tatiana's apartment has been thoroughly trashed; someone is looking for something. Tatiana and Olena were also chased by a silver Benz shortly after Lev told her to go to my place. In retrospect, I should have told you about it earlier. Shit, this isn't good. Katerina, what can I do? I can be there tonight."

Mikheil knew what they were looking for and suspected Katerina knew too. She had to have known. She was Arkadiy's right-hand person and well aware of the hundreds of millions of rubles floating around out there. Playing dumb could be a lifesaver for both of them.

"Mikheil, have Tatiana call me right away. Is Lev's mother there with you?"

"Yes, she's upstairs resting now. Shit, how am I going to tell her her son that has just had brain surgery is missing. This is terrible."

"Mikheil, listen to me we have great guys looking for him. I'll call Vlad now and have him call you. Stay put with Olena."

It was 10:00 p.m. by the time the security team were all at the corporate headquarters of Abramov's empire. They had taken over the large conference room with the huge mahogany table that ran down the middle of it. Each of the men were already very busy over the past week locking down and securing parts of the Abramov empire. This consisted of organizing a brigade of armed men and the physical lockdown of sensitive documents at the various businesses. They were all a little flustered and disorganized. Arkadiy's death alone was a huge shock and there had never been any plans laid out in the event of such an attack. Katerina was unofficially in charge because of her overall knowledge of Arkadiy's affairs. Between Vlad and her they felt they were starting to get a handle on things but now with Lev's abduction, there was a brand-new battlefront.

Of the three men from the security team all of them were ex-KGB. All fought in Afghanistan except for Ivan. Ivan Breslov was the tech geek of the bunch, the youngest at 28 years old. His sole job was overseeing all video surveillance and electronic security for all of Arkadiy's businesses as well as getting the empire connected electronically. It was a world foreign to all the other guys in that room.

"Ivan, I'm putting you in charge of getting any video from the hospital. I've already talked to the head of security but that's looking like an uphill battle. We'll see if the FSB guys can help us there but don't count on it. If we need to, find the second in charge of hospital security and pay him whatever it takes to get what we need. Also, contact the security detail at Arkadiy's businesses, have them review any footage for anything out of the ordinary."

"Pavel, contact the police chief in Topki and see if he has any useful information. See if he knows any of the FSB guys that have been checking out that part of the country. With any luck, maybe one of us will know one of them."

Pavel Vasiliev was very quiet and difficult to read. He had lost his left foot and sense of humor in a military firefight. Pavel paid great attention to detail except when it came to his appearance. He looked like Jerry Garcia had defected. He was overweight with long hair and a beard. The only thing missing was the tie-dye shirt.

Dmitri Koskov, sat off in the corner awaiting his assignment. He was known for being a little high-strung. The type that would hit first and ask questions later. A hair trigger would describe his demeanor, this coupled with a 6' 5" solid frame made him extremely dangerous. He looked like he was in his mid-30s, ten years younger than his actual age. Unlike his colleagues he didn't drink or smoke; his spare time was spent in the gym and making up healthy green drinks that tasted like fermented cabbage.

"Dmitri, I need you to look into the attack on Konstantin Berezovsky. It happened about five days after Arkadiy was killed, there might be a connection. Find out which hospital he's in and see if you can get in and talk to him. Tell him we're looking for Lev. He knows Lev from the Presidential Club."

Vlad briefed the team about the conversation he had with Mikheil about Tatiana's place being destroyed and the car chasing her. He told them he'd update them after speaking with Tatiana and would make finding the silver Mercedes his priority.

Wednesday, October 9, 1996

"You can't do that you fucking idiot," came from third base at the blackjack table.

"If I want to split tens that's my fucking business," was Dryga's slurred reply.

A six landed on the first ten. "Hit it." A seven followed.

"Fuck!"

"Bust," said the brawny dealer dressed in a white tuxedo shirt and black bow tie.

A three flew from the dealer's hand covering the second ten.

"Hit me."

"22 bust," was the last words Dryga heard from the dealer as he left the table swearing. His foray into blackjack didn't fare any better than his poker career. Despite having paid down the poker debt to save his kneecaps from being cracked he was now down tens of thousands of rubles to very scary guys. As an FSB officer, he came across some of their work. They were sadistic bastards capable of unimaginable torture. Litskevich could also attest to that; they had come across a corpse that had been burned alive. The examiner later revealed to them that the victim's fingernails were all missing and he had been scalped prior to his fiery end.

Dryga ascended the basement stairs of the greasy spoon diner greeted by blinding sunlight. "This can't go on any longer," he muttered to himself as he made his way to his car. A hand grabbed his shoulder and he immediately swung catching the grabber in the jaw with a right hook. A hook from his left side hit his and his right knee hit the sidewalk. He bounced up and ran for the car. The two attackers ran to their car that was already running and a short pursuit ended with the drunken Dryga crashing his beat-up Lada into a concrete construction barrier. He was pulled out of his vehicle in a daze and thrown back over the hood. He took a punch to the face, a few in the kidneys with a reminder that he needed to come up with some cash very soon.

Litskevich's phone rang two hours before his shift was about to start.

"Alex, I need you to come and get me. I've had a bit of an accident," Dryga said slowly and deliberately trying to sound sober.

It didn't work. "Are you fucking drunk?" came the reply on the other end.

"I may have had a few."

"Where are you, you asshole?"

"Was that Igor?" Alexander's wife Nataliya asked as she walked up behind him in the kitchen wearing one of his white shirts.

The shirt was held together by two buttons making his departure that more maddening. "Yes, I have to pick him up. He's got himself into a pile of shit again."

"You don't have time for coffee and me?" she said with a wink.

He left the apartment with an audible groan.

Lev was in and out of consciousness, his head was pounding with no idea what day it was. The container stank of piss and shit and the music did not stop. The Devil Went Down to Georgia had played hundreds of times and the bright light in the container never went out; he was losing his mind. He had been there two days, but it seemed like two months. Protecting Tatiana and his mother was the end goal, but he knew others would be in mortal danger once these fuckers got what they wanted. It was obvious they had taken Arkadiy out to get control of his vast assets and once they had a taste for what was out there their hunger for more would just grow. He knew he was going to break, it was just a matter of when.

The music stopped and Members Only guy appeared staring down at him with the goons in the doorway.

"Empty the shit bucket, I'm going to puke," Members Only guy ordered.

"How is your stay so far? Are you enjoying Charlie Daniels?"

"Fuck you!"

"Look, my friend, you know we'll get what we want. We always do. You're not the first guest here. Save us some time and your sanity. I want to know why you were going to Achinsk. Who were you going to see there?"

"Why is that so important? I'm just Arkadiy's driver. You're wasting your time with me."

"Was Arkadiy's driver and will be joining him shortly if you don't answer any of my questions."

Lev could tell Members Only guy was starting to get frustrated and he was getting some satisfaction from that, but he knew things were going to heat up when with a wave of the hand one of the goons was summoned over to his cot.

"My colleague is here to give you some incentive to answer my questions." With a nod of the head, Lev was picked up off the cot and hurled against the container wall. When he hit the floor a booted foot stepped heavily on his right hand. Fuck this guy is strong Lev thought.

"Okay, okay get off my hand," Lev loudly yelled. "We were going to see the CFO; the books were off."

"What is the CFOs name? How much were the books off by?"

"I don't know. I really don't."

"Are we talking thousands? Hundreds of thousands?"

"Use your head. Do you think Arkadiy would fly out there over thousands of rubles?"

Members Only guy nodded again, and a boot ended up in Lev's stomach.

"I'll use your head as a fucking football if you talk to me like that again."

"Next question. What business did Abramov have with Berezovsky?"

"I don't know. They were friends." Lev was lying but he was now getting a clearer picture as to why he was there. Berezovsky was a mathematician who made a fortune in the automotive industry and later went into broadcasting as Russia was privatized. Arkadiy loaned or bought into some of Berezovsky's businesses but that was about all he knew. He caught wind of things here and there, but the details were closely guarded. Lev couldn't be sure, but he didn't think even Katerina knew what their dealings entailed.

"How did Abramov and Berezovsky meet?"

"I don't know. They were members of the Presidential Club."

"Who else did Arkadiy have dealings with?"

"I don't know. I haven't slept for days. You fuckers haven't helped in that department."

"I'll give you some time to think about it."

The container door closed. Silence.

Relief. Lev thought. Two minutes later The Devil Went Down to Georgia started again.

"Fuck!"

Like on the bus ride to Minsk Tatiana awoke with a startled jump and drool oozing from the side of her mouth. She wiped it away looking at her fellow passenger on her left to see if it was noticed. A friendly smile from the elderly woman next to her indicated it was. She smiled back and turned to look out of the window hoping to avoid idle chit-chat. She didn't sleep well at the hotel in Minsk; she cried and tossed and turned all night worried about Lev. She had gotten the message from Mikheil and called Vlad giving him all the information she could about the men that were following her and the silver Mercedes. Poor Lev, how much more could he take. She knew he had been taken, he didn't just wander off or go into hiding. Don't hurt him, don't hurt him. She could feel the tears coming back but she fought them off. Hold it together she told herself, it was so important now to go unnoticed.

Unlike the airport in Minsk, the Zurich airport was sleek and modern. Tatiana pulled her wheeled suitcase through the long concourse with a bag over her shoulder. She would need to do some shopping soon as she had left in such a hurry. She exited the terminal and climbed into the back of a very clean taxi that smelled of fake pine trees. It was at that moment she realized she had no idea where she was going.

"Please take me to the Marriott, city center."

"Yes, ma'am," came a reply with what sounded like a German accent.

Tatiana was zoned out; her mind was in a dozen different places. The only thing that caught her attention during the 15-minute cab ride was beautiful Irchel Park, it brought back childhood memories of her and Lev. The taxi pulled up to the main entrance of the hotel which was located under a walkway that connected two massive buildings. Panic struck her; she didn't have Swiss Francs. She explained this to the taxi driver asking him to wait. Inside the hotel, she explained her predicament to the hotel clerk who then summoned the manager. The manager was very accommodating making a loan to cover the fare with her passport held as collateral.

"I've got to get my shit together," Tatiana said out loud to herself as she walked back to the cab.

With that crisis resolved she found a nearby bank where her rubles were converted to the local currency. She also planned ahead for the next leg of her journey and got some pounds sterling. Now she could check in and call Mikheil to see if there was any news on Lev.

"Mikheil, please tell me they've found Lev," she asked with an optimistic lilt in her voice.

"No, I'm sorry."

Tatiana felt a physically sinking feeling in her stomach with that news, Mikheil could sense her pain on the other end of the line.

"I just talked to Katerina; Litskevich and Dryga, the FSB guys, they are meeting with Vlad and his team any time now. I'm sure between all of them it's just a matter of time before they find him. Hopefully, there will be some video from the hospital, with that and the description you gave of the guys and their car we'll be able to get Lev back. How are you holding up?"

"I feel sick. I've thought about coming back and seeing if there's something I can do." Tatiana thought that if she turned over the black book this would all end and they would let Lev go but turn it over to who.

"Tatiana, Lev had you leave for a reason. He told me about the plan to meet you in London. I'm sure that meeting is going to happen. Everything is being done on this end and Olena is safe with me, although she is worried about you and Lev."

"Tell Olena I'm fine and not to worry; I'll see her soon." She then thought about her own mother. It was probably best to leave her in the dark, besides she didn't have a clue as to what was happening.

"Where are you staying in Zurich?"

"I'm at the Marriott city center. I'll check back in with you later today. Hopefully, you'll have some good news."

"Let's hope. Take care of yourself."

"Thanks, Mikheil."

Litskevich and Dryga were in a good mood; they finally caught a break with two floppy disks in hand containing video footage from the hospital. One floppy showed Lev standing in front of the hospital with a bag in his hand waiting for Elisei. The other of the gray van pulling up, Lev being tased by two burly guys and hurled into the back. They were called into the office and gave Kovalyov an update on what they had. This put their boss in a good mood too, but it wasn't enough to satisfy him.

"Where are you guys on locating our tax attorney, Magnitsky?"

"We're still at a dead end there, sir," Litskevich replied.

"I'm getting a lot of pressure about finding him. I really need you guys to focus on that. There is someone very high up really pushing."

"We're on our way to meet with Abramov's security team to exchange information about the Drozdov kidnapping. We'll get back on it as soon as we're done there."

"Please get on it. The heat is becoming unbearable."

"Yes, sir."

"Unbelievable. That prick is never happy. I thought he'd be ecstatic we're making progress in this case but all he does is adds shit to our workload. He's still going on about the attorney."

"Fuck him," muttered a bruised and hungover Dryga.

"At least we'll make someone happy. I'm sure Abramov's guys will be happy with this video footage."

"Are you sure it's a good idea sharing that with them?" Dryga said apprehensively.

"Why wouldn't we share it with them? Our workload is nuts and it's more eyes looking for him."

"I don't think it's a good idea. This is an agency investigation, and these are civilians. There's a possibility they could mess things up."

"Normally I'd agree with you but we're getting a lot of pressure to find this Magnitsky guy. We can't be everywhere."

"Fine, let's just concentrate on Magnitsky, screw this case for now. It can wait."

"What the fuck are you talking about? We've just got a big break and you want to put it on the back burner. No, that's just wrong," Litskevich said raising the decibel level.

"What you're doing is just going to create more problems that we're going to have to clean up."

"I'm going to share what we have. A man's life is in danger, we'll deal with the fallout later."

Dryga stared out of the window not saying a word for the rest of the ride.

Lev had officially lost his mind and was at a point he no longer had anything to lose. He was fried, thirsty, and hungry despite the stench of his prison cell. Time was running out; it was time for action. He lay in wait. The nightmarish music didn't stop, the searing light never went out. The shit and piss-filled bucket was his only weapon, he was ready with it. He stood by the container door for hours. He drank the last of his allotted water and added the byproduct as more ammunition.

Finally, the squeak he was so patiently waiting for. Wait for the first guy to step in he thought to himself. The hooded thug stepped in and was met with a face full of piss and shit. The hood quickly came off with a simultaneous guttural yell. Lev then used the now empty bucket to drive the rim of it into the nostril of the unhooded thug driving it upward and then the bottom of the bucket into the head of his collapsing foe. The second thug caught Lev with a right to the cheek when Lev was in a downward motion with the bucket. He fell backward but quickly got back on his feet now bucketless. He charged at the bear man striking him with a right to the jaw. It had zero effect. The hooded bear man struck him with a left to the cheek followed by a quick and powerful right to his temple. He was KO'ed.

It looked like a board meeting but with the CEO of the company missing at the Abramov headquarters conference room. Gathered around the large conference table were Litskevich, Dryga, Vlad, Ivan, Pavel, Dmitri, and Katerina. She sat at the head of the table taking charge as she was used to doing. This was something none of the men in the room were comfortable with but there weren't any complaints. Katerina was very pleasing to the eye, especially today in a tight-fitting navy-blue pencil skirt and white silk blouse.

"I understand you have some promising news officers."

"Yes," Litskevich said taking the lead. "We have security footage of Lev being abducted at the hospital. The footage shows him being thrown into the back of a gray UAZ van by two big guys after they tased him. From the footage, we have grainy pictures of the two kidnappers and a partial license plate that starts with the number 515. You each have copies of the pictures in front of you."

The group took a minute studying the grainy black-and-white images before Vlad started with a series of questions. "Do you have any idea who these guys are? Who they're working for? Have you been able to locate the van? Do you have any witnesses from the hospital?"

Dryga cut him off before he could get to his next question. "We just got the security footage an hour ago and haven't had time to look into any of this yet. We thought we'd come to you guys first, and see if you could work with us. Our workload has us all over the place and we know time is of the essence."

Litskevich laughed to himself. Moments ago, his partner was dead set against working with these guys, now he's coming across like their partner in all this. He chimed in, "Vlad, have you guys been able to come up with anything?"

Katerina, Vlad, and the team had a discussion prior to the arrival of the agents about sharing what they had discovered so far. It was consensus that they would keep Tatiana's account of events secret for now. There were a few reasons for this. One, they needed to be sure they could trust the FSB and Litskevich and Dryga, all of them were very aware of the corruption that existed. Two, they wanted to see whom they were dealing with. The wild east was a complicated place with warring factions all vying for money and power. If they could narrow it down to a couple of Abramov's rivals, they could feed that info along and have the FSB do some of the dirty work. Third, Tatiana was safer the fewer people knew about her.

Katerina stood up and walked around the room giving a summary of what was done so far. Her Chanel No. 5 wafted behind her slightly distracting the men.

"Ivan has contacted the security departments of Abramov's holdings and has them combing through video footage for unusual activity. Dmitri is looking into rivals that would benefit from the power gap that's been created and Pavel has been in touch with Major Petrov in Topki. The Major hasn't been helpful at all. He just says it's under official investigation and to speak with the FSB for any updates."

"I'll talk to Major Petrov and ask him to keep your team appraised of any news," Litskevich said. "As to Vlad's questions, we will be looking at all those things, but it will take a little time. We have a number of other cases we are working on but realize how important it is to find your colleague. Vlad, we will give you updates as soon as we have them and would appreciate you doing the same, this way we won't be duplicating efforts."

"Understood lieutenant. We appreciate you taking time out of your busy day and seeing us today."

The meeting concluded with handshakes.

Tatiana was safe in Zurich making plans for the following day. She tried to sleep after checking into her hotel but just laid there; her mind was racing. She got up, entered the code into her hotel room safe, and took out the black book, making notes from its back pages. It didn't take an economist to figure out the abbreviations of the listed banks that had what looked like account numbers and PINs beneath them. SBC, Swiss Bank Corporation would be her first stop tomorrow, then CS, Credit Suisse. Lastly would be SGW, S. G. Warburg. She wondered to herself why Arkadiy had picked three of the largest and concluded that he would not be noticed as much if he went with small boutique banks.

While she was copying addresses from the phone book, she heard a loud grumble. It was her stomach saying feed me, with everything going on food hadn't entered her mind. She jumped into the shower and figured on an early dinner before calling Mikheil again for updates on poor Lev.

Tatiana forced down dinner, but it wasn't enjoyable. She knew she had to keep up her strength, food was simply just fuel. On her way back from the restaurant she stopped at a dress shop to find a conservative business outfit for her bank visits the next day. In her mind, the mid-length skirt and matching gray jacket were a costume for her new role. Black three-inch heels completed the look.

Once back in her room she put on the new outfit and did a dress rehearsal playing her part as well as that of the imaginary banker. Her goals were to get some cash to finance her travels, cover living expenses for the next few months, and to ascertain the cash balance of each account. Once in London she would set up several accounts and have the Swiss funds wired to them. Having worked in a bank she knew the importance of not setting off any alarm bells. A wrong word or misstep could cause major issues. She decided to call it a night after several run-throughs and got ahold of Mikheil. There hadn't been any progress, poor Lev was still unaccounted for.

Thursday, October 10, 1996

"Housekeeping." Knock, knock, knock. "Housekeeping."

"No thank you," Tatiana called out with a raspy morning voice, wondering where she was for a second.

She had fallen into a deep, deep sleep right after the phone call with Mikheil. I should call him now; she thought before going down for breakfast.

The phone rang and rang before a timid, grandmotherly voice answered, "hello."

"Hi, Olena, it's Tatiana. How are you?"

"I'm okay, sorry it took me so long to pick up. The only reason I did is I thought it might be you. Mikheil left early this morning. I could tell he was anxious; he went to Moscow to meet with Katerina. He was pacing around and said he had to try and do something to help."

"Is there any news?"

This question sent Olena into tears, followed by gasps of "I'm sorry, I'm sorry. No, no."

"Olena, it's going to be all right," she said encouragingly. She could tell the sobs had been building over a number of days.

"Are you all right?" Olena inquired.

"Yes, but worried sick like you. Mikheil hasn't heard anything yet?"

"No, I think he thought it best to see the security team. He wanted to get a real sense of what was happening. All he kept hearing is there wasn't any new information. He was feeling very helpless like all of us."

"How is Jacques?"

"He is good. We've become good friends. He follows me around meowing and likes to watch TV with me, but I think he really misses you. I sometimes see him looking in all the rooms like he's looking for you."

"I miss him a lot. Please give him a big hug from me and tell him I miss him."

"I will. You made it to Zurich without any problems?"

"Yes, just a bad case of nerves a few times but everything has gone smoothly so far. I'll be here until tomorrow, then on to London. Lev's plan was to meet me there in a week and a half. I can't wait to see him. I'm sure he's going to be there; he has never let me down."

"He's a good boy," Olena choked out.

"I'll let you go. Stop worrying, it's going to be all right. I'll check back with you soon." With that, she hung up the phone as she felt her own tears beginning to well.

After a good breakfast and a long, relaxing shower she put on her makeup, put her hair up in a bun, donned her business attire, and left the hotel with the attitude of a millionaire. Tatiana noticed she had received glances from a couple of men in the lobby. You own this she thought. One stop first though, I need to pick up a briefcase, partly for looks but also for practicality. She couldn't just stuff thousands of pounds into her purse.

"I need 25,000 today," Dryga said into the pay phone trying not to sound desperate.

"I can come up with 20,000 but you better have something for me."

"Always, relax. There's security footage of your gray van and two of your guys from the hospital."

"Can they make out who they are?" Members Only guy, also known as Miroslav Jablokov, asked.

"I don't think so. The images are pretty grainy, but they should still lay low. Have you gotten any information from our guy?"

"Nothing. We have a bit of a problem there."

"What kind of problem?"

"He's kind of out of it now. He's taken a blow to the head."

"I thought you guys knew what the fuck you were doing."

"Relax, I'll have your money for you. Leave the rest to us."

This better not turn into a mess Dryga thought as he hung the phone up. He already had enough mayhem going on.

Lev came to but barely. Everything around him was foggy, he was dazed. The never-ending light was still never ending but there was one bit of relief, silence. He turned his pounding head to see a couple of bottles of water that were placed just beyond his reach. He tried to get to his feet, but his body wasn't going to allow that. His mouth was so dry he could hardly swallow. He made another attempt to get to his feet but collapsed. He was now dreaming of mama; they were in the kitchen making cookies. It was Tatiana's 6th birthday, and she was coming over.

"Are they ready yet?" Lev repeatedly asked as the smell of the sweet treats permeated the house.

"Not yet, not yet," his mama said sounding mildly annoyed.

"Hi Lev," Tatiana's voice said from behind him. She never knocked; she was like family and was prone to just turn up. "What did you get me for my birthday?"

"You'll have to wait and see. Did your mama make a cake?"

"Yes, a big chocolate one with sprinkles."

"I'm bringing sugar cookies with jam on them."

"It's going to be a good party. All of our friends will be there, and my mama said she has a big surprise. My papa left an hour ago to get it."

The cookies finally came out of the oven and were plated. Iosif, Olena, Lev, and Tatiana all walked over to Tatiana's house with cookies and a present in hand. Tatiana was greeted with a big surprise; her papa had gotten a pony for the day. This was going to be a great party.

"Is this my pony?" Tatiana screamed with delight.

"Just for the day," her father quickly made clear.

"Can I ride him, please?"

"Yes, the birthday girl can have the first ride," her papa, Ilya, said as he lifted her up.

This is going to be the best party.

The party was over for Lev. He was woken up by a gray-haired, hoodless Members Only guy slapping his face, "wake up buddy."

Fuck, my head. He was trying to focus without any luck. His eyes were blurry and all he could smell is the foul breath of his capture. He quickly lost consciousness again.

Litskevich and Dryga were hot on the trail of the tax auditor Magnitsky, this was making their boss very happy. He was spotted leaving a bank in

Tsaritsyno, the neighborhood of his in-laws. They hadn't realized it until then, but they weren't the only agents looking for him. "What was up with this guy to garner so much attention?" Litskevich asked a shrugging Dryga. They sped across town to meet up with two other FSB agents, Turov and Mikheyev.

"We almost had him, but we lost him in the metro station. He got on a train as we got to the platform. We radioed for help and hope to get him at a stop further up but that's a long shot."

"Do you know why we are looking for him?" Dryga asked the agents.

"Apparently, he works for a big hedge fund and there's missing tax money, a lot of money," Turov informed them.

"What's a hedge fund?" was his next question.

"It's an investment vehicle for rich people," Mikheyev answered.

"Aren't you the smart one," his partner joked.

"There must be a massive amount of money involved. Our boss informed us he's getting a lot of heat from some people pretty high up. It's taken priority over an RPG attack on a very powerful man," said Litskevich.

"We've gotten the same sense of that," added Mikheyev.

The two teams went on their way empty-handed knowing they'd probably be seeing each other again soon.

Tatiana got out of the taxi in front of the Swiss Bank Corporation. It was a surprisingly modest white, three-story building with blue architectural accents that gave it a modern feel. She strutted toward the receptionist like a runway model asking to see someone in regard to making a large cash withdrawal. She had only sat for a minute when a middle-aged, overweight, balding gentleman came over and introduced himself.

"Hello, I'm Peter Kohl. I understand you would like to make a withdrawal. Please come with me."

Tatiana knew from her banking experience that the secretive Swiss banks conducted business using numbered accounts and in Arkadiy's case a second PIN. She also, wasn't surprised not to be asked her name, although she was prepared to introduce herself as Katerina Grigoryev.

They entered an efficient, medium-sized office adorned with family photos.

"Please have a seat. A form was slid in front of her. Please put your account number and PIN on this with the amount you wish to withdraw."

Tatiana wrote the numbers down hoping she would not start trembling as she jotted. The amount entered was 10,000, underneath she added the words pounds sterling hoping that would not create an issue. She slid the form back to Peter who looked it over and then summoned the receptionist.

"Miss Schmidt?"

In just a few seconds Miss Schmidt appeared in the doorway and walked over to Kohl's desk picking up the form.

"May I also get the current balance of the account please?"

"Certainly," Miss Schmidt said with a smile that showed off beautiful white teeth.

While waiting for what seemed like an hour the pair made small talk about the weather and other topics that wouldn't be the least bit personal. Tatiana guessed this was part of the routine of not being nosy.

Miss Schmidt returned with two stuffed manilla envelopes placing them on the desk in front of Tatiana along with a slip of paper that contained many digits. When Tatiana unfolded it and read what was there a rush of sweat broke out under both armpits. She swallowed hard, picked her briefcase up from the floor, and placed it on her lap. It was opened and the envelopes put inside along with the paper with the very large number on it. Her hand shook as she flipped down the latches. She hoped the tremor wasn't noticed.

"You don't want to count it?" Peter asked.

"No thank you," she said as she got to her feet. "Thank you for your assistance."

She walked through the office doorway hoping her knees wouldn't give out. "Goodbye, Miss Schmidt. Thank you."

"Good day."

Tatiana was in shock. She walked to a café ordering a glass of wine, her nerves needed calming.

The wine worked and she hailed a cab, popping a breath mint on the way to bank number two. This Credit Suisse branch looked like a classic grand old bank; there she repeated the rehearsed routine. The only difference with Credit Suisse is that it had a code word instead of a PIN and she withdrew 5,000 US dollars. To her shock, the account balance was a whopper but not quite as large as bank one. She considered more nerve-calming wine but decided she really needed to keep her wits about her.

Finally bank three, S. G. Warburg, the withdrawal amount was 50,000 rubles which she was going to send to Mikheil and Olena so she could take care of Lev when he finally turned up. The account balance wasn't as much as either of the other two banks but was still large enough that if divided up with all the people she knew none of them would have to work for at least the next couple of decades.

The taxi pulled up to the Marriott. When Tatiana exited, she no longer had the supermodel strut and kept her eyes focused on the ground in front of her. She pulled the security latch over on the hotel room door, dropped the briefcase, stood at the foot of the bed, and fell backward.

The adrenaline still hadn't worn off, she was wired. Now she had a very clear picture of what was going on and knew the seriousness of it all. A plan had to be formulated to safeguard the fortune that she controlled. Breathe she said to herself. Out of the corner of her eye, she saw the red light flashing on the phone. She entered the numbers to retrieve the message and heard Mikheil's voice.

"Tatiana, I just spoke with Katerina, there have been some positive developments. Please call me when you get this."

Tatiana reached for her purse and quickly pulled out a phone card connecting with Mikheil.

"Mikheil, what's going on?"

"About an hour ago Vlad received a call from Litskevich, he provided him with two possible addresses that matched the van and partial license plate number. Vlad's team split up and will call Litskevich if they come up with anything."

"Mikheil, that's great news."

"Tatiana, I have to run now but I'll call you as soon as I hear anything."

"Thank you, Mikheil," Tatiana cried into the phone receiver.

Litskevich's cell rang. "Hello, Vlad?"

"Yes, it looks like we might ha…" The phone cut out.

"Fuck, this cell service," Litskevich said with his face getting red.

The phone rang again, "yes, Vlad."

"The second address you gave me, the machine shop. We think he's here. There's a big, padlocked container in it. We're about to go in."

"No, wait. You have to hold tight we're about ten minutes away. Wait for us."

"Okay, but hurry. Please."

Vlad and Ivan were patiently waiting when they heard the sound of a car speeding up the gravel drive. It was Dmitri and Pavel; it was a relief to have backup.

Dmitri explained it couldn't be the other address. "The building looked like it had been abandoned for some time. There wasn't sign of any activity."

"I need to make a stop," Dryga said.

"It'll have to wait. These guys are about to storm this place. If they do you know the trouble that will cause us?"

Dryga clenched his jaw knowing there was going to be trouble in one form or another.

They pulled up in front of the large garage door greeting Vlad and his anxious team. Litskevich circled the building and climbed up on a dumpster to look through a dirty window about three meters from the ground to get a look at the locked container. There were empty water bottles and fast-food bags scattered around. Someone had been there recently. He elbowed the window sending shards of glass crashing to the floor. He said to the guys watching him, "you didn't see that."

He reached in, undid a latch, and swung the window inward. Litskevich was now inside making his way to a door beside the garage door to let them all in. They entered looking cautiously around before calling out to Lev. The silence was eerie.

"Lev," Vlad yelled. Nothing.

"Lev!"

Litskevich was at the container tugging on the padlock while the others checked other rooms in the shop.

Litskevich pounded on the container door calling out Lev's name. Still nothing.

Pavel come over to the container holding a hacksaw that he found on a workbench and started cutting into the padlock while the others looked on. After 15 long minutes and two replacement blades, the lock released, and the door swung open. Lev lay there unconscious on the cold container floor. Vlad pushed a couple of the guys out of the way kneeling down beside Lev and touching his neck.

"He's still alive! Call an ambulance!"

Vlad gently slapped Lev's cheek, "Lev, Lev. Can you hear me?"

Lev's eyes opened to little more than slits.

"Lev, you're going to be okay. We have help coming."

"Tatiana…"

It was Lev's last word. The ambulance was no longer necessary.

"No, no, no! Mikheil, no!"

Tatiana collapsed to the floor clutching the phone receiver against her head as a sobbing Mikheil told her the horrible news that no one wanted to hear. As soon as she hit the floor she sprang back up to her feet and ran to the bathroom throwing up her room service dinner.

"Tatiana, Tatiana!" Mikheil was starting to freak out even more.

"Tatiana!"

"I'm sorry Mikheil. What happened? Where did they find him?"

"He was being held in a shipping container that was in a machine shop. That's all the details I have for now."

"I'm feeling sick. Hold on."

She got back on the line, "how is Olena taking this?"

"I haven't told her yet. I'm still in Moscow at the headquarters with Katerina. We're all just shattered. I didn't want to tell his mother over the phone."

"Poor, poor Olena. Her only baby!"

"Mikheil, I need to lie down. Please call me if you get a chance later when you are back home."

Mikheil choked out, "I will," and hung up the phone.

Tatiana lay curled up in a fetal position crying uncontrollably.

The ambulance arrived, pronounced Lev Drozdov dead, and put his body into a bag. From the discoloration of his face and head and the fact that he'd recently had brain surgery the cause of death was pretty obvious, but the examiner would have to do an official report. The overworked crime scene guys had the machine shop roped off with yellow tape, were dusting for prints, and bagging items as evidence. Normally with everything that they had already, the hospital security footage, the van details, and all the forensic evidence solving the case should be extremely easy from this point, but Litskevich knew better. If these guys were bratva - Russian mafia - anything could happen. Cases he'd had in the past that looked like slam dunks fell apart when key pieces of evidence disappeared, or witnesses vanished, or all of the above. There were times he wondered why he stuck his neck out.

"Let's grab some dinner, we'll do the report in the morning," Dryga said as they walked to their car.

"Sounds like a plan."

Mikheil walked through the front door of his house to an open-mouthed Olena. She could tell just by looking at him things weren't right.

"Mikheil, what's wrong?" she belted out.

"Olena, sit down." He put his arm around her shoulder as they sat down on the couch. He started crying before he could say a single word, and this set Olena off.

"Please, Mikheil. No!"

"I'm so sorry, Olena. Lev has passed."

A repeated scene of disbelief played out.

"No, no Mikheil. Please tell me it's a mistake. Not my Lev."

"I'm sorry, Olena. I wish I could."

Jacques woke up from a catnap staring at his new friends both sobbing out of control in front of him. He didn't know what to do but rub his head up against Olena's leg. She didn't even notice him, her face was buried in a pillow saying no, no over and over with Mikheil's arm draped around her shoulder.

Friday, October 11, 1996

Katerina marched into VTB Bank and asked the receptionist for access to the safety deposit boxes. She was recognized instantly.

"Certainly, Miss Grigoryev."

She signaled what must have been a code for the safety deposit boxes to a manager who quickly came over and escorted Katerina downstairs to the safety deposit vault. Katerina had a clutch purse under one arm and two rolled-up canvas sacks under the other. She placed them on the table in the center of the room and joined the manager at a large box with two locks. The manager inserted one key, she the other, and the box was unlocked. The manager exited and said to get him if anything else was needed. Katerina, with some effort, pulled on the handle of the box, it was packed with various foreign currencies and gold. Lots of gold. She removed 100 Krugerrands and split them between the two sacks, not enough she thought clenching her jaw. She added 100 more to each sack and locked up the box. This morning she was getting a workout leaving the bank with more than 4 kilos in each hand.

The security team were summoned for a 10:00 morning meeting in the conference room. At 10:01 Katerina walked in with the two sacks in her hands. She emptied them onto the conference room table with a few of the shiny gold coins rolling to the floor. The eyes of the men lit up.

"Gentlemen, there is more than 8 kilos of gold here. The man or men who bring me the head of the man that killed our friend, this is your reward. Meeting adjourned."

Litskevich and Dryga had just completed their report about Lev's brutal demise and were now on their way to see Jamie Firestone.

"Are you staying out of trouble?" Litskevich asked his partner.

"Life is good. I made two weeks' pay last night and got the ex-wife off my back for a while."

"You know you're just going to give it all back. Was it poker or blackjack?"

"Blackjack, it doesn't require as much thought."

"I hope I'm not going to have to bail you out of any more jams. You should find a good woman and settle down."

"You sound like my mother."

"How is your mother?"

"Not good, but they're trying her out on some new medicine, hopefully, that will help. It better it costs a fortune."

They arrived on the 32nd floor and were greeted by the same attractive receptionist, Miss Malkin.

"We're here to see Mr. Firestone."

"I'm sorry but he's out of town."

"When will he be back?"

"I don't know. It could be several weeks. He's been working from the London office for now."

"Is Mr. Magnitsky in the office?"

"No, he's taken a leave of absence. I don't know when he'll be back."

"Okay, is Mr. Duncan available?" asked a now frustrated Litskevich.

"I'm sorry but Mr. Duncan passed several years ago."

"Thank you." And with that, they went on to meet with Sergei Magnitsky's wife, Natasha.

Tatiana was getting stir-crazy cooped up in her hotel room; she forced herself out of bed and was walking along the Limmat River toward

Schindlergut Park. The clean, cool autumn air was working. Her mind was getting clearer but that didn't mean the tears were being kept at bay. She so much wanted to call her mother and hear the comforting voice that would tell her everything would be all right but fought that temptation with all her might. She was taking enough risks talking to Mikheil and Olena and didn't want to put anyone else in danger. Besides, she knew her mother would worry endlessly. Tatiana made up her mind at that moment; she would see her mama in a few days. There was no way she could not be at Lev's funeral. She could not live with herself if she didn't say a proper goodbye to her best friend.

"Mikheil, when is Lev's funeral?" Tatiana was inquiring now back at the hotel.

"Tuesday."

"I'll be back on Monday."

"Tatiana, you can't do that," Mikheil sternly said.

"I will be there for the funeral. Lev was my best friend. I won't miss it."

"Tatiana, we have no idea who we're dealing with. These animals aren't messing around. There's no way of being safe if you don't know who they are. Katerina is making arrangements at this moment to move Olena and me."

"I hope Jacques is included in the move?"

"Definitely."

"How is Squeaky? Is he being a good boy?"

"He's the best. He's what's keeping Olena from losing her mind. She hugs him nonstop, and they sleep together. He's been a lifesaver."

"I miss my buddy so much. Tell Olena I'll see her on Monday."

"Tatiana, I wish I could convince you otherwise, but it sounds like you've made up your mind. Please reconsider. Katerina is also making arrangements to get me a new cell phone. I'll leave you the new number tomorrow. I want you to check in with me every day."

"I will. By the way, there will be a package arriving soon for you and Olena. Take care of everyone there, Mikheil."

Saturday, October 12, 1996

Armed with lined yellow legal pads, a couple of pens, a pencil, and a highlighter Tatiana hit the library on Lagerstrasse finding the finance section. It was Saturday morning and very quiet. If she thought her plan to get some cash and ascertain account balances was tricky, guess again. Tatiana was now in control of a large fortune, so large it had to be carefully managed to avoid unwanted attention. Not just the attention of Russian gangsters but tax authorities and government regulators. One bad move and the fortune could be forfeited or even worse her life could be forfeited. For now, the money was safe in Zurich, but she also knew from the black book there was more out there. She couldn't deal with that now, she had to focus on the three accounts.

Tatiana came across numerous books about the stock market, trading, economic theory, which she was well versed in, and a plethora of stuff about managing your money. The first thing that caught Tatiana's attention was a book about tax havens. These were havens for the money of smart, rich, powerful people for a reason, secrecy. If these havens could hide money from powerful governments with their economic clout, Russian gangsters shouldn't be a problem. They also came with an additional benefit, citizenship, for a nominal fee. She came across an article about a company in London that specialized in these services, Carshalton House. This company billed itself as "Worldwide Residence and Citizenship Planners." A principal of the company, Malcolm Spencer, provided the interviewer with a list of countries that had, as he described, "citizenship by investment" programs. These countries weren't only located in South America and the Caribbean but in Europe too. She noted their Harley Street, London address putting a star beside it. The citizenship aspect of this interested her greatly, after living in a country that had restricted her life and that of her parents, she could now zip off and be out of the Kremlin's reach.

Tatiana left the library for a somber task, one that brought more tears to her eyes. She needed to find a black dress for the funeral on Tuesday. In her wildest imagination, she could never have pictured this happening as young as they were. Life was so good for Lev, he was happy. He was enjoying the good life with Arkadiy and now they were both gone.

Dryga's Saturday morning was a little different, no library was involved here. He woke up with a headache beside a plump blonde woman who was snoring. It reminded him of a joke, what's the difference between a girlfriend and a wife…20 kilos. He checked his ring finger, nothing was there. Relief. He didn't want to wake the naked sleeping beauty, so he slid quietly out of bed and made some coffee. His crumpled-up pants were on the couch; he checked the pockets, but there was barely enough money for bus fare. Bits and pieces of the night started coming back to him. The blackjack table was treating him well and that's when sleeping beauty appeared, but it wasn't long until things went south. Litskevich's words hovered around in his head, "get a wife and settle down." He knew that was sound advice but for now, his goal was to get this lovely lady out of his house, then take care of some pressing business.

Saturday morning for Mikheil and Olena had them sitting at the kitchen table of their new digs with hot cups of coffee and cookies. Jacques was curled up on a living room armchair he had claimed. All of their lives had been turned upside down by recent events. Katerina set them up in a secluded cottage in the country about two hours north of Moscow in a town called Rostov. It was nice and quiet; they were on a picturesque lake, far away from people. Their first impression was this would be a safe place but that only lasted several minutes. Shortly after they arrived

Katerina had gone back to her BMW, opened the truck, and pulled out two rifles. She put the rifles on the kitchen table with two unopened boxes of bullets. Her instructions were simple, do not hesitate to use these.

"Have you ever fired a rifle?" she asked both of them.

Olena shook her head and Mikheil nodded yes.

"Mikheil, please give Olena some lessons. It's important you know how to use these. I hope you won't have to, but just in case. I wish I could have someone from the security team stay with you guys but with everything that's happening we're stretched a little thin."

To reassure Olena, Mikheil said it wouldn't be necessary. They were in a safe place, but his senses were on high alert. There was the constant fear of the unknown enemy. Katerina departed with instructions for them to check in with her a few times a day. Mikheil nodded at the phone on the kitchen wall and goodbyes exchanged.

After their coffee the pair decided to go for a hike, the fresh air was what they needed. Olena and Mikheil both shared stories about Lev and at times had to take a break and sit down when tears overcame them. Olena talked about how he was a great son that always called her to make sure she was okay. It didn't matter where he was, they talked at least every other day. Mikheil shared edited stories, some about their travels together and some about simple childhood memories. A story that put a smile on Olena's face was when he told her about Lev standing up to a playground bully for him. Lev got his ass kicked but he wasn't going to back down. He was the same way on the football pitch, fearless and the other kids were drawn to him because of that quality. At times there was silence as the two walked through the woods strewn with colorful leaves. They were both dreading the day of the funeral. It was going to be tough, but both appreciated the company of the other.

Sunday, October 13, 1996

"I told you I'm on it, you're not dealing with an idiot," Dryga yelled into the phone. "I've had someone following her since Friday and I think I've located the mother."

"Arkadiy's assistant, Katerina?"

"Yes, she was out in Rostov yesterday."

"I don't know what good locating the dead guy's mother will do."

"Lev only had two visitors when he was in the hospital, his mother and a sister who really wasn't a sister. One of them will have something that will help us."

"I hope you're right. The heat is on us now."

"Don't worry, I'm heading out there tonight. I'll be in touch."

After lying in bed until almost noon Tatiana decided enough was enough. As usual, her mind was swimming with a myriad of thoughts. She jumped in the shower and put on her makeup for the first time in days. It was her last day in Zurich, she was going to take in some of the sights. She grabbed a few tourist attraction brochures and looked them over at lunch. If she hurried, she'd catch the last cruise on Lake Zurich and hit the town of Thalwil. She chugged back the last of her orange juice, walked south to Burkliplatz, and boarded a medium-sized boat, the Linth. The sun was out, it was warm enough to shed her jacket. Sitting on the upper deck she leaned back and enjoyed the sun hitting her face. It had been a while since that last happened. When she opened her eyes, the views were magnificent, beautiful towns with church spires piercing upwards and snowcapped mountains in the background. It was easy to see what drew people to first settle here. The boat pulled up to the dock in Thalwil, what a quaint town she thought. Her first stop was a majestic church with postcard views over the lake. Small shops lined the main street, she popped into several of them. It was the perfect way to turn off her mind. The afternoon was finished off at a hotel overlooking the boat dock with a nice riesling and cheese platter. Tomorrow she'd return to reality.

Sunday for Olena consisted of too much reality. She spent much of the day on the phone with Katerina who was graciously making Lev's funeral arrangements. Although it was going to be a very small, secretive ceremony Olena wanted a nice send-off for her only child. At times it was becoming too overwhelming, she had to call Katerina back after a break here and there. She couldn't imagine having to handle this herself; she'd be eternally grateful to Katerina, who also had to take the occasional break. The guest list consisted of Olena, Mikheil, Tatiana, Katerina, and the security team. Vlad contacted several close ex-KGB friends to add to the security team. They would pair up with the existing team members and be in charge of getting the guests to the funeral home. Due to the need for weapons, there wouldn't be a church service, but there would be an abundant amount of firepower distributed discreetly around the funeral venue. Dmitri and his new partner's job was to fetch Tatiana from the airport. Vlad was dead set against this for a number of reasons. First, he pieced together that Tatiana had valuable information, otherwise, she wouldn't be on the run and flying in from Zurich. Second, it was crazy based on this to be coming in via Sheremetyevo Airport. It would involve going through Russian customs and they still didn't know whom they could trust. He had several conversations with Mikheil about this imploring him to talk her out of it. She wasn't going to listen despite the risks involved.

After an emotionally draining day, Mikheil and Olena hit the sack a couple of hours after dinner. Olena was out for the count, but Mikheil woke up after just a few hours. His mind was going nonstop, he decided to sit in bed and read for a bit. While flipping through an old National Geographic magazine that had been lying around, he heard a car engine outside. This caught his attention instantly as they were a couple of hundred meters from the road. He immediately turned off the light and felt around under the bed for the rifle. He debated waking up Olena but decided against it. Katerina's words echoed in his head, "don't hesitate to use it." He wasn't going to hesitate. He slowly and quietly opened the back door which was off the kitchen and crept out into the cool autumn air. The car engine went silent a moment before he exited the house and he saw a large figure of a man walking hunched over towards the house about 40 meters from the car. He fired once and pulled the bolt back to reload. A second shot wasn't necessary, the hunched over man quickly straightened and set a new record for the 40-meter dash. The brake lights went on, the engine fired up and the car was soon kicking up dust. He breathed a deep sigh of relief, dropped the rifle to his side, and entered the kitchen.

"Freeze!" came a ferocious deep voice.

His gun dropped to the floor; he threw his arms straight up in the air almost pissing himself.

Olena was standing two meters in front of him with the rifle pressed against her right shoulder and ready to go Rambo on his ass.

"Olena, it's me! Mikheil!"

She lowered the rifle, turned on the light, and started quizzing him. To say she was upset was an understatement. Jacques, had been woken up by all the commotion, watched all this from underneath the kitchen table, he was visibly upset. His meows distracted Olena, she leaned the rifle against the kitchen wall, scooped him up, and hugged him.

Mikheil called Vlad, who was sound asleep, and told him what had just happened. He offered to come right out but Mikheil told him everything was under control; they'd talk in the morning.

The two of them sat up for the rest of the night drinking tea. Adrenaline would make sleep impossible.

Katerina and Vlad appeared a few hours after the sun had come up. They packed up Mikheil's car and headed to the new location. Katerina and Vlad took the lead, Mikheil and Olena following.

"Shit, I forgot to call Tatiana. There's no way she can come out, it's just way too dangerous."

"Definitely," Olena chimed in.

Mikheil pulled out his cell phone, but the spotty rural reception wasn't allowing any calls to be made or received. They flashed the headlights from behind, put on the turn signal, pulled over at the first gas station they came across and Mikheil called the Marriott.

"Shit, too late!" he announced to the others. "She's checked out. She's probably on her way to the airport."

Tatiana was at the airport and was getting an eerie feeling like she was being watched. Destroyer by the Kinks played in her head, the one about paranoia. She was walking to the ticket counter when her cell phone rang. It could only be Mikheil, I better pick up she thought.

"Tatiana, where are you?"

"Hi Mikheil, I'm at the airport. I'll be seeing you soon."

"Tatiana, you can't come."

As these words were coming out of Mikheil's mouth a large man that had been looking at her quickly raised his newspaper. I'm not being paranoid.

"You're right."

"What?" Mikheil said fully expecting a fight.

"You're right. I'm out of here. Something doesn't feel right."

Keep calm, keep calm she said to herself. "Mikheil, I'm going to hang up now, but I'll call you back shortly."

With that the line went dead; a sense of dread overwhelmed Mikheil's body and then the others when he relayed what had just happened.

The man with the newspaper rose from his seat. Tatiana's heartbeat quickened. Tatiana was fortunate to be in Terminal 2, the train station was located below it. She mingled with a crowd of tourists that were gathered in a group, they sounded French. She looked around but didn't see her stalker.

"Do you have direct service to London?" she inquired at the ticket counter.

"No, you'll have to travel to Paris first, you can take the Eurostar from there."

"When is the next train?"

"Forty minutes from now."

Tatiana handed the clerk cash and a was slid a ticket under the window separating them. As she left the ticket window her stalker appeared at the entrance of the train station. She turned away and weaved through the crowd making her way to the ladies' room.

The women's bathroom was her hiding place for the next 35 heart-pounding minutes. From there she called Mikheil and left a message on his cell phone with an update on her new plans and what just transpired. She left the loo and made her way to the platform, so far so good, the coast was clear. A feeling of relief swept over Tatiana as the train pulled out of the station, but she wasn't totally at ease. Questions ran through her mind; how could someone find her. Could it just be in her head; who were they. The sums of money were huge, and she knew whomever it was would not just go away. She'd have to be on high alert from this point on but for now, the spectacular Swiss mountains would be her distraction. Like her parents, Tatiana had spent her entire life in Russia. Now here she was in Switzerland, had just been to Belarus, and was about to pass through France on her way to London. Her thoughts went back to Lev and all the postcards she received from his travels with

Mikheil and then with Arkadiy. The two of them often talked about taking trips together, but now that would never happen.

The train pulled into Nord Du Gare; Tatiana found the ticket counter for her next leg. Her request for her London ticket was met with, "that will be 465 francs." Shit, she thought, all I have is rubles, Swiss francs, and pounds.

"I don't have francs," she told him and was directed to a currency exchange booth.

After a coffee and a delicious French pastry, Tatiana scanned the station for more stalkers. The coast was once again clear, and she made her way to the platform for London. Most of that part of the journey was spent in a deep sleep and as usual waking up wiping drool from the side of her mouth, then looking around to see if anyone noticed. She was now exiting the train at Waterloo Station and thinking about finding a taxi to take her to a hotel but then she spotted it. Her heart sank, tears filled her eyes, and uncontrollable sobs began. The clock where she and Lev were to meet in just a week from now was right in front of her.

"Are you all right, Miss?" asked an elderly woman with a thick Cockney accent.

"Yes, thank you," Tatiana said as she pulled herself together and made for the exit.

4

Mikheil pulled into his driveway, and he and Olena darted in to pick up a few things before heading to their new Moscow hideout. Katerina, Vlad, and Jacques patiently waited parked in front of the house with Jacques curled comfortably on Katerina's lap. Mikheil was given instructions to make it snappy. A medium-sized package sat on Mikheil's front doorstep, he brought it in and placed it on the kitchen table. This must be the package Tatiana had mentioned, he thought. He opened it to find books, War and Peace, Crime and Punishment, Anna Karenina, and poems by Alexander Pushkin. Why is she sending me books he initially thought. He opened Crime and Punishment up to find the pages hollowed out and filled with rubles. He called Olena over, and the pair opened the cash-filled books and just looked at each other. They divvied up a small portion of the loot, Mikheil stashed the books on a living room bookshelf and soon was off with some clean clothes and supplies. Olena was going to bring Jacques back to their car, but he looked too comfortable to be disturbed, Katerina had a new friend for the remainder of the journey.

Mikheil and Olena's new home was a downtown Hilton. Mikheil now had Vlad as a roommate, and Olena was next door in an adjoining room with Jacques as hers. A bribe of a couple of hundred rubles had to be exchanged to get the no-pet policy overlooked. After the harrowing night with the unwanted visitor, no chances were taken.

Now that everyone was settled Vlad's next order of business was to call the security team and get an investigation update. He had to find out who the enemy was. The first part of the conference call was disappointing. Ivan didn't have anything concrete from CCTV footage at Arkadiy's businesses. Pavel's news was a little more encouraging or discouraging depending on how you look at it. He managed to find out whom several of the FSB officers were looking into Topki activity, the site of Arkadiy's assassination. A familiar name came up, Bogdan Goda, an old army buddy. It had been years since they last seen each other but it hadn't seemed that way. The laugh-filled phone conversation ended with a promised get-together that would surely entail the consumption of lots of beer. The part of the conversation that wasn't funny was Bogdan's warning about Dryga. He didn't have any specific details but had heard rumors of some shady dealings. The message was clear, be careful around this guy.

Next came Dmitri's turn to report and it sent shivers down Vlad's spine. The name Boris Voshkolup, the Solntsevskaya bratva boss, was uttered. He immediately knew things were more likely to get worse before getting better. Boris, a 50-year-old, short, bearded, morbidly obese, Ukrainian was probably the most dangerous man in Russia. He has ties all over Europe, connected to the most politically powerful men in the country. His weapons, drugs and human trafficking, coupled with extortion and murder contracts gave him funds that almost rivaled Arkadiy's. It made perfect sense that he would go after Arkadiy, if he could get control over his assets, he would have businesses to launder all the illicit money. His name came up when talking to Konstantin Berezovsky who was still in the hospital recovering from burns after his car came under attack shortly after Arkadiy was killed. Vlad knew at that moment he had to step up his game.

"Are you Natasha Magnitsky?"

"Who are you?"

"I am Lt. Litskevich, this is Lt. Dryga," he said flashing his credentials.

"What do you want?"

"We are looking for your husband."

Dryga pushed by the two of them only to be met by Natasha's mother who got in Dryga's face. "What do you want? Why are you here?"

He put his hands on her shoulders, moved her aside, and searched the house. "He's not here," he announced to Litskevich.

"Where is he?" Litskevich asked again, raising his voice this time.

"I don't know, I don't know."

"You're coming with us." Natasha was put in the back of the car, and they sped off.

Natasha was put into a small, dingy holding cell with a filthy toilet in the corner. She sat there silently. Her husband warned her this might happen and urged her to leave the country. They had argued furiously about it, but she wasn't going to leave her family, her parents depended on her. She knew her husband hadn't done anything wrong; he had explained to her why he was being sought. His company, Firestone Duncan had been hired by a hedge fund that was accused of not paying billions of rubles in taxes when in fact the taxes had been paid. He had proof of the taxes being paid but this was Russia, corrupt Russia. There had been a police raid on the hedge funds headquarters and the corporate seals were confiscated. The seals were used to illegally transfer ownership of three of the hedge funds companies and tax payments were claimed back and paid just days later to the fraudulent owners.

Natasha's mind went over numerous scenarios about what was going to happen next. Her mother would get in touch with Sergei, she was counting on him to use his connections to put an end to her confinement. The biggest fear she had though was Sergei, what would happen if they got ahold of him. She hoped and prayed that her mother wouldn't lead them to him.

Tatiana had checked in to the Thistle Hotel in Holborn. The friendly driver, who talked nonstop on the ride over had recommended it. As they zipped along the congested streets, he had a story about every block they came across for the 20-minute journey. The front desk clerk had thrown her for a loop when she asked how long she would be staying. She must have looked like an idiot as she finally stammered out "a week." How long was she going to stay she thought. All her plans to this point had been just getting out of Russia and discovering the funds in Zurich.

Tatiana did have a friend in London, Lily. She hadn't seen Lily for about eight years, her junior year of college, but they had kept in touch. The last letter she had received was a thrilled Lily announcing she was pregnant. She would look her friend up, that would help her decide her next step. After unpacking and checking in with Mikheil Tatiana lay down on the bed to relax.

Three hours later Tatiana awoke, still fully dressed, looking around, wondering where she was and the time. It was dark outside and she was shaking off the effects of the deep sleep. Between the constant movement and stress her body had just shut down without any notice. She considered jumping in the shower before grabbing a quick bite but opted for a splash of water in her face and a brush pulled through her bed head.

Tuesday, October 15, 1996

The sky was pewter gray, and a cold wind whipped up dry gold and red leaves as Lev's sendoff group approached the plain, clay-bricked funeral home. Olena had an arm wrapped tightly in Mikheil's as they entered and were greeted by a tall young slender man dressed in black. In a whispered voice he expressed his condolences, escorting them to the room none of them wanted to be in. Centered at the end of rows of chairs was a shiny black coffin with polished silver handles surrounded by a forest of the most beautiful flowers. Olena and Mikheil walked up the aisle, both of their legs feeling like they were wearing concrete shoes. Katerina and Vlad were a couple of steps behind; the security team had fanned out taking their rehearsed positions. Olena stood in front of her son's body, her arms straight down at her sides, tears streaming down her face. Mikheil stood ready with two handkerchiefs, one for each of them. Olena gently touch Lev's hand and told him she would see him and his father in heaven. She stepped back into Katerina's waiting arms, they hugged, Olena's body shaking. Mikheil stood over his friend and memories of their travels filled his mind. Think of all the good times he kept telling himself, there had been many of those. They had known each other for just over 20 years and explored many countries together. There was always the next adventure planned even before the current one had ended but not anymore.

Katerina had orchestrated a nice gathering but felt very helpless that she couldn't have done more for her friend and his loved ones. She especially felt bad that Tatiana, who she knew meant the world to Lev, couldn't be there. The fact they were all there now was extremely dangerous, and she gave a nod to Vlad indicating it was time for them to leave. Vlad went over to Mikheil, put his hand on his shoulder and they started for the door. Katerina stood with Olena, her arm across her shoulder and the two of them said their final goodbye. There wouldn't be a graveside service, it was just too dangerous. As they filed out the remaining security team followed and proceeded back to the hotel. It was a long quiet ride back.

Tatiana spent the morning curled up in bed wearing the hotel robe; her arms hugging an oversized pillow. She cried so much the tears had run out. There had been times when she wanted to reach out to the friend that was no longer there and share a story or a thought like they had done so often before. Her mind also started to think about the future and her next steps. One day at a time for now she said to herself, just get through today. It would be one of the longest of her life.

Back at the hotel Mikheil and Olena camped out on the bed in Olena's room with Jacques comfortably stretched out between them. They stared mindlessly at the TV screen as Babe, the talking pig attempted to entertain them. In the adjoining room, Vlad was heading a meeting with the security team. Now they had an idea of who they were up against a plan had to be formulated about how they would defend themselves and neutralize the threat. What they had at this point was a silver Mercedes, the van plate number, the warehouse where Lev had been held, and Berezovsky's mention of Boris Voshkolup.

"I'll get in touch with Litskevich and Dryga today, see if they've come up with anything," Vlad told the team. "Pavel, I want you to find out what you can about the warehouse, Ivan the van. If Voshkolup is involved we're going to have to be extremely cautious."

The room was sullen and solemn but there was an undercurrent of anger that had them motivated. Katerina's bounty was another incentive, though none of them would openly admit it. Katerina had left the funeral home with a couple of the guys from the security detail that was now permanently assigned to her and went to the headquarters. There was still a multibillion-ruble empire that still needed to be run, things were backing up without Arkadiy's guiding hand.

Litskevich and Dryga were busy working the leads, the same leads Vlad and his team were concentrating on. It was starting to piss off Voshkolup. Not only had his right-hand man, Miroslav Jablokov, aka Members Only guy fucked up and killed the man who could lead them to hundreds of millions of rubles but now he had the FSB to deal with.

"What the fuck were you thinking? The guy just had brain surgery and you're punching him in the fucking head. You're a fucking moron."

"My guys got a little out of control. I'm sorry," uttered Miroslav who was looking down at the floor. He knew there would be this reckoning and had dreaded it.

"What are we going to do now? Abramov's people know there's someone looking for the money now and we have the FSB on our asses too. This is a huge fuck up. Fix it!" bellowed Voshkolup at the top of his lungs.

"We're looking for the sister, I mean friend, the one that was at the hospital, and our guy, Dryga, he's one of the lead investigators. Everything will work out. Don't worry."

"Don't ever tell me not to worry! Get the fuck out of here!"

Wednesday, October 16, 1996

Lily opened the door to a large Paddington bear that blocked the view of her treelined street.

"Are you going to invite me in for a cup of tea?" Tatiana asked in her best bear voice.

Paddington was put on a table and the longtime friends bear-hugged. Tatiana needed the hug more than ever and tears streamed down her face. She didn't let Lily go for more than a minute.

"Tatiana, what's wrong?" asked a worried and puzzled Lily.

Where would she begin, what could she say. None of this had entered her mind she hadn't thought this out before the raw emotions had taken over.

"It's been a horrible couple of weeks."

At that moment a baby started crying at the top of its lungs and Lily's attention was diverted.

"That's Oliver. I'm sorry Tatiana, let me introduce you and then we'll have a cup of tea, you can tell me all about it. I'm sorry."

"I can't wait to meet Master Oliver," Tatiana said with relief as this would buy her some time to figure out what to tell Lily.

The two women stood over Oliver in his crib, he returned their gaze with a smile on his face obviously enjoying the attention he was getting. Lily disappeared for a moment returning with Paddington, Oliver's arms reached upward towards the big plush bear, he let out a laugh and Lily lifted him out. They cooed over Oliver for several minutes and Lily noticed tears welling up in Tatiana's eyes again. She put Oliver back in the crib, took Tatiana's hand, and led her downstairs. Over a cup of tea, Tatiana told Lily of Lev's death and now tears were flowing out of control. Lily had met Lev on his college visits, and the two of them shared a romantic connection. It was never serious, but they had spent numerous nights together when the partying ended both knowing it wasn't going to go anywhere because of the geography. Tatiana and Lily embraced; the obvious question followed, "what happened?"

Tatiana told Lily of the attack on Arkadiy and Lev, but the truth ended there. For a number of reasons, she didn't want to tell Lily why she was running but had to justify not being at her best friend's funeral. She told a vague story that Arkadiy's security team advised anyone close to Lev to go into hiding, adding that she wasn't happy with her job and had been considering a change of scenery for some time. There was an element of truth to that. How it was going to play out and how long she was going to stay in London was a mystery to even herself.

Without hesitation, Lily said, "you're staying here."

"No, I can't," responded Tatiana. "You have enough going on with a new baby and a husband, by the way."

"Trevor won't mind, trust me. The firm has him working so many hours that he comes home eats, sleeps, and is back out the door. He really won't mind. We have a room waiting for you."

"I'll only consider it after you get Trevor's blessing."

"You're trying to kill me. Who sent you?" Litskevich gasped, barely able to breathe.

"You are not free to leave. You will be here all day, don't even think about getting out of that bed," Nataliya ordered while mounted on her husband.

"Kitten, I have to leave now," he said regaining his breath back. "I can't keep the boss waiting."

"I'm the boss this morning and you're going to fuck me one more time."

"Kitten, I'm sorry but I really need to get going."

With a pouty face, Nataliya rolled off and stared at the ceiling. Alexander leaned over, kissed her, and promised a repeat performance after dinner.

"Promise?"

"I'll put it in writing."

"Litskevich, you're late!" Kovalyov yelled as Alexander entered the office that was already occupied by Dryga.

"Sorry sir, the traffic was horrible."

"Save it. First, we have released Magnitsky's wife, Natasha. She wasn't giving us anything, I think we stand a better chance of finding her husband if she's out. I think he might try and contact her, so we'll keep her under constant surveillance. Do you have any leads on him?"

"No, there was the one sighting but we don't have anything new. This isn't going to be easy, he was working for wealthy, powerful people with unlimited resources. We don't even know if he's in the country," Dryga added, his head pounding from the previous night's festivities.

"I've told you guys, over and over; I need this to be made a priority. I'm being asked about this every day. Get with Turov and Mikheyev, make it happen. I want Magnitsky now; I don't give a shit if he's in Timbuktu, get him!"

"Next, what do you guys have on the Drozdov case?"

"The warehouse where he was killed belongs to a holding company in Ukraine, Potsdam Tool and Die. We have our assistant digging into it now. Hopefully, we'll have more by the end of the day."

"Okay, I want constant updates and until Magnitsky is found there will be no days off. Make it happen!"

There goes dinner, was the first thing that ran through Litskevich's mind. Sleeping on the couch was the second.

Dryga broke Litskevich's train of thought. "I'll call Turov and Mikheyev, we'll meet them at the diner and put a plan together over coffee."

"Good, I have a call to make." It ended with, sorry, Kitten.

Before the coffee meeting, a call came in from Vlad. Dryga informed him that they were working on it but there wasn't anything to report.

"You don't have anything on the van?"

"Not yet. Things are crazy here, but we are working on it. Have you guys come up with anything on your end?"

"Nothing, but I'm sensing there is someone very powerful and dangerous behind this."

Dryga's lips tighten into a smile. You have no idea he thought.

Thursday, October 17, 1996

Olena was woken up by frantic knocking on her door. Jacques' head and ears shot up and his eyes went black from the sudden commotion. Olena sprang from the bed and pressed her shoulder against the door.

"Who is it?" Olena asked in a loud whisper.

"It's Vlad, open the door."

Vlad and Mikheil rushed in locking the door behind them.

"What's going on?"

"There are some suspicious guys downstairs in the lobby. Dmitri is keeping an eye on them; the rest of the security team is on the way."

Olena's elevated heart rate quickened with this news and wondered what was next. The two previous days had been filled with boredom. She and Mikheil watched about a dozen movies and played countless games of Durak. Questions about how long they could put up with this had come up several times. Vlad assured them that he would see to a change of scenery as he was also going stir-crazy. Even Jacques seemed annoyed at times by the cramped living quarters.

The room was quiet and filled with tension. About 20 minutes later the phone rang, and Dmitri updated Vlad, the security team had arrived and occupied various spots in the lobby. All six, heavily armed men, that included Ivan and Pavel, took turns taking casual glances at the hotel coffee shop that opened into the lobby. Four men that ranged in age from late twenties to early forties were drinking coffee, smoking cigarettes, and engaging in intense conversation. Dmitri couldn't put his finger on it but something about these guys set off his spidey senses. After about 45 minutes the meeting broke up, handshakes were exchanged, and the men moved to the hotel's main exit unaware of the eyes that were on them. Dmitri signaled with a nod to two of his guys to follow them out to make sure they were actually leaving. The coast was clear. If nothing else, it was a good drill to see how quickly the team could be assembled. Vlad would sleep easier at night.

Vlad and Mikheil headed back to their room, and Olena and Jacques hunkered down for a couple more hours of sleep before another round of movies and card games would commence. Sleep didn't come for all of them, Olena lay there staring at the ceiling with tears streaming down the sides of her face. There was no point in dabbing at them as they would continue on and on until she climbed out of bed.

A couple of kilometers away there was an eerily similar sinister meeting happening with four suspicious characters, but this coffee shop meeting was going unnoticed. The organizer of this get-together was Miroslav Jablokov, also in attendance were the two goons complicit in Lev's death. A man in a baseball cap now had the group's attention.

"You guys need to start laying low. The warehouse and the partial van plate number are starting to lead to you. I'm doing what I can to slow things down but there's only so much I can do. There's also your fingerprints, so to speak, all over the Berezovsky debacle."

The warning was coming from Lt. Dryga who was now lowering the baseball cap closer to his eyes in an attempt to not be recognized.

"Next time Berezovsky won't be so lucky," grunted one of the goons.

"Gentlemen, you need to be more careful. There's only so much interference I can run," Dryga reiterated. "I do have something for you. Our guys have the name of the woman that we thought was Drozdov's sister. She was his best friend; they grew up together in Nizhny."

"The thin one with blond hair, drives the green Mini?" Jablokov asked.

"Yes," replied Dryga who was caught a little off guard by their intel. "Her name is Tatiana Belov. She lives a few kilometers away on Minskaya."

"We know the place. Dumbass here trashed it but didn't find anything, not even a bill with her name on it," Jablokov added.

"Fuck you. Someone was coming, we didn't have time," the goon growled.

"Do you have any idea where she is now?"

"No, I talked to the neighbors, she hasn't been seen in more than a week. I think she may have left the country."

"What makes you think that?"

"I went through the wreckage that you guys left and didn't find a suitcase or passport."

"Do you have any idea where she went?"

"No. She works at Menatep Bank. I'll be heading over there today to talk with her boss, I've been surveilling her mother."

"What does she do at the bank, bank teller?" one of the goons asked.

"She has a degree from St. Petersburg University in economics, she works in the global trading department," Dryga responded trying not to sound condescending. "Let's meet here in three days, same time and we'll share any new information."

"Let's make it two days. Voshkolup is crawling up my ass and is going to want something very soon."

The mention of Boris's name sent shivers up the spine of every man at that table. They all knew that if Tatiana Belov wasn't found life was going to be unpleasant, to say the least. The meeting concluded, Dryga climbed into his smashed-up Lada and Members Only guy and the thugs a silver Mercedes, the hunt was on.

Friday, October 18, 1996

Tatiana woke up to an empty house. It was comforting to be around her friend and the family, but it was also nice to have peace and quiet. She had been tempted to spend the morning in bed but that would have her stuck in her head with a revolving loop of the past week's events. As she brushed back her hair that was now midway down her back, she thought about the last time she had visited a salon, it had been a while and it was now starting to look that way. Add that to the list as well as some clothes shopping, she mentally noted. The bare necessities of makeup were applied, a step back and glance in the mirror satisfied her. She headed downstairs to the kitchen to find a note on the counter.

Have taken Oliver to the doc. Help yourself to anything. Will be back around lunchtime. Enjoy the peace.
L & O.

Needing some fresh air and wanting to check out her new neighborhood Tatiana strolled down the quiet street towards a busier thoroughfare. The houses here in Raynes Park with their manicured lawns, sprawling rose bushes and precisely trimmed hedges were very different from home. Home, she thought, a call to her mama was long overdue. With the clatter of a train in the background, Tatiana was now on a busy sidewalk, and a sudden anxiety came over her. It was triggered by two drivers honking and yelling at each other. She found herself looking over her shoulder as she weaved in and around fellow pedestrians. Her pulse quickened before she reminded herself, she was safe. There was no way she could be found but that wasn't always going to be true, a plan had to be formulated. That plan was going to be determined by her visit to Carshalton House, the residence and citizenship specialists. I'll think about that tomorrow, make that Monday, she thought, today let's just chill. Now it was time for a good cup of coffee and something sweet. The pastries in a bake shop window looked so inviting with so many choices.

"I see someone's been busy," was the greeting she received as she came through the front door with several bags in hand.

"Hi, Oliver. Were you a good boy for the doctor?" Tatiana cooed.

The response was a big smile that was on the verge of laughter. "He was a very good boy," Lily answered for him. "How was your morning?"

"Very nice. I've been exploring the neighborhood and shops."

"I see that. You'll have to show me what you got."

"Nothing fancy, just some of the basics," she said as she pulled out a pair of jeans with long skinny legs.

"Those should attract some attention."

"Wait till you see the top that goes with them." Tatiana was well-built and would definitely fill out the low-cut, tight-fitting blouse.

"You'll have no problem stopping traffic with that outfit. We'll have to get dressed up and have a girls' night out soon. I'll introduce you to some of my friends."

"That sounds like fun. It's been a long time since I've gotten out; I'm long overdue."

"How does tomorrow night sound?" Lily excitedly asked.

"Perfect!" Tatiana's response came with a twinge of guilt. Her best friend was just laid to rest three days earlier and here she was about to hit the town. She quickly rationalized it with, that's what Lev would want, and she truly believed it. Lev always lived in the moment, the last thing he would want is for his friend to mope around with tissues in her hand. It would be nice to make some new friends.

Bang, bang, bang!

Dryga's eyes were coming into focus, seeing the time on the clock by his head, 7:45. Shit, he thought. I've overslept again. He knew right away who was going to be on the other side of the door and the speech that would follow. He opened the door wearing only his boxers reeking of vodka and cigarettes.

"Why weren't you picking up?" Litskevich demanded instantly having his question answered eyeing the phone laying on its side on the living room floor. "Get dressed we need to get to the airport now!"

"What's the hurry? I need some coffee," Dryga said, his speech slightly slurred.

"No time. Turov and Mikheyev have spotted Magnitsky's wife at the airport. We need to leave right now, get dressed."

This news sobered Dryga up, and the two of them dashed out to Litskevich's Lada that was parked by the front door, his car was four years newer and in showroom condition. Dryga pulled out his cigarettes and put one in his mouth; Litskevich slapped it away.

"You know you can't smoke in my car."

"Come on man, you can't drag me out of bed, no coffee, no smoke. I'm dying here."

"Roll the window down. I don't want you stinking my car up."

The chilly fall air and the smell of the cigarette filled the car, it irritated the piss out of Litskevich. He was annoyed by his partner but understood, a few years earlier that was him. Out boozing every night, getting high, and smoking a pack a day. All of this, with the exception of the occasional drink, came to an end when he met Nataliya. She was a strait-laced accountant that wouldn't tolerate his shit. The law had been laid down early. She had left him a couple of times when he tested her, but love straightened him out. He was hoping a good woman would do the same for his self-destructive friend.

They sped into the airport scaring some heavily luggage-laden travelers along the way before ending up at departures. As they exited the car a patrolling policeman yelled, "no parking, no parking." A pair of FSB badges quelled the outburst. After a few minutes, they spotted Turov and Mikheyev who had been there for about half an hour.

"He's going to board a flight to London in about ten minutes. He's over there with his wife Natasha." The moment Turov nodded in the couple's direction Natasha immediately recognized Litskevich and Dryga. It had only been several days since their encounter at the house, they were faces Natasha would never forget.

Natasha leaned forward to Sergei's ear; his head turned toward the agents. He dropped his carry-on bag and a chase was on. The agents were surprised by how quick and agile the tax advisor was. He had dodged an elderly couple and actually leaped over a young boy making it to the far end of the terminal before being tackled by an out-of-breath Litskevich. Turov arrived next, followed by Mikheyev, all three of them now were on top of the struggling Magnitsky. Turov and Mikheyev came in sending several blows to Sergei's head. Natasha's screams could be heard 50 meters away. Dryga who was now walking arrived several seconds later and stopped at the melee with his hands on his knees before pulling out a pair of handcuffs. Magnitsky was cuffed, picked up, and staggering as he was escorted by his frantically crying wife.

"Don't hurt him, don't hurt him," she cried out between sobs.

"I'm okay, I'm all right," Sergei said trying to calm Natasha. Blood was streaming down his face and into his eyes, he wasn't okay.

Saturday, October 19, 1996

Veins were bulging from the fat man's head, his face was beet red, and the air was filled with expletives. Boris Voshkolup was on the verge of a heart attack.

"What am I paying you fuckin' idiots for? It's one fuck up after the next! Every time I turn around, I'm having to fix another problem! I'm fucking sick of it! Now on top of it, I'm having to do your job for you, a job you make a lot of fucking money to do!"

Jablokov, adorned in his black Members Only jacket, and his two goons had felt the room temperature increase a few degrees, sweat was now appearing on the foreheads of the three. The large, wood-paneled office, lined with book-filled shelves felt very small at that moment, almost like a closet. The day wasn't starting out as hoped. The hockey game they planned to attend wasn't going to happen, not after a meeting like this.

"The girl's been spotted in Switzerland, this Tatiana Belov. She was seen at Credit Suisse in Zurich just over a week ago. I've seen the security footage, it's grainy but it's fucking her. I want someone there today; I want her fucking found! You motherfuckers have no idea what's on the line! The next time I hear from you is you telling me where she is, now get the fuck out of here!"

Voshkolup was truly a powerful man with eyes and ears all over Europe. His source of the grainy security footage was a long-legged blond receptionist that Boris had had a liaison with several months earlier, Inga. They met at a loud Zurich nightspot; Inga had caught his attention in a very short black leather skirt and a clingy pink top that left little to the imagination. It turns out Inga was also having a liaison with a married director at the bank. Boris hoped that his chance encounter would lead to a very large payout.

Within two hours of the ball-busting meeting, Jablokov was on a plane to Zurich. He had considered booking first class but was instead crammed into a middle seat with a middle-aged man who hadn't showered that day on his right and an extremely obese young lady with pink hair on his left. He didn't want to push his luck. He decided to leave the goons behind as they would only slow him down and make his stealth efforts more visible. Good thing it wasn't a terribly long flight, he thought to himself.

Katerina had been in touch with Vlad and told him his desired relocation from the Hilton was about to happen. She could only imagine how stir-crazy they were getting hunkered down in the cramped hotel rooms. Another cabin was found southeast of Moscow about 65 minutes from the city center in a town called Popovka. It was eerily similar to the Rostov property in the fact it was on a lake and the town was about the same size. This time though she took extra steps to make sure that she wasn't being followed. The plan involved a vehicle switch that Ivan orchestrated and a couple of out-of-the-way detours. The pair arrived at the cabin in the middle of the afternoon, stocked it with groceries, gave it a quick clean, and scoped out the area for any potential problems. The last thing on the to-do list was leaving a couple of rifles and some ammunition. This final step had saved the day at Rostov, she truly hoped it wouldn't be necessary.

"Ivan, are you hungry?" Katerina inquired.

"Starving," was the reply.

"I am too and I'm not in the mood for greasy spoon crap we'll find on the way back. We'll give the kitchen a trial run before they get here tomorrow."

Katerina had always been used to hitting all the best restaurants all over Moscow. Reservations were the best thing she made but now that she was keeping a low profile her cooking skills had been refreshed.

"What can I do?" Ivan asked.

"Put some good music on, pour us some wine, and boil a pot of water."

"Yes, boss. I think I can manage that."

Katerina had pulled the needed ingredients from the fridge and cupboards and was on her way to making a very good bolognese. The wine was flowing, the music had her hips moving with her dark hair swaying across her back. Ivan, standing in the doorway, took notice. He had never seen this side of his very attractive boss before. The conversation also flowed as they talked about their favorite restaurants and night spots.

The meal was served and more wine with it. Katerina shared her travel experiences with Ivan who was in awe. He had only left Russia once and that was as a teenager to visit relatives in Poland. Katerina, on the other hand, had traveled the world. Most of her travels were business related with Arkadiy, the stories had them in stitches. There was one trip where she, Vlad, and Arkadiy had boarded Arkadiy's Gulfstream late one afternoon, and they all started drinking champagne and doing shots of vodka. A few hours into the flight they all fell asleep and woke up when the plane was touching down. The flight attendant opened the cabin door, the pilot stood waiting for them to exit. Arkadiy whispered to Katerina and Vlad, "where are we?" Laughter filled the cabin before the pilot graciously announced, "welcome to Barcelona."

The wine, the memories, and the stress of the past couple of weeks had taken its toll on Katerina and the laughter turned to tears. Ivan, a bit beyond buzzed, immediately hugged Katerina who had been in the middle of clearing the plates. To his surprise, Katerina grabbed the back of his head, and his lips were met by hers. Kissing his boss had been a frequent fantasy during the security meetings. Katerina was hot, and he wasn't alone in this fantasy, but he couldn't believe what was happening. It was quickly getting better when he felt a tug at his belt and his pants button released. His dick immediately became rock hard; he didn't waste a second unbuttoning her pink silk blouse. It fell to the floor exposing a see-through white lace bra that soon was on the floor too. Katerina's right nipple was in Ivan's mouth, in a breathy whisper she ordered him to bite it. Ivan then hiked up her skirt and lifted Katerina off the floor carrying her into the bedroom while she kissed his neck. Katerina reached back while lying on the bed to undo her skirt, Ivan noticed this, and it was pulled past her ankles in seconds. Ivan pulled Katerina's G-string to the side and drove his cock into his boss over and over as Katerina gasped "yes, yes, fuck me, fuck me," into his ear. The faded smell of her perfume lingered in his nose as the pair came in unison. What the fuck just happened went through Ivan's mind while he was catching his breath.

"Yes, mama I'm all right. I'm sorry I haven't called."

"You've had me worried beyond belief. I left message after message on that machine of yours. Is it working?"

"Mama, I'm in London. I'm on a work assignment. They sent me here last minute; it's kept me very busy." Tatiana was hoping the bank hadn't tried calling her mother or that story would be blown.

"London? What do they have you doing in London?"

"The bank is setting up a trading desk here."

"Why do they need your help setting up a desk?"

Tatiana couldn't hold back, and a laugh was heard on the other end of the phone.

"What's so funny?"

"Sorry, mama. They are doing banking stuff here; I'm working with the bankers."

"Why didn't you just say that Miss Hoity Toity? When are you coming back?"

"Right now, it looks like a few weeks, but it could be a little longer."

"And you're just telling me now," her mama said sounding a little hurt.

"Mama, I'm sorry. Everything has been happening so fast and they've had me working day and night."

"Have you seen much of London?"

"Not, yet. I've been here about five days and it's been a whirlwind. I'm hoping to catch some of the sites tomorrow. Mama, I have to go but I'll call you on Sunday. I love you."

"I love you, Tati."

Tatiana hung up the phone and breathed a sigh of relief. That went well, she thought to herself, but sadness overwhelmed her. When would she be able to go home again. When would she see her mama. Where would she be a week, a month, or a year from now. It was all too much to think about. Adding to her stress was the guilt of her mother all alone. The sudden passing of her father five and a half years earlier from heart failure shattered her and her mother. Her papa had doted on them, and he was so proud of her when she graduated with her degree. Her thoughts were interrupted by Lily and Oliver coming through the front door.

"Hello!" Lily called out pushing a stroller into the front hall with a bag of groceries.

"Let me help you with those."

"I have good news. I talked to the girls; we're all set for our big night out tonight. Let me put Oliver down, he's been cranky, and I'll give you the details."

Sunday, October 20, 1996

"Good morning, your royal highness."

"Good morning," Tatiana replied staring down into her coffee cup avoiding eye contact with Trevor.

It immediately came back to her. Things had gotten a little crazy, to say the least, last night. She was being helped through the front door with Lily under her arm supporting her and announcing the queen was home. The laughter this invoked woke Trevor up and the pair were asked to keep it down.

The night had started out mellow enough with a pleasant dinner at one of Lily's favorite curry houses. They were joined by Charlotte, Camile, and Anna and the festivities began. With stomachs full of biryani, masala, and naan the next stop was a local pub, the Fox and Hounds. Lily took notice right away of Tatiana's downing of a pint of lager and calling for another round before the others had barely touched their drinks. Lily also noticed the wad of pound notes in Tatiana's purse, she knew she was going to have to keep an eye on her mate tonight.

The taxi pulled up outside the Fox and Hounds and the ladies slid in, Tatiana's entrance was a little less graceful. "Where to ladies?"

"Piccadilly Circus," Tatiana bellowed out.

"Why Piccadilly Circus?" Charlotte asked.

"I like the name of it. Piccadilly, Piccadilly," Tatiana said while laughing hysterically.

"Let's do Covent Garden," Camile interjected. "I know a fun club there that's open late."

"Piccadilly, Piccadilly," Tatiana continued still laughing.

Lily took charge and instructed the driver to Covent Garden. Tatiana pushed out her bottom lip, her pout had all the girls laughing. "We'll do Piccadilly another time, promise," added Anna.

The half-hour cab ride gave Tatiana some time to sober up a little, but she was still tipsy. When the taxi pulled up to the trendy club, Pipeline, Tatiana insisted on paying, dropping hundreds of pounds on the taxi floor in the process. This had all the girls looking at each other and kneeling down to recover the trove of cash.

As the night went on Tatiana and Anna bonded. Unlike the other ladies, Anna was unattached and liked to get out and mingle. Anna's black hair with maroon highlights started the evening up in a tight bun but was now flowing freely on the dance floor. The ladies stood back watching Tatiana and Anna dancing; it didn't take long before they noticed they each had a new partner in the strobe-light-filled space. Before the song had ended Tatiana's arms were around the neck of her Italian-looking dance partner. Lily was about to hit the dance floor and break up the embrace, but Charlotte grabbed her arm and said, "let her go." Based on previous conversations Lily felt Charlotte was probably living vicariously through Tatiana at this moment, she backed off while keeping an eagle eye on her friend.

"Shots, shots, shots," was the rallying cry the bartender heard over the loud music from Tatiana while her arm was draped across the shoulder of her new Italian friend, Antonio. Anna chimed in and shots of chilled Stolichnaya were lined up in front of them. The vodka instantly disappeared, and the chant started again, this time from Anna who had her arm around the waist of her new friend from the dance floor. The three ladies who were observing this from a couple of meters away decided it was time to call it a night. As Lily approached the second round of shots disappeared and Tatiana was now lip locked with Antonio. Lily knew she had her work cut out for her but was surprised that it took just a light tap on Tatiana's shoulder to have her full attention. As Tatiana separated from Antonio her face was white as a sheet. Lily sprang into action having seen that look from her college days. She grabbed Tatiana's hand, pushed through the crowd, and pulled her through the bathroom door ignoring the cries of the ladies in the queue. The rest of the ladies followed causing a ruckus in the hallway which Camile attempted to quell with repeated sorrys. With all the stalls occupied the sink turned out to be the best option and a couple of girls scooted back groaning at what came next, Tatiana filled the sink with the spicy Indian concoctions from earlier in the evening while Lily held her hair back. This caused a shift in Anna's stomach, but she managed to keep it together. "Scene," Camile announced, a sheepish exit followed.

Ivan awoke to the smell of coffee and bacon. He pulled his naked body out of bed putting his boxers on still not believing what had occurred seven hours earlier. It was going to be awkward, but he was fine with it, he was the man, he thought to himself. His strategy was to play it cool like this kind of thing happened all the time. After hitting the head, he strolled into the kitchen to find a showered and fully clothed Katerina plating breakfast.

"How did you sleep?" she asked.

"Great, and you?"

"Very well," was the reply without giving a hint of what happened last night away. "We should get on the road soon. I don't want Vlad and the others worrying about us. I'm sure they're going to find this place an improvement over the cramped hotel."

"Definitely," Ivan responded wondering to himself if it was normal for women to act indifferently like this after a passionate evening. At 28 and having nerdy tendencies his experience with the opposite sex was limited.

Ivan helped Katerina with the breakfast dishes, they pulled the cabin back together and were soon on the road. The drive back was filled with relaxed conversation but nothing of a really personal nature. It was clear to Ivan that last night was a one-time event, one he would never forget.

Jablokov was digging into a large breakfast at the Marriott restaurant right off the lobby. It was ironically the same hotel Tatiana had stayed at 10 days earlier, but he didn't know that. He realized that his impromptu trip had been poorly planned, nothing of real value was going to happen on a Sunday. The upside was being out of Moscow and the reach of his raving mad boss. After an after-breakfast cigarette and shower the plan was to locate Credit Suisse, then catch some of the sites around Zurich.

Now that the bank he was going to visit on Monday was located Miroslav decided to check out some of the high-end shops that were scattered in the neighborhood. He was seeing a couple of ladies at home and thought they'd be impressed with an expensive gift from a foreign country. His first stop was Chanel where he picked up two scarves and two bottles of the signature perfume. The next stop was Gucci where he picked up a purse for girl number two and lastly Prada, a large handbag for girl number one. A couple of beers were now in order for being such a good guy.

Sitting at a quiet steakhouse bar across the river from the Credit Suisse branch he'd be visiting Miroslav was plotting out his approach to finding Tatiana. He knew that he would get a little more information from Inga, his boss's squeeze, so what next. Check all the hotels near the bank to see if she was still in Zurich. It would have been a good idea to bring a couple of his colleagues with him to speed the search up; hindsight he thought.

"I'm sorry ma'am but no one is seen without an appointment."

"I've traveled all the way from Moscow, surely you can find someone that can spare a few minutes for me," a still slightly hung-over Tatiana said with some irritation.

"Miss Lynch, I'm free. I've just had an appointment cancel."

"Hello, my name is Malcolm Spencer. You are?"

"Katerina Grigoryev," Tatiana said trying to sound unrehearsed.

"How can I help you?"

"I have questions of a confidential nature involving citizenship."

"Please follow me."

Tatiana was soon sitting in a very British mahogany paneled office in a comfortable padded leather chair as Malcolm pulled out a legal pad from his desk and jotted notes. He started the meeting with a speech he's given more than a hundred times before that explained the confidentiality that was afforded to his clients and the basic fee structure for his services. Tatiana, aka Katerina, nodded in agreement and went on to admit this was not her true identity, but would reveal it when necessary. Mr. Spencer explained that he was used to that kind of secrecy and would do what was necessary to allay her fears, he asked what she was looking to accomplish. Tatiana explained that she was looking to move funds from Switzerland to a safe place and would need to relocate due to safety concerns. It was obvious by Tatiana's questions she had done her homework; Malcolm was impressed.

"How much money is involved?"

"Ten million pounds to start with."

Tatiana now had Malcolm's attention. He often had meetings with potential clients who thought 20,000 pounds was sizable and worth his while, but those meetings never lasted long. "There are a number of countries that are very agreeable to granting citizenship to high-worth individuals without having to disclose too much information about themselves or the source of their funds. Since I have a meeting in about 15 minutes; I would like to put together a plan that I'm sure will satisfy your current needs. Would it be possible for you to return on Thursday with a couple of passport photos, at the same time?"

"Certainly. Thank you, Mr. Spencer."

"Please, call me Malcolm."

With that Tatiana left Carshalton House with a sense that she had accomplished an important task, one that would help her sleep much better at night.

Mikheil, Vlad, Olena, and Jacques were settling into their new digs. Their body language made it clear that they were glad to be out of the cramped confines of the Hilton, back to the country with fresh crisp air and space to roam and not tripping over each other. There had been a couple of moments of tension between Mikheil and Vlad but that was to be expected. Olena and Jacques couldn't have gotten along better. Jacques was lapping up all the attention he could get.

Mikheil unpacked his suitcase, then went for a walk by the lake and through the woods. The colorful leaves crunched under his feet, a reminder that the crunch would soon come from hardened snow. He had talked with Vlad about how long they would have to be in hiding; who knows became the standard response. Mikheil still had money left from the books Tatiana had sent but that would last only so long, he couldn't keep telling his boss at the restaurant that his sick mother was still sick. At some point, he'd have to return home.

Olena had also taken a walk exploring her new surroundings thinking about what was in store for her. Every day was filled with the grief of losing her only son, she realized that grief would be there until the day she died. Her thoughts also pondered returning home, getting back to the circle of friends she dearly missed and needed so much now. Mikheil had been so sweet listening to her stories about Lev, but she was worried about becoming a burden. It was apparent that he was having a hard time as well missing his best buddy.

Miroslav Jablokov slept a little later than he'd wanted. His Sunday ended with drinks at the hotel bar, it was a visit that had been quite interesting. While feeling the effects of some after-dinner cognacs he invented a story about his girlfriend abruptly leaving him. She had taken his money, stolen his car, and left it at the airport; he suspected she had been here at the Marriott. At least that's what his credit card statement told him. A sympathetic bartender, or at least one working for a good tip, listened intently and offered his assistance. The description of her Miroslav provided was of no help but a flirty night auditor who enjoyed free after-work cocktails was able to confirm that a Tatiana Belov had stayed there for almost a week. The only thing that didn't jive was no credit card was ever used, a minor detail that was soon overlooked by Miroslav's new friend that was now a couple of hundred francs richer.

Jablokov, who was in a good mood, knowing he was on Tatiana's trail headed to Credit Suisse. It was an unusually warm morning that made the 15-minute walk pleasant. Upon entering the bank, he was met by a friendly receptionist who offered her assistance, "I need to see Inga Sommer please."

"May I ask your name?"

"I'm a friend of Boris's, she'll know what it's about."

"Certainly, sir. I'll get her."

A few minutes later the receptionist returned with the stunning Inga in tow. Wow thought Miroslav, the boss does have good taste. After an introduction and hearing of the requested favor, Inga suggested they meet at lunchtime at a café across the street. She did not want to be seen with the mobster's associate in the lobby of the bank. Inga had done her due diligence after meeting Boris quickly realizing she wasn't dealing with someone who could be called an upstanding citizen. At the same time though she was intrigued and excited by this dangerous and powerful man.

Jablokov milled around the city for about an hour zipping in and out of several shops before his lunchtime meeting. This time the shopping he did was for himself, he ended up with a Rolex souvenir. He decided to wear it to his lunchtime meeting hoping to impress Inga. If she was impressed and he did manage to get her attention he knew it would be a very dangerous liaison, but this woman would definitely be worth risking his life for.

"Hello, Miroslav. I hope I haven't kept you waiting long," Inga said standing in front of the seated Miroslav.

"No, I just got here," he said standing up and pointing to the seat across from him.

As they both sat Inga said, "I can't stay long. I must get back but have something for you. It's not much but I hope it will help."

Flashing his best flirty smile and his new Rolex Miroslav said, "anything would be useful."

Used to this kind of attention Inga said in a business-like tone, "I did some digging and Miss Belov had visited the bank a week and a half ago but hadn't identified herself. She met with a bank officer, Ms. Klein, and left with an envelope of cash denominated in US dollars."

"The account the money came from; how much is in there?"

"I wasn't able to find that out. It's an anonymous account accessed by a password. Based on whom she spoke with and a couple of other things I suspect there is a large amount of money in that account. I'm sorry I don't have more for you. I will try to investigate more but can't promise anything. The privacy of these accounts is kept top secret, it is Switzerland you know," she said with a giggle.

Miroslav took the giggle as Inga flirting and asked her if she was free for dinner that evening. He was quickly shot down with, "I don't think Boris would approve." A bead of sweat broke out on his forehead, he hoped Inga hadn't noticed and said with a chuckle, "he doesn't need to know." A smile from Inga indicated that the secret non-meeting was safe. They parted with a handshake, Miroslav enjoying the view as she walked away.

Tuesday, October 22, 1996

"Magnitsky, you have a visitor."

Sergei propped himself up from the bed and planted his feet on the ground with great effort but standing would be the real challenge. Several ribs were badly bruised, a couple of them possibly broken. An uncontrolled groan escaped as he thrust himself up and he caught the edge of the bed. His back was wet with sweat as a result of the exertion and pain. A cough sent excruciating pain through his body; the only thing worse would be a sneeze.

"Hurry up or we'll send your visitor away!" the guard growled.

Sergei was escorted by the guard past dozens of steel doors like the one he had just come from. Yells and animal noises echoed all around him, it was only the second time he had made this trip and it was unnerving. The pain with each step made the journey to the visitor room seem extra long but he couldn't wait to see his wife. He hoped like hell it would be her. There she was, Natasha, the love of his life, and tears streamed from his eyes. She looked up at him, her hair messed up from the wool hat that was now on the table and tears streamed along with uncontrollable sobs.

"What have they done to you?" she asked while rising to her feet and stepping forward to hug him.

"Sit down," the guard ordered. There would be no hug. Sergei was a little relieved since it would have revealed injuries that he didn't want his wife to know about.

"I'm okay," he said trying to comfort Natasha.

"You're not, your face is all swollen your eyes are black and blue. What have these animals done to you?"

"Natasha, please keep your voice down."

She buried her face in her hands trying to regain control of herself, if she didn't the consequences could be never seeing her husband again. It had taken three days to locate him as he had been moved to two different prisons. Their meeting today would never have happened if it wasn't for the dogged efforts of Bill Browder, the man that hired Sergei's firm for the tax issue.

"How did you find me?" he asked.

"I didn't, Mr. Browder did. Jamison told him what happened, they've been working day and night to find you and get you out of here. I feel so helpless, look at you." More tears followed.

"Natasha, please I'm okay," Sergei said with a wince that was noticed by his wife.

"You're not. I'm going to do everything possible to get you out of here. We're talking with a couple of lawyers; it's taken longer because of the weekend."

"How are Stanislav and Nikita?"

"They're all right. They miss their father dearly."

"I miss them so much; I think about them all the time. It's what is going to get me through this. Do you know what they are charging me with?"

"Theft."

"What? That's crazy. Are they saying I stole the tax money?"

"Yes. There haven't been any formal charges yet, though."

"They are claiming I stole billions of rubles, but I have documentation of payment of the taxes."

"Jamison provided that to the FSB. A Department K, have you ever heard of it?"

"No. It must be a new division."

"It is, they are an economic counterespionage unit."

"This is bullshit!" Sergei cried out getting the guard's attention.

"I know darling. We are working on it. It's just taking some time because Mr. Browder and Jamison are working on this from London. They're afraid they'll end up in here with you if they come back, then they'd be no help at all."

"I understand. This whole thing is a fucking mess."

"I know. You'll have to keep your spirits up. We're going to get through this."

Natasha attempted to make small talk to lighten the mood, but it was useless. Emotions kept overcoming her. Eventually, she blew a kiss to her husband as she was escorted out of the visitor's room. Tears filled their eyes as they mouthed goodbyes and both wondered if this would be the last time they saw each other.

Katerina entered the lobby of the office to find a gentleman sitting in the reception area. The receptionist followed her into her office, informed her he was an attorney, and had requested a meeting. Katerina looked at the business card she had just been handed and asked the receptionist to escort him to the conference room and to have Pavel or Dmitri join them.

"Hello, my name is Salvadore Ortin," he said standing and looking Katerina over from head to toe.

"Hello, I'm Katerina and this is my associate Dmitri. How can we help you?"

"First, I was wondering if we may speak alone as this is a confidential matter."

"What is it about?"

"Mr. Abramov's estate."

"Dmitri will be staying."

"Very well. Are you the person currently managing Mr. Abramov's assets?"

"Yes, I'm overseeing everything with the assistance of his attorneys."

"May I ask who they are?"

"Not until you tell me why you are here."

"It is of a delicate nature. Are you sure we can't talk alone?"

"Mr. Ortin, please don't waste my time. Why are you here?" Katerina asked starting to lose her patience.

"It turns out Mr. Abramov has a son. His name is Nicholas, he's nineteen and lives with his mother in Barcelona."

"You are sure that Nicholas is his son?" Katerina replied without hesitation. She was a little surprised but only a little, Arkadiy did have a reputation.

"Yes, and we will gladly have him provide DNA to confirm this."

"Please get that to me; once confirmed I will set up a meeting with our attorneys."

"I will have the results within the next few weeks and get them to you."

"Thank you, Mr. Ortin."

After Mr. Ortin left Katerina asked Dmitri to keep what he had heard confidential. He agreed and informed her of the upcoming security meeting later on in the day.

Vlad stood at the head of the conference room table. Katerina and the security team had assembled for the after-lunch meeting. Vlad started by giving an update on what Litskevich relayed to him and what he had already strongly suspected, that Boris Voshkolup was behind Lev's death. The warehouse where he was killed, Potsdam Tool and Die, was owned by a Ukrainian company that was a subsidiary of Voshkolup's holdings. The gray van involved in the kidnapping was registered to Potsdam. It had taken some teeth pulling to get this information and was given with strict instructions to protect the source. It was unheard of for the FSB to share information with civilians, but Litskevich was burned out and was counting on a return favor to help him solve this case. Not only this case but possibly the attempted assassination of Konstantin Berezovsky also. The wild, wild east was producing new victims if not on a daily basis but a least on a weekly one. The team now had to decide on a plan of action; one wrong move and lives would be lost.

"There's no way we can get to Voshkolup," Vlad stated emphatically. "He's just too well protected. I checked him out as soon as I got the information," after all there was the incentive of the Krugerrands.

120

"We need to find out who the key guys in his organization are," Pavel added.

The rest of the team quickly agreed, with Katerina adding, "I want their fucking heads." Even knowing Katerina's no-bullshit approach to things, her passionate outburst caught them by surprise.

"We now know we are dealing with a vicious psychopath. Katerina, do I have permission to add additional people to the security team?" Vlad inquired.

"Definitely, whatever you need. We're not only going to play defense but we're going to cut off the balls of these pricks and feed them to them."

Security details, assignments, and schedules were discussed. The meeting concluded with everyone knowing what they had to do. The enemy was now known, and war had been declared.

Wednesday, October 23, 1996

"Please, no smiling."

"Sorry," Tatiana said as she stood in front of the white screen at the back of the Raynes Park pharmacy having her passport photos taken.

"They'll be ready in an hour."

With an hour to kill Tatiana set off to the shops to buy a few gifts for Lily and the family. The first item was a blue jumpsuit with Taz the Tasmanian Devil emblazoned on it for Oliver. For Trevor it was a tea mug with her Royal Highness in all her regalia, she wondered if he would find it funny, and for Lily some lavender bubble bath. After picking up her photos she would hit the butcher shop for a leg of lamb and the greengrocer. The last stop was for a couple of bottles of wine; a surprise dinner would be nice she thought.

Jablokov touched down in Moscow at about 2 p.m. He took a taxi home, dropped off his luggage and gifts, then made his way to see Voshkolup. It was a trip he wasn't looking forward to making; it never was but at least he had something for his boss that would spare him his wrath. At least the wrath would be spared if Inga hadn't mentioned his advance towards her, that did make him a little nervous.

"What do you have for me?" was Boris's first question, no hello or how was your trip?

"She was in Zurich."

"I know that you idiot, we had the bank surveillance pictures. What else?"

"She was staying at the Marriott in the city center checking out early on Monday the 14th."

"What about Inga?" Boris asked with a grin.

Miroslav's heart dropped into his stomach; he felt the room temperature increase. "Yes, she was helpful. Tatiana left the bank with an envelope filled with US currency. She spoke with a bank officer that usually deals with high-net-worth clients, so we must be talking about a considerable sum. Inga wasn't able to come up with a figure."

"I'll have our FSB guy check out flights to the US that day and see if she was on any of them."

"Good work." Miroslav was tossed an envelope of cash. After his gifts were paid for there was some drinking money left over.

Vlad's team was as busy as ever. Vlad pulled the key team members together after the meeting with Katerina to discuss the Krugerrand reward. He suggested that they work as a team dividing the reward equally. He wanted them to work as a cohesive unit and not a bunch of lone wolves. There wasn't any descent, they knew it would be a team effort that would bring these thugs down.

The team had been working with a renewed vigor now they had Voshkolup to focus on. Ivan and Pavel bribed a librarian at a local university to let them spend the night and research old microfiche newspaper articles about the Solntsevskaya bratva boss. There were reams and reams of articles about the Russian mafia but surprisingly little was written about their newfound adversary. He had managed to stay out of the limelight; they wondered if he was smart or if journalists were just too terrified to mention him. After several cups of coffee, just before the sun was about to come up, Pavel had come across a couple of extremely rare photos of the big man. In both of the photos, a well-built, salt-and-pepper-haired guy in a Members Only jacket was by his side. He was about 40 and fit, what they would imagine as a "right-hand" man. They printed the poor-quality pictures and left to go home to get a couple of hours of sleep. The librarian was pleased to collect her cash and do the same.

Thursday, October 24, 1996

"Hello, Jacques."

Jacques was on Olena's lap purring and rubbing his head against the telephone receiver. He recognized his mama's voice. Olena then placed the receiver next to her ear and gave Tatiana an update as to what was going on. Vlad had instructed her and Mikheil not to give out too many details, like their location, over the phone since they didn't know who could be listening. Olena repeated Vlad's instructions to Tatiana, she was relieved to hear Tatiana was safe, staying with a friend. Tatiana was glad to hear Jacques was in good spirits and had gained a kilo but asked Olena to ease up on the treats. She didn't want her buddy getting fat and keeling over from a heart attack before she could make it back to him. Getting back was a subject both ladies avoided since they knew of the uncertainty that lay ahead. Just as she was asking about Mikheil he came through the door. Olena held up the receiver handing it to him telling him it was Tatiana.

"Tatiana, how are you? Keeping safe, I hope."

"Hello, Mikheil. Yes, I am. Are you keeping well?"

"Yes, much better now. I was just out for a nice long walk. It's great to be able to get fresh air even though it's raining and on the chilly side."

"It's the same here. Has there been any progress in tracking down the murderers?" Tatiana asked while choking back tears.

"There has been some progress but I'm hesitant to talk about it on the phone. Let me just say they are working very hard; we hope to see some results in the near future. Sorry to be so vague."

"I understand. I'm glad to hear that and that everyone is well. I don't want to tie up my friend's phone, so I'll go. Please give Jacques and Olena a hug from me and please keep an eye on Jacques and the number of treats he's getting."

"Olena is spoiling him, but I'll keep an eye out. He is getting big."

"Thank you, Mikheil. Hugs and kisses, talk again soon."

Tatiana dabbed a tear from her eyes then jumped in the shower to get ready for her appointment with Malcolm Spencer. She was very curious to hear what he had come up with. As she came downstairs, she was greeted by Lily who had Oliver in her arms burping him.

"Don't you look nice," she commented.

"Thank you."

"Hot lunch date?"

"No, nothing like that. Just a business meeting. I've looked up an old contact and I'm going to look into some possible job opportunities."

"That's great. Does that mean you might make a permanent move here?" Lily said with excitement.

"It's possible," Tatiana responded cringing inside. She hated lying to her friend that was being so kind to her but there was a possibility that she could end up staying in London.

"Hello, Ms. Grigoryev. Mr. Spencer will be with you in just a minute. Please have a seat."

"Thank you," Tatiana said noting a much friendlier greeting than the first one.

"Ms. Grigoryev, how are you today?" Malcolm said opening the office door and signaling for her to enter.

"Very well and you," Tatiana said noticing his impeccably tailored olive-green suit.

"Based on the bit of information you've provided me I've put together a plan."

"I'm excited to see what you have come up with."

"First, we're going to get you a new passport. For about ten thousand pounds you'll be the proud holder of a Marshall Islands passport."

"Marshall Islands?"

"Don't feel funny you've never heard of them, few people have. They are a chain of islands halfway between Hawaii and the Philippines. They are sparsely populated with about 50,000 people."

"Why do they issue passports to people that aren't citizens?"

"Cash, plain and simple."

"Does the passport make me a citizen?"

"No, but we can make that happen if you wish. The passport will make it very difficult for the Russian government to track you. That is what you want?"

"Yes. I will give you more details as we proceed."

"At your leisure."

"The second thing we are going to do, with your approval, is set up a couple of holding companies. I have all the details in here," Malcolm said holding up a leather-bound folder. "The purpose of the holding companies is to give you the ability to move money around with total privacy. Your name will not appear on any documents."

"Is this all legal?" Tatiana asked with a puzzled look.

"One hundred percent. We're in the business of solving problems not creating them."

"Getting back to the citizenship issue. How could you make that happen?"

"It's quite simple, really. Dozens of countries offer citizenship with investment in their countries. Some countries require as little as 100,000 US dollars, it can go as high as one million. Are you comfortable with what we've gone over so far?"

"Yes, very," Tatiana said. She really was to the point; she told Malcolm her real name and all the events that had transpired. The only detail left out was the funds that sat in two of the banks. Mr. Spencer would have to prove himself first.

Their meeting concluded with Tatiana signing some forms and giving Mr. Spencer her passport pictures. He informed her that the process didn't take very long and that everything should be in place within the next 30 days. She could call anytime to get a progress report. This was easy she thought leaving the office with fewer worries.

"Lt. Dryga, I haven't been able to find a flight manifest with the name Tatiana Belov on it for Monday, October 14th to the U.S." his FSB associate informed him.

"Please keep checking. Look at the Sunday before and the Tuesday after and call me the minute you find something."

Friday, October 25, 1996

"Have you been able to get a name for that face?" Vlad asked Ivan.

"I'm meeting with a couple of guys today that know Voshkolup, they can probably come up with something," Pavel interjected.

"Okay, I'm meeting with Litskevich and Dryga today, hopefully, they'll be able to come up with a name."

"Dmitri, Berezovsky is out of the hospital now and will be at the Presidential Club this afternoon. I want you to see if he can identify this guy and give you anything on Voshkolup. I don't want you to spend the day there. In and out, there's a lot to do."

"Yes, boss. I'm sure Berezovsky will be very happy to help us after what they did to him. That poor guy, have you seen how badly he was burned?"

"It's horrible, but we're not 100 percent sure Voshkolup was behind his attempted assassination."

"It has his fingerprints all over it, besides it works well for us to have someone like Berezovsky on our side."

"True. Let's all meet for dinner this evening, we'll discuss what we've all found. It will be on me, there might even be some drinks involved."

"Tatiana, how are you?" screamed a thrilled Anna into the phone.

"Great. What are you doing tonight?"

"Nothing, why?"

"I think we need to get out on the town."

"Just the two of us?"

"Yes, I tried to talk Lily into coming out tonight, but she doesn't think she'll be up for it. Motherhood you know."

"I would love to. Do you have anywhere in mind, like Piccadilly?"

"Very funny. I'll leave it totally up to you as this is your town."

"Do you like live music?"

"Definitely."

"I have just the spot for us. I'll swing by Lily's place at eight, we'll go from there."

"Perfect!"

Miroslav Jablokov. The name was repeated by Pavel, Vlad, and Dmitri. There was now zero doubt about the identity of the man they were looking for. Soon as business for the evening had concluded Ivan was calling for shots to the waiter. Katerina had joined them for dinner and was throwing them back with the guys. Ivan was really glad to see her with his hopes up for a return engagement. Katerina was looking super-hot tonight in the tightest jeans, four-inch high heels, and a skin-tight sleeveless top that left absolutely nothing to the imagination. She was wearing the perfume that filled his nose just five days earlier. He repeated to himself, play it cool.

Pavel noticed Ivan looking at Katerina with puppy dog longing and sat next to him. "Could you imagine what that would be like? She would kill you."

Ivan just smiled. He so much wanted to say something but instead just called for another round of shots. The shots soon disappeared, and Ivan was pulled up on the dance floor that really wasn't a dance floor by a pretty young thing that had been secretly eyeing him for a while. Katerina's eye caught his, and a coy smile was exchanged, Ivan was clearly in demand, and it stunned him. He had gone the previous year with just one hook-up to now being the center of attention, what was happening.

Ivan's evening didn't go exactly as he wanted. While his dance partner was using the ladies' room he casually walked over to Katerina and with the courage from the vodka asked her to dance. The reply was a friendly shove to his left shoulder, "go have fun with your new friend." It was clear their night of passion was going to be just that, one night.

"Shots, shots, shots," was a now familiar cry Anna was hearing from her new friend. They were standing at a loud dive bar in Camden. The band was covering Clash songs and doing a hit-or-miss job of them. A brief struggle that resembled a mosh pit scene erupted behind them as two pairs of guys in their mid-twenties fought to supply Tatiana's request.

"What do you want?" A tall skinny guy with a crew cut and neck tattoo from the winning team asked.

"Fuzzy navels."

"Fuzzy navels for the ladies, we'll do a couple of Jaggers," he yelled with a thick Irish accent over the band's rendition of London Calling.

"Cheers," Anna called out hoisting her shot glass in front of her, clinking with her new friends.

"Let's dance," Tatiana said slamming her shot glass on the bar.

"We don't dance," the tall skinny guy said.

Tatiana grabbed Anna's hand and they were off. When they returned from the dance floor now wet from sweating Tatiana's "shots, shots, shots," cry started again. The request this time was met by a pair of guys that looked like they had come straight from the office. After a round of drinks and small talk about where everyone was from and what they did for a living, it was decided to move on to a new venue just half a block away. The music was more to the liking of the girls and unlike the previous guys they had met these guys, Dave and Michael enjoyed dancing. Their ties tucked into their pockets and the lady's arms around their necks, tongues were now being exchanged. When the beat of the music picked up with the real Clash's Should I Stay or Should I Go the couples returned to their table where more drinks soon arrived.

It turned out that Dave and Michael were roommates and lived in neighboring Russell Square. Michael suggested they head back to their place for a nightcap, the girls nodded in agreement, and the couples were soon crammed in the back of a black taxi snogging all the way.

"We're here ladies and gentlemen," announced the cab driver.

They all separated exiting the taxi laughing and walking toward the flat in a zig-zag pattern. After very quick drinks the couples made their way to the bedrooms and weren't seen again until late morning.

Saturday, October 26, 1996

Sergei awoke to the 6:00 a.m. roll call at Butyrka Prison. Breakfast, if you could call it that, was served a short time after consisting of a chunk of rye bread uncooked in the center and a clump of tea with a pot of hot water. He ate the bread each day with the same thought how am I going to do this day after day for months on end. Each day it seemed an inmate had reached their breaking point and like clockwork, it ended with a cell door opening, the shuffle of guard's feet, groans and screams ending when the latest victim was hauled away to solitary. After a few bites of bread and a couple of swallows of tea, he lay down on the bed and tried to sleep. It was very difficult because even after several days his ribs weren't feeling any better, his breathing was becoming more labored, then there was the smell of human waste that continuously hung in the air. He had requested a doctor's visit but each time it was met by a snicker. This was day eight of his incarceration, his only escape was sleep and it came only after an imaginary talk at the breakfast table with his wife and sons.

Tatiana used her key trying to sneak in as quietly as possible. She knew everyone would be up after all it was almost noon but hoped she wouldn't be noticed. No luck.

"Good morning, sunshine or should I say good afternoon," was Trevor's greeting. "Look what the cat dragged in," he called out to Lily who was standing in the entrance to the kitchen with a cup of tea in hand.

"Looks like someone had fun," said a grinning Lily. "Where did you end up last night?"

"I'd rather not talk about it," Tatiana said with a raspy voice. "I'd just like some coffee and go to bed."

"Was he hot?" continued Lily.

"Who said there was a guy involved? I might have just crashed at Anna's last night."

"Not with hair like that you didn't."

Tatiana thought, busted, as she ran her fingers across the back of her head. "I'm not going to talk about it" and with a whisper came, "not in front of Trevor."

Lily giggled. "There was a call for you a couple of hours ago from Mikheil, he said it was important for you to get back to him."

"Did he say what it was about?"

"No, he left a message on the machine while we were out this morning."

"Thank you." With that Tatiana put her coffee down and went straight to the phone. Mikheil answered on the second ring.

"Tatiana, I'm so glad to hear from you. I got some news from Vlad this morning, a lot has been going on. His team was able to identify Boris Voshkolup's, right-hand man."

"Who is Boris Voshkolup?" Tatiana interjected.

"I'm sorry, I'm jumping ahead a bit."

"Voshkolup has been traced back as the owner of the warehouse where Lev was killed. He is the head of the Solntsevskaya bratva, the Russian mafia; we've identified his right-hand man. His name is Miroslav

Jablokov and Litskevich informed Vlad that he had been in Zurich just a few days ago."

"What are you telling me? Do they know who I am?"

"I don't know, things are starting to move quite quickly here. It might just be a coincidence, but Vlad wanted to keep you in the loop. You need to be careful."

"Has Vlad been working with the FSB?" a worried Tatiana asked.

"He has, they have been exchanging information but don't worry they don't know about you. Vlad hasn't told them everything."

"Are you sure?"

"Yes, I've been under Vlad's watch the entire time, he's a straight shooter. He would have told me."

"Thank you, Mikheil."

"Tatiana, please keep your cell phone on in case I need to get a hold of you, and don't worry I'll keep you updated with any developments."

"Thank you, thank you."

Litskevich was successful in identifying Jablokov but a question had been raised when he was working with an assistant on the flight manifests to Zurich. The assistant that routinely did this kind of work had mentioned Dryga's investigation of Tatiana Belov's travels and said she was still looking into it; nothing had been found so far. Litskevich said he'd pass along the update but when he said the name Tatiana Belov, Dryga said, "who?" He let it go thinking the assistant probably had confused the investigator and it was a different case, there was always so much going on.

When Litskevich spoke to Vlad and Jablokov's identity had been confirmed Vlad brought up the Berezovsky attack inquiring about a possible connection. The manner of the attacks was slightly different, Berezovsky's car had been blown up, his driver killed. They were traveling to a business meeting through Moscow's congested streets in his bulletproof Mercedes, and a car they pulled up next to was detonated. Arkadiy's attack happened by RPG in the middle of nowhere. It was the timing of the attacks, just days apart, that raised questions in Vlad's mind. Litskevich said he would look into it, and he did. The Berezovsky file was quite thick, and it contained a lot of information, it would take days to comb through.

Sunday, October 27, 1996

The sun had been up for three hours illuminating a dust-filled apartment. Dryga was looking forward to hitting his pillow. It had been a long frustrating night that started out at the blackjack table in the dingy basement of a Chinese restaurant and ended up at a poker table at a local social club filled with cigar smoke. Neither game was successful, he lost a month's rent; it wasn't a good night. What now he thought as he noticed the red light flashing on his answering machine.

"It's Jablokov," call me.

"I just want to sleep," he said out loud to himself.

"I need an update on that girl, Tatiana Belov. Voshkolup is going ape shit about this."

"I'm working on it. Really, I am. It's Sunday, if I go in and press them on it it will cause problems. I was asked about her by my partner yesterday and I played dumb. I'm going to get some sleep and think about how I'm going to handle this. I expect to have something for you by tomorrow."

"Please, I don't want to be called into his office and deal with the maniac. You have to get me something."

"Tomorrow." Dryga hung up the phone his pillow was seconds away.

Sunday wasn't a good day for Magnitsky. Roll call was called and he couldn't get out of bed, the pain from his ribs was just excruciating. He lay there groaning and a guard called for the nurse, the doctor was off enjoying his day of rest. The nurse removed Sergei's heavy cotton pullover, he thought he was going to pass out raising his arms above his head. She wrapped his upper torso with a stretchy bandage that seemed to offer a little relief, this was followed by a few aspirins. The pullover was pulled back over, and pain shot through his body. He asked if the doctor would be able to see him. "You'll be fine," she said and exited.

Tatiana, Lily, Trevor, and Oliver were leaving the Hyde Park Corner tube station for a day out in the park. The sun was out but a strong chilly wind blew across their faces giving them all a rosy glow as they hiked around the Serpentine. Oliver had the luxury of a stroller; Tatiana was happy to be the driver. "This park is huge," Tatiana said for the second time. Trevor took this as a cue that they had done enough walking, it was time to grab some food and drinks. They ended up at a restaurant at the end of the lake and were soon enjoying sandwiches, wine, beer, and Tizer for Oliver.

"Tatiana, how did your meeting go on Thursday?" Trevor asked.

"Fine," her heart rate quickened; she wondered how he knew.

"Do you think you'll have a problem finding a position with one of the big banks here or are you staying with Menatep?"

She realized it was the story she told Lily, replying with an "I'm really not sure."

"I have a few friends that work with some large investment firms, they are always looking for good people. With Russia opening up I'm sure you'd be in high demand. Let me know if you want me to put the word out."

"That would be fantastic," Lily said beaming.

"It would, I'm really loving it here in London. I'll have a better idea in the next few weeks as to what's going on with my assignment here."

"When do they plan on putting you to work?"

"I have done a bit of research and submitted a couple of reports. I expect they'll have more for me this coming week," Tatiana said lying through her teeth.

"When did you do that?" Lily asked with a puzzled expression.

"Last week. I was able to send the reports electronically using the library computer."

"So, it hasn't been all holiday for you?"

"For the most part, it has but things will get busier. I would like to stay but there is so much up in the air right now; I'm taking it week by week."

"Let me know if I can help," Trevor added.

After a relaxing hour at the restaurant, Oliver started getting restless, and they headed back to the tube. Tatiana was deep in thought on the way back, it was time to tighten up her story and make plans for a possible departure. Mikheil's news left her feeling unsettled.

"Who wrapped him with the bandage?" the doctor cried out obviously annoyed. "Guard, get an ambulance, right away."

Sergei was rushed out of the prison on a stretcher and was soon on an operating table. An x-ray revealed that the stretchy bandage that the nurse wrapped around his body caused his left lung to fill with fluid. The bandage had pushed a rib into the lung, it needed to be drained.

Sergei, with an oxygen mask over his mouth and nose, was coming in and out of consciousness. The ceiling lights of the hospital corridor were passing in a long blur. The gurney he was now on entered the operating room; he was staring at a big, bright round light. He wondered if that would be the last thing he ever saw. He was hoisted onto the operating table; the clear oxygen mask was removed; it was replaced by a rubbery-smelling black mask. He felt very lightheaded and then nothing, he was out.

A nurse wiped his torso down with alcohol and commented on the horrific bruising she was looking at. The doctor said, "Butyrka," nothing more needed to be said. Using a needle, a tube was inserted between Sergei's ribs into the lung, and immediately a yellowy pea soup-like fluid emerged filling the clear bag. They had just saved Sergei's life.

An hour later, against the advice of the surgeon, Sergei was leaving the hospital and was on his way to the prison infirmary; two guards were his escorts. He was still groggy from the anesthesia but despite that was handcuffed to the stretcher that was sitting on the floor of a prison van. Every bump felt like another punch to his battered body. There was no ambulance for the ride back.

"Lt. Dryga, I haven't been able to find a Tatiana Belov on any flight manifests out of Zurich. I've looked at all flights to the US from Zurich on Sunday, October 13 to Tuesday, October 15, and nothing. I even looked at flights back to here on those dates, and still nothing. Do you want me to continue to look?" asked the FSB associate, Miss Balakin.

Not wanting to draw any more attention to his search he thanked the associate and said he would take another approach. With any luck, nothing more would be said about this. Dryga's brain was churning. Where would this woman, with plenty of cash go and how would she get there. Was she traveling under her own name. He had to make a call he wasn't looking forward to before his partner joined him for a busy day of work.

"Miroslav, I don't have good news. I haven't been able to come up with anything. She did not fly to the States or come back here, at least not flying. It's possible she's traveling using an alias."

"I thought you fuckers knew everything about everyone. What am I going to tell the big man?"

"I'm doing my best. I must be careful, questions about this are starting to be raised by my partner. Our research associate has already said something to him. I played dumb about it."

"We pay you a lot of money, that's going to come to an end very quickly if you don't come up with something."

"I know, I know. I need to go, my partner just got here." The phone went dead.

Litskevich, who was usually on time to the point you could set your watch by him, was several minutes late. He explained to Dryga that traffic was snarled up due to a shot-up car and a few bodies strewn in the street on his way in. There weren't any investigators at the scene yet, he was hoping it wouldn't be assigned to them. There was only so much they could handle.

"Look at this!" Litskevich said standing at his desk waving a piece of paper in the air. He handed the page to Dryga.

"Incredible!" Dryga cried out trying to sound excited.

"This places Jablokov at the metal shop where Drozdov was killed," referring to the fingerprint report.

Litskevich continued on to the accompanying pages. It was Jablokov's lengthy criminal record, and it was what he would expect of a high-ranking mafia member. It contained petty theft from an early age to assaults and truck hijackings. All the charges in the past five years had ended with dismissals or acquittals. In Russia that meant only one thing, powerful friends.

"Let's talk to Kovalyov and figure out a plan. Now that we know we're dealing with Voshkolup we need to be very careful."

Litskevich knocked on the Major's open door. "Do you have a minute?"

"Not really, it's Monday morning and bodies are already starting to pile up."

Shit thought Litskevich, please give those cases to someone else. He started talking very quickly in the hope to avoid any upcoming assignments.

"It'll just take a minute. I think we might have a break in the Drozdov case."

"Drozdov?" Kovalyov questioned sounding irritated.

"Abramov's guy," Dryga clarified.

"Okay."

"We have tied Voshkolup's right-hand man's fingerprints to the metal shop where he was killed. The metal shop is owned indirectly by Voshkolup and the van used in the abduction was registered to the business. This has Solntsevskaya written all over it."

They now had their boss's full attention and could see the wheels turning in his head. "We need to proceed very carefully," were his next words. The three men spent the next half hour behind closed doors coming up with their next steps. Dryga interjected a couple of times with his thoughts on how they should approach this but was overruled by the boss. The next few days would be crucial in putting this case to rest.

Thursday, October 31, 1996

Three days had passed since a light blanket of snow turned everything white, Mikheil and Olena were talking with Vlad about their hiding out. They expressed to him their appreciation for looking out for their safety but had had enough. Even though the cabin in Popovka was an improvement it was a major interruption in their lives. Soon they would be stuck inside again for possibly weeks on end. Vlad totally understood, even being able to switch off with another security team member and travel into the office for meetings, he was growing weary of the hiding too. He agreed he would talk to Katerina about them all resuming their normal lives.

Three days passed since Litskevich, Dryga, Mikheyev, and Turov, the elites of Dept. K had gathered to put a plan together to infiltrate Voshkolup's home in Kuntsevo. It was coincidentally the same neighborhood where Arkadiy had lived, only a few streets over. It was a contemporary bunker-like structure constructed of thick concrete surrounded by a three-meter-high gray stucco wall. It stood out from all the traditional styled homes on the street. Cameras jutted out from every corner of the home and at numerous points on the surrounding wall. Various tactics were used to get a close view of the bunker where Voshkolup did the majority of his business. This involved intercepting a package from a courier and posing as him. They also posed as linemen and with high-powered binoculars noted possible entry points. These points were limited as most of the windows were narrow slits, too narrow for someone to squeeze through. It was ultimately decided that they would simply enter through a back door in the dead of night. Listening devices would be planted in several strategic locations.

The plan to enter had been delayed by a day because of something they didn't anticipate, fresh snow. It would have indicated every step that was taken on the vast property. Fortunately, warmer weather was in the next day's forecast, and most of the snow melted. The entry plan involved a power disruption from the main grid as well as the backup generator. From then on it involved simple locksmith techniques.

By day three everything was in place, the bugs, a tap on the phone, and surveillance of Jablokov. It was decided they wouldn't follow Voshkolup because of the fact he rarely left his home. Why would he. Their break-in had discovered an indoor swimming pool, a library, a snooker room with video games, and pinball machines. There was even a spa and a bowling alley in the sprawling complex.

A white contractor van located around the corner from the house was manned by Mikheyev and Turov, the pair listening intently, each wearing headphones but not hearing anything.

"I got something."

"It sounds like a vacuum cleaner," responded Mikheyev listening to Turov's headphones.

"That's what it is. Now we know at least one of the bugs is working," said Mikheyev. "I'm still not getting anything as he flipped a switch between two of the listening devices."

Dryga and Litskevich were in separate cars, Dryga's beat up, pieced together Lada and Litskevich in his immaculate, spotless one. They were in contact by radio, taking turns being the lead car tailing Jablokov. It was usually an effective method used to avoid detection if the tailed person hadn't been tipped off. Litskevich was starting to get frustrated and they had only been doing this for a day.

Jablokov had driven around for an hour, apparently for no reason. There had been a stop at a laundromat to pick up some clothes, a long lunch, more driving to nowhere, a stop at the park, and then home. He was glad that they'd be switching off with Mikheyev and Turov tomorrow, sitting in the van drinking coffee and eating ponchiki.

The first half of Tatiana's week began at lunch with Anna that morphed into a bar-hopping happy hour. The two of them toured a good part of Soho, Tatiana financing the boozefest when there wasn't a gentleman around to supply the libations. Lily, who was putting a late dinner on the table, heard the door open and called out thinking it was Trevor coming home from the office. "It's me," said a slightly slurring Tatiana picking up a chip from a still-hot baking sheet.

"Where have you been?" Lily asked.

"Where haven't I been," responded Tatiana. "I'm drunk."

"I can see that. Was Anna your partner in crime?"

"Most definitely. She's so much fun. You'll have to join us for the next crawl."

"Someday," Lily said trying to hide the fact that she was annoyed. "Dinner's ready, grab a plate."

"Thanks, but I'm not hungry. I think I'm going to go for a nap."

Lily fed Oliver and put a plate together for Trevor who had just walked in. He inquired about Tatiana and was given the low down. He could see Lily wasn't happy and sensed she was starting to feel like she was being taken advantage of.

Tuesday began with Lily hearing Tatiana talking and giggling to someone while descending the stairs. She was on her phone with Anna, it sounded like plans were in the works for another night out. Lily didn't want to be confrontational so she let it go but decided it might be time to chat with her friend about her late nights, make that early mornings, and party lifestyle. She knew her friend was going through a lot with the loss of Lev and all of the uncertainty in her life now, but she was tired of feeling like a guest in her own home. She didn't want to sound like a mother and lecture Tatiana so she decided she'd get a sitter for Oliver; the two of them would do lunch.

"How is your mother doing?" Lily inquired.

"She's well. I feel very guilty though. I'm always making excuses why I can't see her, I miss her a lot."

"It was the same way with my mom but since Oliver came along, I see her much more. There's no way I can keep her away."

"How are you coping? I know it's been tough for you."

"I'm fine, Lily. Like everyone I have good days and some bad ones, but overall, I'm fine."

"I worry about how you cope with things sometimes. I don't want to sound like a mother, but your partying and drinking worry me."

"I'm fine, really Lily. Thank you for your concern."

Lunch continued with girl talk and plans for a day-long shopping trip in the near future. It ended with hugs and plans to meet at home in a couple of hours. Lily went off to pick up dry cleaning and groceries and Tatiana told of a visit to her imaginary office. Tatiana went to the library instead. She went to the familiar finance section and did some more reading that would help her manage the fortune she was now in control of.

Friday, November 1, 1996

Dryga stumbled out of a cheap hotel on the seedier side of Moscow, exactly where he wasn't sure. It looked vaguely familiar, but he had only seen that part of town for minutes sober. The woman he'd left upstairs, Olga or Helga, had been a lot of fun, they both said they'd see each other again but that was very unlikely. He lit a cigarette and set off on a mission to find his car so he could get the workday started. There wasn't any time to go home, shower, and put on clean clothes, he knew this would become a topic of conversation later.

"Where have you been?" was Litskevich's aggravated greeting. "We need to relieve the guys in the van."

"It's a long story."

"It always is. Man, you smell like shit. I'm not going to be in the back of the surveillance van with you all day smelling like that."

"Are you serious?"

"Yes, go home and clean up. I'll meet you in the van."

Litskevich donned his coveralls, looking like a tradesman of some kind, walking a couple of blocks to the white van. He knocked on the door, and an FSB officer he had never worked with emerged. They stood outside, he was given an update. There was very little to report. Voshkolup had a female friend over and there was hours of chatter between the two. They ended up in the bedroom, where there was no bug, and she left a few hours later. "Maybe we should have put one in the bedroom for entertainment purposes," Litskevich joked. Ultimately there wasn't anything that would interest the FSB and the first guy left. He entered the van, exchanged small talk with officer number two, then he left. He was now alone monitoring four listening devices by himself, fortunately, all was quiet. An hour later there was a knock, and a better smelling Dryga entered.

"Has there been any activity?"

"Nothing yet. I thought you would have brought some coffee."

"Sorry. I'll get some soon. Thanks for covering for me."

"You owe me."

They sat silently in the van for an hour, still no signs of life. Dryga needed a smoke and offered to do a coffee run. Perfect timing Litskevich thought as he was starting to feel a little drowsy and could use some caffeine. Several minutes after Dryga had left a bug was picking up some activity, it was coming from Voshkolup's office. Papers were being shuffled; the creak of an office chair was heard. Minutes later there was a knock on the door.

"Ya, come in."

"Boss, we might have something on that Belov girl."

There were then some footsteps and about ten seconds of silence before the conversation resumed.

A couple of things caught Litskevich's attention and sent a sinking feeling deep into his stomach. First was that name. He had heard it before, his mind was racing to place it. Second was the pause in the conversation, the fact there was no continuity to it. Something wasn't right. Dryga returned with a couple of coffees.

"Thanks."

"Did I miss anything?" Dryga asked.

"The big man is having a meeting." Litskevich unplugged the headphones, and they listened over a small speaker.

"Is that Jablokov?" Dryga asked knowing it wasn't.

"I don't know."

Voshkolup talked about "his fine piece of ass" from last night, and the other guy talked about some of his recent conquests but nothing of a business nature. After several minutes of this they said their goodbyes, the door closed, there was some more paper shuffling and then Voshkolup left the office. Ten minutes later they saw a large black Mercedes with dark-tinted rear windows pass their van. They assumed it was the big man going off somewhere for lunch.

Litskevich sipped on his now cold coffee. Something was definitely wrong. He wasn't being paranoid, be cool he thought to himself. A couple of hours later they were monitoring sporadic senseless phone conversations but mostly silence. Small talk about sports and movies was exchanged between the partners during the moments of bug silence but Litskevich couldn't shake the feeling that he had a rat in the van with him. They had worked together for more than five years; over the last few he had seen Dryga's life spiraling downward. He couldn't shake the question of whether he was on the take. This was one of Litskevich's longest days of his life. He couldn't get out of this van fast enough.

Vlad's team had been doing some reconnaissance and surveillance work of their own with surprising results. Pavel and Dmitri befriended a couple of the thugs that worked closely with Jablokov. It took a couple of *chance* encounters at a bar that sported a couple of pool tables, their names were Anatoli and Mo. They were both secretive, which was expected, and claimed to be in sales. When asked what they sold, out came, "you don't want to know". It was left at that. Pavel and Dmitri knew the importance of taking it slow and not spooking these guys. Under different circumstances, these guys seemed like they could be fun to hang with.

Ivan was using his research skills to find out everything he could about Voshkolup and Jablokov. There wasn't a whole lot; this was where Vlad would have to do more schmoozing with Litskevich. Ivan did come across something interesting though. Voshkolup had just been placed on the FBI's ten most wanted list described as the most dangerous man on earth. He was wanted for fraud by wire, racketeering, mail fraud, money laundering, aiding and abetting, securities fraud, false SEC registration, false filings with the SEC, and falsification of books and records. Ivan wondered about the arms dealing, murder, and extortion. He figured the FBI would leave those charges for the FSB to deal with.

Ivan had a chance to lock eyes with his old flame Katerina the day before when they had a meeting, she was given an update on their progress. She was wearing the same perfume she had on in the cabin and it brought back memories of that night. He knew deep down it would never happen again, but he would always hold out hope.

Saturday, November 2, 1996

"Tatiana, I don't want you to panic but your name has come up in the investigation," Mikheil said in a calming voice.

"What?" was the panicked reply.

"It's okay. We don't believe they know where you are."

"How is this? Who are the they?"

"I don't have all the details, but I just got off the phone with Vlad and one of the FSB officers asked him about you. Naturally, he played dumb but doesn't know how long he can get away with it. Vlad has been giving Litskevich tidbits of information in return for updates on their investigation. It's been give and take with both sides only giving up what they need to. He's assured me he'll end all communication with the FSB if pushed for information about you. He hasn't even asked me where you are."

"Are you and Olena safe?"

"Yes, from everything Vlad can gather we haven't appeared on anyone's radar screen. He expects that we should be able to get back to our normal routines within the next couple of days. The reason I'm telling you this is so you can have a plan B if Voshkolup and his guys identify you."

"I think Voshkolup and his guys know who I am since they were probably the ones that trashed my place. It has me wondering how the FSB has come up with my name."

"Vlad was wondering the same thing. I think you need to be prepared to bolt from where you are with a moment's notice."

"I think that's a good call. I'll start putting a plan in place. How's Jacques doing?"

"He is good but still getting bigger. I keep telling Olena to stop giving him treats but you know how she is."

"I miss him and you and Olena. Please thank her for taking such good care of my buddy."

Tatiana hung up the phone her mind racing. Slow down she thought, one step at a time. She couldn't do anything in haste that she would regret later. She went upstairs to her room, the house was nice and quiet, and she lay down on the bed.

"What the fuck is this? came over Dryga's radio." It was an obviously annoyed Litskevich.

"What's going on?"

"I've just been cut off by a couple of assholes who are now on Jablokov's ass. This isn't looking good."

"Where are you?"

"I'm on Kutuzovsky about a kilometer from Third Ring."

"What are they driving?"

"It's a black Saab, plate Y513PT78."

"I'll see if I can get in front at Third Ring," Dryga said while putting a flashing light on his roof and flooring his sputtering Lada. "Come on you piece of shit," he cried out. Fortunately, the car heard his cry and seemed to come to life. Traffic reluctantly moved over as he was speeding down Third Ring towards Kutuzovsky. He removed the flashing light from the roof, making a dangerous right-hand turn in front of the Saab. Now with the assholes between them, Dryga said, "get ready" locking his brakes. The asshole's car skidded to a stop with Litskevich's doing the same, all bumpers now just millimeters apart. With guns drawn the assholes were ordered out of their car.

"Put your gun down," Litskevich called to his partner. He instantly recognized the assholes. "It's Vlad."

"What the fuck is going on?" Dryga yelled as drivers cautiously inched around the three stopped vehicles.

"What are you guys doing?" Litskevich asked and realizing it was a dumb question as it left his mouth.

"Sorry, man," Vlad said now leaning on the front fender of his car, Ivan looking on still visibly shaken at almost being shot.

"What were you thinking? If we didn't shoot you the guys you were following would have without so much as a thought. Get out of here before we attract more attention. We'll talk later."

Ivan climbed into the passenger seat looking quite pale. Vlad looked at him and said, "time for a drink."

Miroslav and Anatoli pulled up to Voshkolup's gate, drove 30 meters, and parked in front of the garage. They were met at the front door by Mo who led them to the snooker room. The snooker room had been swept for bugs where they could talk without FSB ears.

"What happened today?" Voshkolup asked, looking mildly irritated.

"We were being followed by Dryga and his guy then a black Saab started riding our ass. They backed off a bit when Dryga boxed the guy in, and they were pulled from the car," Jablokov recounted.

"Any idea who these guys are?"

"Not yet. I'll talk to Dryga later."

"Could it have been one of Berezovsky's crew?"

"No idea. I've never seen these guys before."

"I got the Saab's plate number," Anatoli added.

Voshkolup signaled to the two men to follow him down the hallway to his office.

"Miroslav, how was your date last night? Get any?"

"I always do boss." The pointless conversation continued for Turov and Mikheyev for several more minutes and then the pair departed, this time without a tail.

Litskevich spent the previous night tossing and turning. His mind ran through a possible explanation for Dryga's denial of knowing Tatiana Belov on more than one occasion. Then there was that gap in conversation he had heard from the bug in Voshkolup's office. His gut told him his partner was dirty, that feeling was backed up further by his freewheeling lifestyle. How was he supporting a chronically sick mother, four kids, a wife, and the numerous women that rotated through his life, not to mention the gambling losses.

Litskevich and Dryga were now back at headquarters giving their boss, Kovalyov a verbal rundown of the day's events. They were cautioned to be very careful and warned about the dangerous bratva boss.

"Keep eyes in the back of your heads," was the caution given as they left the office.

The partners said their goodbyes and wished each other a nice day off. Dryga drove off while Litskevich fumbled around in his car for missing imaginary keys. Once the coast was clear he exited his car and went back inside.

Sunday, November 3, 1996

Sergei awoke in a new cell, just several doors down from his original cell at Butyrka. His breathing had been normal for a few days, the ribs were healing. Movement was still painful but slowly improving, just don't cough or sneeze he thought. The greatest pain he was experiencing though was the mental anguish from not seeing his family. He wondered if they were told of his emergency surgery and when he would see them again. He was feeling very lonely and isolated. While in the infirmary he had a couple of fellow prisoners to chat with, as well as the nurses that were tending to him. When would he see his lawyer, also came to mind. He had been locked up for almost 10 days and not informed of any charges. His whole life was in limbo.

"Alexander, what is wrong? You've been quiet all day and you haven't been hungry," Nataliya said while laying on top of him on the couch.

"I'm sorry but there's a lot going on at work."

"There always is, what is going on now?"

"I really don't want to talk about it. It's looking like some bad shit."

"You can't tell me you're dealing with bad shit and expect me to let it go. What's going on?"

He knew he had just opened a can of worms and decided to tell his wife everything. It was probably a good idea since it could become an issue for her if things got nasty. If Dryga was crooked and dealing with Voshkolup who knows how this could all play out. He told her of the airline manifest search and the surveillance, but not mentioning Voshkolup's name. He also relayed his suspicions about Dryga affording the keep of his family, the boozing, and gambling. The regret he was starting to feel was he didn't suspect something sooner. Although he couldn't put his finger on a specific incident there had been a few times when things didn't feel right. He attributed it to friendship clouding his judgment.

Now that he had talked to his boss about it, he was also dealing with feelings of guilt. What if he was wrong. What if there was an explanation for it all. He decided he would rely on his gut and as Nataliya pointed out it was what made him a good investigator.

Tatiana spent much of her day cleaning. First her room and bathroom, then helping Lily with the kitchen. The thought in the back of her mind was not wanting to leave a mess behind if she needed to make a quick getaway. All her clothes were neatly folded, ready to be packed away in a suitcase at a moment's notice. Thoughts raced through her mind as to what she would tell her friend if she left hastily. Where would she go was another consideration. She would set up a meeting with Malcolm, get a progress report, and put some tentative plans in place tomorrow if he could see her.

Tatiana helped with the Sunday roast beef dinner and was helping clear the dirty dishes. After a cup of tea and a chat with Trevor and Lily, Oliver began screaming at the top of his lungs. It was his bedtime; he was getting cranky. She decided she needed a break from the house after being inside all day. Walking Raynes Park Streets for about twenty minutes a refreshment was in order; time for a glass of wine. One glass she thought, she didn't want to be read the riot act from Lily.

"Litskevich, you're going to be in the van surveilling Voshkolup, Dryga you're flying out to Kemerovo. Now we know who we're dealing with I need you to check flight manifests around the time of the RPG attack and visit Major Petrov in Topki again. I want you to show him Jablokov's picture and pictures of Voshkolup's associates, let's hope we can identify a suspect."

"Yes, Major Kovalyov, but is it necessary to travel out there? I could do the research from here and do an ID electronically."

"I'm not sure if the Topki police department is that technically savvy, besides I need you out there really digging for information. I want you to talk to people now we have possible faces to tie to this. There's a flight leaving in two and a half hours, I need you on it."

"Litskevich, stop back here after Turov relieves you. I want to comb over the bug transcripts with you."

"Yes, sir."

Litskevich worried about how the meeting with the boss was going to play out. It looked like the plan was to keep Dryga at a distance until suspicions about him could be investigated. He wondered if separating them may cause Dryga to think something might be up. He didn't seem out of sorts by his assignment but just said a couple of days out in the country would be a nice break.

Tatiana had a restless night's sleep. She thought another glass of wine would help after she got in, but her mind would not stop. At an early breakfast with Trevor, Lily, and Oliver that elicited a, "you're up early" from Trevor, Tatiana fibbed about an early meeting at the bank when in fact she was dying to get in touch with Malcolm Spencer. Whenever she walked out of Carshalton House there was a feeling of accomplishment and relief like something was being done to build a protective wall around her.

After breakfast and a shower, Tatiana was out the door and, on the phone making her appointment. She was placed on hold for a few minutes while the receptionist conferred with Malcolm about fitting Tatiana in. She had explained that it was important for her to see him this morning and Malcolm, sensing the urgency, adjusted his schedule for a 10:00 meeting. Ms. Belov was a VIP client.

"Mr. Spencer, thank you for seeing me on such short notice," Tatiana said noticing he was wearing another very nice expensive suit.

"Please, it's Malcolm."

"Sorry, Malcolm."

"What can I help you with?"

"First, do you have any updates as far as the passport?"

"Well, it's only been about a week. I would expect it to take a couple more weeks. Has something happened that might make it necessary to speed things up?"

"Yes. I may have to leave the country in a hurry. Can something be done to speed the passport process up?"

"Certainly. I've run into situations where things need to be expedited and they can be, however, it will take an additional fee. Something like that involves greasing some palms if you know what I mean."

"Of course, I do. You know I'm from Russia," they chuckled at that.

"How soon do you need the passport?"

"Can you have it by next week?"

"Consider it done. I do have some good news; I believe the setup of your holding company is just days away. We'll be able to move funds immediately after we get confirmation."

"That is very good news," Tatiana said trying not to sound excited but feeling her heart beating a little faster. The thought of getting some more cash to Mikheil and Olena was a priority. It would give them peace of mind and the ability to move around a bit more freely. Malcolm concluded their meeting by saying he would be in touch with any updates and to expect a call soon.

Tatiana exited the office buttoning up her wool coat as she hit the cool damp London air. She pulled out her phone and called Anna.

"Anna let's do lunch."

"I can't Tat, I have this thing to do called work."

"Blow it off."

"I can't. Let's meet up after."

"Okay, that will work. I'm in the mood to have some fun."

"You do know it's Monday."

"Quit sounding like an old woman. I'll meet you at the Fox and Hounds at 5:30."

"Ciao, bella."

Litskevich got a call from Turov that they were heading his way. A minute and a half later Jablokov was at the gate, two minutes later Turov and Mikheyev were driving past the surveillance van. Jablokov had been in the house for five minutes, there was no activity coming from the bugs. He and Voshkolup were conducting their meeting in the snooker room again. This meeting had such a sinister tone to it that made Jablokov so uncomfortable he felt a shit coming on.

"Are you sure you want it handled that way?" Miroslav said trying to sound diplomatic and not set off the big man.

"Definitely, I want a message sent."

Finally, Litskevich picked up activity but as he predicted it revealed nothing, just small talk. This pretty much confirmed his initial hunch, he felt better relaying his concerns to his boss but it gave him a sickly feeling that his partner likely had crossed sides. He called Kovalyov with an update, it was decided at that moment they had been compromised and the listening surveillance was terminated. They would meet later and discuss the tracking of Jablokov.

Tuesday, November 5, 1996

Vlad was relieved to get back to a more normal routine. There was still the burden of having eyes in the back of his head but now they were just looking out for him. Mikheil and Olena had each returned to their homes, Mikheil to Kubinka, and Olena to Nizhny. Each was using the same story about a family emergency when asked by friends where they were for the past month. Eyebrows were raised and lectures were given about them being inconsiderate for not telling anyone, but they would all get over it. Mikheil had the added challenge of having his boss put him back on the schedule bartending at the restaurant he worked for the past three years. His absence lost him his prime Friday and Saturday night shifts but at least he got a few nights back. The bulk of his bills would be covered.

"Vlad, have you heard from Mikheil and Olena today?" Katerina inquired calling him after he just arrived home.

"Everyone is good. Is everything calm over there?"

"Yes. Things have been a little too calm. I'd like you to set up a meeting with Litskevich soon, have him update us on what he's learned."

"I'll reach out to him first thing in the morning."

"Are you still at the office?"

"Yes, but I'm almost done. I'll be leaving shortly."

"You're not alone there are you?"

"No, Pavel is here. Don't worry I'm being careful, one of the security team is always with me and they follow me home each day."

"Good. I don't want us to start letting our guard down."

"Thank you for looking out for me. I'll see you tomorrow."

"Good night."

Vlad went over to the fridge and stood there looking at the only two things in it, half a carton of milk and a pizza box with three slices of pepperoni pie left. Deciding what dinner was going to be was a no-brainer. Just as he was reaching inside the fridge, he heard the apartment doorknob move. He was relieved to realize it was locked, he reached for the Glock strapped underneath his arm and turned out the kitchen light.

As he hit the switch the door burst open, he started firing in the direction of the light coming in from the hallway. The light was almost gone as the frame of the door filled with bodies and the flash of automatic weapon fire. He was on his stomach on the kitchen floor squeezing off rounds as quickly as he could pull the trigger. Bits of cabinet, then plates and glasses were raining down on his head in a blizzard-like fashion. The kitchen was filled with thick smoke, the gunfire not ceasing or even slowing down. His gun emptied and he was reaching for a fresh cartridge when he felt it. A hot searing pain in his left shoulder, then one in his thigh. That was the last thing he felt as the next shot entered his skull; it was all over.

Vlad left his apartment for the last time on a stretcher, his body encased in a black body bag. The apartment filled with Moscow police and the smell of gunpowder that started at the elevator 20 meters away. There was a lot of chatter and pictures being taken but that came to a halt.

"FSB, I need everyone out," announced Mekheyev waving his ID above his head.

The GUVD Moscow police officers obediently filed out, as if expecting the interruption.

"Holy shit," Turov uttered to his partner. "This was Abramov's head of security's place?"

"Yes. That's him on the floor. I'm calling Litskevich now; the crime scene unit is on its way."

Turov surveyed the damage with his notebook in hand. The refrigerator had at least a dozen bullet holes, cabinet doors that remained were hanging by a single hinge, kitchen tiles were shattered like glass and the linoleum floor had a large puddle of blood. The blood by Vlad's head had been stepped in and made footprints that led out of the door. Scattered randomly everywhere were 39mm shell casings, hundreds of them. This was AK-47 ammunition; several AKs were probably used in this attack he thought. A note was made of the visible bullet holes inflicted on Vlad; he counted seven but knew the coroner would probably find more. It was clear that the cause of death would be a single shot to the head. These guys meant business and he knew exactly who these guys were.

After Mekheyev hung up his phone he said shaking his head, "it's a coincidence this happened within hours of being pulled off our surveillance detail."

Turov just nodded.

Litskevich turned up just minutes after the crime scene unit. "Holy shit," was his first words, "this is going to be a war," was his next. He looked down at Vlad and swallowed hard, they had gotten along well almost to the point of being friends. Now this young, healthy guy who he'd been laughing with just days before was lying in a bloody mess. It was going to be a very long day.

Dmitri, Pavel, and Ivan were all gathered in the conference room. The meeting was called for by one of Katerina's assistants just ten minutes earlier, just minutes after they arrived. "Where is Vlad?" Ivan asked to shrugging shoulders.

Katerina entered with Litskevich; they knew right away something bad had gone down. It was obvious Katerina had been crying and was about to start again. Litskevich was visibly shaken too.

"I have some horrible news," Katerina said breaking the silence.

A pin could be heard dropping as they awaited the words to come from her mouth, "Vlad has been killed."

They sat there in stunned silence before Dmitri asked, "what happened?"

Litskevich stepped in as Katerina broke down attempting a response. "Armed men broke into his apartment last night and gunned him down. We've reviewed security camera footage; four masked men were seen entering his building at about 11:00 p.m. The police were called by neighbors and arrived about 11:30, we got there just after midnight."

"Did you see him?" Katerina quietly asked.

"Yes. I'm sorry but he didn't suffer," he said putting his arms around her. Katerina went into uncontrollable sobs causing tears for everyone in the room, including Litskevich. She hated when she lost control of her emotions and left the room. The guys in the room dabbed at their eyes with shirt sleeves quizzing Litskevich, getting as much information as they could. He warned them not to do anything and that the FSB would handle it. He knew that warning had fallen on deaf ears and deep down was glad. He wanted justice for Vlad as much as they did.

The guys in the conference room assumed Katerina was in her office crying uncontrollably. Wrong, that wasn't her style. She had moments of weakness like anyone, but she was steely when she needed to be.

"Konstantin, it's Katerina Grigoryev," she said into the telephone receiver.

"Good morning, Katerina."

"Unfortunately, there's nothing good about it. Our head of security, Vlad, was murdered last night, gunned down by four guys with AKs in his apartment."

"That's terrible, I'm really sorry to hear that."

"Things are getting fucking crazy and it's all leading back to one man."

"I know exactly who you're talking about."

"I'm tired of playing defense. Between our organizations, we have the resources to stomp this fucker into the ground. Let's meet up later today with our security teams."

"Yes."

Wednesday, November 6, 1996

Tatiana woke up wondering where the hell she was. She hoped she hadn't weakened and been lured to a strange guy's house. Her bra and panties were still on, a good sign she thought. Anna, that's right, she had been out boozing with Anna. She put on her jeans and blouse making her way out to the kitchen; Anna was hovered over a cup of tea looking like she felt.

"Good morning, lover," was the greeting.

"Good morning," Tatiana replied racking her brain wondering if Anna was referencing something that happened in her bed last night, she decided to let it go. "How many places did we hit last night?"

"A few. It was a wonder we made it out of the last place with our lives, the guys in there were all over us."

"Do you have work today?"

"Yes, but I called and told them I'd be a little late. You're such a bad influence. Tatiana, I have a question for you. I hope you don't think I'm being nosy."

"Shoot," Tatiana said fixing herself a cup of tea.

"I noticed you're not short of cash. You've been very generous; I was wondering what's up with that?"

"The bank pays me well and Lily doesn't accept any money for room and board so I'm, how you say, flush."

"Well, thank you but you don't need to pay for everything," Anna said feeling that wasn't the whole story.

"Talking about work, I'm going to need to make an appearance myself today."

"What do you do there?"

"I'm an economic forecaster; I'm working with the new trading desk they're setting up here. Boring, boring stuff."

"It's a lot more interesting than being an office manager at an advertising agency."

"Do you like it?"

"Yes, the people I work with are great, but I want something more challenging."

"Have you ever thought about going back to school?"

"Yes, but between the time and money, I really don't see that happening."

A seed was planted in Tatiana's head then her phone rang. It was Mikheil. "Tatiana, I have some bad news."

Dryga was woken up by his phone ringing. He was still in Topki at a budget hotel; he was hoping it was his boss summoning him back to Moscow. He hated the country.

"Where the fuck are you?"

"Miroslav?"

"Yes."

"I'm in Topki."

"Where? It doesn't matter. When will you be back, the boss is losing his shit? There's a lot going on."

Dryga was in the dark. Litskevich hadn't been in touch with him and a call to the office was going to be the first thing he did after breakfast. "I should be back tomorrow unless something comes up here."

"Call me the minute you get back," the phone went dead.

Dryga lay there thinking but stomach pains put a stop to that. There's always a fire to put out somewhere he thought to himself. Eat first, then run around and look busy was the goal of the day.

Katerina's day started with a packed conference room at Konstantin Berezovsky's headquarters. She traveled across town with Dmitri, Pavel, and Ivan. Getting up to the 18th floor was a high-security ordeal that involved a pat down and metal detectors. The guys were required to leave their weapons in lockers in the lobby, this was overseen by a half dozen large men all sporting AK-47s. It made Katerina think about how lax their security was, it was time to step things up today.

"Katerina, lovely to see you. I wish it was under better circumstances," Konstantin said walking from his seat at the head of the conference room table and giving her a warm hug. He noticed her perfume and like all men took notice of her stunning appearance. Have a seat he motioned to Katerina and the team. She was seated to his right; the conference room table was flanked by just over a dozen men all built like rugby players. Most of them had had broken noses and looked the part of capable protectors.

Konstantin took the lead as he was used to doing. "Gentlemen, Katerina and I have spoken at length and have called this meeting to put a plan in place. As you know their head of security, Vlad, was murdered in his home by heavily armed thugs less than 48 hours ago. Up until now, we have all been playing defense against our attackers. Part of the reason for that was we weren't sure who we were up against. That has changed, we know the organizer of the attacks is Boris Voshkolup. You all know him and his reputation for unrelenting, horrific violence; all you need to do is look at my scars as evidence of that. The plan is to first put together an army of men, arm them to the teeth with whatever they need, and take this fucker down. Money will be of no object and the man that brings me his head will never have to work a day again in his life. His family will never have to work a day in their lives either."

"Dmitri will be head of security for our group," said Katerina.

"Viktor is our security chief," said Konstantin with Katerina nodding at him. They had been introduced 15 minutes earlier. At 42 Viktor looked like a no-nonsense guy with piercing blue eyes, specks of gray in his hair, and scars on his face that looked like a road map. At 6' 4" and 240 pounds of muscle, there wasn't a tough guy in that room that would want to go head-to-head with him.

Viktor rose from his seat nodding to Konstantin; Konstantin nodded back giving him the floor.

"I would like to express my condolences to Vlad's colleagues. I met him several times and he was a solid, dependable guy. I've never heard a negative thing said about him, he seemed like a great guy and I'm sure he'll be missed a lot."

Thank yous and nods were exchanged.

"I'll be working closely with Dmitri, and we'll be taking on as many good guys as we can find. It's important that we recruit guys we know we can trust. If you have any military friends that would like to join us let Dmitri or me know. We won't be fucking around. Again, I'm sorry for the loss of Vlad, let's make sure we won't be having a meeting like this with one of us not in attendance."

The meeting was adjourned; Konstantin and Katerina remained in the conference room making further plans.

Thursday, November 7, 1996

"Katerina, have you gotten a hold of Mikheil or Olena?" Dmitri asked.

"Shit, no. There's been so much going on I forgot. These are going to be horrible calls, but I need to make them now. I'll have you meet them at the train station later today. Could you bring them back here?"

"Not a problem, I'll check back with you later for the details."

Katerina's calls went as expected with one unexpected issue. Olena had barely settled back to her old routine, with Jacques now part of it. She enjoyed waking up in her own bed and did not want to go through the upset of another move and interruption in her life. It took about 20 minutes of convincing and a bit of background on their enemy before Olena agreed to return to Moscow.

Mikheil was in complete shock at the news of Vlad's death. They had become quite good friends with all the time they spent bunking together. Plans had even been made to grab some drinks the next time Mikheil was in the neighborhood. At first, Mikheil resisted the idea of returning and disappearing off the map but the idea of ending up with bullets in him like his friend pushed him toward common sense. He put a call into his boss at the restaurant, told him he wouldn't make it in for his shift tonight and was swiftly fired. One less thing to worry about Mikheil thought as he hung up the phone.

Katerina's next call was to Vlad's grieving family. His father took the call and told him that she would pay for the funeral and the family would receive Vlad's paycheck for the next year. Vlad often talked fondly about his parents, particularly his father. They had and still went on hunting and fishing trips together, each enjoying the wilderness.

The sadness combined with rage in her was a dangerous combination. Katerina was hard as nails but the hurt inside her made for a ferocious adversary. The pain was going to be fuel for action and would not cease until the objective was achieved. She wasn't going to stop at Jablokov, the big man was going down as well.

Dryga was getting antsy and wanting to get back to his routine, one that wasn't good for him. He went through the motions doing what was expected but reporting to his boss essentially nothing. This angered Kovalyov confirming his suspicions that Dryga was crooked. He had the FSB assistant who specialized in flight manifests research the same thing Dryga was supposed to be working on and she pulled up a couple of names that were closely tied to Voshkolup's organization. They had flown into the Topki area around the time of the Abramov assassination, he felt sure these were the guys. Anatoli Kazinski and Mohammed Raffael had extensive files with the FSB and worked as mercenaries in various skirmishes around the globe. If he was going to hire a team to take someone out these guys would be his pick.

"Dryga, I want you to keep digging, there must be something there," Kovalyov demanded.

While these words were uttered an investigation was underway by two trusted FSB officers handpicked by Kovalyov. The orders were very precise, be thorough, fast, and talk to no one but me. Even Litskevich was in the dark.

"What the hell?" Lily exclaimed as Tatiana walked into the kitchen. Even Oliver, who was being fed did a double take.

"You like it?"

Lily's mouth hung open like a fish gasping for air searching for something nice to say. Nothing came out except a halfhearted, "yes, it's different."

Tatiana's locks were cut back just below her shoulder and had gone from blond to a shiny jet black. Black lipstick and a couple of piercings were the only things needed to complete the Goth transformation.

"You don't like it?"

"It's just so different. Why the change?"

"I've always had the same look, all my life. It was time to do something completely different."

"Yup, won't they say something at work?"

"I don't think so, at least not to my face. Besides it's not like I'm the face of the bank."

Lily noticed Tatiana's transformation over the weeks, and it worried her. Tatiana was going out more and more with Anna. She knew Anna wasn't that much of a bad influence but more of a catalyst for what was happening. Trevor had expressed some annoyance at what was going on. If it continued another heart-to-heart would be necessary. Maybe she would arrange a lunch date with Anna and see what she could unearth since a strain on their friendship was setting in.

"Magnitsky," the guard called out.

Waiting for what seemed like an eternity, Sergei got the call. His ribs were feeling better, and he was finally getting an hour a day in the exercise yard. In his whole life, he would have never imagined that an hour outside in a freezing cold yard with six-meter walls and wearing a coat that had been worn by hundreds of men before him would be such a treat.

He joined several others in the yard and walked the perimeter of the yard with them exchanging small talk and grumbling about the food. They didn't know his name and he didn't know theirs; everyone went by nicknames that were often random and made up on the spot. Forty minutes into his yard time a guard approached him and said come with me. His stomach collapsed on itself until he heard, "you have a visitor."

Inside he shed the smelly coat and was led to the visitor room where a beaming Natasha stood waiting for him.

"Sergei," she cried out and sobs of happiness followed with words that couldn't be deciphered. "You're looking so much better." He had no idea what she was talking about since he hadn't seen himself in a mirror for weeks.

"Natasha, I've missed you so much," he said with a huge lump in his throat. "How are the boys?"

"Great, they're doing well in school but miss you dearly. Nikita is on the school volleyball team and Stanislav is getting straight As. They each made you a card, but they wouldn't let me bring them in, maybe they'll give them to you once they've been inspected."

They held hands across the table knowing they were pushing their luck. Some guards permitted it while others would holler "no touching."

"How are you holding up?" Sergei asked, genuinely concerned. "I'm fine. My parents have helped me through this. I don't know what I would do without them."

"Have you had a chance to speak with the lawyer?"

"Yes, there still haven't been any charges filed yet. The lawyer is pressuring for your release on that basis. Mr. Browder and Jamie are doing what they can. They have a team of investigators looking into it and they are starting to find some alarming activities by government officials that make this look like a thoroughly thought-out fraud. The lawyer isn't optimistic that charges won't be filed since there are billions of rubles that have gone missing. He feels this is something that goes to the top and is doing what he can to prove it. His only fear is he could end up here with you or worse."

Sergei went silent. He didn't like the sound of that and realized Natasha was putting on a brave face for his sake. He gathered himself and did the same. The half-hour they spent together seemed to vanish in minutes and the dreaded words, "visiting time is over," was announced. Sergei gave Natasha's hand a last squeeze mouthing the words "I love you" before he was led away. Natasha mouthed the words back with a tear in each eye.

Friday, November 8, 1996

Tatiana Belov
DOB: 6/6/1966
Place of Birth: Nizhny Novgorod Hospital
Father: Ilya Belov
Mother: Valentina Belov nee Skol
Education: Graduated School 118 6/84, St. Petersburg University, Bachelors, Economics 6/88
Employment: Menatep Bank 9/92 to present
Current Address: 431 Minskaya Street, Fili-Davydkovo, Moscow
Previous Address(es): 124 Troitse Avenue, St. Petersburg
Criminal Record: None

Litskevich held Tatiana's one-page file in his hand wondering where to begin. By all indications, she was no longer in Moscow, likely not even Russia. What was the interest in this woman, he pondered. His first stop would be her current address but knew that would be fruitless, next on to Menatep Bank to speak with a supervisor. Now he wasn't tied up with surveilling Jablokov he had a bit more time on his hands.

He glanced at the page again, and this time something caught his eye, Nizhny Novgorod Hospital. Nizhny, wasn't that Lev's hometown. He grabbed the Drozdov file and yes, there it was. Looking at the date of birth, they were the same age and both living in Moscow. Were they boyfriend and girlfriend he wondered. Questions began to swirl around in his head. His first inquiry was going to be with the assistant that handled the flight manifests to see if she had any updates and if those updates were passed along to anyone, like Dryga.

"Miss Balakin, could you see if there has been any flight manifest information on Tatiana Belov? Also, could you please tell me if any other inquiries were made of her and by who?"

"Yes, Lt. Litskevich. I will look into it and get back to you within the next few hours."

"Thank you."

169

Viktor pried open the long wooden crate. Dmitri assisted removing the lid, exposing the contents to about a dozen burly guys surrounding them. The crate contained six AK-47s, and there were three more crates below. The guys donned in body armor adorned with magazine clips and Rambo knives had night vision goggles in their hands and were instructed to grab a gun. They formed a long row about two meters apart and were instructed to load their weapons. Bursts of automatic gunfire could be heard from a kilometer away as targets were soon being shredded.

"Can you hear that?" Dmitri said into his cell phone.

"How can I not?" replied Katerina holding the phone away from her ear.

"That's the sound of Voshkolup's nightmare," he chuckled.

"Are these guys going to be ready soon?"

"Very soon," Dmitri confirmed in a confident tone. "These are all battle-hardened guys. We're just shaking off some rust, but they should be ready to go within the next day or so."

"That's good news. Are Olena and Mikheil settled in?"

"Yes, they're tucked away. I spoke with Mikheil, everything is good on their end."

"I'll check in with you later then."

Dmitri returned to the group; combat training resumed.

"The big man is getting pissed," were the words blasting out of Dryga's phone.

"Trust me I'm doing what I can which is a lot. You have no idea. I'm still stuck out here in Topki, they're trying to tie you guys to the RPG attack. I'm doing what I can to slow things down, but the shit is going to come out."

"Leave that for the big man to worry about. He wants info on the Belov girl yesterday. Smoke is coming out of his fucking ears. Do you understand?"

"Okay, okay. I'll get the fuck out of here today but that's likely to create some problems."

"I don't care, just get me something on Belov or we're both fucked. He's not messing around."

Dryga hung up the phone and realized what a deep pile of shit he was in. He'd jump in a car this afternoon and make the drive back; only one problem it was a two-day drive, 48 hours. Flying was his only option. On his way to the airport, he kept thinking about his boss, with any luck there wouldn't be any calls.

"I'm sorry sir but I don't have any available seats to Moscow until the morning," said the husky, middle-aged man.

"It's very important you get me on a flight today," Dryga said while flashing his FSB credentials.

"Let me see what I can do." A seat magically became available. "I can have you on the 22:10 to Moscow."

"You don't have anything sooner?"

"I'm sorry, sir. It's the best I can do."

"Fine, I'll take it," said a relieved Dryga. He wasn't thrilled because that still meant he wouldn't make it back until early Saturday morning. He drove back to his hotel and decided to rest up knowing he had a hectic 72 hours in front of him.

Saturday, November 9, 1996

"Tatiana, this has to stop. It was 3:30 when you came stumbling in the door, you woke the entire household up."

"Lily, I'm so sorry. I know I'm starting to become a burden."

"Tat, you're not a burden, but Trevor is starting to get a little stressed out."

"Let me talk to Anna maybe she'll let me stay with her."

"I don't want you to think we're throwing you out."

"No, I totally understand."

"The girls hugged. I'm sorry Lily."

Tatiana realized she was pushing her luck. Lily and Trevor had been so good to her, the last thing she wanted to do was wear out her welcome.

Dryga was in a cab on his way home. He wasn't able to sleep on the overnight flight. The only thing he could think about was grabbing a couple of hours of sleep before making his way to the office. How was he going to pull this off when he was supposed to be in Topki. He would figure that out later, sleep was the priority, but first what was that smell. It was the full garbage can with week-old trash, as tired as he was it needed to be taken out.

Miss Balakin was a busy woman and wondered why she was getting multiple inquiries for the same task. Tatiana Belov, her again. She remembered Lieutenant Litskevich's request and called him.

"Lt. Litskevich, Lt. Dryga was just here requesting flight manifests for the Belov woman."

"He was there in the office?"

"Yes, just five minutes ago. I told him the same thing I told you; I hadn't found anything."

"Thank you, Miss Balakin. If any more manifest requests come in for her, please let me know."

Within minutes Litskevich was on the phone with Kovalyov passing along what he just learned.

"It can't be, he's in Topki."

"I just got a call from Miss Balakin, he was just here."

Kovalyov had what he needed to confirm all suspicions, there was now zero doubt. He called the officers investigating Dryga, a rat trap was now being constructed but not before he had a chance to fuck with him a bit.

Pavel, Mikheil, Olena, and Jacques were settled in their new luxury three-bedroom suite at the Moscow Ritz. Katerina was well aware of the upset in all their lives and decided to pamper them a little. Mikheil was still in shock over Vlad's death and could see Pavel was taken aback even more. Vlad was such a large part of their lives, now they were going to be burying him in two days. Like Lev's funeral, all details would be secret until the last minute; security around the event would be extremely tight. This would be the first assignment for the new security team recruits. Ivan came to the hotel to fill in for Pavel, he was going to meet with Vlad's parents at the funeral home and put together a ratcheted-up security plan for Tuesday's funeral. Nothing was going to be left to chance, the handful of guests would be transported by armed security to and from. Two snipers would have bird's eye views of the funeral home and inside there would be at least one security personnel for each guest. One of the challenges Pavel faced was the more urban setting than the one for Lev's funeral. This meant more traffic and more people had to be paid attention to.

Vlad's parents were still very shaken from the week's events but greeted Pavel with hugs. They appreciated his efforts and were grateful for an ear at this difficult time. With heightened security, they were unable to gather with many family members and get their help during this hellish time.

"Pavel, thank you so much for everything you have done," Vlad's father said.

"Yes, and please thank Katerina for us, she has been wonderful," Vlad's mother added.

"You're both very welcome. I wish there was so much more I could do. Is there anything you need?"

"Nothing, Katerina has taken care of everything and more."

"I just wish we could have our Vlad back," his teary-eyed mother said and was soon being hugged by her husband.

"Have all the arrangements been made to your satisfaction?"

"Yes, the funeral director has been wonderful," Vlad's father said still in a comforting embrace.

"I think we should get you both home now, remember to call me if you have any concerns or if there's anything you need."

Two security team members escorted them home, they would be there until it was time to return on Tuesday.

Sunday, November 10, 1996

"Mr. Voshkolup, I just returned from Topki yesterday. While there I was assigned to look into flight manifests around the time of Abramov's demise and came across Anatoli's and Mo's names. Without a doubt this will tie it to you," Dryga said standing back, watching Boris slide a ball into a corner pocket.

"As I told Jablokov I don't give a shit about that." Boris did give a shit about that though. This would mean FSB headaches as well as additional heat from Berezovsky and not to mention the pending retaliation from Abramov's guys. Things were going to get tense, which made finding Belov even more important. Battles like this were going to be costly, his survival could depend on getting his hands on the fortune he suspected Tatiana now controlled.

"I need to find Belov. She didn't just disappear from the fucking planet."

"You know I haven't been able to trace her to any flights from Zurich."

"Then why was I?" Boris bellowed at the top of his lungs.

"What are you talking about?" Dryga asked trying not to look scared shitless.

"She was scheduled to fly out of Zurich the day before Drozdov's funeral but never boarded the flight. You didn't know that?"

"I don't know what to say."

"I do, you're a fucking idiot that's costing me a lot of money for nothing."

"My next plan was to look for her in London. I did discover a possible link."

"What's that?" Boris asked now calming down a little.

"She has a school friend there."

"You're just finding this out now? Who is this?"

"Her name is Lilian Murray, that's all I have for now."

"When will you have more, I need that information fucking yesterday?"

"I'll pass along everything to Miroslav. I don't know when I'll have time to look into it more, they have me stuck in Topki. I'm not supposed to be here now."

"I want everything you have now. I feel like my time is being wasted and I'm not going to put up with it. Do you understand?"

"Yes, sir, I promise I'll have more very soon."

Dryga left Voshkolup's compound knowing he better come up with something. His FSB job was in peril and a very dangerous man upset with him, not an enviable position to be in. The question running through his mind was when. He would have to have Jablokov do some of the legwork.

Tatiana was getting her stuff together; she spoke to Anna about sharing her flat and was welcomed with open arms. Tatiana's only fear was putting a strain on this friendship by either bolting without any notice or overstaying her welcome. She did warn Anna that her plans were up in the air and as expected the response was "whatever."

Anna's flat wasn't too far from Lily's, just a short train ride in nearby Surbiton. It was a nice London suburb just south of Raynes Park that lacked some of the hustle and bustle. Anna's flat above a Bulgarian restaurant was a short walk from the train station but with all her stuff Tatiana sprung for a taxi.

"Welcome to your new home," Anna said opening the door and handing Tatiana a key.

"Thank you," Tatiana said, pleased that Anna was making it so easy for her.

"Will you be all right sleeping on the couch? We don't want to start any juicy rumors."

"Anna, that's perfect. Where should I put my bags?"

"You can put them in the bedroom. I made a little room in the wardrobe for you."

"Thank you so much, this is going to be fun. Please tell me if I start to get on your nerves."

"Pish posh, it's going to be fab."

"Yes, and pish posh we'll go to Piccadilly."

The girls hugged singing, "Piccadilly, Piccadilly, Piccadilly."

8

"Magnitsky, up against the wall."

"What?"

"Up against the wall?"

"What is going on?"

Sergei was yanked up out of his bed with his cheek pushed against the cold concrete wall by two stocky guards, a third placed shackles around his ankles, then around his waists locking his hands to those chains.

"What is happening?" Sergei inquired hoping to avoid being roughed up.

"Court," the guard who just applied the restraints answered.

He was hurriedly led out of the cell and through the prison corridors with his feet tripping up along the way. The two gloved guards with hands cupped under his armpits brought him back to his feet without slowing for a second. Shoved into the back of a windowless van and falling onto a prisoner making the same journey he recovered his balance until the van quickly accelerated throwing the half dozen men towards the back. They could hear the guards in front chuckling as the van made swift and jagged zig-zag movements throwing the occupants around like sacks of potatoes. This went on for the 25-minute trip, he realized the shackles weren't only to prevent escape but to protect these sadistic pricks from strangulation.

Sergei and his fellow prisoners were being stored in a 3-meter by 3-meter white room with obscenities etched all over the walls and even under the bench that ran around the perimeter of it. One at a time a name was called, and the room became a little less crowded. Magnitsky was called out leaving only two. He was led into a windowed room; a man in a gray suit stood up and introduced himself.

"Mr. Magnitsky, I'm Fyodor Chaika. I've been hired by Bill Browder to represent you. They have brought serious charges against you, we're here today to enter a plea."

"Please thank Mr. Browder for me. I very much appreciate his efforts. What are the charges?"

"Theft, embezzlement and tax evasion. I have been given all the facts; the charges are ludicrous. The whole thing stinks of corruption on the highest levels. You are facing the rest of your life in prison if convicted and I'm afraid to tell you the conviction rate in our country is more than 99 percent. We have an uphill battle."

Sergei's stomach dropped; he became visibly pale. "Is there anything you can do?" he asked looking Fyodor in the eyes.

"What makes the charges so ludicrous is they are accusing you of stealing 5.4 billion rubles and the circumstances around the money going missing. The government doesn't deny that the taxes originally due were paid but that you claimed they were unjustly paid and three days after you made that claim it was refunded back to you."

"Have you ever heard of something so ridiculous in your life?"

"Never and I've been practicing law in Russia for more than 30 years."

Fyodor looked like someone that had dealt with the frustrations of life in Russia for decades. He had large dark bags under his eyes, strands of long gray hair combed over his bald head, and a right leg that was always in constant nervous motion. The stress was also apparent in his chain-smoking habit. Sergei hoped his legal proceedings wouldn't last very long, he wondered how much longer his lawyer's abused body would hold out.

"What will happen next?"

"We will be called before the judge sometime today; you will enter your plea of not guilty. They will then remove you from the courtroom and take you back to the prison."

Attorney and defendant talked for a few hours. Sergei described the beatings during and after his arrest, the broken ribs, and the surgery that followed. He also recounted the very limited contact with his wife, the inability to even send her or anyone a letter. Fyodor took notes of this promising to do everything he could to get this nightmare to stop. The conversation turned to more relaxed topics while they waited to see the judge. Getting updates on his favorite sports teams and finding out what was happening in the world made the wait enjoyable. It had been so long since he had had this kind of social interaction and sorely missed it.

Dryga exited Kemerovo Airport just after lunchtime, he was starving. The breakfast on the plane was a stale ponchik and lukewarm coffee. He approached his rental car in the airport parking lot; shit he thought, the driver's side front tire was flat. He popped the trunk pulled out the jack and reached for the spare, but it wasn't there. The flat tire was the spare. He threw the jack back in the trunk grabbed his bag and made his way back to the terminal, he'd have to arrange for another rental. The diner would have to wait.

Finally, he made it back to his hotel. Time for some rest, but the red light on his hotel room phone was flashing. He retrieved the message, make that messages.

"Lieutenant, where are you? You're needed back here ASAP. Call me when you get this." The same message was repeated several times.

"Shit, shit, shit," he yelled loud enough to be heard next door.

"Major, it's Lieutenant Dryga. I got your messages."

"Where have you been?"

"I'm back in Topki."

"I need you here, right away. We have a break in the Abramov investigation. Be on the next flight," the phone went dead.

"Shit, shit, shit," this time it was loud enough to be heard at the front desk. He checked out of the hotel and made his way back to the airport. Coincidently enough he found himself in front of the same husky, middle-aged ticket agent.

"I need a ticket on the next flight to Moscow."

"Déjà vu," he said and skipped the part about not having any seats available, he remembered the FSB credentials. "Unfortunately, a flight for Moscow just left half an hour ago but we do have another leaving in three hours."

"Can you please direct me to the bar?"

"Bar Milton is near gate 13 you'll be leaving out of gate 9."

"Thank you," said a very frustrated and thirsty Dryga. He would not be arriving in Moscow sober.

As expected, Litskevich didn't get any leads about Tatiana Belov from the flight manifests and there wasn't any answer to his repeated knocks on her apartment door. A nosy neighbor, however, informed him she hadn't been seen in weeks. He was now on his way to Menatep Bank.

The Menatep headquarters located in central Moscow was a historic ornate cream-colored building with gold trim. For the average citizen, parking would have been impossible, luckily for him, his credentials landed him a prime spot that even included an escort to the human resource department. He was introduced to a fellow Alexander, the head of the department, who told him Ms. Belov was on leave due to a family emergency, but Alexander also added that there was an inquiry about her from a bank in London just the week prior and is why he remembered her as easily as he did. It was an aha moment that was confirmed by her frustrated supervisor. Her boss, Mr. Popov, hadn't heard from her in weeks and was getting fed up with the situation. When human resources informed him about the London call, he had reached his limit. He was going to grill her the first chance he got and now there was the FSB asking questions. It was all too much.

Litskevich now had something to go on – London.

Tuesday, November 12, 1996

Dmitri and the security team all rose early donning their black, funeral suits. They were suits tucked in the back of closets so as not to be seen and give constant reminders. Every time they were put on it was hoped it would be the last time. Just as Dmitri finished getting dressed his cell phone rang.

"It's Viktor, can we get together half hour earlier? I want to make sure everything is in place."

"I'll do my best, but it might be 20 minutes earlier."

"Fine, I'll see you at the funeral home soon."

Once the security team at the funeral home was in place the remaining security force was to meet at the Abramov headquarters to escort the guests to the funeral home. Katerina arranged for cars and was overseeing all non-security-related details. Vlad's parents were still in shock and Katerina was doing everything she could to make it easier for them.

Dmitri left the funeral home with Viktor in charge of the security team there and made his way to the headquarters. There would be four cars that each contained two security team members and their wards. Each car would take a different route to the funeral home with Vlad's parents occupying the first car. Katerina and Vlad's sister Olga would be in car two, and two of Vlad's closest friends would be in car three with Mikheil and Olena in car four. Each security team member was prepared for whatever came at them with AK-47s between their legs, semi-automatic pistols at their sides, and walkie-talkies in hand. So far it was smooth sailing.

"Katerina and Olga have just arrived," Pavel heard over his walkie-talkie. He was riding shotgun with one of the new recruits at the wheel. The Moscow rush hour traffic had subsided, and they were cruising along at a good pace. Suddenly a black Volvo in front of them locked on its brakes, and two masked men emerged with AK-47s, riddling the car with bullets.

Get down! Pavel yelled as he and the driver opened the doors sliding out onto the ground and returning fire. Mikheil threw himself over Olena who was now on the floor, small pellet-sized glass shards covered his back as the sound of gunfire continued to fill the air.

"I've been hit!" Pavel yelled out with his finger still squeezing off a constant stream of rounds at the Volvo.

"My guy is down," the new recruit called out as he ran to the back of the car. The lone surviving gunman was now outgunned and took a bullet to the forehead. His black balaclava dripped blood into his eyes; he folded hitting the ground like a ragdoll. The gunfire stopped, and everyone's ears were enveloped by loud ringing. The driver called back to Mikheil and Olena, "are you all right?"

"Yes," came back two muffled cries.

"Stay down," he ordered as he helped Pavel up and into the passenger seat. "Where are you hit?"

"Upper arm and vest," Pavel groaned as warm blood oozed down his right arm.

The driver closed the door and raced around to the driver seat, amazingly the car was still running. He picked up the walkie-talkie and said, "we've been ambushed, the attackers are dead; Pavel was hit in the arm, I'm on the way to the hospital."

"Do you need assistance?" came back over the walkie-talkie.

"No, send several guys to GMS Hospital. We'll be there in five minutes." He sped off with the tires leaving chunks of rubber on the road.

Dmitri and Ivan met them as they pulled up to the emergency room entrance. Dmitri helped Pavel out of the car and into a wheelchair, asking him how he was doing. Fortunately, the driver had instructed Mikheil to apply a tourniquet to Pavel's arm and it was greatly slowing the bleeding.

"I'm okay but if it hadn't been for my vest, it would be a different story."

Dmitri instructed Ivan to take Olena and Mikheil back to the hotel, they herded Pavel into the emergency room yelling, "gunshot, gunshot!"

When Katerina received word of what happened, she was about to postpone the funeral service and send everyone home. Viktor stepped in suggesting they hunker down for a while and think it through. His reasoning was that the security team was scattered, emotions were running high, and they were all off balance now.

"Let's wait to hear how Pavel is doing, I'll talk with the team, and we'll decide what to do shortly. We're all safe here now."

Katerina, whose adrenaline was peaking, agreed. She tracked down the funeral director told him what happened and asked him if he could spare a glass of vodka. The vodka did the trick, now it was just a waiting game.

An hour had passed when word of Pavel's condition was relayed; he was okay. They were going to keep him in the hospital overnight. Dmitri was on his way back to the funeral home. The driver would stay with him until relief came.

Katerina went ahead with the service; it was a very sad goodbye with tension in the room that could be cut with a knife. Not the sendoff she wanted for her dear friend.

Kovalyov received word about the attack and immediately called Litskevich. Within an hour Litskevich was at the hospital getting details of the ambush from a drug-induced Pavel. There wasn't any doubt about who the responsible party was, but it would be confirmed when the bodies were identified. Litskevich decided to take advantage of Pavel's state.

"Why is Tatiana in London?"

Pavel had nodded off. Litskevich gave his face a gentle slap hoping not to get the drivers' attention. "Pavel, why is Tatiana in London?"

"She is visiting Lily," he said dreamily.

"Who's Lily?"

"Her school friend."

At that moment the driver walked toward the bed asking how he was doing.

"He's out of it," Litskevich replied. "I'll talk to him later and see if he can be of more help."

Mikheil and Olena were back at the hotel suite with Ivan and were visibly shaken. After a call to Tatiana, Mikheil sat holding Olena's hand, both saying nothing, and Jacques sat pressed against Olena's leg. They were soon joined by Katerina and Dmitri who were trying to be cheery and lighten the mood, but it wasn't happening, the stress was written all over Katerina's face. She had been dealing with so much that even her

185

resilient self wondered how much more she could handle. It was at that moment a switch went off in her head. She was either going to crawl up into a ball and give up or fight.

"Dmitri, call Viktor and Konstantin we're having a meeting at headquarters in two hours."

Tatiana's call from Mikheil left her shaken, so much that she hadn't even asked about her buddy, Jacques. She felt guilty they were going through so much shit and she was safe and sound in London, but for how long. Arkadiy, Lev, and Vlad were dead, Pavel shot, and Mikheil and Olena were almost killed; it was clear that the bratva would stop at nothing to get their hands on what she now controlled. It wasn't going to happen. Her thoughts turned to her new passport when her cell phone rang. It was Malcolm's secretary Miss Lynch with news that her passport had just arrived, and Malcolm wanted to meet with her. Good timing, she thought.

Wednesday, November 13, 1996

Twenty masked men outfitted in full combat gear surrounded Voshkolup's compound. It was just before sunrise; security cameras were sprayed with paint and every inch of the grounds was covered by automatic weapons. Two men in front of the house armed with RPGs would start things off by taking down the garage and front doors hoping to force its occupants out the back to the awaiting team. Orders were simple, take down any man emerging from the house with lethal force.

5-4-3-2-1 was heard over the walkie-talkies then BOOM! The doors disintegrated, and instantly three shiny vehicles were ablaze, a Rolls-Royce Silver Shadow, a Lamborghini Countach, and a Range Rover. Smoke billowed from the front hallway and out of the now-missing front doors. Several guns were trained in that direction, but no one was expected to emerge from there. Moments after the BOOM the front gate toppled down; a chain attached to an old UAZ-469 made short work of it. There was activity coming from the back of the house as a back patio door swung open.

"Hold your fire, hold your fire!" came blasting out of all the walkie-talkies. "They're women."

Four of the team swept in pulling them to the side of the house. Viktor approached asking the bare-footed pajama-clad ladies where Voshkolup was.

"He's not here," they both screamed at the same time with tears running down their faces.

"Where is he?"

While the questioning was going on Dmitri lead a group of about a dozen men through the open back patio doors. They fanned through the mansion confirming over the walkie-talkies what the women had just told Viktor. The questioning of Voshkolup's staff revealed he left about eight hours earlier and would be gone for a few days, his whereabouts was unknown. Computers, laptops, and files were carried out to the vehicles in front. The last of the security team to leave the house had a flame thrower strapped to his back. After the upstairs of the mansion was ignited a couple of squeezes of the trigger had the downstairs going. The security team quickly departed with the compound lighting up the morning sky. Round one was complete.

Litskevich had it, a picture from St. Petersburg University. It was of Tatiana Belov, Marina Grachyov, and Lilian Murray, taken at an event of foreign exchange students graduating from the program. He knocked and entered Kovalyov's office to share the news and get an update on the Dryga situation.

"You're not going to fuckin' believe this," Kovalyov said hanging up the phone. "Voshkolup's mansion in Kuntsevo was stormed and burned to the ground."

"Shit," Litskevich said trying to sound surprised, he instantly knew who did it and pondered what he should say. "Was Voshkolup there?"

"No, he wasn't there, but two maids were and escaped from the inferno unharmed."

Too bad, his job would be much easier if that piece of shit had been taken out, Litskevich thought to himself.

"Do you know who's responsible?"

"Come on, don't fuck with me. You know it's Abramov's people, there were about two dozen of them. They were armed to the gills in full combat gear. They even had a fucking flame thrower, and it happens a week after their head of security is gunned down in his apartment."

Litskevich gave a sheepish grin; he couldn't play stupid anymore. "Do you think this is the start of a war?"

"Damn right I do. I need you to talk to that woman, the hot one, and put a stop to this shit."

"Katerina?"

"Yes. We want to take down Voshkolup but not this way."

"What's going on with my partner?"

"He's going to be reassigned, for now, you're going solo. You're not to discuss any cases with him or pass on any information."

The word reassigned triggered a number of thoughts in Litskevich's head, none of them good. He knew at that moment Dryga's days with the FSB were numbered. As he left the office, he realized he had forgotten to tell him about Belov, just as well he thought, it was going to be a busy day.

Tatiana entered Malcolm's office, he was smiling and waving a brand-new Marshall Islands passport in front of him. "It arrived yesterday," he said handing it to her.

"Olga Olenska, I like the new name. Thank you. It's a relief to have this, I might need to use it very soon." Tatiana was starting to feel comfortable with Malcolm and really needed to unload on someone. If she couldn't trust him, the person who was orchestrating her escape who could she.

"There are some things I need to tell you, but I need some assurance it won't leave these office walls."

"Tatiana, our business is based on trust and confidentiality, please tell me what is on your mind. It will go no further than here, and it will help me assist with future plans."

"My best friend worked for a very rich and powerful man that was killed. The same people that killed him killed my friend but not before he passed along the location of large sums of money. The bratva, the Russian mafia, is after this money. I fear they will find me soon."

"Shit," slipped out of Malcolm's mouth. "I'm sorry, you caught me off guard. Okay, well that makes the next news I was about to pass along timelier and more relevant. I've set up a holding company for you to make the funds you currently have easier to move without your name being attached to them. Its name is CTW Strategic Assets. It's been set up by a company on Harley Street, just down the road from here, we work quite closely with called Formations House."

"I've heard of them when I was doing some of my research."

"They're very good at what they do and have been around for some time. Do you expect to have more funds coming in the near future?"

"I do."

"Will it be of a similar amount we previously discussed, 10 million pounds?"

"No, more. Four to five times more." Although Tatiana trusted Malcolm she wasn't 100 percent there yet. Let's see what he can do before she unloaded the full monty his way, she thought.

"Does CTW stand for something?" Tatiana asked.

"Circle the Wagons. It refers to a defensive strategy used in the old westerns. There has also been a Cayman Island bank account set up in that name. With your permission, we'll wire some funds from Zurich today to fund it. How much would you like to do?"

"I like the name. I can picture John Wayne saying that. Let's do 20 million pounds."

Without batting an eye Malcolm went on, "I'm glad because you're stuck with it. Well, actually not, because of the additional funds I'd suggest we set up a couple more holding companies and I'll explain why. CTW is going to be bought by one of the new holding companies for one pound. This time I'll have you pick the name of it."

"Okay, let me think. How does LD Travel sound?"

"What's the LD for?"

"A close friend."

"That should work. I'll need you to come up with another."

"BCJ Enterprises," Tatiana came back with after a couple of minutes of thought.

"The BCJ?" Malcolm inquired.

"Black Cat Jacques."

"That shouldn't be a problem. So, let me give you the details of how it will all work." Malcolm pulled out a legal pad and started to jot it out.

"CTW will be bought by LDT and then you'll be CTW secretary."

"My typing skills are a little rusty," Tatiana interjected. There was an awkward silence until Malcolm realized Tatiana was just playing with him.

After a chuckle, Malcolm continued, "you'll also be the secretary for BCJ and the director for LDT. Formations House will place vetted individuals as secretaries and directors in the remaining openings with your approval."

"This all sounds extremely complicated."

"It is supposed to, just think if it's complicated to the person behind it all an outsider doesn't stand a chance of figuring it all out. That's why I've noted it all on this pad for you; I'll give you a copy before you leave. All this is just for starters as assets are acquired more companies will be formed giving additional layers of protection."

Usually, when Tatiana left Carshalton House it was with a feeling of relief. This time her head was spinning but knew she was in the hands of a trusted professional who was at the top of his game.

Thursday, November 14, 1996

"Oh my God, oh my God," Lily breathlessly exhaled. She looked through the front door that was splintered around the deadbolt to see her house in shambles. Grabbing the handles of Oliver's stroller she sprinted to the neighbor's house and banged on the door. There was no answer, of course, she thought, they were at work. She reached into her handbag dialing 999.

"999, what's your emergency?"

"My house has been broken into. I need the police."

Two police cars arrived simultaneously with a third following a minute later. Three policemen and a policewoman swept the house with guns drawn reporting the house clear to the arriving officers. The policewoman stayed with Oliver in the gated front garden while Lily surveyed the damage with one of the officers.

"Is anything missing?" he asked.

"Not that I can tell." The TVs were still in place, and no jewelry appeared to be missing, but all the drawers were pulled out and overturned or their contents tossed on the floor. It was clear whoever was there wasn't there to rob the place, they were looking for something. She called Trevor next.

"Trevor, we're okay but the police are here, someone has broken into the house."

"Are you sure you're all right?"

"Yes, the police are here now. It doesn't look like anything was taken."

"I'll be right home."

After the officers dusted for prints, they advised to have all the locks changed when the door was repaired and remit a list of missing items, if necessary. They would have a report available the next day for the insurance company. Two of the officers stayed until Trevor arrived.

Dryga hoped for a day off, he was on the brink of exhaustion from his travels back and forth to Topki. He spent the previous day chasing leads given to him by his boss that went nowhere. This day started being summoned by Kovalyov for an early morning meeting; he hoped it would be related to a case he was working on or a new one but had a feeling deep down something ominous awaited him. As he approached Kovalyov's office his feelings were confirmed, his boss and two large men occupied the small office. He was called in and introduced.

"This is Lt. Maslov and Lt. Yukhantsev."

Dryga held out his right hand to Lt. Maslov, but his hand didn't leave his side. Not good he thought, he felt his stress level rise.

"These gentlemen have some questions for you please go with them."

Dryga was led around the corner towards the interrogation rooms and entered the first one available.

"Please have a seat," Lt. Maslov said.

Lt. Yukhantsev placed two file folders on the table and pulled a tape recorder from his jacket pocket. "Myself, Lt. Yukhantsev, and Lt. Maslov are with Lt. Igor Dryga at FSB headquarters, Moscow." He looked at his watch and said, "it's 8:17 on Thursday, November 14th, 1996."

"Lt. Dryga, do you know a man by the name of Miroslav Jablokov?" Yukhantsev asked.

"Yes, I know of him. He works for Boris Voshkolup."

"Have you ever had any personal dealings with him?" Maslov asked.

"No," came an immediate response from Dryga as his palms began to sweat.

"Have you ever met with Boris Voshkolup?" Yukhantsev asked.

Another negative response followed.

"Have you ever received any payments from either of these men?"

"No." Dryga's stomach was now in knots. "What is this all about?" he asked trying to take control of the questioning.

Yukhantsev opened the top folder that was filled with enlarged color photos. It wasn't looking good for Dryga at this moment. It contained dozens of photos of him and Jablokov, a few of them with him receiving fat envelopes from Miroslav. One in a diner where they regularly met and a couple on the street. Dryga knew he was done. His mind was racing trying to think of a defense.

Maslov asked, "have you ever spoken with Boris Voshkolup?"

"We, my partner, and I are investigating him. Voshkolup is suspected of killing Arkadiy Abramov."

"Have you ever spoken to Voshkolup?" Maslov asked raising his voice this time.

"No!" Dryga yelled out knowing he was fucked.

This time Maslov pulled out a tape recorder, one very similar to the one recording the interrogation, he placed it on the table hitting the play button. It was slightly muffled, but Voshkolup's voice was heard followed by his. I am so fucked he thought over and over.

"We're not done Dryga."

"I want to speak with a lawyer."

"You will but a few more questions first. How have you been able to lose hundreds of thousands of rubles and still pay for your mother's medical bills? What about your ex-wife and kids?"

"I don't always lose when I gamble. I've had some good days."

"That's not what we heard," Maslov said removing handcuffs from underneath his jacket. "Please stand up."

194

Dryga rose to his feet, his knees feeling weak like they might give out at any moment.

"We are placing you under arrest, hands behind your back," announced Maslov as he placed handcuffs around Dryga's wrists.

"You are being charged with public bribery. More charges will likely follow," Yukhantsev stated without any emotion.

Dryga was led through the office with the eyes of his colleagues glued to him. It was the longest 50-meter walk of his life. He caught the gaze of Litskevich on him and turned his eyes towards the floor. At that moment Dryga wished he was dead.

Lily started the call under control but quickly lost it when she told Tatiana about the break-in. By now the contents of the dumped drawers were put back but everything would need to be washed and cleaned before she would be even slightly comfortable again. Tatiana's mind was set in motion by the news. She was terrified at the thought that she had put her friend and her family in danger and so thankful Lily and Oliver were out when it went down. Her thoughts went now to Anna, what was she exposing her to. These thoughts were further cemented by Lily's next news.

"The only thing that appears to be taken are some old letters and bits and pieces from my uni days."

"That was it?"

"That's all I can tell at this point. Why would someone want that stuff?"

Tatiana wanted to rush over and be with her friend but realized it would put Lily in danger. She knew it was time to leave. She had pondered her next move and when she had looked at the Marshall Islands on the map Australia jumped out at her.

"Lily, I'm so glad you and Oliver are all right. I'll check in on you tomorrow," she said before making her next call.

"Miss Lynch, it's Tatiana Belov, I need to see Mr. Spencer. It's very important."

"Mr. Spencer is with a client at the moment. Can it wait until tomorrow?"

"No, I must see him today. Please tell Malcolm, I mean Mr. Spencer, it's very important I see him today."

"He is here until 5:00 o'clock; I'll ask him to stay if you can be here at five sharp."

"I will be there, thank you very much."

Tatiana hung up the phone and started packing before her meeting. It was imperative she saw Malcolm to make sure any paperwork was signed and he was aware of her new plans.

Friday, November 15, 1996

Tatiana left a note for Anna, it said a last-minute work assignment popped up and she had to fly back home. She thanked her for her hospitality and said she'd be in touch soon. Tatiana wasn't sure if she would be in touch anytime soon. She would rather look like an inconsiderate friend than put Anna in danger. The note ended with an apology for not saying goodbye in person and had 200 pounds on top of it. Tatiana knew Anna would doubt the work story but hoped the money would convey the message there weren't any hard feelings.

Tatiana only unpacked a few items for her stay at the airport Hilton, very close to Heathrow. After just a few calls to the airlines the night before she managed to secure a first-class flight to Sydney for that morning. She worried she might be spotted at the airport by the thugs that had trashed Lily's house and her ticket purchase less than 12 hours earlier might raise a red flag. At least I was smart enough to book a two-way ticket she thought.

A shuttle bus dropped Tatiana off just meters from an airport entrance close to the British Airways ticket counter. She pulled her large, wheeled suitcase through the maze of black stanchions and stood in a short queue before the ticket counter. With a head nod a pleasant-looking uniformed ticket agent summoned her asking where she was flying to and her name. Tatiana's reservation was found, and she was asked for a credit card for the 3,242 pounds that were due.

I'll be paying cash she told the ticket agent whose eyebrows were physically raised by that news.

"No worries, I'll just need to get my supervisor."

Tatiana's legs started shaking; she hoped it wouldn't be noticed.

"Thank you, Ms. Olenska," the supervisor said as Tatiana handed her the cash. A feeling of relief came over Tatiana as the supervisor began counting it. When finished the supervisor apologized for the formality explaining they rarely received large sums of cash, it was just an airline policy. Tatiana's cash supply was starting to get very low but fortunately, Malcolm was on top of things. Tatiana's last-minute visit confirmed the wire transfer to the newly set up Cayman Bank account from Swiss Bank Corporation. Those funds could be drawn upon as soon as she set down in Sydney.

With boarding pass in hand and through the security checkpoint Tatiana sat at a bar near her gate. It was still well before noon, but the glass of wine couldn't have come too soon. It was clear to anyone watching that she was on edge, Tatiana hoped no one was. I better order something to eat, you never know how long it will take to get food on the plane she thought. A breakfast croissant arrived followed by a second glass of wine, her nerves were starting to calm.

"Now boarding first class passengers on British Airways flight 518 to Sydney." Tatiana at first ignored the announcement but realized she was in first class. She stood and scanned the crowd for anyone that looked out of place or was looking at her, it had become instinct, especially at airports. The coast was clear, Tatiana walked toward the ticket agent examining the boarding passes and was soon on the jet bridge approaching the plane. Her blood pressure was elevated even as she was greeted by a handsome flight attendant named Chad. It was her lucky day the seat next to her was vacant. Chad offered her a glass of Champagne that she quickly said yes to. With the Champagne half-finished the jet roared down the runway lifting off. The higher it went the lower Tatiana's blood pressure went. A sense of relief flowed through her body.

"Katerina, it's Salvadore Ortin on line one."

"Who?"

"Salvadore Ortin. He's an attorney from Barcelona."

"Shit, I can't deal with him now. I'm buried."

Seconds after hanging up the phone it rang again. "He says it's very important; he needs to meet with you."

"See if Monday afternoon works, if not sometime later in the week."

Katerina started thinking about their prior meeting. If he was contacting her, it likely meant one thing, the man he was representing *was* Arkadiy's son. This could change everything; would that be a bad thing though. Katerina's head was in constant motion handling all the various business interests, meetings with lawyers, accountants, and overseeing the security team. Arkadiy had done a good job putting great people in place that ran these departments, but it was more than a full-time job to choreograph it all. While thinking about this the phone rang again.

"What now?" Katerina asked with an annoyed tone.

"Lt. Litskevich is here to see you."

"I'm sorry. Please show him in."

Litskevich gave Katerina a hug and passed along his condolences for Vlad's death.

"How are you holding up?"

"I'm okay," she said swallowing hard.

"We have identified the dead gunmen that attacked Pavel and the driver, they were Voshkolup's guys. Speaking of Voshkolup, you wouldn't have any idea who it was that stormed and burnt down his house?"

"His house was burned down?" Katerina answered fighting back the temptation to smile.

"Katerina, I'm just the messenger. Please let the FSB handle it."

"Most definitely."

"Off the record, I hope whoever is after him fries the fucker. On another matter, the name Tatiana Belov keeps popping up. Are you familiar with her?"

"No, should I be?"

"I have a feeling you're holding out on me. Based on everything that has happened I understand why."

"No," Katerina attempted to interject.

"It's okay. My interest in her is simple. Her name keeps coming up and I strongly believe she's in danger.

I don't know how she ties into all of this, but I think she's in

Voshkolup's crosshairs. I didn't want to get into this, but I think you should know Lt. Dryga has been arrested. It's believed he's been feeding Voshkolup information."

"Wow, that's a shock!" She started thinking about all their interaction and now worried about how they may have been compromised. Did Dryga have anything to do with Vlad's murder. What is the interest in Tatiana and why had she left Russia. She wanted Litskevich out and to immediately meet with the security team.

"It was very much a shock; we've been partners for more than 5 years," Litskevich said shaking his head.

"Thank you," Katerina said knowing Litskevich would pick up the subtle acknowledgment that the news about Tatiana and Dryga was useful. Deep down she knew he was on their side but too many lives were at stake to trust him.

Saturday, November 16, 1996

Igor Dryga had gone back and forth from the holding cell to an interrogation room. He refused to make a statement until he'd seen a lawyer and that didn't happen until late the previous day. An hour later he was thrown into a windowless van and transferred to Butyrka. His nerves were shot from the lack of sleep, cigarettes, and plenty of fear. Being a cop in prison meant his days were numbered. He desperately needed help from Voshkolup but knew it was unlikely since he could no longer be of any benefit to him.

While being booked into the prison he was asked his occupation, "FSB officer," he mumbled under his breath.

"What?" loudly asked the guard.

"FSB Officer," Dryga looked around after repeating himself, he was relieved to see no one appeared to be paying attention. He was given a stiff black uniform, ordered to the next room to put it on, and bag the clothes he was wearing. Next, he was given a course gray wool blanket, and a rubber pair of sandals and escorted down a corridor, along with five other prisoners that were each dropped off at their new homes before he ended up at his.

He shared a cell with seven other guys; the stench was horrific. Several times the urge to vomit had been fought off, it was a living hell. He lay in his bunk pretending to sleep to avoid interaction with his cellmates. After a few hours, exhaustion took over and he fell asleep.

Mikheil had spoken with Katerina and was very worried. He relayed to her that several attempts to reach Tatiana had all calls going to voicemail right away. The news she'd received from Litskevich was extremely troubling, the idea that another funeral could be in the works freaked her out.

"Mikheil, keep trying. If we don't hear from her soon, I'll put Dmitri on it."

An hour after that exchange Mikheil's phone rang. "Where are you?" Was his first question, number two was. "Are you okay?"

"Mikheil, I'm fine. Do you really want to know where I am?"

"No, yes. It's probably not a good idea for you to tell me but I won't rest until I know."

"I just landed in Sydney. I'm at the airport waiting for my luggage. I saw your calls and instantly felt horrible. I'm sorry I didn't tell you I was leaving."

"You're all right though?"

"Yes, things were getting crazy in London. Lily's house was trashed, I didn't feel safe."

"No need to apologize, you did the right thing. One of the FSB agents looking into Arkadiy's death was asking about you and his partner has been arrested."

"Do they want to arrest me?"

"No, your name came up in the investigation. The FSB agent connected you to Lev but it's not clear what the interest is."

"You said the FSB agents' partner is in jail, what for?"

"It was believed he was feeding information to the bratva boss, Voshkolup."

"Mikheil, I'm scared. They trashed Lily's house; she has a family you know. If anything happened to them, I wouldn't be able to live with myself."

"Are they okay?"

"Yes, nothing was taken just some college stuff. That is how I know it was Voshkolup's guys. If they could come close to tracking me down in London, I'm probably not safe anywhere."

"Let me talk to Dmitri, and see what he has to say."

"Please don't tell anyone where I am."

"I promise I won't. Get some rest and call me later in the day or tomorrow my time."

Tatiana's brain was turning faster than the baggage carousel and her suitcase went by her unnoticed.

Boris Voshkolup was having a rough day and the crew of his 160-meter mega yacht, the Blue Whale, were made well aware of it.

"I can't believe you ran out of Dom; we've only been out at sea two days."

"I'm so sorry, sir," a very nervous stewardess clutching her tray to her chest said leaning over the large pink man sprawled out on a deck chair in the bright Black Sea sun. "Can I get you a bottle of the Veuve Clicquot instead?"

"Forget it, I'll take a piña colada instead. Tell Jablokov I need him now."

"Yes, sir."

"Miroslav, you're blocking my sun. Sit down. What have you found out about the attack on my home?"

"Nothing yet. I've been asking around and put out word about the half million-ruble reward but still nothing. Whoever it was was well financed."

"No shit. Commando gear, AKs, night vision goggles, a fucking flame thrower. Have the helicopter take you back to Sochi and I'll have a plane waiting for you. I want you back in Moscow today to track these fuckers down. My guess is it's Berezovsky's or Abramov's people but I have so many people after me I need to be sure so we can focus our resources."

"Yes, sir. I'll report back to you the first I hear anything."

"Check with Dryga."

"I've been trying to reach him but he's off the grid."

"Keep trying!"

"Yes, sir," Jablokov said springing to his feet. Minutes later he was in the air with Sochi in sight.

Lily picked up the phone after the first ring. "Tatiana, I've been trying to reach you. Is everything okay? I spoke with Anna, she said you're back in Moscow?"

Tatiana knew Lily would be worried if she hadn't tried to call her and made it a priority as soon as she checked in to her hotel. "Yes, Lily everything is fine. I apologize for not calling you sooner but between travel and this new work assignment, I haven't had time to breathe. Are you and Trevor back to normal after the break-in?"

"Not really, we've both been on edge. All the locks were changed and Trevor had a security company out yesterday to install an alarm system. It's left us very unsettled."

Tatiana felt a twang of guilt hearing this. She was trying to think of a way she could get some money to them without implicating herself in the mess she likely caused. "I want to thank you guys for putting up with me and my antics. You both were so kind. My new work assignment came with a pay increase and a bonus for the last-minute move, I'll be sharing a bit of it with you."

"Tatiana don't be soppy; it was our pleasure having you."

"What time is it there?"

Tatiana's head started to spin. "It's…"

Tatiana disconnected the call. She almost told Lily Sydney time instead of Moscow time. After a quick calculation, she called back and apologized for the disconnection. That was a close one she thought.

Sunday, November 17, 1996

Dmitri woke up with a pounding head. He, unnaturally, had hit the booze hard and was looking for a bottle of aspirin. He and Ivan went out with Anatoli and Mo, playing pool and chatting up the ladies. It had been about two weeks since they had seen them. They considered bringing Pavel along, but some questions might be raised about his arm in a sling.

Dmitri knew it was risky meeting Voshkolup's guys out, but they weren't alone. Several of the new recruits were also partaking in some spirits at the bar, they were armed in case Dmitri's cover was compromised. Dmitri knew he was taking some serious chances pressing these guys for information about their boss, but vodka had a way of relaxing lips. Mo made a comment about things heating up in their line of work; Dmitri inquired how. Anatoli nudged Mo but Mo ignored him and continued. He told them about their boss's house being burned down and there was a very large reward in the offing. Dmitri exchanged glances with Ivan.

"What happened?" Ivan asked inching into the conversation.

"Our boss is a very powerful guy; he was out of the country and his house was torched. You may have heard of it."

"Is that Voshkolup?" Ivan asked doing a good job playing stupid.

"It is."

"I read about it in the paper," Ivan continued.

"We know a lot of people. We'll keep our ears open," Dmitri added while sinking the six ball into a corner pocket. He changed the subject knowing things were about to get very interesting.

Shouts of roll call and banging on the cell door had Dryga waking up freezing cold with a headache. Saturday night was a booze fest in cell D209. One of the occupants, who worked in the kitchen, had a container of prison-made moonshine. A gourd was hollowed out, filled with sugar, and a week later white lightening. It hadn't taken much before Dryga was comatose in his spinning bunk. He laid there hoping he had kept his shit together and hadn't said anything that would come back to haunt him. He wasn't alone in his pain, all the other participants appeared in equally rough shape. One of them wasn't going to be eating his breakfast today, he was off in the corner heaving his guts out into the disgusting shit-stained toilet.

Two hours after breakfast the men were herded from their cell to the frigid prison yard. The only way to stay a little warm was to keep moving, which meant walking the perimeter of the 50-meter by 100-meter walled-in yard. A few minutes into his stroll his thoughts were interrupted by a fellow inmate asking him what he was in for.

"Auto theft," lied Dryga. And you?

"Burglary. My buddy and I would cut into the roofs of pharmacies and steal money and drugs. It was profitable while it lasted. Did you steal many cars?"

"You're not going to believe this, but it was the first time. They found me passed out in it. I was totally fucked up. I'm still waiting for my trial."

"Good luck with that. I have to go back and see how much time I'm going to get."

"Do you think you'll get off lightly?"

"No, after they figured out it was us, we were linked to eight other jobs. I'm going to be in for a while."

Yard time was over and Dryga lay in his bunk pondering how he was going to extricate himself from this mess. He came to the conclusion, based on what they had on him, his only way out was to rat on Jablokov and Voshkolup. It would mean living his life running from the bratva, but it was better than rotting away in this cesspit.

Magnitsky was in a building very similar to Dryga's less than a hundred meters away. The difference being he was the lone occupant of his cell. Magnitsky often wondered why he didn't share a cell when he saw many others not far from him crammed in like sardines. What made him special. He sorely missed social interaction but was glad he didn't have to deal with the possible nightmare situations like being beaten up or worse, raped. His only concern on that front was the psycho guards. What type of person would choose to spend each day of their life in a place like this; you would have to be a little off, he often thought.

Magnitsky's days were long, but he managed to get ahold of a book, For Whom the Bell Tolls, from a fellow prisoner for a pack of cigarettes. A book was gold, it kept his mind occupied and helped pass some of the long, long hours. When he wasn't reading much of his time was spent thinking about his wife and family. It had been ten days since he last saw Natasha; he constantly worried about how she was getting along without him. Hours were spent remembering their first dates, their wedding day, the birth of their sons, and just many of the routine things that made up their days together. What he wouldn't give to be lying in bed with her spooned next to him with his arm draped over her belly. His nose buried in her long hair.

From what Natasha told him he knew there were people working on getting him out of there, but not knowing how long it would take made him crazy. Not having a date to look forward to was like doing a job without a finishing point. Uncertainty was his biggest enemy.

Tatiana spent her day as a tourist. The first stop was Circular Quay and the Sydney Opera House. She bounced from outdoor cafes around the harbor sipping wine and trying out new dishes while absorbing the Australian sunshine. She gazed up at the Harbor bridge and saw a row of people scaling it to its apex, something to put on the to-do list she thought. She wandered in and out of the quaint shops and boutiques that were scattered around The Rocks. For Tatiana, the day was a day off from worry. It was still there for all the people she cared about and that could be harmed by their association with her, but she realized she needed to be selfish and give herself some time to relax and enjoy herself. Tomorrow she would get back to reality plotting out her next moves.

Oh shit, was Katerina's first thought as she entered the lobby of her office. The receptionist nodded in the direction of the man waiting, it was Salvador Ortin.

"Mr. Ortin, how are you this morning?" her acting job put a smile on Salvador's face.

"Good and you?"

"Great, join me," she said leading him into her office. "I take it you have some news for me."

"Yes," he said handing her a sheet of paper.

That sheet of paper from a DNA laboratory confirmed what she suspected on Friday when he was setting up their meeting; Arkadiy Abramov had a son. An heir to his multibillion-ruble empire. Her new boss was going to be a 19-year-old boy who lived with his mother in Barcelona. She had put it out of her mind over the weekend because she simply couldn't wrap her head around it but now it hit her square between the eyes.

"Mr. Ortin, how would you like to proceed?"

"We should meet with the company's legal counsel and lay out a succession plan."

"Very well, I will contact them this morning and present them with this document. How long will you be in Moscow?"

"As long as it takes. I've had a few weeks to prepare a series of proposals, I'd like to share them with you and the lawyers. My preference has you staying on and running the show as you've been doing. You will be given a substantial pay increase should you elect to stay."

That was music to Katerina's ears, but she held back her excitement.

"Mr. Ortin, I'll do whatever I can to make it a smooth transition, but I must warn you this is Russia and things don't always go smoothly. Are you aware of the potential dangers?"

"Dangers?" Salvador asked with a puzzled look on his face.

"Unfortunately, yes. You come from a country with laws that protect individuals and businesses from threats and violence. It took centuries for those laws to morph into a system you take for granted. Here those laws and procedures are just being put into place. There are many criminals and corrupt politicians that will kill to prevent such a system from existing. Mr. Abramov spent his life cultivating business relationships that were often complicated, quid pro quo agreements that had little, or no documentation associated with them."

"I'm not totally naive to the way things work here, that is why we would like you to stay on. Is that something that might interest you?"

Katerina paused and thought, she wasn't acting this time. Arkadiy had paid her very well over the years, she was in a position to walk away and live a life of luxury. She was also a fighter and knew Arkadiy's life's work would be looted and destroyed if she was to walk away.

"Mr. Ortin, I'm not playing games but I'm going to give it some serious thought. So much has happened and I've been running on adrenaline. Our head of security was killed, another security team member shot, and then there's the reason why you're here. I'm not sure I'm up for it."

It wasn't until she said those words that it hit her; the seriousness and craziness of what she had been dealing with. It was a series of events that started becoming the norm when it wasn't normal at all.

"I understand and am very sorry for the loss and what you and your team have gone through. I will commit anything you need in the way of security and resources to keep everything going. I hope you stay on. I realize your importance and as I have said you will be taken care of very handsomely."

The meeting ended with a handshake that became a hug. Katerina had a feeling of satisfaction that her efforts were noticed. Arkadiy would be proud she thought.

"Litskevich," came a shout from Kovalyov's office.

"Yes, Major," he said standing in the doorway of the office.

"I have something on that Lilian Murray from our London contact."

"Great, what is it?"

"Several days ago a police report was filed, apparently the house she lives in with her husband and son was ransacked. There wasn't anything taken. It looks like the burglars were looking for something specific."

"What about Tatiana Belov? Was there anything about her?"

"Nothing for certain but there was a woman that fits her description staying at their home for at least a few weeks. There hasn't been any sign of her for about a week."

"Where is this going?" Kovalyov asked looking up from the file on his desk, but the doorway was empty.

After exchanging the last of her pounds at the airport and paying for a few nights of accommodation Tatiana was down to less than $20. Again, she neglected the time difference and realized she'd have to call Malcolm in the middle of the night to get him during business hours to get the details of the wire transfer. The soonest she would have some money would be 24 hours later; McDonald's would be her best friend.

With almost no cash Tatiana hit a local market, picked up a loaf of bread, lunch meat, a bottle of water, and boarded a bus for Bondi. With a towel and sunscreen in hand, the beach would be the perfect place for a cheap afternoon. Sydney was so different from London, it seemed to have more color and a cheerfulness about it. People here seemed happier, and in a better mood. Could this be her home in the future she wondered.

The bus ride from the Travelodge at Martin Place to Bondi was 35 minutes but seemed to take only 10. Stepping off the bus into the sunshine Tatiana realized she forgot her sunglasses; she rarely needed them in London. She inhaled the sea air and strolled the curved beachline before finding a semi-quiet spot on the sand. It was a beautiful cloudless day with a slight breeze.

She pulled out a Cosmopolitan magazine, laid on her stomach, and soon fell asleep. She dreamed she was living in a beach house and was the host of a swanky party. All the ladies exited expensive shiny cars driven by their dates dressed in tuxedos. Everyone walked around, mingled with champagne flutes in hand, and chatted over soothing chamber music. Lily and Trevor were there dreamily dancing staring into each other's eyes.

The peaceful dream came to a startling end when a soccer ball bounced off her butt and she was being apologized to by a group of giggling teenage boys. Even with the sunscreen, Tatiana noticed her pasty white skin was turning bright pink; she had been asleep for an hour. She put on her white shirt and explored the area before taking the bus back.

With beach stuff dropped off and fresh from a cool soothing shower Tatiana hit the local Pitt Street KFC. She wondered why all the things that were so bad for you tasted so good.

The next stop was walking dinner off in the Royal Botanical Gardens. She was amazed at the exotic tropical plants that were so perfect she wondered if some of them were fake. Around the park were numerous birds she had never seen before, not even in books.

It was going to be dark soon, so Tatiana ambled back to the hotel. She was still feeling the effects of jet lag; she turned on the TV and set the alarm for one a.m. It was a good thing because she was fast asleep minutes after hitting the bed.

The irritating buzzing of the alarm woke Tatiana up, the TV still on. She wondered for a minute where she was and then why the alarm had gone off. That's right, I need to call Malcolm.

"Hello, Malcolm. It's Tatiana. I made it to Sydney safe and sound. How are you?"

"That's great to hear, I'm fine. I suppose you're calling about the fund transfer."

"Yes, I'm literally down to change."

"Well, I received confirmation about 45 minutes ago. One hundred thousand Australian dollars was received at Commonwealth Bank. What time is it there?"

"One a.m."

"You will be able to draw on that account first thing in the morning. Do you have a pen and piece of paper, I'll give you all the details?"

"Go, Malcolm, I'm ready."

The call ended with Tatiana requesting a check for 2,000 pounds be sent to Lily and Trevor. She wanted to send more but knew that would raise questions. She would figure out a way to make it up to them soon.

Tuesday, November 19, 1996

Prison life was already starting to take its toll on Dryga. He pulled himself out of bed for roll call but went back skipping breakfast, which meant more for his cellmates. A deep funk took over his brain; it had an almost paralyzing effect on his body. He lay there drifting in and out of sleep, his goal was to make the day end. He passed on a lunch of salty water, managing to sleep until dinner. He forced down a couple of spoonfuls of porridge. It was on the dinner menu every day of his stay except Sunday. Sunday's meal consisted of a boiled potato with an unidentified piece of meat. He had heard about the torture that went on at Butyrka but didn't realize all the inmates experienced it three times a day with these foul meals. The meals and the stench of raw sewage. Dryga went to sleep that night trying to ignore the hunger pains. He really needed to talk to his lawyer; he'd do anything to get out of this place.

Katerina's day started at a large conference table with tasty pastries and a choice of coffee or tea. She never minded visiting the company's law firm because of the treats that were readily available. She and three other attorneys occupied only one end of the large table discussing the matter involving Salvador Ortin.

The head of the law firm, Mr. Novikov started off the meeting by summarizing what was known so far and laying out a few possible options. "The first approach we could take is to let young Nicholas take the reins and assist him in running it. We would have to make sure Mr. Ortin knows the complexities involved and that we would insure everything continued to run smoothly with the appropriate compensation to all the key players if Nicholas played a silent role."

"Do you really think he'll go along with that with the billions of rubles of assets involved?" asked attorney Mr. Gusev.

"His only other option, to avoid the collapse of everything, would be to bring in his own management team. Since he's in Spain he would have to bring in Russians, where would he start?"

"He would have to be made aware of the pitfalls of doing that," Katerina added. "It's crazy out there. You know the dangers we face on a daily basis, and we have a pretty good idea who the enemy is. Imagine the power struggle that would ensue with new management."

"I agree. Mr. Ortin needs to know the consequences of such a move," Mr. Novikov added. "Another option and this doesn't get repeated outside of this room, is we take a severance package for our hard work, turn everything over to young Mr. Nicholas, and walk away."

"Can you imagine the mayhem that would follow?" Mr. Ivanov said chuckling with the others joining in.

"Another possibility is the liquidation of everything but that won't be as easy as it sounds."

"Why is that?" Mr. Gusev inquired.

"Many of the business units have partners that do not appear on any paperwork. There are agreements in place that keep things running smoothly. If one partner feels slighted it could lead to serious conflicts. Katerina can attest to that."

"Yes, gentlemen. Many of the partners Mr. Novikov is referring to are government officials. These are powerful men that can squash any deal or put a monkey wrench into the works if they don't like what they see."

"Understood, again the complexities of Russian business," said Mr. Ivanov.

"Gentlemen, I suggest we convene again in a few days with Mr. Ortin present and discuss what we have gone over with him. Part of the strategy is not to speed things along. He has to be made aware that this could turn into a very long drawn-out process if he wants to be unreasonable."

"Thank you, Katerina. We'll wait to hear from you."

Tatiana left Commonwealth Bank with $5,000 leaving the new CTW account with a $95,000 balance and her McDonald's days in the rearview mirror. The first stop was a nice breakfast of fresh fruit salad, a croissant, and a couple of cappuccinos, next the salon.

She had grown tired of the black hair she'd used as a disguise; it was back to blonde. Shopping was next, the items in her current wardrobe were heavy and colorless, time to show off some flesh and sandals, don't forget the feet she thought.

Arriving back at the hotel with several large department store bags hanging from her arms she piled into the elevator filled with pink tourists. It was time to ditch the Travelodge but go where. It was a decision that didn't need to be made right away.

Lunch was next on Tatiana's to-do list. It was a bit of a walk, but she made her way to Darling Harbour and came across numerous dining options that were so different from London and day and night from Moscow. It took forty-five minutes to decide on a Mexican place with a large outdoor seating area. Like the day before the weather was perfect and she found herself needing frequent applications of sunscreen. The sunglasses weren't forgotten today. After a delicious avocado dip and chips with a couple of glasses of a nice local sauvignon blanc it was time to make her way back.

Calling home to mama was the next priority, one she had neglected for a while, but first there were some calculations to be made to get the times straight. She would call at 6 p.m. to reach her mother at 10 a.m. Moscow time; it would be 7 a.m. in London.

"Hi mama, how are you?"

"Tatiana, I'm upset with you. You have been ignoring me."

"Mama, I'm so sorry. You know how it is, they have me working day and night."

"What time is it there?"

"Seven o'clock," Tatiana said without hesitation.

"What is the weather like?"

"Cold and drizzly," Tatiana anticipated that question researching London weather ahead of time.

"Make sure you dress warmly. I don't want you catching a cold."

"Mama. I'm fine. Is everything going well with you?

Yes, just the usual, the arthritis in my fingers is acting up again."

"Make sure you wear the gloves I gave you for Christmas."

"Yes, yes. There were a couple of men asking about you last week, they said they worked at the bank. What was that about?"

It was a question she wasn't anticipating and stammered. "I don't know, maybe it was part of a security clearance thing. Did they say who they were?"

"No, just from human resources, something about a background check. They seemed a little surprised you were in London."

"Mama, it's a big bank and all the departments don't always share information. I'll ask around and see what it was about."

Was it the FSB or bratva Tatiana wondered. Her move to Australia now seemed a good one but she wondered for how long.

"Mama, I have to go. I'm running a little late. I promise I will call sooner next time."

"You better. I love you, Tati."

"I love you, mama."

The call left Tatiana very unsettled. How could she find out who those guys were and what they wanted. If they were FSB they would have likely identified themselves as such. She had to assume the worst, it was the bratva.

Wednesday, November 20, 1996

Mikheil and Olena had been staying in the suite at the Ritz for almost two weeks now and boredom set in in a bad way. Mikheil missed his buddy Vlad and the sadness he felt occasionally came out in anger that was directed at Olena. Olena understood but it was hard to ignore especially since her life was upset by all the terrifying events. Her only son had been murdered and there were times she crowded Mikheil, it was just motherly instinct coming out. Dmitri took them out on day excursions and other members of the security team had taken them out on day trips to parks and museums, but it was no replacement for having control over your usual routine. There was a discussion with Katerina about getting another house in the country but with things heating up, she wanted to make sure all the security team was nearby.

Mikheil suspected things were heating up. Dmitri swore him to silence, he wasn't even allowed to tell Olena about the bonfire at Voshkolup's and now he hadn't seen Dmitri for a few days. The times he saw Dmitri last he noticed a change in his demeanor, he was more serious, and his mind was elsewhere. After witnessing the attack by Voshkolup's guys and the anguish it caused Olena he hoped Dmitri and his team planned something that would help end this nightmare.

A bribe paid by his lawyer to a corrupt guard got Dryga the visit he desperately wanted. Leonid Kozlov was waiting patiently for his new client; it had been close to an hour.

218

"Lt. Dryga, I'm sorry I mean Mr. Dryga," Leonid said in a now hushed tone as they shook hands.

"Did you have any problems getting in?"

"No, the money-grubbing bastard was waiting for me."

"Don't worry I'll reimburse you for that," said a grateful Dryga.

"Mr. Dryga, I haven't had a chance to review your case. Can you tell me a bit about it?"

"You know I'm accused of public bribery?"

"Yes. What are the circumstances?"

"They claim I was providing Boris Voshkolup and his men information."

"According to some wiretaps and photos, yes."

"Based on your experience do they have a case?"

"Probably."

"Okay, but I need to get out of here. I'll give them anything they want," Dryga said leaning in close to Leonid's ear.

"Are you sure that's a good idea? Voshkolup is a nasty character. Going against him will likely result in a not-so-good ending."

"If you spent a day in here, you would understand why I'm willing to take such a chance."

"As your lawyer, I really shouldn't suggest this, but wouldn't you be better off keeping Voshkolup on your side and seeing if he could make things a little more comfortable for you in here?"

"Not a chance. It's hell here, besides if I approach him about what you suggest he could easily take that as a threat and the result would be the same or worse."

"What do you have on him that the FSB would want?"

"I have names of Voshkolup's key associates and a long list of very questionable activities. I also know about some of his partnerships and of some corrupt government officials that aid his operations."

"I understand you really want out of here but are you sure you want to go that route? It makes me extremely nervous as your attorney even to present such an offer. It puts me in a very treacherous spot." Leonid's mind was no longer paying attention to what Dryga was saying. His thoughts went to the safety of himself and his family. He was wishing that he never heard the name Igor Dryga and didn't want to be sharing a room with a marked man.

The men said goodbye with Dryga thanking him for coming. Leonid couldn't get out of Butyrka fast enough.

For days Litskevich was going around in circles, he knew this Belov woman played a significant part in the Abramov case. Voshkolup was interested in her for a reason, it was either information, money, or both. A light bulb went on in his head, "we might have something on that Belov girl," from the bug before it went silent. He felt stupid, he had played that over and over in his head for weeks and hadn't thought to trace Voshkolup's guy, Jablokov, and his travels to trace Tatiana. If they had found her, they would not have gone looking for her and the big man wasn't about to be jetting here there and everywhere.

"Miss Balakin, it's Lt. Litskevich," he said over the phone in his friendliest voice.

"Yes, lieutenant." Miss Balakin didn't sound pleased to be hearing from him.

"I need a big favor."

"You and everyone. What is it?"

"I need you to look at the flight manifests for Miroslav Jablokov flying out of Moscow around the first of November."

"What is the destination?"

"I don't have one but start with France and Switzerland."

"You know this will take a while."

"I do but please make it a priority. It's very important."

"Ya." And the phone went dead.

Litskevich knew he'd be at a dead end if nothing came of this.

Thursday, November 21, 1996

Miroslav Jablokov was having a heated discussion with several men at the back of a smoky dinner. He was stressed out and adding to the smokiness. Voshkolup was getting very frustrated with him, the shit was now running downhill. He learned earlier in the week that his FSB connection had been arrested. This created a number of headaches from a lack of credible intelligence to the possibility of a snitch with useful information being on the loose. It made his job of finding the Belov woman so much more challenging. Then there was the assault on his boss's compound. He knew it wasn't going to end there and the huge reward being offered wasn't yielding any leads as to who was behind it. He had a strong suspicion but had to be careful of starting a war and provoking another enemy. They were already spread thin.

"You guys have no idea how pissed off he is. I have been blasted every day this week now that he's off the boat."

"What do you want from us? The Belov girl has vanished again. We checked out the bank where she works or worked, but no one has seen her. She was in London staying with her friend but she's not there now. She's vanished."

"You have to keep looking! Mo, have you gotten anywhere finding out who attacked the compound?"

"No, we're asking around, but you know we have to lay low. We can't exactly be running around asking who burned down our boss's house, you know that Voshkolup guy."

"Anatoli with all of your contacts you haven't come up with anything?"

"No. We're not dealing with a bunch of street thugs; this was a very organized and skilled bunch of guys."

"That should make it all the easier to find out who!"

"I'll keep working on it, but you know as well as I do it was Abramov's people."

"That's what I'm thinking too but we need to be sure," Jablokov said sounding frustrated. "I'm really spread fucking thin now losing two guys and overseeing all the new guys we have providing security. The big man is growing increasingly paranoid; he has good reason to be, someone is trying to kill him and us. Keep that in the back of your minds!"

Dmitri and Ivan hadn't been able to sleep much over the previous several days. They were on heightened alert knowing they would be suspected of the Voshkolup attack and were very busy making plans for round two. Pavel, who was now out of his sling, and Viktor met with them in Sculpture Park on this unusually warm but overcast day. They were joined by Mikheil and Olena who quickly took off in different directions enjoying their own bit of peace and quiet.

"Guys, we can't let our guard down," Dmitri said starting off the picnic table meeting. "Viktor, have your guys been able to locate Voshkolup?"

"Yes, he's staying on Shvedskiy Tupik at a luxury apartment about a kilometer from the Kremlin. It's heavily secured with more than a dozen men. He's been there for a few days now, he rarely leaves."

"Okay, let's keep tabs on him. If he becomes accessible even for a minute, I want to know. Has Jablokov been seen there?"

"I haven't had anyone watching 24/7 but we haven't seen him lately. Do you want me to have Voshkolup's place watched?"

"Yes, very discreetly. If Jablokov is spotted I want to know instantly. Next to Voshkolup, he is our next priority. Ivan and I are hoping to run into two of his guys at the bar where we play pool tomorrow and set a trap. I have a few security team members that will be joining us."

Tatiana's last couple of nights were restless ones. She hoped the move to Sydney would provide a little peace and relaxation but that wasn't the case.

The conversation she had with her mother worried her. Who were those men. Another call to her mama was going to be necessary soon but a few things needed to be put into place quickly. The first thing was to get her out of Russia, but where. Tatiana considered flying her out to join her in Sydney but quickly shot that idea down. She didn't know how long she'd be there herself.

Her mother always talked about the south of France, the French Riveria, a place she had fallen in love with from old movies. A move there was a distinct possibility since money wasn't an issue. How could she make that happen without setting off alarm bells. An idea popped into her head. Her mother was a dressmaker by trade and worked at a local clothing store doing alterations. She would buy a little dress shop for her and tell her mother it was owned by a banking client that was getting out of the business. She would need a little help to pull it off and that's where Malcolm would come in handy. Perfect, she called Malcolm later that night.

"Malcolm, it's Tatiana how are you?"

"Very well, Tatiana. I see you received the funds; I've been monitoring the account there."

"Yes, this call is to thank you for that and also ask another favor."

"How can I help?"

"I need to get my mother out of Russia and set her up in a dress shop in the south of France. I'm trying to do this without her realizing she might be in danger."

"I see. Where do I come in?"

"I need you to find and buy a shop for her."

"All right. It's something I don't exactly have experience with but I'm sure I can figure it out. Can you give me a few weeks?"

"I'm sorry to do this to you but I need something right away. Could you have something for me in a week?"

"I can't promise but I'll do my best."

"I'll give you a 10,000-pound bonus if you can pull it off."

"Thank you, Tatiana I appreciate that. I will do my best and be in touch soon with any news. How is everything else going?"

"It's gorgeous here Malcolm. I'm loving it. I might have to make a move again soon, but it'll be somewhere here in Australia."

"Is everything okay now?"

"Yes. I just want to go somewhere I can start fresh and set up some roots, at least for a little while."

"I understand. I have to run, take care, Tatiana."

"Thank you, Malcolm you're the best."

Tatiana hung up the phone with the usual relief she felt after talking to Malcolm. He really was the best.

Friday, November 22, 1996

Leonid Kozlov had an important meeting, it started with a pat down by a 6'6" gorilla and being led to an opulent, ornate dining room.

"Please have a seat," the looming giant grunted.

Leonid placed his black leather briefcase on the floor next to him, while the gorilla moved to the corner of the room. Nothing was said, this made the room start to feel warmer. After several minutes footsteps were heard on the hardwood floor from a hallway leading to the dining room. A large, bearded man wearing a bright red tracksuit entered with another gorilla following closely behind. The gorilla moved to another corner of the room; the large man sat down at the head of the table.

"Mr. Kozlov, how can I help you?" the bearded man asked; the gorillas had no intention of making the meeting a private one.

"I have some information of a delicate nature that I think you'll find very useful," Leonid said with perspiration now visible on his forehead.

"What makes you think it would interest me?"

"I recently had a meeting with Igor Dryga."

"I see."

"He expressed to me, his attorney, that he wants me to make a deal for him."

"He's in prison, what kind of deal does he want to make?"

"One that would be detrimental to you if made public. Information about your people, your organization; he wants to try to negotiate his way out of prison."

"Why are you telling me this?"

"Because I don't want any complications in my life."

"You think I would cause you complications? Don't be silly, I'm just a businessman. Thank you for coming, Mr. Kozlov," Boris said with a slight emphasis on *Mr. Kozlov*. He rose from his seat and left the room. Leonid took that as his cue to leave and was followed to the door. He left not feeling like he completely accomplished what he set out to do but felt better about his situation. He wouldn't be lying awake staring at the ceiling tonight.

"Hello, Katerina. I presume this is Mr. Ortin, I'm Mr. Novikov," he said shaking his hand.

"Salvador Ortin. It's nice to meet you."

"This is Mr. Gusev and Mr. Ivanov."

"Gentlemen, it's a pleasure to meet you," Salvador said exchanging handshakes with the men.

They all took their spots around the conference room table with Katerina sitting next to Salvador. Katerina placed herself next to him intentionally, she wanted him to feel like she was his ally.

"Mr. Ortin, what is it you would like to see come from this meeting?" Mr. Novikov began.

"Katerina was good enough to present me with an overview of the consortium of businesses. It's very impressive and I'm in awe of how she and her team have managed to keep everything running since the tragic event that occurred almost two months ago. My client, Nicholas, had no idea who his father was until his mother, Melina, read about the attack. She had always known Arkadiy was Nicholas' father and he was quite successful but didn't know to what extent. Melina was hesitant to contact me about this and even more hesitant to pursue it, but she realized it shouldn't be her decision. She talked to Nicholas who decided to explore the next steps."

"As I explained to Mr. Ortin, we will assist him in any way possible no matter what is decided," Katerina said secretly having a definite preference as to the outcome.

"Does Nicholas have an idea as to how he would like to see things happen?" asked Mr. Novikov.

"I explained he would have the option to liquidate everything and walk away with a big windfall, but it could take years and years to complete that option. He was also told of the option to bring in his own management team, but I strongly advised against that. The businesses are being well run; it wouldn't make any sense."

"I do agree there," Mr. Ivanov chimed in.

"After reading about his father and his extraordinary accomplishments Nicholas would like to keep all the teams in place and run it all as a silent partner. He would hate to see all his father's efforts wasted."

"I'm sure we all agree that that is the best option," Mr. Gusev said.

"Yes, yes," came the unanimous response from the others.

"We'll get started on drawing up all the necessary documents and getting the transfer of the business units in place. When are we going to meet our new boss?" asked Mr. Novikov.

"Nicholas will be in town next week; I'll make arrangements with Katerina to bring him by."

The meeting ended with smiles and handshakes and a feeling of relief from all of the involved parties. Katerina left with Salvador heading back to headquarters. There were still many things to go over.

"Dmitri, I believe you have met Mr. Ortin," Katerina said entering Dmitri's office.

"Yes, how are you today?"

"Very well, thank you."

"Dmitri, would you please get Pavel and Ivan and join us in the conference room."

"Certainly, we'll meet you there in a few minutes."

Katerina and the team gathered soon after. "Gentleman, Mr. Ortin and I have just returned from the lawyer's office and have some interesting news; I'll get right to it. Arkadiy, it turns out had a son. His name is Nicholas Leon and he lives in Barcelona. We have DNA evidence that supports this, and this gives him legal rights to Arkadiy's holdings. Apparently, with all of his business acumen, Arkadiy never had a will."

"That's unbelievable, even I have a will," "Dmitri said.

"It's true despite my efforts to have him make one," Katerina added. "The good news for everyone is nothing is going to change as far as anyone's roles here. Mr. Leon is leaving everything in place and will be a silent partner."

"Gentlemen, I understand the challenges you have been going through and I appreciate what you have all done. I think, and I have expressed this to Nicholas, that he'd be crazy to change anything. I've made him aware of the risks he'll face taking this new role but am confident he'll receive top-notch protection from you."

"Will Mr. Leon be moving to Moscow?" Pavel asked.

"We will be setting up a residence for him here. He will be staying at his father's house when in town but will likely be spending the majority of his time in Barcelona. This will mean some changes to security details but I'm sure something very agreeable will be arranged."

The meeting, surprisingly, went on for hours. Salvador had no idea of the complexities involved with all the different business locations and the monthly routines in place to monitor them all. It was further complicated by the current threats and hostilities. It made him realize the importance of leaving the current team in place. The meeting adjourned; Dmitri and Ivan confirmed plans to meet for drinks and pool later. The other security team members would be there too.

"Nostrovia," Ivan said raising a glass to Dmitri.

"Nostrovia, but take it easy, remember we're still working." Just as he said that three men entered the bar. "Dmitri," said Anatoli, "how are you, my friend?"

"Great, good to see you again."

"Mo, how are you? Who is your friend?" Ivan asked while shaking his hand. Ivan's mind was racing, he knew exactly who he was. His look at Dmitri confirmed it.

"This is our friend and colleague Miroslav."

Dmitri stepped in gripping his hand with a very firm handshake, "nice to meet you Miroslav." His adrenaline was soaring as he did this. They had hoped to set up a meeting to snare Jablokov but here he was in the flesh. Drinks were ordered, and they played pool like it was an ordinary night, but Mo and Anatoli didn't see the bathroom meeting between Dmitri and a member of the security team that was backing them up.

"It's going down tonight," Dmitri said into Ivan's ear as he pretended to discuss a pool shot.

"Shots," Ivan called out.

"I understand from your friends you're looking for some information about an attack on your boss's place."

"You know something?" Miroslav asked looking directly into Dmitri's eyes slurring slightly.

"Yes, but what kind of reward are we talking about?"

"100,000 rubles for starters."

"We'll talk outside later," Dmitri said to a very interested Miroslav.

"These guys are getting really fucked up," Ivan said to Dmitri as he poured another shot on the floor.

"Keep it up, I want them disabled."

A few hours into the partying Mo announced he was calling it night. One down, Ivan thought.

An hour later Anatoli and Miroslav were saying their goodnights.

"We have some business to discuss, remember?"

"I'll wait for you outside," a now visibly drunk Miroslav relayed.

A security team member confirmed passing by Dmitri that Mo and Anatoli had departed. It was on.

Saturday, November 23, 1996

Katerina awoke to the ringing of the phone next to the bed, it was 2:10 a.m. She had just fallen asleep.

"Hello."

"It's Ivan."

"What Ivan?" she said with irritation expecting a drunk hookup request.

"We got him!" he excitedly said.

"Who?"

"Jablokov, Miroslav Jablokov."

"Shit, where are you?"

"We're at the truck repair shop."

"I'll be there in half an hour."

Katerina pulled on a pair of jeans, dragged a wool sweater over her long-sleeved t-shirt, and was about to leave. "Forgot something," she said out loud, turned around, and entered the dining room. Hanging on the wall supported by two decorative pegs was a meter-long razor-sharp Samari sword. She carefully took it down placing it in a case that sat underneath on a credenza. The case was closed with a brass latch, she threw on a coat and was off.

Ivan was standing by the door of the garage, opened it when he recognized Katerina's BMW. She entered the garage carrying the dark wooden case and set it on a workbench.

"Great work guys. Where did you find this murderous piece of shit?"

"He actually came to us," Dmitri said with a grin as he pulled Jablokov's head back by his hair.

Tied securely to a metal chair, Jablokov was wearing his signature black Members Only jacket, sweating like he was in a sauna. He was surrounded by the six members of the security team with Pavel at his side. Pavel whose wound was healing nicely did not want to miss this day.

"Remove his gag," Katerina ordered. "Who else was involved in Lev Drozdov's death?"

"I don't know."

"I'm only going to ask you one more time. Who else was involved in Lev Drozdov's death?"

"I don't know."

"You lying piece of shit." With that, Katerina spun launching a roundhouse kick that landed her dark brown boot squarely in Miroslav's mouth dislodging several teeth that he was now spitting on the concrete floor. The room was silent except for the moans coming out of Jablokov's bleeding mouth. Katerina walked over to the workbench, removed the sword from the antique case, and brought it over to Pavel carefully giving it to him by the handle.

"Off with his fucking head!" she yelled and left the building.

"Hello."

"I found the information on him."

"Who is this?" Litskevich asked on his Saturday morning off.

"It's Balakin. I found the information you requested on Jablokov. He flew to Zurich on October 19th and returned October 23rd."

"Miss Balakin, I owe you big time. I'll be bringing you chocolates on Monday."

"You better, I was here until 11:00 last night researching this stuff. You were off by a week and a half on when you thought he left."

"It'll be a big box of chocolates. Thank you." He hung up the phone as Nataliya was entering the living room.

"Who are you buying chocolates for?" she asked with a pensive look.

"It's not what you think, baby. Miss Balakin worked very hard for them."

"And I didn't," Nataliya said grabbing Alexander's left ear and leading him back to the bedroom.

Dryga lay in his bunk feeling depressed. He hoped his meeting with Leonid would have yielded instant results but knew this was wishful thinking. Nothing happened that quickly in Russia. The idea of being plucked from prison two or three days later was nuts but with some luck maybe Leonid would have some good news for him on Monday.

"Yard!" was yelled into the cell and all of Dryga's cellmates exited their bunks, he was the last one out. They all walked the noisy corridor toward the yard entrance where the old, tattered coats hung on hooks, the search for the one with the fewest holes began. Being the last one there Dryga's had a huge rip on the side under the left arm, it was going to be a chilly hour. The circular march around the yard began. He intentionally hung back from the others. He just wanted some alone time, some time to think. What if this was going to be his routine for years to come. How was he going to manage. These thoughts had run through his head over and over, the answer was always the same. It wasn't going to happen. One way or another it was going to end and soon.

Tatiana knew her days in Sydney were limited so her Saturday was spent being a tourist. First stop today was the top of the Sydney Habour Bridge. She booked a bridge climb the day before and was suiting up in coveralls for a quick training run-through. She was a little nervous because of a slight fear of heights but those fears were quelled when she slid into the harness and saw the system in place to ensure no one ever got blown off into the harbour below. As the group climbed out onto the structure a warm breeze whipped across Tatiana's face; she felt her pulse increase slightly.

The blonde young lady with a thick Aussie accent, who was their guide, quickly put everyone at ease with a mix of history about the bridge and jokes she had probably told hundreds of times before. As they climbed higher on the riveted thick steel beams the breeze got stronger, the sun seemed brighter and the views more spectacular. The Sydney Opera House glistened in the sunlight and the ferries departing Circular Quay seemed like toys leaving a white trail of seawater behind them as they headed to various destinations. The people on the ferries were probably watching her, she thought, as she had marveled at the climbers she eyed days before. At the bridge summit, she took in the views that included the Botanical Gardens she enjoyed so much with a sense that she had accomplished something remarkable. It wouldn't be long until she was back at a harbour side café eating lunch with a chilled glass of white wine staring up at the new wave of bridge conquerors.

Sunday, November 24, 1996

Nicholas Leon strolled down bustling Las Ramblas with a beach towel over his shoulder wearing leather sandals and a new pair of stylish Ray-Bans. He was going to the beach to hook up with some friends.

The idea that he was a billionaire hadn't sunk in; he hadn't even wrapped his head around the number yet. How much was a billion he contemplated, a thousand million. Shit, that's a lot he thought. I guess I'll be treating today. His mother strongly advised him against telling anyone about his new status in life. They will all find out fast enough and when they do everything will instantly change.

"Enjoy these days," she said, "you'll soon be moving on to a new chapter of uncertainty."

There were no truer words because as he walked, he was being followed, not by a couple of people but several. They had hidden microphones and earpieces and were switching off surveillance at regular intervals. Even a trained expert would have trouble detecting them. Nicholas would eventually come to know his stealthy stalkers but for now, he was just enjoying a Sunday as a teenage kid. His stalkers had been pulled together by Katerina and Dmitri, he didn't realize it, but he was in excellent hands.

Boris Voshkolup was finishing his huge breakfast that included doktorskaya kolbasa, syrnikis, and blinis when his driver stuck his head into the dining room to announce the car was in front.

"I'll be there in a minute," he said as he guzzled the last swig of coffee from a large mug.

As he entered the foyer a butler, who looked more like a bodyguard, held his very large coat up by the shoulders, assisted him in putting it on, and then opened the door. The driver opened the rear passenger side door and the big man slid in.

"What is the smell?" he inquired as the driver entered the running Rolls-Royce.

"I don't know sir, but I'll run inside and get some air freshener."

Boris looked over to his left and noticed a red towel on the seat next to him. He lifted it up and started to violently vomit all down the front of him and on the seat in front. The head of Miroslav Jablokov was looking up at him. He pulled on the door handle, rolled out of the car ending up on his hands and knees, continuing to vomit. The driver ran out with the air freshener in his hand and helped him to his feet. Boris had absolutely no color left in his face and was visibly shaking.

"Sir, what's wrong?" And then he looked in the car and threw up in his mouth before turning away.

"Tatiana, it's Mikheil." Tatiana just entered the lobby of her hotel when her cell phone rang. "Can you talk, are you alone?"

"Mikheil, I'm just getting on the elevator. Can you hold on for a couple of minutes?"

"Yes, Tatiana."

"Mikheil, how are you?"

"I'm well."

"How is Olena and Jacques?"

"They are both very well."

Tatiana entered her room. "Mikheil, I'm alone, is everything okay?"

"Yes, I'm going to be brief. They got one of the responsible parties. It's been dealt with."

Tatiana immediately got the message. "Mikheil, say no more. Got it. Am I safe?"

"In one word, no. I don't know when I'll be able to tell you that but it's not now. Based on what I've been told things will likely get worse you need to be more careful than ever."

"Not what I wanted to hear, but Mikheil thank you for the news. Please tell Olena I'm thinking of her every day and give Jacques a great big hug from me."

"I will. Be safe."

Sergei Magnitsky just woke from a deep sleep. His sleeping habits had improved since he started doing some exercises in his cell to help kill the time and get himself in better shape. He was up to a couple of dozen sit-ups each day which would have been unthinkable a week earlier. Each one required immense effort. After finishing a set, a sudden jolt of pain shot through his body and an audible groan emanated as his arms crossed his stomach; his knees rose up. Something wasn't right. At first, he thought maybe he just overdid it with the exercises but soon realized it was more serious.

"Guard'" he called out. Nothing. "Gua…" the pain made it impossible to complete the word.

"Guard." Nothing.

He lay in the fetal position until the morning. When roll call went unanswered, he was found, his shirt and sheets drenched in sweat. A stretcher was called for, he was taken to the infirmary.

10

Tatiana's wardrobe had expanded since she landed in Sydney. Packing now required two large suitcases and a backpack, and they were stuffed to capacity. She called around to a couple of camper rental companies, and in an hour one was going to pull up in front of the hotel and would be hers for the next few weeks. The plan was to drive north and explore the coast. The great thing about her plan was there wasn't much of one; the beauty of not knowing where she was going was no one else knew either.

Before her departure, a late breakfast was squeezed in and water, snacks, and other necessities were purchased for the trip, including a new disposable phone. It was almost two months since she drove last, coupled with driving a large vehicle on the opposite side of the road had her a little apprehensive, but she was ready for a new adventure.

"Hello, my name is Donny, this is Karl," Donny said pointing at the guy waving who pulled up right behind the camper van.

"Hello, I'm Tatiana." When she introduced herself, she thought this will be the last time I'm Tatiana for a while.

"Have you ever had a camper van before?"

"No, this is a first for me."

"I have some paperwork here that needs to be filled out. They told me at the office you'll be leaving a cash deposit, is that right?"

"Yes, my credit card was lost."

"No worries," Donny said as he counted the large bills and put them in an envelope. "Let me walk you around and show you some of the features. This is a new Mazda Bongo Friendee, you're only the second person to have it."

"It still has the new car smell," Tatiana commented.

"That it does and see how the roof pops up, a lot of extra space there."

Donny had been very thorough showing off the obvious features as well as some hidden ones and fifteen minutes later Tatiana was on the road with a full tank of petrol, destination unknown.

Litskevich was now on to something, but he was getting frustrated. His search for Tatiana Belov was starting to gel but a few other cases he was working on, now partnerless, kept diverting him in different directions. Tatiana's trip to Zurich made total sense, it was a banking hub and the attention she was getting from Voshkolup very likely meant there was a large sum of money involved. He needed to talk to Jablokov but couldn't locate him. He had spent days looking for him, he was possibly the only link, or at least a link that would save him a massive amount of time putting all this together.

"I'm Lt. Litskevich, I need to see Igor Dryga," he said to the guard in charge of visitation at Butyrka.

"Who are you?" he said ignoring his introduction.

"Lt. Litskevich," this time pulling out his credentials.

"And who is it you wish to see?"

"Igor Dryga."

The guard opened a large ledger book and scrolled through several rows of names before instructing him to wait several meters away on a well-worn wooden bench. Half an hour later he was summoned and led to a private visitation room.

Litskevich flashed his credentials to the guard standing in the doorway watching over Dryga. "Please give us several minutes." The guard stepped away allowing Litskevich to close the door behind him.

"Igor, what the fuck?" he said embracing his old friend.

"Alex, it's so good to see you. I take it my lawyer Leonid Kozlov has spoken with Kovalyov."

"No? I'm here on my own. Igor, what have you done?"

Dryga buried his gaunt face into his arms that were resting on the table. Litskevich reached over and squeezed his shoulder.

When he raised his head up his eyes were tearing up. "You have no idea what it's like in here."

"Man, you really fucked up. We're you really supplying information to Voshkolup?"

The room was silent for what seemed like minutes. "Alex, you have no idea the pressure I was under."

"But you were helping that monster."

"I didn't know that at first. I had some big losses at the tables and most of it went away if I helped a guy that knew a guy. I just got pulled in deeper and deeper before I knew who was behind it all."

"You dumb shit. Why didn't you come to me? We could have turned the tables on this piece of shit. Sure, you would have lost your job, but you could have avoided this," Litskevich said raising his arms in the air.

"When I saw you, I thought this was going to be my chance. My lawyer hasn't talked to anyone there?"

"I'll look into it, but I'm not aware of any deals. I wanted to see how you're doing, see if you might be able to help me locate Jablokov."

"I'll help you wherever I can. Please tell Kovalyov I'll give them any information I can I need to get out of this fucking place."

Dryga gave his old partner a list of places where Jablokov might be found and information that he could use as leverage to make him more willing to talk. He asked Litskevich to check in on his mother and ex-wife and tell them he was well. The prison meeting ended with hugs and a promise to do what he could to get his friend out of this mess. When Dryga returned to his cell he was asked who was visiting him, "just a friend," he said.

It was only a matter of 80 kilometers of driving before Tatiana felt at ease driving her new home. She made her way from the M1 to the scenic A1 taking in the salty breeze with all the windows down, her hair blowing all around. It was then she started thinking about practical matters like a sleeping bag, flashlight, lantern, pots and pans, and basic camping gear. Four hours in she decided to stop in Port Macquarie, pick up her gear, hit the supermarket, and give cooking out a crack.

Tatiana pulled her camper to the front of the Anaconda Store and a young man with a nametag that read Jimmy assisted her in loading the equipment into the back. He told her of a local park just outside of town where she could set up camp for the evening, a place she wouldn't be bothered and had nice views overlooking the ocean. It turned out to be the perfect spot for the first night of her vagabond adventure. After an hour of relaxing in her new fold-out lawn chair, Tatiana popped up the roof and unfurled her sleeping bag in the back of her van. She lowered the windows down a crack, locked the doors and she was out minutes later.

Tuesday, November 26, 1996

Nicholas was picked up at his home by a chauffeured Maybach limousine. The driver wore a sharp, tailored navy-blue suit complete with a cap, opened the rear passenger door for him, and then deposited his suitcase and carry-on in the trunk. He asked his mother to come along but she thought that would send the wrong message. The head of a billion-ruble conglomerate couldn't be seen with his mama on the first day of work.

The Maybach pulled into a part of Barcelona Airport Nicolas had never seen, it was a private gate at Terminal 2. The driver said something to a uniformed guard and the barbed-wired topped gate slowly opened with the aid of a noisy motor. The limo proceeded along slowly for a couple of hundred meters pulling up to a white shiny Gulfstream jet.

"Wow," came out of Nichols' mouth.

The driver chuckled, "this is your ride."

The rear door opened, and Nicholas stepped out at the same time the Gulfstream's door opened and steps extended for his entrance.

"Welcome, Nicholas. I'm Brittany," a friendly attractive young lady said as he entered the climate-controlled interior. The captain stuck his head out from the cockpit with a warm hello and a promise of a smooth flight to Moscow.

"Please let me know if there is anything you would like. Can I offer you a glass of Champagne?"

"Yes, please," Nicholas said trying to not sound eager.

The captain walked back into the cabin while the flight attendant popped a bottle of Moet Chandon informing Nicholas a couple of members of the security team would be joining them shortly. He just finished saying that when they entered the cabin.

"Hello, Mr. Leon; I'm Ivan and this is Yuri. We'll be heading back with you to Moscow." At that moment the jet engines fired up causing a slight vibration to the champagne glass sitting on the pull-out table in front of him. "Please feel free to ask us any questions you might have," as they both took a seat a couple of rows away.

Nicholas literally pinched himself. This can't be happening, I can't wait to tell my friends about this and then the words of his mother popped into his head; "things will instantly change." He then realized how right she was. He would have to be very careful to whom he gave access to his new life. Off the top of his head there were only three, maybe four close friends, guys he'd known from childhood that he could fully trust not to take advantage of him.

The jet finished taxiing down to the start of the runway, then the engines revved to a low roar and the jet lurched forward. He looked out of the window; within seconds they were off the ground.

"Can I get you something to eat?" Brittany asked. "We have a selection of tapas for starters."

"That sounds great, please bring enough out for all of us," motioning towards his security team. Nicholas was going to use this moment as an opportunity to gather information about the myriad of questions swirling through his head from Ivan and Yuri. The second glass of champagne relaxed him, so he didn't feel self-conscious asking about some of the things he was about to experience for the first time. Ivan was happy to take Nicholas under his wing. He pictured what it would be like if their roles were reversed.

Tatiana had an okay night of sleep waking up once because her sleeping bag was too warm; the windows of the van needed to be lowered a little more. Her memories of camping were as a young girl with her parents, the family crammed into a medium size tent, and her father waking her and her mother up with his snoring. When she woke up this morning the sun was bright, and there wasn't a single cloud in the azure blue sky. Crawling out of her sleeping bag she popped the side door of the van open, set up the bottle-top propane stove, and boiled water for her instant coffee. She dunked a couple of biscuits into the coffee, that was breakfast. Minutes later she was back cruising the A1 northward. The vast beaches she kept coming across at various segments of the highway were so inviting that she pulled over, put her swimsuit on, and dove into the crashing waves. It was a nice break from the tedious driving.

After driving for about five and a half hours Tatiana had enough. For the past hour, she debated with herself about finding a place to camp near the Gold Coast or staying at a posh hotel. The hotel won out. She pulled her camper van up to the beautiful Hyatt Regency, entered the lobby that screamed luxury, especially after camping, and inquired about a vacancy. She decided she was going to register under her new alias, Olga Olenska. Fortunately, she had her new passport as proof she was Olga if needed.

"Ms. Olenska, we'll just need a $500 dollar cash deposit since you don't have a credit card available," the front desk clerk stated.

Olga located an envelope in her purse handing the cash over.

"You'll be in room 711. Do you need help with your bags?"

"Yes, thank you. I'm parked in front."

"I'll have someone right over."

The first thing Tatiana aka Olga noticed was the temperature of her nice room. She hadn't realized how hot it had been. The next thing that caught her eye was the huge swimming pool and the inviting bar seven stories down. She put on a dry swimsuit, slipped on her sandals, pulled on an oversized t-shirt, and headed down.

Sitting down at the poolside bar she ordered a piña colada complete with a pineapple wedge and cherry, but before she could take a sip a voice came from over her shoulder.

"Good day, how are you?"

"I'm fine. How are you?" she asked looking at the man standing just off to her right up and down, taking a sip of her drink.

"My name is Matthew. It's nice to meet you," he said extending his hand.

"Ta…Olga," was her response with a slight stammer. She hoped she wasn't blushing.

"From your accent, I take it you're not from around here."

"No, Russia. From your accent, I take it you are."

"Local compared to you. I'm from Cairns, about 1,700 kilometers up the road."

"What brings you to the Gold Coast, Matthew?"

"Holiday. Taking a break from things and you?"

"The same."

The pair continued chatting over another drink and made plans to meet up for dinner later that evening. Tatiana was already enjoying the local scenery and she hadn't even left the hotel yet.

Dryga had another restless night, caused by a feeling of unease. He knew his chance to get out would be soon or not for a very long time, if ever. The FSB would want his information or would prefer to make an example out of him. If it was the latter his days would probably be numbered. He tried to sleep after breakfast, but it was difficult in the dank smelly crowded cell, fresh air was desperately needed.

"Yard!" was called into the cell. Dryga had finally just dosed off. He rubbed his eyes and marched down the corridor with his cellmates. The coats were donned, and they were soon outside on a chilly day walking the yard perimeter. One of his cellmates walked up beside him and started chatting.

"Dryga, what is it you're in for?"

"I thought you knew, auto theft."

"Ya, that's right. You?"

"Drugs. I'm going to be here for quite a while. I got nine years for a little bit of hash oil. Unfucking believable. How long are you in for?"

"I don't know. I'm waiting for my trial. Hopefully not nine years."

The conversation continued until his cellmate was called over to a group standing by the door. Dryga walked alone for a couple more minutes when "everyone in" was called. He started walking to the door to join the others. They had just entered the building when the door slammed a few meters in front of him. He was now in the yard alone. He approached the door and pounded on it. There wasn't a response. He pounded on it again, this time it opened, and two large guys emerged from it pushing him backward. The door then slammed shut, there were just the three of them in the walled yard.

Dryga's heart started to pound, he knew he was in trouble. He lunged at the guy who was a bit larger first and as he lunged, he saw it, a small shiny shank. He managed to knock the arm back with his left hand and land a blow to his attacker's face with the right. As he made contact the other guy came up from behind driving a knife into his neck. The pain was like molten metal poured into him, and he went down, his legs unable to support him. Attempting a call for help but nothing came out of his mouth. He looked at his right hand now covered in blood after grasping his neck. The two men dropped their weapons and the door opened as they approached, it shut right behind them. Dryga lay on the cold ground clutching his neck with warm blood trickling through his fingers. He looked up toward the sky to see blackbirds. A murder of crows, how ironic he thought.

Wednesday, November 27, 1996

"Litskevich."

What was up that couldn't wait for him to at least take off his coat he thought as he made his way to Koyalyov's office.

"Yes, Major?"

"I have some bad news. Dryga's been killed."

"What? That can't be, I just saw him," as Litskevich said that a tsunami wave of guilt rushed over him. Had his visit put him in danger. Did he cause the death of his friend. He left the headquarters, raced to the prison, and made his way to the infirmary. As he stood waiting for the doctor, he found himself wondering why he was there. Nothing could be done now his friend was dead. When the doctor did emerge from the examination room, he explained who he was and asked for the details of Igor's death.

"I don't have any details of the events surrounding your friend's death. All I can tell you is he was mortally stabbed in the neck. He lost a tremendous amount of blood."

"Where did this happen? Who were the guards on duty?"

"Again, I don't have any details. You'll have to request a report from the warden's office."

"I want to speak to someone in charge now."

"I can't help you with that; I have many patients to see. You'll have to excuse me."

"This is bullshit! Heads are going to fucking roll!" Litskevich said storming off.

In a twist of fate, Litskevich's yelling was overheard by patients confined to their beds in the infirmary. One of them was Sergei Magnitsky. He was sleeping, recovering from lifesaving gallbladder surgery, and was in and out of consciousness. I know that voice he thought before drifting back to sleep. Sergei had been on death's doorstep. If surgery was delayed another hour, he would be in the fridge next to the man who helped put him in Butyrka.

Tatiana woke up from a pleasant dream. She was laying on the beach being fed piña coladas by young hunky guys, and one of them was massaging her neck. As she opened her eyes though reality was setting in; her head was feeling the effects of the night before. The afternoon had started with a couple of piña coladas and wine during dinner ending with a Grand Marnier to cap the evening off. Despite her aching head, a smile came across her face.

Dinner with Matthew was very nice, filled with interesting conversation and ending with a drawn-out passionate good night kiss that would have led to more if she hadn't given him a gentle shove away from her hotel room door. She had plans to pack, jump in the camper van, and hit the road and told Matthew that but as she lay there, she thought what's the hurry. Not being on a schedule of any kind she went to the front desk to pay for another night before going to breakfast.

A big, hardy English breakfast of bacon, sausage, eggs, beans, and toast had just been placed in front of her when a familiar voice came from behind.

"I see someone is hungry."

She looked over her shoulder to see Matthew standing there. She smiled and motioned for him to join her.

"Good morning," she said.

"Good morning. I thought you'd be long gone on your journey."

"Me too, but I decided to stay another day."

"Did I have anything to do with that decision?"

"Listen to you, Mr. Full of Himself. Maybe."

Matthew smiled. He knew it was going to be a great day. Breakfast was complete and remembering something that Olga said the night before he told her to meet him in front in half an hour. He had a surprise. Olga exited from the automatic hotel doors to find Matthew in an open Wrangler Jeep.

"I hope you brought your sunglasses," he called out.

Olga pulled them out of her bag and climbed into the jeep. Where are we going?

"It's a surprise. Don't worry I'm not taking you out to the bush. It's about an hour and a half away, but it's a nice drive. We'll stop for a dip on the way. Do you have a swimsuit?"

"No. I'll just have to watch you."

There wasn't a stop, the drive went by in a flash as they talked and laughed nonstop all the way. They turned off the highway when Matthew lowered the radio announcing they were almost there, their destination was Currumbin Wildlife Sanctuary.

"Perfect," Olga exclaimed. "I really want to pet a koala." This guy is something else she thought to herself.

"Dryga's dead," Mo said to Voshkolup as he entered the dining room.

"Good," Voshkolup responded not even looking up from a large plate of lasagna. "You're sure he's dead?" he asked now looking up into Mo's eyes.

"Yes, I spoke with the guard 45 minutes ago."

"You took care of him?"

"Yes, he's been paid."

"Good. Sit down. There's some more urgent business that needs to be discussed. First, I want Abramov's bitch brought to me, Katerina Grigoryev. I don't have proof that she's behind Miroslav's death but I don't need it. My hunch is good enough, bring her to me. Second, I need to find that Belov woman, she just can't have vanished. I already have guys looking for her, I need you to get with them and find her. The next time we speak you better have something for me. Do you understand?"

"Yes, sir."

The big man went back to his lasagna. The meeting was over.

Thursday, November 28, 1996

Tatiana lay in bed deep in thought, she was very conflicted about what to do next. In just two days she had grown quite fond of Matthew. He seemed to be the perfect match for her. He was two years older than her but at 32 had a maturity about him. He owned a construction company that he started from scratch, was blonde, tall, and muscular, and had a surfer dude look about him. What more could I ask for she thought. She also realized by allowing him into her life he would be in danger. Knock, knock. Tatiana jumped. She got out of bed and looked out of the peephole; it was Matthew. She opened the door and was greeted by a kiss.

"Good morning, Matthew," she said pulling away, the kiss giving her butterflies in her stomach.

"Good morning, Olga. Want to come out and play?"

She was going to tell him she was checking out today but couldn't. "What do you have in mind?"

"I have a meeting in Brisbane with a client this afternoon, it won't take long. Would you like to come with me, we can do lunch, you can shop, and then we'll explore the city?"

Play hard to get she thought, but an instant reply came, "give me half hour to get ready."

"Have you had breakfast?"

"Does it look like it?" she said pulling strands of messy hair in the air.

"I'll meet you in the restaurant downstairs."

So much for playing hard to get she thought as she stepped into the shower. Her mind drifted to yesterday when they were driving back from the wildlife sanctuary. They made a stop at the beach and took a dip, Matthew in his swimsuit, she in her shorts and a bra. Luckily, she hadn't been wearing a lacy see-through one. They played in the sea and exchanged kisses as the waves crashed against their bodies. After drying off in the sun they found a local seafood restaurant that seemed to be popular with the locals filling up on shrimp, crab, and buttery lobster. The sauvignon blanc tasted really nice with the drive back preventing a second bottle but one was waiting for them at the hotel and enjoyed watching a picturesque sunset. It had been the perfect day. Her daydreaming had her running late for breakfast, she called down to the restaurant.

"Please tell Mr… Please tell the good-looking blonde gentleman waiting I'll be there in 15 minutes."

The hostess laughed saying she knew exactly who she meant.

Litskevich spent the night tossing and turning. Nataliya tried to comfort him, but she knew it was useless. She pointed out to him that his visit to the prison was unlikely the cause of Igor's death, that he was being a good friend trying to help him out of the mess he was in, and that he had always been there for his friend. He tried to listen to her and said those things over and over to himself, but thoughts of Igor's last moments played in his head repeatedly. He vowed he would find out who was responsible and have them locked away.

"Major, I went to Butyrka yesterday to try and find out what happened to Dryga and got nowhere. Can you contact the warden and get some answers?"

"No," Kovalyov said while shuffling papers.

"I know you think he was a traitor, but he was trying to fix his mistakes."

"I don't think he was a traitor, he was a traitor. He was working for that piece of shit, Voshkolup; he was part of the bratva. I know you helped him out in the past, shit came out when he was being investigated but you never crossed the line. You were his friend, and he took advantage of you. In the end, he got what he deserved."

"Everything you say is true, but we can't let the person or people responsible for his death just walk away," Litskevich said exasperated.

"I have dozens of open cases where bratva thugs are reining terror all over the city, the country, in fact, I'm not involving myself in this. If you want to look into it in your free time, go ahead. I'm not going to stop you."

Litskevich walked out of his boss's office frustrated. Everything he said was true, but he felt he owed his friend justice even if he was flawed. If nothing else looking into his death might relieve some of the guilt he was feeling.

He jumped into his car, drove to the prison, and spent the next two hours being given the run-around. He went to four offices, at first trying to meet with the warden and then settling for just a copy of the report detailing the incident. Litskevich left with nothing.

Katerina's day was a very busy one. It started with gathering reams of documents for the company's attorneys pertaining to the transfer of ownership. By lunchtime four banker's boxes had been filled for their request and odds were a couple more boxes would be filled by week's end. Next was a lengthy meeting with Nicholas in which she went over a report she put together of all the company's enterprises, what they each did, where they were located, who the key staff members were, if there were partners involved, and different nuances each one had. She was surprised by how quickly he was absorbing all the information and his interest in it all. He had just finished high school and was in his first year of business school at a university in Barcelona. The plan was for him to get his degree while figuratively running his late father's business. By the time he got his degree, he would probably be able to teach some of the classes he was now attending.

Katerina's final meeting in her grueling day was with Berezovsky, Dmitri, and Viktor. It was a highly secretive meeting that took place in a private dining room at an upscale seafood restaurant on the Moskva River. Dmitri and Viktor did most of the talking after they finished a meal that started with Beluga caviar and ended with flaming bananas Foster. The two men provided details of the most aggressive attack planned on Voshkolup at his Shvedskiy Tupik apartment. This time they would be sure he was there for the show.

The meeting concluded with both Katerina and Konstantin buzzed, walking to their waiting respective cars. Konstantin was accompanied by Viktor and Katerina with Dmitri. Each car had a security team member driving and one riding shotgun, they were on heightened alert. Berezovsky's car was in front and made a quick right turn out of the restaurant parking lot, and Katerina's car went left. She leaned into Dmitri and said quietly into his ear "I haven't forgotten about the reward for Lev's killer." This put a smile on Dmitri's face, he had thought about it but knew there was so much going on. At that moment they felt their bodies pressed a little more firmly against the backseat as the car accelerated and the driver announced they might be followed. Dmitri instructed Katerina to get down, the three men all pulled out Glocks from underarm holsters, the man to the driver's right reached under the seat and now had an Uzi as well. The driver made a couple of last-second turns hoping he was just being paranoid, but each turn cemented his suspicions and those of the car's occupants. After trying to elude the pursuing vehicle for about a kilometer the first shot was fired, it shattered the rear window above Katerina's head. Dmitri turned back returning fire at the BMW that was 30 meters behind but missed. More shots came from the BMW with a couple of them hitting what sounded like taillights.

"Hand me the Uzi!" Dmitri yelled as he punched away at the rear windshield fragments. He started firing at the BMW striking its windshield.

The security team member riding shotgun had his window down and was pumping off shots as fast as he could pull the trigger. Some of the shots making contact with various parts of the car. The front seat passenger could be seen kicking at the shattered windshield trying to knock it out when one of the shots made contact. He was stopped in mid-kick.

"Katerina, stay down!" Dmitri yelled as they were being tossed about as the driver was making sharp turns through Moscow streets trying to keep them in motion. Dmitri and his partner continued firing as the pursuit surprisingly continued. Dmitri wondered how the driver of the BMW could keep up as well as he did with a windshield as shattered as it was.

"They're slowing down, I think I hit the radiator," Dmitri shouted. "Stop!" was his next word.

The driver now swung open his door, the BMW was now being peppered by bullets from the Uzi and two Glocks. One more shot came from the BMW going over the driver's head and then the only shots that followed were from the security team. Clips were replaced; Dmitri and shotgun were now out of the car continuing to fire while they approached the now silent BMW. Inside were three badly bleeding bodies. The driver swung open the driver's door of the BMW and saw the driver was still alive.

"Who sent you?" he yelled.

"Fuck you!" was the response.

It was his last words as a bullet entered his forehead.

Shotgun pulled open the front passenger door to find his guy with two holes in his face. Dmitri went to the back to inspect the damage; he was shocked to find Anatoli laying there with several holes in him. Dmitri added a couple more for good measure.

Friday, November 29, 1996

Tatiana's day in Brisbane with Matthew was another perfect one. It started with a pub lunch on the river that had a spectacular view of the Story Bridge. The slight breeze kept it very pleasant as they enjoyed a pint, and ate fish and chips watching the boats drift by. Unfortunately, lunch had to end when Matthew looked at his watch and excused himself for a meeting that was a short walk away. He gave Olga a kiss and they agreed to meet back in front of the pub in an hour and a half. Tatiana made her way over to Queen Street; she always had an uncanny ability to find the best shopping spots. Two things that struck her about Brisbane were how friendly the people were, and the women dressed so nicely. Her mission today was to find a nice outfit for dinner tonight.

Despite missing Matthew, the hour and a half flew by, and Olga saw him standing in front of the pub.

"I see you've been busy," Matthew said eyeing the numerous bags strung across Olga's arms.

"I love the shops here," she said with an ear-to-ear smile.

"Let me take a couple of those bags for you."

"I wish you had come shopping with me, you could have helped me pick out some things."

"It looks like you've done all right without me."

"How did your meeting go?"

"Great. It looks like I'm in the running for a large build-out job here in Brisbane. It's just a matter of some adjustments to the contract but it looks very promising. It would keep my guys busy for about three months."

"That's great news."

They made their way to the river and had a nice walk holding hands. "I have a surprise for you tonight; I've made a dinner reservation for us at that French restaurant near our hotel. It will be my treat." Tatiana at that moment was very happy but also very conflicted.

Sergei was feeling better emotionally and also physically. He enjoyed the company of a couple of patients next to him in the infirmary. The days went by much quicker having people to talk to and they would have gone by even quicker if he still didn't have the nagging pain emanating from his abdomen. At least it wasn't the stabbing debilitating pain that brought him there he thought. Another benefit of the infirmary was he was able to write a letter to his wife and gave it to a nurse. He promised she would receive a gift from his wife when she received it.

"Magnitsky!"

Shit, he thought.

"You're going back to your cell."

"But I'm still sick. I'm still having severe stomach pains. Ask the doctor."

"Not severe enough, according to the doctor. You'll be getting your rest elsewhere."

There was no point arguing. He was put in a wheelchair and taken back to the cold stinky cell.

Katerina, Dmitri, and the security team members were safe. They survived the evening with just a few minor cuts and scrapes.

"Konstantin, are you okay?" Katerina asked, calling from the hotel suite they had just checked into.

"Yes, why?"

"We were followed from the restaurant and shot at."

"Are you all right, was anyone hurt?"

"Just the bad guys, Voshkolup's. Three of them now are dead."

"Are you safe?"

"Yes, it wasn't safe to go home. I'm shaken up but the guys seem to be taking it in stride."

"You know for sure it was Voshkolup?"

"Yes, Dmitri recognized one of the dead ones. There's no doubt."

"We'll see if we can put the plan into action more quickly. It's gotten to a point where it's us or him and I prefer the latter," Berezovsky said.

"Talk tomorrow. Stay safe."

Konstantin didn't sleep at all that night. Thoughts of the attempt on his life played over and over in his mind, he was tired of living in fear.

Tatiana stood in front of the mirror admiring her purchases from earlier in the day. It was a fitted white dress with a black bow in front at the waist and matching shiny white high-heeled shoes that added several centimeters to her thin stature. Black opal earrings with a matching necklace completed the look. Just one more thing was needed she thought reaching for the Oscar de la Renta perfume.

Matthew greeted her in the lobby with a "wow." She locked her arm in his and they walked a couple of blocks to the restaurant. Upon arrival, they were promptly seated which worked out well for them as they were both famished.

"Bonjour," said the waiter.

Tatiana's mind went straight to her mother. She had been so enthralled with Matthew she had forgotten about calling Malcolm. Guilt swept over her.

"Olga? Olga? Is everything all right?"

"I'm sorry Matthew. I have a couple of things on my mind."

"Is everything okay? You had a very worried look about you."

"I'm fine. It was just some work stuff that popped into my head. It can wait until next week."

"Yes, I'm sure the bank will be fine. Cheers," Matthew said raising a glass of white wine.

"Cheers," Olga said.

It was obvious to the waiter his customers were very hungry. It didn't take long before a couple of chocolate eclairs were brought to the table.

"I noticed you haven't been your chatty self this evening. What's on your mind?"

"I'm sorry, Matthew. It's not only work but I'm having such a good time."

"And that's a problem?"

"Yes. I have some decisions to make, and you are complicating them. I'm starting to feel something for you, I'm not sure the timing is right."

"I'm definitely feeling something for you too. I love every minute we spend together. Here's what I suggest, we take things day by day and see where it goes."

"You won't be upset if I run off in a day or two."

"Yes, but we'll figure something out. Deal?"

"Deal."

For several minutes passionate kisses were exchanged outside of Olga's hotel room door.

"Are you sure you don't want me to come in?"

"Not tonight, Matthew. I've had a lovely day and an even better evening. See you tomorrow?"

"You better."

Tatiana entered her room to a flashing red light on the phone. I bet it's a message from Malcolm. It was, he asked her to call him at home. After their chat, a call was placed to her mother.

"Mama, how would you like to move to France?"

Saturday, November 30, 1996

"Tatiana, I've thought about it and yes, I'm ready for a new adventure."

"Mama, that's fantastic. What changed your mind?"

"When you told me that most of the customers were Russian, and I would be able to work as much or as little as I wanted, I thought what the hell. My biggest concern was leaving my friends but as you said they can come and visit. Also, what if business isn't that good, how will I pay you back?"

"You're going to love Antibes; I've heard it's gorgeous there. Don't worry about the money. Pay me what you can when you can. It's the least I can do for you."

"Why is there such a rush to get me there? A week isn't much time to pack all my things and say goodbye to everyone."

"The old owner is moving abroad and wants to go over all the customer accounts with you, show you all the equipment, and introduce you around."

"This is so exciting."

"Mama, one thing though and it's important. Please don't tell anyone where you're going, at least at first.

"Why?"

"Part of the issue is the old owner has some tax issues. I'm working with someone here at the bank who is going to transfer the business to a corporate entity, take care of the tax issue and then put it in your name. I know it sounds complicated and it is a little but it's important we keep this quiet until these details are worked out."

"What am I going to tell my friends?"

"Tell them that you're going on holiday. Tell them you're going to be cruising the Mediterranean for a couple of months. Since you're keeping your house there, they'll believe you."

"It is starting to sound very complicated."

"Mama, trust me you'll be in good hands. Someone from the bank will meet you in Antibes and get you all set up. There is nothing to worry about."

"I trust you, Tati."

"Mama, you're going to love it there. I heard the weather is great and it's just like the movies you always talk about."

"I love you."

"Love you too."

Tatiana's next call was to Lily, who was thrilled to talk to her.

"Tatiana, we've been so worried about you. We tried calling you on your cell phone, but the number is no longer in service."

"I'm sorry Lily, stupid me, I lost it and haven't replaced it yet."

"That's what Trevor said, trying to calm me down. Another reason I was trying to reach you is the check you sent. You didn't have to do that. I'm giving the money back next time I see you."

"Lily don't be silly. It's the least I can do, besides the bank is working me so hard I don't have time to spend it anyways."

"Everything is going well?"

"Yes, besides working 12-to-14-hour days."

"I'm reading in the paper about some of the crazy things going on there. People being blown up and shot. Are you safe?"

"Yes, of course. They're only going after the rich ones, I'm not there yet. How is Anna?"

"Anna is good, but you really need to call her. She wasn't pleased with you leaving without a proper goodbye."

"I will definitely call her in the next day or two. Please tell her that if you talk to her."

The ladies said their goodbyes with a hug going out to Oliver. After hanging up the phone Tatiana was left deep in thought again but was soon asleep. Her last thought was Matthew. What was she going to do.

Voshkolup's luxury apartment was strategically located. That became apparent when plans to use a sniper to take him out were being discussed. It wasn't a very tall building, only three stories high but it was on top of a hill. A bird's eye view wasn't available into it. Berezovsky came up with a solution, use an electric utility bucket truck, and put the sniper in the bucket.

At 6:10 a.m. the security team divided into two groups of fifteen, dressed as utility workers, and closed down Shvedskiy Tupik with wooden barricades. Two men directly across the street from the apartment armed with AKs, walkie-talkies, and high-powered binoculars gave the men a count and location of Voshkolup's beefed-up security. It had doubled from previous counts, it stood at 20 now. There were several men on the street, several at the door, several patrolling the grounds, and the rest in the apartment itself.

At 6:16 the order came from the lookouts, "it's time to move." Two armored vehicles disguised as utility trucks edged up from either end of the road each containing six guys. A couple of guys with wheelbarrows filled with guns, ammo, and grenades walked behind the trucks, and several guys followed them. At 6:17 the order to fire was given. Men from the armored vehicles emerged from the windows and the back of the trucks firing AK-47s. The men they were firing on hadn't been caught sleeping, the sight of the trucks had them on heightened alert and they immediately returned fire. A rain of gunfire was also coming from the apartment and had taken out a couple of members of the security team. Grenades were lobbed at the front of the building and two men by the street were blown to bits, all the men in the apartment building entrance were a bloodied mangled mess.

"I got one in the apartment," said a lookout that was coordinating the troops.

"I got two," the other lookout announced as they hit the ground one after the other.

But the bullets from the building continued to pelt down on the trucks below.

"On three," called out a man by one of the wheelbarrows, and grenades were launched up onto the balcony of the apartment. Two men came crashing down, a huge gaping hole was left where they had been firing from.

"Bring in the truck," was heard over the walkie-talkies. The driver of the bucket truck inched up the street firing a pistol while he drove. A man on the deck of the truck also fired away as he steadied the slowly extending bucket with a rope. A couple of bullets ricochet off the side of the armored bucket before it was fully extended.

"Now!" The order over the walkie-talkies was heard and a man rose from the bucket brandishing an RPG. The next thing heard was a giant whoosh followed by shards of glass and chunks of concrete showering down on the few survivors left below.

"Move out!" The bucket truck continued to roll forward still taking and returning fire until it dropped out of sight. The armored vehicles passed each other also being peppered with bullets until no longer seen. The men occupying the vehicles all quickly exited and jumped into the backs of waiting trucks with smoke still coming out of the barrels of their weapons. One man had been left on the battlefield, one was dead on the floor of a truck, and several were wounded. A doctor was waiting a kilometer down the road for the wounded.

Litskevich was leaving his favorite breakfast spot with Nataliya. They were walking down the street about to detour through the park on their way home when his cell phone rang.

"Litskevich, it's Kovalyov, I need you to meet me at Shvedskiy Tupik. We have a real fucking mess here."

"That's Voshkolup's street, isn't it?"

"Yes, there's been a massive attack on his apartment, there are bodies everywhere and parts of the building are missing. Voshkolup has been taken to the hospital, the piece of shit is in bad shape."

"Shit, I'll be right there."

Nataliya looked at Alexander and simply said, "go." She knew the drill and could tell there was nothing that was going to get their day together back. Litskevich ran down the street turning back to his wife mouthing the word sorry.

Sunday, December 1, 1996

Should I stay or should I go now
If I go there will trouble
If I stay it will be double

The Clash had followed Tatiana to Australia. They were playing in the background, and she was wondering if it truly was a sign. She

264

deliberately skipped breakfast at the hotel restaurant opting for a coffee shop a few blocks away. Joe Strummer was imparting his wisdom. It gave her some space and time to think. She knew if she ran into Matthew, she would run off with him for the day and probably most of the evening. This wouldn't help her make a logical decision about what to do next.

Back in her hotel room Tatiana took a piece of the cream-colored hotel stationary, wrote a short letter to Matthew, packed her bags, and checked out leaving the letter at the front desk for him. The valet brought the camper van to the front doors, and she slipped away undetected. A sappy love song came on the radio as she drove north along the beach road to M1, "turn that off," she said out loud.

"Get out of the way," Litskevich said with his credentials drawn as he shoved past a guy the size of a moose. He stood over Voshkolup, tubes ran from poles into his arms and nose, he was on a respirator and a monitor kept track of his heartbeat, blood pressure, and oxygen level. Bandages wrapped his head and various body parts; he was burned badly and had shrapnel removed from all over him.

"What are you doing in here?" the trauma doctor asked from the doorway.

"Lt. Litskevich, FSB," he said raising his credentials again.

"You're not going to get any response from him."

"I can see that. When do you think I will be able to?"

"The doctor approached Litskevich and said in a low voice, probably never. As you can see, he's in really bad shape. We have another surgery scheduled for this afternoon. Between the metal in his body and the burns, we don't have much hope of saving him."

"I wouldn't put too much effort into saving this piece of garbage but if you do, please call me."

Dmitri, Pavel, and Ivan entered the conference room to see Katerina sitting at the head of the table. In front of her were the 300 Krugerrands that had occupied that spot six weeks earlier.

"Guys, a lot has happened over the past two months; it's been brutal. I can't tell you how much I appreciate your devotion. You guys have put your lives on the line and never once bitched or questioned a thing. She stood up circling the table with three large thick envelopes in her hand giving one to each of them. There's three years' salary there and I still don't think it's enough, but if you stick around there'll be more, I promise. I understand the dangers we all face and will understand if any of you decide to call it a day. I've gotten word that Voshkolup is still alive, just barely. I'm not going to rest until he's eliminated from the face of the earth."

"I'm with you," Dmitri said.

"Me too," Pavel and Ivan each said.

"I understand all the guys wounded will be all right?"

"Yes, the two that were lost were Berezovsky's guys," Dmitri added.

"I've talked to Konstantin. He's naturally upset but understands, he's still all in. I will be meeting with him tomorrow; Dmitri I would like you there."

Dmitri returned to the hotel where he was staying with Mikheil and Olena. They had caught wind of the operation from news coverage they'd seen on TV. Olena ran over and bear-hugged Dmitri, her arms not quite long enough to make it around the big man.

"I'm so glad you're safe."

"From what?" Dmitri shrugged.

"Nothing. I'm just glad," she said stopping herself from saying more.

Mikheil then hugged Dmitri. "I'm so happy to see you in one piece. Are Pavel and Ivan okay?"

"Yes, of course."

"Let's go for a drink," Dmitri announced.

"You're not going without me," Olena said grabbing her coat. Jacques was the only one left out.

"Let them in," Berezovsky called out to Viktor. He was in the middle of an important business meeting but knew it would be pointless to deny the FSB agents waiting in the lobby entry.

"Konstantin Berezovsky, you need to come with us."

"Where are you taking me?"

"FSB headquarters, we have some questions for you."

"Pertaining to what?"

"We'll explain later. You must come with us now."

"Viktor, call the lawyers," Konstantin called out as he was led out of the lobby toward the elevators.

Two of Konstantin's lawyers were waiting at FSB headquarters, though they arrived 20 minutes after he did.

Berezovsky was in an interrogation room, but it wasn't much of an interrogation.

"One of your employees was killed at the scene where there was an attempt on Boris Voshkolup's life."

"And?"

"We are charging you with attempted murder."

"My lawyers will handle everything from here."

"You don't wish to make a statement?"

"No."

Berezovsky didn't get a chance to confer with his attorneys and was soon passing by them handcuffed. "Make the call," he said.

Litskevich learned from Mikheyev and Turov that Berezovsky had been arrested. It made sense to him; he knew Abramov's people were likely involved too and with good reason. The firepower and organized nature of the attack pointed to a well-funded team with a sound motive. He was tempted to have another meeting with Katerina but figured it would be a waste of time. He already wasted the good part of a week looking for Jablokov.

"Guys, I feel like I've been running in circles for the past couple of months. The Abramov murder keeps getting more complicated every day. Abramov's driver, a key guy to him was kidnapped and murdered. This has led me to Miroslav Jablokov who is nowhere to be found. Dryga's connection to him led to his demise. Abramov's head of security was gunned down in his apartment. Voshkolup's compound was burned to the ground and the second attack, it looks like, has accomplished its mission with dozens dead and Voshkolup hanging on by a thread."

"It's clear Voshkolup is behind it all and the people he is targeting are fighting back. He sees the opportunity to create mayhem, seize control of these businesses and use them to legitimize his crooked fortune. We were called in to investigate the attempt on Berezovsky and all along it's pointed to Voshkolup but we can't prove it," Mikheyev said.

"I've been hoping that that piece of shit, Voshkolup, just dies but you know he's got guys that will take over where he leaves off," Litskevich added. "It's added reason for me to locate Jablokov."

"Who would be next in line to move up if it turns out Jablokov was one of the crispy critters we recovered from Shvedskiy Tupik," Mikheyev asked.

"Probably Anatoli Kazinski or Mohammed Raffael."

"It won't be Kazinski. We pulled him out of the back of a car the other night with a bunch of holes in him," Turov said updating Litskevich.

"My hope was to possibly turn Jablokov but Raffael would work."

"Good luck there," Mikheyev said. "Have you seen his file? He's a heartless son of a bitch who is all about money. Yugoslavia, Tajikistan, and most recently Chechnya are all on his resume along with scars left from a few bullets. You'd be better off with Jablokov; he's a boy scout in comparison."

"Something else that has come to mind with Dryga was his Topki trips. He was initially assigned there to keep him out of the way while he was being investigated but he returned to Moscow at his own expense and met with Voshkolup. I suspect he learned something of interest prompting the return. According to his report, nothing new was discovered but I'd like you guys to head out for a couple of days and see if you can find anything. I'll talk to Kovalyov today about that."

"We're swamped but if this is a missing link to a lot of the shit that's been going on it would be worth it."

"I'll get on Jablokov and Raffael. Let's meet up in a few days and see what we have."

Mo understood from discussions he'd had with Jablokov the importance of finding Belov and with all the shit hitting the fan there was no better time. He always had a knack for hunting down prey. With the resources now available it had just gotten easier. Jablokov had showed off the Rolex from Zurich and spoke about a last-minute trip to London that was called off. If she was still in London Jablokov would have traveled there. He picked up the phone and said, "meet me at the yacht."

Tuesday, December 3, 1996

Tatiana's drive from the Gold Coast had been anything but uneventful. After a few hours on the road, she had an extremely close call with a kangaroo. Cruising along in the camper van and singing along to a Goo Goo Dolls CD she spotted a roo on the side of the road; it completely surprised her springing out in front of the van causing her to lock on the brakes. The massive animal about 60-70 kilos, collided with the front bumper as she skidded to a stop knocking it on its side. It scrambled up and managed to make it to the other side of the road but only barely. A car coming from the other direction almost made it a hood ornament. She couldn't shake the look in the animal's eyes at the point of contact. It left her on edge for the rest of the drive to Airlie Beach.

Airlie Beach was postcard gorgeous with turquoise waters framed by palm trees. The tropical breeze off the water that fluttered into the beach bar made the after-drive drink even better. Tatiana's destination on this leg of the trip was Cairns, she had covered about two-thirds of it and was hoping for a wildlife-free experience for the remaining 600 kilometers the next day.

As she finished her second fruity cocktail, a house specialty called the Quench My Desire, she thought about Matthew. Tatiana hoped he wouldn't be upset by her brisk departure and as she did during the drive there debated whether she would look him up when in Cairns.

The bartender was extremely friendly, almost uncomfortably so; recommended a very nice casual burger joint. It was a welcomed break from all the seafood she had gorged on. After a buzz from the last drink and a full stomach, she made it back to the van, kicked off her shoes, crawled into the sleeping bag, and slept until early morning. She was woken up by a boat firing up its engine several hundred meters away. She slid into her bikini, grabbed a towel, and went for a dip. What a way to start the day she thought.

Natasha Magnitsky's day started with a trip to Butyrka. She received her husband's letter and was demanding to see him. At first, her request was very calm but grew increasingly agitated with each denial. She explained to the stone-faced guard that was in charge of visitation that her husband was very ill. She just wanted to make sure he was all right. The denial came over and over even as tears streamed down her face; it was no use.

After leaving the prison she paid a visit to Fyodor Chaika expressing her frustration to him. He was very understanding and empathetic but patiently explained, between puffs on a cigarette, there was nothing he could do regarding visitation. He was able to pass on a bit of encouraging news. Mr. Firestone and Mr. Browder had given an interview with The Times in London, and the article had been picked up worldwide. He explained that international pressure could possibly expedite the matter but also cautioned that the Kremlin might choose to dig its heels in instead. Natasha returned home only to cry more into her mother's arms.

Berezovsky left FSB headquarters after an overnight stay flanked by his lawyers. His hair was ruffled, and his tie was crooked as he hurriedly tried to pull himself together anticipating newspaper photographers that gathered outside. There weren't many waiting as his release was unexpected; most detainees that entered rarely exited but Konstantin was connected. A call was made to Yeltsin which led to several more calls before Kovalyov received word no charges would be filed. It had been explained to him that an employer isn't responsible for an employee's actions outside of work. It made perfect sense, but he knew Konstantin was at least partially responsible for the attack on Voshkolup. Kovalyov was at peace with the release secretly hoping the attack would accomplish the mission it had set out to do.

Berezovsky climbed into the back of a black Mercedes and sped off with a Range Rover containing four burly men following very closely behind. He called Katerina and got an update on Voshkolup's condition. It wasn't good news; he was still alive.

Voshkolup was still alive, but that hadn't been the case for two and a half minutes the day before. On Sunday a second surgery was performed to remove shards of metal that were dangerously located near his spinal cord. There were signs of improvement, the possibility he had turned the corner. But on Monday he went into cardiac arrest, and his heart stopped beating. His bodyguard was ordered from the room and the trauma team jumped into action with a defibrillator shocking him back to life. The whole time this was going on Voshkolup never became conscious.

"Armen, it's good to see you," Mo said giving his friend a warm hug as he boarded the Blue Whale.

"It's good to see you're well. Word has it you're running the show and standing where we are it looks like it."

"There's a lot going on right now as you can imagine but I really have no interest in "running the show." I've spent most of my life looking over my shoulder; it's time to move into less risky endeavors. What can I get you to drink?" Mo said motioning to the fully stocked bar behind him.

"A Moscow mule," Armen said with a smile.

"You'll have to get it yourself then. My bartending skills are limited to beer or vodka shots."

The bar had everything Armen was looking for as well as a Louis XIII cognac. "Did you see this?" Armen said pointing to it.

"What is it?"

"It's cognac, 30,000 rubles a bottle," he poured each of them a healthy shot into a crystal snifter. Mo took a big sip and spit it out on the Persian carpet.

"What are you doing? You just spat 1,000 rubles on the floor."

"You can keep that shit," Mo said grimacing and wiping his mouth. "I'll stick with my Stoli."

"What's up, why did you pull me down to this dinghy?"

"I need your help finding someone."

"You know that's my specialty. If I can't find them, they likely don't exist. Who?"

"Tatiana Belov. Jablokov was looking for her, he told me the big man was putting a lot of pressure on him to find her. He had tracked her to Zurich and then London, but she's disappeared again."

"Poor Miroslav? What the fuck happened there?"

"Honestly, don't know, don't care."

"What makes her so important?" asked Armen.

"You know about Abramov, right?"

"Yes, Boris had him taken out a couple of months ago."

"Yes. This Belov woman was childhood friends with his right-hand man. Jablokov got too rough with him and killed him. It was believed he had all the details about secret accounts and a bunch of other shit."

"You know if the big man's looking for her there must be something big there."

"Exactly. After what went down in Chechnya, you're one of the few people I can trust. I need you to keep whatever we discuss to yourself."

"If you can't trust the person who had your back in firefights who can you," Armen said taking a long swig of the Louis XIII.

A day laying on the beach, reading, and taking an hour-long nap was just what Tatiana needed. Returning from the beach around dinner time she caught a glimpse of herself in one of the camper's mirrors, she was golden brown, sporting a tan like she had never seen before. Her hair was blonder from the effects of the sun, giving the appearance of the surfer chicks she had envied. I could really get used to this she thought.

Her stomach reminded her it needed some food, and she remembered seeing a market about a kilometer up the road. There she picked up a premade salad, chicken drumsticks, and potato chips. It was a tasty barbeque dinner.

As she ate her thoughts went to Matthew, everything was perfect, but she was lonely. Tatiana missed their chats, his humor, and the way he took charge of a day and introduced her to new experiences. He was very comfortable to be around, and he was a good kisser.

Tatiana had one last glass of wine while reading a local paper and decided to hit the sack. She had been asleep for a couple of hours when her cell phone rang. It was Malcolm.

"Hello, Malcolm," she said sounding a little groggy.

"It sounds like I woke you."

"It's okay. How are you? Is everything all right?"

"I'm well and everything is fine. I just wanted to give you an update. Through a colleague I've found a Russian gentleman to pose as the tailor shop owner for the shop you're purchasing for your mother, his name is Gennady Mitov. He'll be perfect as he used to be a tailor; he's retired now. How is your mother doing?"

"Malcolm that is perfect. You think of everything. Mama is great, she is very excited about the move but a little worried too. She's always lived in the same town and she's going to miss her friends."

"That's understandable. I'll do whatever I can to make it an easy transition for her."

"Thank you, Malcolm. I'll pass all the information on to her; we'll firm up plans within the next day or so." Tatiana crawled back into her sleeping bag but didn't sleep, her mind would not turn off until the sun started to come up.

Wednesday, December 4, 1996

Litskevich's search for Jablokov went nowhere. He was starting to think that maybe he vanished off the planet; with his line of work that was very likely. Let's focus on Mohammed Raffael he thought and pulled his file complete with mugshots. Mikheyev was right, this guy was bad news, it won't be hard picking him out of a crowd with the head and neck tattoos. It was clear from the lengthy file that this guy was fearless. Most people when shot tend to avoid encounters with bullets, this guy went looking for more. The pay for mercenaries must be extremely good. When Mo wasn't involved in international skirmishes, he was in the bone-breaking business doing several years for assault and extortion.

Now that Voshkolup was incapacitated and Jablokov was MIA, it was likely Mo was going to take a more high-profile position. With the compound burned to the ground and the Shvedskiy Tupik residence missing a roof where would this gang of psychos meet?

"Major, did Turov and Mikheyev go to Topki?"

"Yes, they left yesterday."

"Good. I've been trying to locate Jablokov without any luck, so I've turned my attention to Raffael. If I can find him there's a good chance Jablokov will turn up too. Can we spare a couple of guys?"

"That's tough with all the shit going down. What for?"

"Voshkolup has a country house and a huge yacht. I'd like to get some surveillance on them."

"I can spare one guy; you'll have to be the other one."

"Okay, I can live with that."

Where are you going?

"I'll take the yacht. It was last seen in Sochi. If I get eyes on Jablokov I will arrest him for Lev Drozdov's murder. We have the fingerprints from Voshkolup's warehouse where the murder took place and with Voshkolup in his current condition there'll be no interference."

"Get me the country house details. You have a couple of days then I need you back here."

Tatiana's road trip continued a little later than planned due to her sleepless night. By the time she ate and packed up, it was almost 11:00; she'd arrive in Cairns for a late dinner. It was straightforward driving taking A1 north and encountering some of the most beautiful white sand beaches along the way. As usual Tatiana's thoughts were all over the place. She was worried about her mama, she thought about Mikheil and Olena, Lily and her family and Anna, don't forget to call Anna. But the overriding thought was Matthew. As hard as she tried, she couldn't shake him from her mind.

Nicholas was still getting used to his new space and living alone for the first time; well not really alone. There were at least a dozen security team members within shouting distance from him at all times. Security had been recently stepped up, but he wondered if it was always going to be like this. At first it made him feel important, but it quickly became more of a nuisance.

His father's house gave many clues about the man he never met. There was a closet still filled with racks of nicely tailored suits, clothes, and shoes. He tried a few of the suits on and they were a perfect fit; he would have Katerina leave him his favorites. The rest would get picked over by the security team and staff members. This stuff was too good for charity bins.

There were also framed photos of Arkadiy with famous people from all over the world, many of them he'd seen on the evening news or in newspapers. It left him wondering if he was ready for all of this.

Each day presented a challenge learning about all the businesses he legally controlled, but there were also the challenges that came from the changes in his daily routine. Gone were the days of walking out the front door and meeting friends at the local café or bar.

And then there was his mom, he hadn't seen her in a week, and he missed their chats. They talked on the phone, but it wasn't the same. He would talk to Katerina and see about a get-together with her and his friends soon.

Sergei Magnitsky was having zero luck seeing his wife, he didn't even know if she received the note he tried to get to her from the nurse in the infirmary. In the note, he told her he was well but knew Natasha would question that with the note coming from a nurse. He hadn't thought about that at the time.

The past several days passed a little more quickly, he managed to trade some cigarettes for another Hemingway book, The Sun Also Rises. Part of the torture of prison for him was boredom. He had a very challenging job that kept his mind in constant motion; to think that was replaced by a single book fell quite short. While sitting there with the dog-eared book on his lap the cell door opened. It wasn't mealtime, what the fuck was up, he thought. "Magnitsky, come with me." He followed the guard with another guard trailing behind. A door at the end of the long corridor was opened by the lead guard revealing a table and two chairs, a squatty man in glasses and a black suit occupied one of the chairs.

"Have a seat," he ordered.

On the table were two white pieces of paper and a pen.

"Sign it," he said.

"What is this?" Sergei asked.

"You can read it first if you like then sign it."

It was a confession to the theft of 5.4 billion rubles of tax money.

"I'm not signing this," Sergei said with his adrenaline starting to surge.

"You will sign it."

"No, take me back to my cell," he said standing up.

One of the guards stepped forward and drove his fist into Sergei's diaphragm muscle sending him to the floor but not before catching his head on the edge of the table on his way down. He lay there clutching his stomach, gasping for air with blood streaming from his forehead onto the floor.

"Get up and sign it."

Sergei tried to speak no but nothing came.

The guard stepped forward again launching his foot into his stomach. Sergei's mouth now was filled with vomit. He spit it out and gasped for more air.

"Sign it!" The pages floated down beside his head with the pen dropping in front of his eyes. It was the last thing he saw before losing consciousness.

I'm going to like it here, Tatiana thought as she walked along the esplanade that ran parallel to the water. Cairns had a sleepy feel to it but with enough going on it wouldn't get boring. She took a seat at a sidewalk restaurant and ordered a healthy seafood salad that paired very well with her wine. While eating she found herself looking at tall blonde men walking by. She knew Matthew would be back from his business trip and just maybe he'd be out and about tonight. While sitting there and enjoying her second glass of wine she noticed that Cairns did have a lot of good-looking men. Guys that were fit and rugged, they must be here for the diving she pondered. The weather had gotten warmer the further north that she drove and tonight would be perfect for that third glass of wine, but she would get some sleep instead, all the driving left her in need of rest.

Tatiana walked north on the esplanade after she found a campground just south of the airport; it was only a couple of kilometers away. According to her time zone calculations, Anna would be getting home from work in an hour. I'll get a campfire started and have that glass of wine in the meantime.

"Tatiana, I'm not happy with you."

"Anna, I'm sorry to leave the way I did. Everything happened so fast."

"It took you long enough to call."

"I know, again I'm so sorry. Work really has been nuts; I barely have time to eat."

"That's what Lily was telling me. I miss having my drinking buddy around."

"I miss you too. Are you staying out of trouble?"

"No, I met this guy, Mick and we've been seeing a lot of each other. How's your love life?"

"Complicated, I've met someone too but I'm so busy."

"That's why I haven't heard from you, it's not work. What's his name?"

"Matthew. He's perfect but the timing isn't right."

"When is it ever? You need to prioritize, work isn't everything. One day you'll be old and realize that."

"You're right. Have you gotten out with Lily?"

"We have plans for lunch with the girls on the weekend. I wish you were coming."

"Me too. I have to run but I promise not to wait so long to call."

The girl talk ended, and the fire was just glowing ambers now, Tatiana closed the camper van door. She dreamed about being back in London. It was a good dream being surrounded by friends, everyone drinking and laughing.

Thursday, December 5, 1996

Litskevich landed in Sochi and was making his way to the Aeroflot ticket counter; his return ticket needed to be corrected it had a Saturday night return, not the Friday he needed. It was especially important as it was Nataliya's birthday on Saturday. Standing next in line for the ticket agent he noticed the man being served had tattoos on his head. It can't be he thought. The man turned leaving the counter, it was, complete with the confirming neck tattoo, Mohammed Raffael.

"I need to change this ticket," Litskevich said putting his return ticket on the counter. I need to be put on the flight that the man you just served is on.

"He's your friend?"

"Yes."

"Do you want first class also?"

"Yes, please."

"Let me see if I have something available. You know there will be an additional charge."

Litskevich handed her a credit card.

"You are in luck; I have a seat available."

While waiting for the flight to depart he called Kovalyov and gave him the news. Arrangements were made for surveillance from the airport. So much for his Sochi holiday.

Katerina and Konstantin met at his office to discuss their next step. They were both pleased at the damage and the lull the attacks had caused, at least for now. It wasn't time to rest they both agreed. Voshkolup needed to be finished off. The report they had managed to obtain still had him on death's doorstep but that wasn't enough. "This evil prick needs to die," said Konstantin.

"We need to get someone in the hospital to pose as a doctor or nurse," Katerina said.

"You know security is very tight."

"Yes, we've already checked it out. There are layers of it."

"I can imagine but when will we get a chance like this again."

"I agree," Katerina said nodding.

Viktor was called in and over the next hour, the plan was completed. If everything went well Boris would be out of the ICU very soon, but not going home.

Tatiana's mother heard a knock at the door and put the dish towel down wondering who it was. A courier was there handing her a thick cardboard envelope. She opened it revealing a purchase agreement for the tailor shop owned by Gennady Mitov to BCJ Enterprises. She read the eight-page document over but didn't see her name on it, then she remembered the tax issue Tatiana told her about. Her jaw dropped when she saw the 635,000 franc purchase price. That sounds like a lot of money she mumbled to herself. It was all starting to become real.

"I'm here to see my client."

"What is the name again?"

"Sergei Magnitsky."

"I don't have him listed," the visitation guard mumbled.

"Has he been transferred?" asked Fyodor.

"I don't have him on the prisoner list."

"Either he's been transferred or released. I'm his attorney, I demand to know where he is."

"Let me get my supervisor."

"Mr. Magnitsky is unavailable," the supervisor stated.

"What do you mean he is unavailable?"

"He is ill. He's not permitted any visitors."

"But I'm his lawyer."

"I'm sorry. You'll have to come back."

"When?"

The conversation ended there. Surprisingly, this wasn't the first time Fyodor experienced something like this at Butyrka. When it had happened in the past it wasn't a good sign. He knew he needed to pull out all the stops to help his client.

Fyodor's hunch was right, Sergei wasn't in good shape. He was unable to hold down any food, the pain in his abdomen was unbearable and it wasn't improving. Sergei just lay in bed doubled over clutching his stomach. He never in his life experienced pain like this before. Despite numerous pleas to see the doctor, he was told to quit the act. The blood in his stool wasn't considered proof enough that he wasn't acting.

"Dmitri, we need to talk. I can't do this any longer." Mikheil had all he could take of living at the Ritz. The boredom and isolation were too much, his only companions were Olena, Jacques, and some of the security team members that rotated through. He wasn't alone in these feelings, as Olena was also getting more vocal about her frustration with the situation. Something had to be done soon or they would just pack up and leave, taking their chances with the bratva. They had been made very aware of the risks involved with the attack on their car going to Vlad's funeral, but they'd had enough hiding for months, their lives were on hold.

"Let me talk to Katerina," Dmitri said. "Things are a little quiet right now with Voshkolup incapacitated but I'm not sure that will last."

"You have to come up with some kind of plan or we're both leaving. We've had enough."

Tatiana's day was spent exploring the Great Barrier Reef from the Ocean Quest. Snorkeling in calm crystal clear Coral Sea waters she saw green sea turtles, grouper, dozens of neon-colored fish species as well as coral formations that didn't seem real. She would never look at the ocean the same way again now knowing what lived below. She discussed with the dive leader, John, who was from Northampton, England about getting certified for scuba diving. She made up her mind there and then signing up for classes when they were back at the dive shop. At the dive shop, Tatiana took advantage of the outdoor shower before making her way back home to her van.

After all the sun, fresh air, and exercise Tatiana was starving, and the esplanade's seafood restaurants were calling. Sitting outside at a place called Splash as the sun was going down was spectacular, the air temperature perfect, and the smells of the seafood cooking made her hungrier. A whole freshly caught lobster appeared before her; it was now her favorite meal after devouring it.

Her thoughts went back to the Gold Coast and the wonderful meal she'd had with Matthew at the French restaurant. The debate about whether to call him was still going on in her mind. A snifter of Grand Marnier arrived after the remains of the lobster were taken away. She had just put her glass down and there he was, Matthew was walking along the esplanade with a tall thin brunette; her heart sank deep into her stomach. She looked away and then back again, he hadn't seen her. A lump formed in her throat; she used her napkin to dab away the tear that formed. A number of thoughts went through her mind. Maybe they were just friends, maybe a work associate, but her gut told her that wasn't the case by the way they were talking and their body language. Decision made she thought. The great day had just become an okay one.

Friday, December 6, 1996

Litskevich was fine with handing surveillance of Raffael over to other Dept. K FSB agents as he exited the airport. He recognized them from the office, they had made eye contact but that was it. It had been a tiring day traveling to and from Sochi but before returning home he stopped to meet with Kovalyov.

"I would like to bring him in for questioning," Litskevich said with a desperate shrug.

"You know we don't have anything on him that would stick, just suspicions."

"It would put him on notice that we're watching him."

"I don't want to do that. You still haven't found Jablokov. He's going to be our best bet at finding him," Kovalyov patiently said.

"You're right."

"Now our mole, Dryga isn't helping them. Let's set up surveillance again."

"That makes sense. We'll have Raffael's location soon; we can get some bugs set up and keep tabs on him and we'll know if Jablokov turns up."

"Exactly."

Mikheil and Olena were in their rooms packing; Jacques was asleep on the couch in the living room oblivious to it all. Dmitri spoke with Katerina; plans were put in place to let them return to their homes. They would both still have around-the-clock security; a team member living with them. Stories were concocted about who the security team members were so not to draw unwanted attention to them by nosy neighbors. For Olena, it was a nephew staying with her and for Mikheil a roommate. It wasn't a perfect plan and Dmitri explained the risks that still existed but they both were fine with it.

Katerina wasn't fine with the new arrangements and told Dmitri so. If anything happened to them, she would feel responsible, and something very well could. These thugs they were at war with would stop at nothing for power, revenge was an added bonus. Mikheil and Olena said their goodbyes to each other and to Dmitri. Cars pulled up in front of the hotel, they were off. Dmitri checked out of the hotel and went home; it was something he was looking forward to as well.

Tatiana spent most of the day at the beach. She was feeling sad at what she witnessed at dinner the evening before and was trying to give Matthew the benefit of the doubt. She convinced herself at one point that the brunette was probably just a casual friend. She picked up the phone and was about to call him.

"No," she said out loud putting the phone down. If things get serious and you have to suddenly run off, you're just going to break his heart. Leave him alone. To keep herself busy Tatiana did something she'd put off for a while, cleaning out the van. It was long overdue, and an unpleasant odor was developing. Two hours later the van was spotless, it was time to eat. She hiked down to the market picking up some Italian sausages for the grill. The esplanade was out of the question.

Sergei spent the entire day in intense pain. He continued to beg the guard to see the doctor only to be told he was faking. Three trays of food sat on the floor untouched except for the nibbles taken by the cockroaches. Sweat was dripping from his head; his shirt was soaked through. "How can I fake this?" he said using all his energy. He reached under his bed and felt around for a pen he had hidden, found a scrap of paper, and slowly wrote: I love you Natasha, Nakita, and Stanislav. He folded the scrap in half and put it in his pocket. Looking at the cinder block wall his mind started to drift to birthdays and family dinners where everyone was smiling and enjoying being together. A jolt of pain shot through his stomach, and he let out a long quiet drawn-out groan.

"Shut up you faker," yelled a guard that entered his cell. Sergei was clubbed in the head and died.

Saturday, December 7, 1996

"Happy birthday, kitten."

"For me?"

"Of course."

"They're beautiful," Nataliya said picking a card from the long-stemmed red roses. *You are the love of my life, I couldn't imagine it without you. Happy Birthday XOXOXO*

"Thank you, baby. You are the sweetest."

At that moment the phone rang. "Don't answer it, don't."

"Kitten, I have to. Sorry."

Nataliya's bottom lip stuck out, she knew her special day would be spent alone. Every birthday her husband had been pulled away from her. She thought she would get used to it, but it hurt every time.

"We need you here in an hour."

"Can we make it two, it's Nataliya's birthday?"

"Sorry, no." The phone went dead.

"Kitten. I have a reservation at that new steak house at 7:00. I promise we'll have a nice dinner and go dancing after."

"Promise?"

"I'll be home by 6:00 even if I have to quit."

"You better."

Litskevich got off the elevator walking towards Kovalyov's office. Turov and Mikheyev were already there.

"Good morning, gents. How was Topki?"

"We have a major break in the case, one that was uncovered weeks ago by Dryga but never reported. Anatoli Kazinski and Mohammed Raffael flew into Kemerovo the night before the attack on Abramov. Their names were on a flight manifest on 9/29 and again on 9/30," Turov said.

"Unfucking believable," uttered Litskevich under his breath.

"It had been a well-planned attack. A terrorist threat was called in prompting the closure of Kemerovo Airport. They knew Abramov would divert, and they lay in waiting," added Mikheyev.

"So, we're taking Raffael in now," Litskevich eagerly asked.

"No, not yet," Kovalyov firmly responded. "We're sticking with the plan; we've started moving on it. We followed Raffael home from the airport and kept an eye on his place. He went out shortly after getting back, we had a couple of guys wire his place. Get the van and let's listen in. I'll leave it up to you guys to set up a schedule. Not only do I want Raffael but Jablokov too."

"This is great news. I'll start surveillance until 6:00, after that I'm a dead man," Litskevich volunteered.

"A dead man?" Kovalyov asked, having the full attention of the room.

"Yes, Nataliya will kill me. It's her birthday."

"My name is Natasha Magnitsky, I demand to see my husband Sergei Magnitsky now!" she said for the second time.

"Come with me," Natasha followed with a sense of accomplishment and anticipation. Finally, my persistence has paid off she thought sitting in a windowless office. A man in a prison guard uniform entered the room, he seemed more important than the rest having more stripes on his shoulder.

"Where is my husband?" Natasha demanded.

"Mrs. Magnitsky, your husband has died."

"No. What are you talking about? I want to see him now," she said with tears running down her face.

"I'm sorry, we believe he was having some stomach issues that were undiagnosed. He died last night."

"No. I don't believe you. He's only 37, he can't be dead. If he's dead, I want to see his body," she screamed.

"We'll have his body sent to the funeral home you choose, please fill out this form."

"No, I want to see him now." The man got up and left the room, Natasha was led away by the guard that brought her, bringing the form with her.

Natasha left Butyrka, walked a couple of kilometers in a daze, climbed into a taxi, and went home. She still didn't believe what she had been told. When home she called Jamie Firestone. He was shocked by the news but not completely surprised. He vowed to get to the bottom of this and offered his support in any way possible. Natasha lay down on her bed with her mother beside her. The fight for Sergei had not ended.

Nicholas made plans with Katerina to go home for the weekend and return on Tuesday. He would spend time with his mother and friends and pay a visit to his school to make arrangements to take a break, before returning for the second semester. The Gulfstream took off with Pavel and two other security team members joining him. Pavel overheard Nicholas's request and volunteered to go along. He enjoyed Barcelona and needed a break from the bleak Moscow weather. The second the jet left the ground Pavel's blood pressure dropped; a sense of relaxation enveloped him and the others on the plane. The stress level would increase again once they were back on the ground and back in protective mode.

The highlight of the homecoming trip for Nicholas was going to be the Sunday dinner his mama promised. A seafood paella feast was in store for him and the team.

"Mama, I'm so excited for you," Tatiana said responding to news that her plane ticket arrived; she'd be flying into Nice on Monday and was looking forward to her new life. Another courier had arrived that morning with the ticket and a voucher for a limo ride to Antibes.

"Who is paying for this limo? I can take a bus," Valentina exclaimed.

"Mama, you are a businesswoman now. You have to arrive in style."

"And who is paying for this?"

"Mama, relax and enjoy. The bank is going to make sure the business transition goes smoothly. When you get there take the first few weeks to relax and get to know your new home."

"Tati, this is like a dream."

"I'm happy for you. I had a very nice day myself. I had my…" Tatiana was going to say scuba lesson but stopped herself in time. Yes, they probably have scuba lessons in London but that would seem out of place. Tatiana continued "…step aerobics class today."

"Why do you need that? You are too skinny as it is."

"Thank you, mama." The conversation continued talking about clothes to bring to France, restaurants, and finished with her mother suggesting she join her in France after she settles in.

"Mama, I'd love to see Antibes. As soon as you're settled, I'll visit."

Tatiana missed her mother a lot and wondered when she would see her. Knowing she was safe and happy took a ton off her mind. Tatiana's stomach reminded her it was dinner time, so she took a walk to a new part of Cairns off the esplanade, by the lagoon. There she found a variety of restaurants, she settled for Thai food tonight. There were a lot of people out, fortunately, Matthew wasn't one of them.

Sunday, December 8, 1996

Tatiana's morning started in a classroom at a local secondary school with nine other students learning about Boyle's law. Like all the scuba students she was dying to put on the scuba gear and get in the pool. It was day two, there would be four more days to go. The instructor, a cute young blonde girl originally from Sydney named Elizabeth was fast-tracking them as everyone was picking it up fairly quickly. Four hours in the classroom and two hours in the pool, soon they'd be in the sea doing certification dives. Tatiana who was going by Olga was enjoying the social interaction and forgetting about all the shit that had been flooding her mind.

"Okay, guys. Let's take a fifteen-minute break, I'll see you at the pool with your suits on."

They all filed out and Tatiana found herself chatting with a young Ukrainian woman, Cindy, who now lived in Buffalo, New York. They were dive partners the day before but had little chance to get to know each other. Cindy recently broke up with her boyfriend of three years, jumped on a flight, and made a similar trek north as Tatiana had done. Also, like Tatiana, she had gone on a snorkel trip and decided to take the classes. Now at the pool, they continued chatting and giggling to the point Elizabeth had to interrupt them. Plans were made to meet up at a pub on the esplanade that evening.

Litskevich's afternoon of surveillance the day before yielded nothing. He sat alone in the van for six hours and Raffael had been home for only the last hour of his shift. When he was there it was just to grab a bite to eat and watch some TV. He was hoping Turov and Mikheyev came up with something, the idea they could be doing this for weeks bothered him. It was getting quite cold out and they couldn't sit there with the van running all the time. When he got home Nataliya was in a beautiful black dress and was putting on her makeup for their night out.

"Hurry, jump in the shower. I don't want us to lose our reservation."

He followed orders, they were soon out the door. The dinner that followed had them both stuffed and the wine and cognac a little tipsy. They walked to a bar just down the street from the steak house and a couple more drinks followed between dances, but Nataliya had other activities in mind.

"Let's get out of here," she said while grabbing his crotch.

"Check," Alexander yelled.

Litskevich soon found himself back at the van, he was relieving Turov who had an uneventful night.

"I didn't get anything but there was some phone activity while Mikheyev was on." Turov departed, and he climbed into the back of the van. It was 6:30 in the morning and as expected Raffael was sleeping.

He used this opportunity to review the recordings from the night before and there it was.

"Where the fuck have you been?"

"What do you mean? I just got back from Sochi. You know that."

"I left you a message to call me."

"And I'm calling you. What's up?"

"I know where that Belov went. She's in Sydney. She flew there from London three weeks ago."

"Are you fuckin' kidding me? Sydney, Australia. You're sure."

"Yes, it cost me a lot of money to find that out. You owe me big time."

"Armen, you're the best. Are you sure she's still there?"

"Not positive but I'm going tomorrow to track her, I'm bringing Sasha with me. I have a couple of other guys working on this too. They're tracking down friends and family of hers. I need some funds."

"Stop by before you leave, I'll take care of you."

Litskevich was pumping his fist in the air. They were doing his job for him, and he was in awe of them though he would never admit it. They were always one step ahead of him. He realized he needed to up his game and take the lead. Litskevich sat there wondering who this Armen was. He looked around the van and found the camera with the telephoto lens. We'll find out really soon he thought.

Nicholas woke up with a massive hangover. His head was throbbing, he felt like he was going to throw up. The afternoon started out harmless enough with a nice lunch with his mother at a local café, next came a late dinner with his friends, followed by the casino. His friends were oblivious to Pavel and his partner following their taxi and shadowing their moves. They also didn't realize that Nicholas was footing the bill for everything until they were at the blackjack table and had set them up with 15,000 pesetas each.

"What's going on, did you win the lottery? You get back from a vacation in Moscow, you paid for dinner, and now this?" Juan asked.

Nicholas brushed it off with, "we'll talk about it later, let's play cards."

It wasn't long until they had blown their money at the casino and moved on to a club nearby at the beach. There was a line outside with a couple of dozen people in front of them. Nicholas walked up to the doorman, slipped him a tip, and waved his friends in. Pavel decided it would be too obvious and they waited outside.

Having to yell over the very loud music Jorge asked, "come on man, what's up?"

Nicholas realized that he was going to have to tell his friends something. "I have come into a bit of money. It's too loud in here to talk. I'll tell you more later, let's get some drinks and talk to those ladies over there at the bar." As they left the third bar Nicholas told the guys about his Russian father, that he had been killed, and left him some money. It opened up the floodgate with lots of questions.

"Guys, I'm not going to get into all of it now. Let's just say that I've been taken care of. I won't have to worry about money anymore. Let's keep this to ourselves."

"That's fucked up," Juan who was a little drunk said.

"It's his business," said Miguel coming to his defense.

"How much money?" Juan pressed.

"It's not our business, leave it alone," Jorge chimed in.

"Come on," Juan persisted.

"Leave it alone," Miguel said raising his voice a little.

"Guys, give it time. I'll tell you more in time." Nicholas realized that he would have to tell the guys more. His life had changed and if he wanted to see his friends, they would need to know the truth. The night ended at an all-night tapas café. Pavel was exhausted and happy to call it a night.

12

Pop, pop, pop! "We need security up here at the ICU now!" said a nurse into the phone crouched under the counter.

"Take cover!" a doctor was yelling.

"He's got a gun. He's in the stairwell," someone called out.

The two gorillas guarding Voshkolup ran toward the stairs with one of them pushing the door open and slamming it against the wall with a loud thud. They saw a man dressed in black descending the stairs with a gun in his hand. The lead gorilla fired a shot missing his target. "Get back to the room," he yelled to his cohort.

It was too late. By the time the second gorilla made it back, a nurse was doing chest compressions and calling for the paddles.

"What's going on?" the gorilla called out.

"He's flatlined, get out," was the response, he was shoved out of the way by a doctor entering the room.

"Clear." The paddles administered by the doctor shocked the big man's chest. He didn't budge.

"Hit him again," an older doctor entering the room called out.

"Nothing."

"Again!"

After three more attempts still nothing. "Call it. He's gone," was announced as the other gorilla entered the room still catching his breath.

"Fuck! They got him."

"The motherfucker got away!"

A security guard standing behind the gorillas said into his walkie-talkie, "lock down the hospital," but by then it was too late. Katerina's and Konstantin's team was out; phone calls to Dmitri and Viktor were made informing them that their mission was successful. The shot of fentanyl into the IV line worked. The big man was no more.

Natasha Magnitsky was surrounded by security, two layers of it. She was at the funeral home making arrangements for Sergei's burial. Orders were given by Bill Browder that no one was to get near Natasha or the children. All their possessions were packed on a private jet waiting for them, it would leave for London on Wednesday, moments after the funeral. Natasha begged her mother to come with them, but she refused. She stubbornly said that she wasn't going to be chased from her home by terrorists. Natasha respected her mother's viewpoint but had her children to think of. The idea of a fresh start in a new country was very appealing if only her Sergei was joining them.

Word made it back to Raffael that Voshkolup had been killed. He ordered the killers to be found, and he would personally deal with them. In reality, he didn't give a shit, the orders were for show. His concern was finding the woman that knew where Abramov's money was hidden. Armen and Sasha were on their way to Sydney and hopefully, the Belov woman would be located soon. In the meantime, he needed to assign someone to take care of funeral plans for Boris. He wasn't aware of any family so it would likely be up to him. It was at this moment he wished Jablokov was alive. He was the person closest to the big man that he knew of.

Tatiana and Cindy finished their lesson and the session in the pool.

"Olga, up for a glass of vino?" she said with a smile.

"Thanks, but no thanks, Cindy. I have a few errands to run but tomorrow maybe?"

"Sounds like a plan. See you tomorrow."

Actually, Tatiana wanted to hit the beach and call her mother before she left for France; she caught her just in time.

"Mama, are you all packed?"

"Almost, just a few more things to go. I'm a little nervous, I've never been on an airplane before, you know."

"Mama, you'll be fine."

"Tati, the car the bank is sending will be here soon I need to finish packing."

"Mama, I don't want you to be late call me tonight. Love you."

"I love you, Tati."

Tatiana was relieved that her plan was going off without a hitch. She would call Malcolm in a couple of hours to check in and make sure there'd be no surprises.

It was time for dinner and Tatiana considered calling Cindy to join her but if they drank like they did the night before it would be a long one. She wasn't up for that. Tatiana also thought that the more time she spent in Cairns the more likely she'd run into Matthew. A part of her was fine with that but her logical side told her it would cause trouble. She took a stroll to the market and picked up some ground beef, buns, and cheese. It was a booze-free burger night.

Tatiana spoke with Malcolm between meetings, he told her he talked with Gennady Mitov. He was in Antibes, everything was going according to plan. The sale of the tailor shop to him went very smoothly and the transfer to BCJ Enterprises went without a hitch. He stressed the importance though of making sure her mother never saw the Chain of Title of the tailor shop or she might wonder what was going on. If that ever did happen Tatiana would explain it away with the complicated tax issue but hoped to avoid that. She was anxiously awaiting the call from her mother. Knowing she was out of Russia would take a load off her mind. Five hours later that call would come. Valentina checked into her Antibes hotel, she was safe. Tatiana would sleep well.

Tuesday, December 10, 1996

"Hi Olena, it's Mikheil."

"Hi, Mikheil. Are you all settled in?" she asked, just walking in the door. Her security nephew was behind her with a bag of groceries.

"Yes, it's good to be back home."

"It definitely is. Even Jacques seems happier, he was out exploring the garden today."

"Make sure he doesn't run off; Tatiana would never forgive you."

"He was safe, I had him on a harness, besides I would never forgive myself. He's become my best friend."

Olena and Mikheil were unaware that their conversation was being recorded by one of Armen's men. Voshkolup had sent guys periodically to Nizhny to Lev's mother's house looking for her. Armen had been one of those guys and now it finally paid off, she was back home after being who knows where. The phone line was tapped and the recordings were retrieved each night when they slept. Another clue to finding Tatiana was coming together.

"Cindy, are you all right?"

"Yes, yes, she said with a couple of coughs in between."

"Cindy, you're doing fine. It just takes practice," Elizabeth said swimming over.

"Olga, you're such a natural at this," Cindy said.

"Not really. I was coughing like you yesterday when I was practicing mask clearing at the beach after yesterday's class. Like Elizabeth said it just takes practice. You'll get this."

Two hours later they were enjoying happy hour drinks at a beach bar that Tatiana noticed earlier in the week. The conversation started with how they ended up in Cairns. Cindy had always been fascinated with Australia and saw a real estate show on TV that featured Cairns. Buffalo already had its first snowstorm of the year; she had broken up with her boyfriend and couldn't see herself spending the winter cooped up pining over a guy.

"Olga, what was the draw for you?"

Tatiana anticipated such a conversation telling Cindy of an unfulfilling job as a government clerk and the dread of another Russian winter. She told her about Matthew and that she wasn't sure where she would be from one week to the next. She didn't want to be tied down; it was all about freedom. She didn't like lying to Cindy but leaving any clue about herself could be deadly, when Cindy pulled out her camera Tatiana panicked.

"Sorry, I don't do pictures," Olga said, as Cindy was handing the camera to the bartender for a picture of them together.

"Come on, one picture," Cindy begged.

"Please, it's going to sound strange, but I really hate having my picture taken."

Cindy could tell Olga was serious quickly putting the camera away.

Olga could tell by the look on Cindy's face that she was confused and taken aback by her response. She quickly changed the subject by saying, I love this song. She sprang from the barstool dancing next to Cindy who got up and danced too. It wasn't long before they left the beach bar to a place with better music and a real dance floor complete with a fantastic light show. They both danced for hours and were getting a little drunk. Cindy reminded them of the early scuba class; they should call it a night. They said good night, Cindy's hotel was nearby, and she headed out on foot across the parking lot. Tatiana didn't feel like a hike back to the camper and walked over to a waiting cab on the street. Just as she was climbing in someone called out, "Olga." Tatiana didn't notice Matthew running after the departing taxi.

"Shit," Matthew said as he walked back into the club.

Litskevich walked into Katerina's office with a look about him that meant business.

"Lieutenant, how can I help you today?"

"I'm not going to mince words. This shit has got to stop!"

"What are you talking about?"

"Voshkolup."

"I heard he didn't make it. What a shame," Katerina said coldly.

"I know you likely had a part in one way or another with the shit that has gone down, but it has to stop now. I'm under increased pressure to find those responsible, and if any evidence emerges that you had anything to do with the attacks, I'll have no choice but to arrest you and anyone else involved."

"What makes you think I'm in any way involved."

"Cut the shit, Katerina. Drozdov's abduction and murder, Vlad being gunned down, the attacks on your people. I get it but understand Voshkolup was connected to some people very high up, very high. You have no idea who you're messing with."

"I'm not messing with anyone."

"I'm not going to say anymore. One more thing, the Belov woman, she's been traced to Sydney."

"Lieutenant, I promise I won't give you any reason to visit again but if you'd like to stop by for coffee sometime feel free," Katerina said turning on the charm.

Litskevich exhaled and left.

Wednesday, December 11, 1996

Mikheil quickly returned back to his old routines and some of them weren't great choices. He had gotten together with friends he hadn't seen in months and a bit of scotch, vodka, and beer was involved. He struggled through his front door with the assistance of his security "roommate," running straight for the bathroom. Several minutes later he emerged feeling better and soon was comatose in bed. Waking up with one of the worst hangovers ever he uttered the familiar phrase, "I'm never doing that again."

While Mikheil was out partying the tape recording Olena's calls was switched out and the calls listened to. Armen's guys were trying to figure out who this guy Mikheil was. It was clear from the conversation he was in hiding with Olena but why. One of the guys pointed out that he mentioned the Belov woman's cat. Was he her boyfriend.

Tatiana and Cindy both arrived late for their second last scuba class, Cindy by five minutes, and Tatiana by ten. It was clear by their raspy voices and makeup-less faces they'd had a late night. They went through the day's lesson that ended with a reminder that their exam on all their classroom work was tomorrow followed by a final test on all the pool work. This included rescues, removing and putting on all their gear underwater and a 30 length of the pool nonstop swim.

"Make sure you guys get an early night," Elizabeth said to the class and looking at Tatiana and Cindy.

"Was it that obvious?" Cindy whispered to Tatiana, who was giggling.

The two of them agreed there would be no boozing after class, it would be an early night. They walked to a Mexican restaurant, ate fresh fish tacos, and drank cokes. As they ate plans were put into place for their open-water certification dives. "We need to get through the classroom tests tomorrow," Cindy reminded Olga in a worried tone.

"No worries, we have it down. Once we get our certification let's go out on a liveaboard for a few days."

"That would be awesome," said Cindy.

With full stomachs, they called it a day making arrangements to meet early for their last class to study for the test. As Tatiana walked back to her camper, she imagined buying a house in Cairns and making it home. She would discuss that possibility with Malcolm when they spoke again.

Natasha, Stanislav, and Nikita Magnitsky walked behind Sergei's coffin in Preobrazhenskoye Cemetery. They wore heavy black woolen coats on this frigid day as did the dozen men walking next to them. The difference was the men were all armed with semi-automatic pistols under their unbuttoned coats and were ready to use them at the slightest provocation.

The entire scenario was a blur for Natasha who still hadn't come to terms with her young husband passing. The boys stood on either side of their mother holding her hands, they were equally in disbelief. None of them could imagine life without him. Words were spoken by a clergyman and the last tribute of the ceremony was Natasha dropping a red rose on the coffin as it was lowered into the ground. She courageously fought back tears. She imagined she was being watched and wasn't going to give those monsters that satisfaction. Minutes later one of the men in a black coat whispered in Natasha's ear, Sergei's family was led away to a black limousine. At that moment Natasha broke down, and tears streamed down her face, Nakita handed her a handkerchief. They sped away to the airport following a black car full of armed men and were followed by the same. It was the Magnitsky's last moments in Russia.

"Mo, we're in Sydney. We got in late yesterday, one of the flights was delayed but we're good," Armen reported.

"Any word on Belov?"

"Nothing on our end but my guys in Nizhny are on Drozdov's mother. She was talking to a guy we thought might be Belov's boyfriend, a Mikheil. They got into the house and found postcards from her son Lev when he was traveling in Europe, he was traveling with this Mikheil. They went to school together and it turns out his last name is Ramazanov, he lives in Kubinka now. I have someone setting up surveillance on him as we speak."

"What are you and Sasha doing now?"

"We've started hitting hotels but aren't coming up with anything yet. You know how it is, it could take a while."

"Call me as soon as you get anything."

Thursday, December 12, 1996

"Mikheil, it's Katerina. Where the hell have you been? I tried getting ahold of you all day yesterday."

"I'm sorry, I was under the weather. Spent the day sleeping and had the phone off."

"You can't do that. You had me very worried. I was about to send someone out there to check on you guys."

Mikheil wasn't going to rat out his "roommate" who was sleeping one off too. "Sorry. What is going on?"

"I got some news Tuesday afternoon. Apparently, Tatiana has been traced to Sydney, I don't have the details of how this came about but you need to get word to her."

"Will do. I'll call her when I hang up with you."

"Mikheil, what is the interest in her? I know she and Lev were childhood friends. Is she in danger?"

"Katerina, I don't have many details myself but when we see each other again I'll tell you what I know." Mikheil was relieved Katerina didn't press him, it gave him more time to come up with a plausible explanation, but right now he needed to call Tatiana.

Elizabeth, Tatiana, Cindy, and a few scuba classmates were out celebrating passing the course and now qualified to take the open water certification. They hit a local Irish pub and were toasting their instructor.

"To the best scuba teacher. Everyone passed thanks to you, Elizabeth," Cindy said with a glass of wine in the air.

"You guys were a good class. Thanks for your hard work, you make me look good."

Tatiana started chanting, "shots, shots, shots."

Everyone looked at her wondering who this person was. The quiet reserved woman was turning into a party animal. Elizabeth and Cindy gave in.

"Okay, one," said Cindy.

"Me too, but nothing really strong," acquiesced Elizabeth.

"Three kamikazes," Tatiana called to the bartender.

The shots were downed, and the dancing started.

It wasn't long before the other students that joined them made their excuses and left the three party girls tearing up the dance floor. After several songs, Tatiana made her way back to the table and checked her phone. Three missed calls from Mikheil. Shit, she thought and went outside where it was quieter to return the call.

"Tatiana, I've been trying to get you."

"I see that. We've been celebrating passing our scuba classes," she said with a slight slur.

"Tatiana, listen to me. I've gotten word from Katerina that you've been traced to Sydney."

"No, no." Tears were welling up in her eyes. At that moment Cindy walked out of the pub and saw her friend upset.

"Olga, what's wrong?"

Tatiana held her finger up and mouthed the words "it's all right."

Cindy got the message she wanted to be alone and went back inside.

Mikheil told her this information was received on Tuesday, she should make a move soon.

"I was really starting to like it here, Mikheil. I could see myself making a home here."

When Tatiana returned Cindy asked what was wrong. Tatiana quickly made up a story of having to return home because her mother was sick.

"Is there anything I can do?" Cindy asked.

Tatiana told her her mother was having an issue with her stomach and required surgery. She'd have to go home within the next few days. This explained why Tatiana had a distant look on her face for the rest of the evening as the remaining two women continued to party. Tatiana was thinking as the girls danced about what her next steps were. Where was she going next.

"It's been confirmed, she's still in Australia," Armen relayed to Mo about 16 hours after Mikheil called Tatiana.

"You found this out from a tap on this Mikheil's phone?"

"Yes, apparently, she was celebrating passing scuba lessons."

"That means she's likely on the coast somewhere," Mo concluded.

"That really doesn't help in Australia," Armen said.

"It should. When I think of scuba diving in Australia I think of the Great Barrier Reef," Mo said with a little frustration in his voice.

"We'll get up there. It's a good place to start. When is the big man's funeral?"

"Tomorrow at two. There's a lot going on as you can imagine. Please just find Belov so I can concentrate on all the other shit that's going on right now."

"Yes, boss. Consider it done."

Friday, December 13, 1996

Malcolm could tell Tatiana had a few but after hearing her predicament, he totally understood.

"I was really starting to like Cairns," she said to him pleadingly.

"Tatiana, you can't stay somewhere you're not safe. Look I don't know all the details of what you are dealing with but based on the amount of money and people involved I can imagine."

"It's more."

"I'm sorry, what?"

"It's more. A lot more."

"Okay. Let's get you out of there first and we'll figure something out. Are you okay for money right now?"

"Yes."

"You can't come back to London; they've traced you here before. How does New York sound?"

"Okay, I'm going to miss the sun and the beach but there's always shopping."

"I'm glad to see you're looking at the bright side."

"I'll need a bit more money then."

"I'll take care of it," Malcolm said rolling his eyes. "Make your way to New York, check in with me along the way and we'll get this mess sorted."

"I love you, Malcolm."

"I love you too," he said with his eyes rolling again.

Tatiana woke up feeling a little groggy after her afternoon/evening out. She remembered her conversation with Malcolm, it jumped her back to reality. "I've got to get moving," she said out loud, first breakfast though and she walked to the esplanade. I'm really going to miss it here she thought, her phone rang.

"Olga, how are you feeling on this lovely morning?" Cindy cheerfully asked.

"Hi, Cindy. I'm okay but wished we hadn't done those last shots."

"Get over it, you only live once. What are you doing?"

"Just grabbing some breakfast. Want to join me?"

"I had mine a couple of hours ago. I'm at the beach and wanted to see if you wanted to join me, we can make plans for our open water dives."

"Cindy, I would love to, but I have to speed up my departure. Mama was admitted to the hospital last night and the surgery was moved up to Monday."

"Olga, I'm so sorry to hear that. When are you going back to Moscow?"

"I'm not sure. I'm going to the travel agent after breakfast and see what they can do for me."

"Call me and let me know. Take care, let me know if there's anything I can do."

Tatiana felt horrible lying to Cindy, she was so nice, and she could have pictured them being friends decades from now. Future dive plans were put on hold.

Armen and Sasha were back at the Sydney airport. They discussed splitting up, one going to Cairns and the other somewhere else, but they couldn't decide on the somewhere else so were traveling together. The earliest available flight was at 2:15, they'd be in Cairns for dinner. Their morning was spent taking in the sights around the Sydney Opera House and The Rocks then rushing to the airport. They had 20 minutes to spare before their flight took off.

The pair got off the plane making their way to the car rental counter. They were deep in conversation about hockey and walked right past Tatiana who was sitting in the terminal waiting for them to clean the plane Armen and Sasha just departed from. It was a flight that went back and forth between Sydney and Cairns four times a day. It was Friday the 13th but it was Tatiana's lucky day, she had come within 20 meters of a torturous death.

Tatiana's day was stressful and busy. Not only were travel arrangements made but she had to contact the camper rental company and tell them their camper van would be left in Cairns. She was informed of a large fee that would be incurred by doing that. She told them she would stop by when in Sydney to square up her account. It appeased them but she could tell it wasn't an arrangement they were happy with.

Flying out of Cairns Tatiana found herself thinking about Matthew again. She was glad he hadn't been pulled into her mess especially now she was fleeing. He was a nice guy and didn't deserve that.

The flight went by quickly with the help of an inflight movie. Soon Tatiana was jumping into a taxi at Sydney Airport. She considered going back to the familiar Travelodge but thought it could be risky, "take me to the Hyatt," she said to the taxi driver. With her hair tucked under a large sunhat, she checked in as Olga Olenska and went straight to her luxurious quarters overlooking the harbour. Room service arrived with a seafood feast and a cold bottle of sauvignon blanc. If she had to stay put this was the way to do it.

Litskevich, Turov, and Mikheyev met with Kovalyov after a fruitless week. They were no closer to taking down the cagey Solntsevskaya bratva. It was decided to hand off the around-the-clock electronic surveillance to junior agents. Raffael and his guys could have been arrested on a number of "minor" offenses but with their clout nothing would stick. There was an increasing backlog of extortion, kidnappings, and murders to investigate but Litskevich would keep Tatiana Belov in the back of his mind. Instinctively he knew there was something big there, he just couldn't put his finger on it.

Saturday, December 14, 1996

Armen and Sasha hit pay dirt, or so they thought. The scuba hunch had been the right one and they believed they were hot on the trial of Tatiana Belov aka Olga Olenska. Armen entered the dive shop where Tatiana signed up for her lessons and spoke with the clerk at the counter.

"I'm interested in taking scuba lessons."

"Well, you've come to the right place mate," he said enthusiastically.

"I met a fellow Russian woman the other day that raved about you guys."

"Oh, let me think."

Elizabeth had just walked from the backroom and caught part of the conversation. "You must be talking about Olga."

Armen pretending to think. "Blond, slender about 30, medium height?"

"Yes, Olga. She was in our last round of classes."

"I ran into her at the hotel," Armen said.

"That can't be her then, she was camping in a camper van," Elizabeth excused herself realizing that maybe she was being a little too chatty.

Armen left with a pamphlet and a promise to return soon. Sasha was waiting in the rental car. "We got her, she's going by Olga, we got her."

It took most of the day, chats with numerous people in the few campgrounds in the area but the camper was traced to a rental car company by the airport. It was dropped off that morning full of camping provisions still inside. It was clear that Tatiana left in a hurry. Armen quizzed a representative at the rental car place that didn't have any details on the previous renter, but he did offer Armen a sweet rental deal, complete with camping gear if he took it and returned it in Sydney. Armen passed.

"Tatiana, no need to apologize. I've been very busy too. Mr. Mitov has been great showing me the shop, but I'm worried about him. I think he might have sold the shop because he is losing his mind. He was showing me around town and seemed to get lost easily and he doesn't seem to remember people in the neighborhood, but he is very nice."

Leave it to mama to find a glitch in the plan she thought. "Do you like it there?"

"It is gorgeous. It's better than I could have imagined."

"Mama, that is the greatest news I could get. Do you think you will be busy?"

"Mr. Mitov said he will get me as much business as I want, having connections all over the place. The last few years he was turning business away he told me. Tati, when are you going to visit?"

"Mama, I'll let you get settled in first but can't wait to see the shop and have you give me the grand tour."

"Are you still working too much?"

"Yes mama, but I'm thinking of taking a vacation soon."

"Come here for your vacation," Valentina implored.

"Soon, mama." She hung up with that familiar guilty feeling but was thrilled her mother was happy. Now it was time to pack and head to the airport, she wasn't looking forward to the extremely long flight to LAX. Tatiana found herself running late, she planned to stop at the camper rental company and pay them, there just wasn't time. She stuffed $1,000 into an envelope and asked the front desk clerk, "is there a courier service available?"

"Certainly, Miss Olenska," was the reply.

Airports made Tatiana nervous and rightfully so. She checked in and being flush with cash she upgraded to first class. It was very costly but worth it; she'd arrive in Los Angeles much more rested and better fed. Going through security Tatiana had a bit of a scare, she was pulled off to the side for a random search. Asked to remove her shoes and her carry-on bag thoroughly searched she was then okayed to proceed. It was a good thing I upgraded to first class she thought; it brought the amount of cash she was carrying to below the level that would have demanded a lot of unwanted scrutiny. A glass of wine was in order to calm her frayed nerves. Finally, the announcement she had been waiting for, "now boarding first class for United Airlines flight 815 to Los Angeles."

Armen and Sasha were back at their hotel still in Cairns having a drink poolside.

"Not having any airline connections here it's going to take a little longer to find out where she's heading," Armen said while watching a couple of college girls splashing each other in the pool.

"We still have those guys watching the woman in Nizhny and that guy, Mikheil in Kubinka right?" asked Sasha.

"Ya, let's hope they get something for us."

Tatiana emerged from LAX into an awaiting taxi. They pulled out of the airport terminal into the California sunshine and headed to Santa Monica. With a one-day layover, Tatiana was going to fit in as many sights as she could. Driving along the LA streets she noticed signs and billboards everywhere vying for her attention, it was so different to Cairns. Stepping out of the taxi she could smell the ocean air which didn't have the same Queensland humidity, it was somewhat cooler. She was now experiencing winter in California and had been enjoying an Aussie summer all in the same day. She actually gained four hours crossing the international date line.

Tatiana pulled back the sheers from the window and looked out to a stunning view of beach, palm trees, and ocean. Directly below her window five stories down was the hotel pool, she would never tire of views like this. Looking to her right she saw a familiar sight, something she had seen on TV and in movies, the Santa Monica pier. She was going to take a nap but instead put her sandals back on, grabbed her purse and sunglasses walking a couple of blocks to the iconic landmark.

People were everywhere posing and taking pictures of each other, and performers were trying to pull in an audience for a payout at the end of the show. Smells of cotton candy, hot dogs, and pizza filled the air reminding Tatiana she hadn't eaten in a while. She went into a restaurant at the end of the pier and sat at the bar. There were more stunning seaside views. She ordered a glass of Napa Valley white and a platter of seafood; both were also things she would never tire of.

Back at the hotel, it was dark out, the pier was fully lit up with every color imaginable and she was getting sleepy. She put on the TV and lay down on the bed. The first-class accommodations on the plane really paid off as she slept soundly for a good part of the journey. Jet lag wasn't going to be an issue. After a good night's sleep, Tatiana would be ready to sightsee and then catch her flight to New York.

Sunday, December 15, 1996

Tatiana stepped out of her hotel after a large breakfast and returned to her room to grab a sweatshirt. It was nice out but a bit cooler than what she'd become accustomed to. She walked south for about 35 minutes along the boardwalk to Venice Beach. It was a memorable Sunday walk coming across the greatest cross-section of people imaginable with also a large number of different smells from weed to urine. It was definitely an experience she was glad to have done but after an hour it was time to move on. After a half-hour cab ride, Tatiana was walking Hollywood Boulevard. It too was interesting but also very seedy. It was time for another cab ride, this time to the Griffith Observatory. This is more my speed she thought. There were fascinating exhibits, spectacular views of the city, million-dollar homes in the hills, and looming in the distance the Hollywood sign. It was time to get back to the hotel, grab her bags and head back to LAX.

Armen and Sasha were heading to the Cairns airport. They were going back to Sydney and back to Moscow unless intel pointed them in another direction.

"I don't want to leave here," Sasha said throwing his suitcase into the back of the rental car.

"I'm with you on that. Between the women and the weather, I'd gladly hang here indefinitely."

"Fuck ya!" Sasha added.

Before boarding their flight, they checked in with Raffael. He wasn't happy and told them they needed to move faster.

"Mo, we're doing everything we can," Armen explained. "You don't have any information about where she's gone from here?"

"No, I've been in touch with your guys, and nothing is coming from the phone taps. We'll have to take it to the next level if we don't get something soon."

Armen knew what the next level was, it wouldn't be pretty. The only problem with that is it would bring a lot of added heat to everyone involved. He preferred the covert route.

Tatiana touched down at LaGuardia and she was feeling the effects of her travels. While in Los Angeles she booked a couple of nights at the Marriott near Times Square. She was confident she'd have no problem blending in with the trove of tourists in town for the Christmas season. A present to herself would be a new warm coat and winter clothes to replace the ones she ditched in London. For now, though her only thought was on getting some rest.

Sydney didn't turn out to be a restful place for Armen and Sasha. It was their last night in Australia, and they were determined to make it a memorable one. They returned to The Rocks, had dinner, and partied with a group of young ladies whose cruise ship was docked nearby. When they scurried off minutes before their boat departed it was onto numerous drinking establishments along Pitt Street before settling down at a rock and roll bar called Frankies. Hours of flirting and drinking finished with slices of pizza but unfortunately, no ladies. It was a long zig-zag walk back to the hotel where they fell asleep snoring still wearing all their clothes including shoes and jackets. It was going to be a long flight home.

13

Tatiana stared out of the Marriott window 22 stories up with a cup of coffee she had brewed in the room. She wasn't appreciating the spectacular view of the city that never sleeps although she had slept very well; she was thinking about her constant running. No matter where she went the bratva were tracking her. Her mother thought she was in London; Lily and Anna thought she was in Moscow, it was only Malcolm, Mikheil, and maybe Olena that knew her location. She trusted all of them with her life and knew they would never knowingly betray her, but it was possible they were inadvertently leaking information.

New York was calling loudly, Tatiana wanted to get out and explore but she had a plan to put into place first. She went down to the hotel gift shop and bought a map of the U.S. While eating her room service breakfast she took the hotel stationary making her to-do list.

1. Get burner phones.
2. Call Malcolm, tell him change of plans, stayed in LA instead, extended stay in Santa Monica.
3. Call Loews in Santa Monica, business associates traveling in.
4. Call Mikheil, staying at quaint inn in Osterville, Massachusetts.
5. Call inns in Osterville tell them about business associates traveling in.

Tatiana then visited the hotel's concierge; he happily compiled a list of Osterville Inns for her. Next, she walked around the corner, she picked up her burner phones and a roll of masking tape. Number one off the list she said. Malcolm, the Loews, and Mikheil were called, two, three, and four done. After calling Loews she realized it was very unlikely a call would be made to her if she wasn't a guest there, so she booked a room and had Malcolm wire funds to them.

"Tatiana, are you short of funds?" Malcolm inquired.

"I'm fine for now Malcolm. I'll explain later."

There were four inns in and around Osterville that she considered even remotely quaint, a call was placed to each. The owners were all very helpful and agreed to call if anyone inquired about her. The burner phones were labeled SM, OST, and NEW, the only thing she needed now was a bigger purse for hauling them all around with her.

Armen and Sasha were back in chilly Moscow. The trip from the airport took longer than usual due to snow. The pair of them grumbled about the shitty weather and agreed they'd go somewhere warm as soon as this bitch was found. When Armen got home, he checked in with his guys doing the surveillance, no calls came in pertaining to Belov.

"I'm back in town. I want those tapes switched out a few times a day and immediately checked. The second you get something for me I want to know."

In the meantime, he would try to get flight manifest information, she didn't leave Australia by boat he thought, or did she.

Tatiana felt better now that she had her plan in place; it was time for some shopping. A warm winter coat topped the list, a hat to make her less recognizable, and some gloves. Macy's had it all. Wearing her new purchases, the only thing left was some boots. The choices were difficult, and she picked up a couple of pairs from a chic boutique. Strolling up Fifth Avenue she came across the Rockefeller Center and marveled at the huge lit-up Christmas tree. The festive atmosphere made her think of home and how she wouldn't be there with friends and family this year.

All the walking and shopping had Tatiana worn out; she reminded herself she didn't have to see everything in one day. On the way back to the hotel she popped into a pizza shop and grabbed a pie to go. It smelled so good it was surprising it made it up to the room in one piece. Kicking off her new boots and climbing into bed with a fresh hot pizza was heaven. She never had pizza that tasted this good before. She now understood the hype.

Tuesday, December 17, 1996

"Armen, I got something."

"What are you talking about?" Armen said waking up from a deep sleep.

"Belov, she's in the States, Osterville, Massachusetts."

"You sure about that?"

"Yes, she called Mikheil yesterday. I looked it up, it's a small place. She should be easy to find."

It was 1:30 in the morning and he knew he needed to move fast; she had slipped away too often before, he called Sasha.

"We're going to the airport; pack and I'll call you back with the details. Belov is in the States, I'm calling Raffael to see if he can arrange a plane for us."

"You know for sure she's there?"

"As sure as we can be. Get ready."

Raffael was awake when his phone rang. "It better be good," he said. He was entertaining an attractive young lady and things were just starting to get hot.

"It is good, Mo. We've located Belov. We need to get to the States, it looks like Boston will be the closest airport. Do you have access to the big man's jet?"

"No, I don't. I've tried and there are a bunch of legal things preventing me from using it. You're going to have to fly out commercially."

"You know that's just going to slow us down."

"I know. In the meantime, I'll see what I can do from here, just get there as soon as you can."

Tatiana awoke looked out of the window and was catching the last wave of the morning rush hour. People were making their last-minute runs into the office as a dusting of snow fell. Room service in the morning was beginning to become a nice routine. It was like having butler service. After a large omelet, crispy bacon, toast, and a couple of cups of coffee it was time for a walk. She had heard about Central Park; it was time to check it out.

Tatiana was surprised to see as many people as there were skating on Wollman Rink. A young man randomly skated around with a shovel trying to keep up with the light snow, but it seemed pointless. She considered renting some skates and giving it a go but thought of the possible attention it could create in large part because of her poor ability to skate.

After the park, Tatiana found herself inside a massive bookstore. She started in the finance section seeing quite a few of those books for the second or third time and then made her way to fiction. She settled on a legal thriller that took place in Biloxi, Mississippi. It would be a good way to pass the time on this snowy December day.

Armen and Sasha made it to the airport by 7:00 a.m. only to find the quickest way to Boston would be a direct flight that wasn't leaving until 10:00 that evening. Frustrated they left the airport with their packed bags returning to Armen's place. The time before the flight was used making calls to the guys doing surveillance only to hear there wasn't anything new to report. Armen pulled out a couple of VHS tapes and the rest of the time was spent watching action films. At 7:00 p.m. they headed back to the airport for the trip to Boston.

Tatiana's afternoon was peaceful, but she was starting to get stir-crazy; a drink was in store. She grabbed a light dinner and then stepped into an Irish pub that displayed a big sign on the sidewalk professing the best happy hour in town. Wine wasn't on the happy hour menu, so she went for an Irish beer on tap just as happy hour was ending. She laughed to herself, she had millions and millions of dollars at her fingertips and here she was worrying about a couple of dollars in drinks prices, old habits die hard she thought. As she sipped on her beer a good-looking guy on her right got one more beer in before happy hour ended and looked her way.

"How is your day going?" he kindly asked.

"Very well and yours?" Tatiana replied.

"Great. It's nice to get out of the hotel."

"I know exactly what you mean."

She noticed this guy stood out a bit. Unlike all the other guys in the bar, he was alone, dressed casually in jeans and a long-sleeved t-shirt.

"Let me guess you're from Poland?"

"No."

"Russia?"

"Yes. You're not from around here, are you?" Tatiana inquired.

"No, I live in the DC area. I came up for a few days to relax, catch an investor conference, and a hockey game."

"I like hockey. We have some great players in Russia."

"I know. We have some great Russian players on my team."

"And that is?"

The Toronto Maple Leafs.

"I've heard of them before. Why the Maple Leafs?"

"I grew up in the Toronto area."

"I see and you live in DC now?"

"Just outside of DC, Alexandria. It's in Virginia, several miles from the Capitol. What's your name?"

This time there wasn't a stutter. "Olga, and you are?"

"Tony."

"It's very nice to meet you, Tony."

This guy is very nice she thought to herself and not bad looking either.

Olga and Tony's evening was flying by. The conversation that started with sports moved to travels and was about to go onto childhood memories and details Olga didn't want to get into. She was feeling very relaxed around Tony, at this point they were holding hands at the bar. Anyone that saw them would think this was date four or five, there was some obvious chemistry going on. Olga got up to use the restroom and looked in the mirror. "What's going on?" she asked herself.

"I need to get going," Olga said after returning.

"Okay," Tony replied a little puzzled by the abrupt announcement. "Can I walk you back to your hotel?"

"That would be nice."

In the Marriott lobby, Tony said he'd like to see her again.

"I would like that." Olga pulled out a piece of paper and copied the top number from it to the bottom of the page, tore it off, and gave it to Tony.

"Can I call you tomorrow?"

"Maybe," Olga said with a flirtatious smile walking to the elevator.

Wednesday, December 18, 1996

"I have intel that the Belov woman is in the States, a small town near Boston."

"And?"

"I want to go."

"Why and do what?" Kovalyov said with an air of annoyance.

"I think she'll help us bring down Raffael and many others in the Solntsevskaya bratva. They're on their way there now to get her. I got it from the wiretap we have on Raffael," Litskevich said.

"First, I need a direct connection. Second, she's in the States, we can't arrest anyone or have them arrested. This is a waste of time. You have several cases that I need you to concentrate on. Forget this woman."

Litskevich knew his boss was right, what was he doing. The only thing he could do was to call Katerina and have her alerted.

"Katerina, it's Lt. Litskevich. I've received information that Tatiana Belov is in Osterville, Massachusetts, and Raffael's men are on their way now."

"How did you get this information and why are you telling me?"

"You know I can't say but you need to get word to her right away."

"Thank you, lieutenant."

The hotel room was pitch-black; Tatiana was woken up by a buzzing sound coming from her purse. Her heart started pounding as she fumbled for the light switch beside the bed, found her purse, and located the buzzing phone. It was the phone identified with the NEW on the tape. Should I answer it raced through her head, she was still groggy.

"Hello."

"Tatiana, it's Mikheil."

"Yes, Mikheil. What's going on?"

"I got a call from Katerina, the FSB guy looking into Arkadiy's death tipped her that you're in Osterville, Massachusetts."

Tatiana's first instinct was to hang up but instead, she said, "yes, it's lovely here. Mikheil how..." Tatiana turned the phone off.

Mikheil sat there staring at the phone trying to figure out what happened.

Tatiana tossed the phone on the bed, her hands shaking. She knew Katerina was getting information from the FSB and passing it along to Mikheil. The FSB must be bugging Mikheil's phone. Why. It was 3:45 and Tatiana wasn't going back to sleep.

Tatiana had hours to think. Mikheil's phone had to be tapped and the only reason would be to find her. Was someone in the FSB crooked. Her first instinct was to bolt and maybe that was what the FSB wanted her to do. Right now, they thought she was in Osterville, Massachusetts, relax and think.

Armen and Sasha touched down at Logan fighting exhaustion. They had almost traveled around the world over the span of a few days and were now driving south towards the Cape.

"I need to pull over. I'm falling asleep," Sasha said battling to keep his eyes open. "Can you drive?"

Armen was falling asleep himself as the car pulled onto the shoulder. "I can't drive, let's sleep for a bit." A minute later the pair were reclined back in the front seats, both were snoring. An hour later they woke up with all the windows fogged up in the running rental car. They were still very tired but not on the verge of nodding off anytime soon.

The road sign indicated they were five miles from Osterville. They discussed what they would do if she was at one of the inns. A note requesting a meeting would be left. Knowing Tatiana would run they would follow and throw her in the trunk of the car at the ideal moment. Before stopping at the first inn a trip to the local hardware store for kidnapping supplies was in order. Sasha selected the first inn on their route, it was the Captain Nelson House, it fit the quaint inn to the letter.

"Here it is on the right," Sasha said pointing. "Don't pull right into the driveway, we don't want the car to be seen."

Armen pulled over to the side of the road about thirty meters from the driveway. "I'll go in by myself."

"Good idea," Sasha agreed.

Armen walked up the steps of the covered porch to the front door. A sign said *Welcome, come on Inn.* As he entered, he saw the office to the right with an elderly man sitting at a desk.

"Hello, welcome to Captain Nelson House. My name is Glen, how can I help you?"

"Hello. I hope you can help me; I'm looking for a business colleague. She is staying here in Osterville and didn't have the room booked at the time we left. Her name is Tatiana Belov."

"You are in luck. I've been in touch with Tatiana. Where did I put that number?" Glen shuffled through the top drawer of his desk and exclaimed, "here it is. Hold on," he picked up the phone and dialed.

Tatiana, who was hunkered down watching a movie in her room heard the buzzing from her purse. Instantly her heart started pounding again. A replay from the middle of the night. It was the phone marked OST. This can't be. "What should I do, what should I do," she said out loud. She stared at the phone and finally answered it.

"Hello?"

"Tatiana?"

"Who is this?" she asked trying to sound intimidating.

"It's Glen from the Captain Nelson."

Tatiana's heart was beating even faster now, her mouth was getting dry. "Hi, Glen. Did one of my colleagues finally show up?"

"He's here now. Would you like to speak with him?"

Tatiana's first urge was to hang up but realized whomever it was was hundreds of miles away. "Yes, please put him on."

Armen was equally surprised when Glen handed him the phone. "Tatiana?"

"Yes. Who is this?"

"I'm so glad to hear your voice. Where are you? We've had a very long trip and we're looking forward to seeing you."

"What do you want from me?"

"Yes, we're looking forward to concluding our deal. Where can we meet?"

At that moment the phone went dead. "Hello, hello," Armen said. "It looks like we've been disconnected. Glen, do you know where she is staying?"

"No, she just left me the number."

"Can I get that from you? I'll try her again shortly."

Glen handed it to him and wished him luck meeting up with his colleague.

Tatiana stood looking off at the New York City skyline with the phone still in her hand. She dropped it and realized the buzzing was coming from her purse, it was the phone marked NEW. What the fuck is going on. After a minute the buzzing stopped, and the message light started blinking.

"Hi Olga, it's Tony. I was wondering if you'd like to go to the hockey game with me tonight. Call me my number is 703 555-5309."

Tatiana's mind was spinning. "Think," she said. Her mind was going at the speed of sound. She knew Mikheil's phone was being tapped by the bratva and probably the FSB or maybe the FSB was tapping the bratva. What a mess she thought. Either way, I can't have anything to do with Mikheil and I need to get word to him that he's being watched. She tried to call Katerina but there wasn't an answer, it was after 10:00 o'clock there, and it went to voicemail. "Katerina, Mikheil's phone is bugged," she hung up. Another movie started but Tatiana didn't even notice, after an hour of staring at the wall she called Tony.

"I would love to go to the game with you."

An hour and a half before the game they met at the Irish pub from the day earlier and had a drink and snack talking about their day. Tatiana made up a story of a lazy, boring day of movies. Tony talked of his investing seminar that was geared around short-term trades. As he explained very short term, the main focus was on day trading, something Tatiana was interested in, but didn't mention her banking job.

They made their way to Madison Square Garden and to Tatiana's delight lower center ice seats. Tatiana was enjoying Tony's company he was very easy to be around, and the conversation flowed except when there was hockey action. The game put them both in a very good mood with the Leafs beating the Rangers 5-1.

"Up for a celebration drink?" Tony asked.

"A 5-1 victory definitely calls for one," Tatiana said taking Tony's hand.

Tatiana was happy to let Tony do most of the talking over drinks. He was an interesting guy with interests that varied from gardening to motorcycles to something they had in common, scuba diving. Tony had been to the Great Barrier Reef and spent a few days on a liveaboard boat.

After the first couple of after-game drinks, they made their way to a place that would be described as a dive bar with a jukebox and people dancing when a good song came on. Party Tatiana kicked in and soon she was calling for shots. Tony at first resisted but gave in when Tatiana called him a pussy. The shots soon led to dancing and then more chatting at the bar. It was clear the shots and drinks were starting to take a toll on Tatiana; the first sign was a drink she knocked over. Tony noticed a change in Tatiana's demeanor. It wasn't long before tears began to flow.

"Olga, what's wrong?"

"Nothing." The tears continued to flow as Tony handed Tatiana a couple of beverage napkins.

"Are you sure? Have I done something?"

"It's not you." The tears were flowing full stream now.

"What is it?"

A drunk Tatiana spit out "they're going to kill me," between sobs.

"Who is going to kill you?"

"I can't tell you. I shouldn't have said anything."

"You can't stop now."

Tatiana let it all out. With each word, it was like having a brick removed from her back. She told Tony about Lev and some of the money in Zurich. About how she was tracked to London, then Sydney, and now to the States.

Tony sat in silence. For a moment he wondered if he was sitting there with a nut job. This was just too farfetched.

Tatiana sensed Tony's apprehension and said, "I know it all sounds crazy but it's all true, trust me."

The way Tatiana looked at him he knew she needed his help, he hugged her and said, "I'm here for you." She did not want to let him go.

Thursday, December 19, 1996

331

Katerina started her day as she always did, listening to voicemails and jotting the down the messages as they came in. "Mikheil's phone is bugged," quickly caught her attention. She was about to call Mikheil's house and stopped, that would be stupid. She called Pavel into her office; he was going to pay a visit to Mikheil and his security team member. He'd bring another phone along with him.

"What the fuck do you mean you talked to her, but you don't know where she is?"

"It looks like we were set up. The innkeeper was expecting us, but he'd never met Belov either. He just talked to her on the phone."

"And you haven't found her there," Raffael said growing more irritated.

"We went to three other inns; it was the same story. We spent the day looking, I think we've just been lured here," Armen explained.

"Stay there for one more day I'll see what we can find out from here."

Tatiana slept well. She woke up with Tony in the bed next to her still fully clothed, she was too. It then hit her, the meltdown and telling Tony about her life on the run. Tony woke up, saw her eyes were open, and put his hand on hers.

"Are you okay?" he asked.

"Yes, thank you."

"I want you to know you can trust me. I'll be here to help you out of this mess you're in if you want me to."

"The first thing you need to understand is these are extremely dangerous people; I don't want you to get involved."

"I want to be there for you. It sounds like you've been through hell with all the worry. I'm sure we can figure something out. Let's start by getting in a good greasy breakfast."

Breakfast consisted of bacon, eggs, home fries, toast, and lots of coffee. It got their brains working. Tatiana told Tony of her work at the bank, one of the Zurich accounts, and the shell companies that were created. Tony was impressed by what Tatiana accomplished so far explaining that he was an active trader. There might be a way to trade some of the money, make enough to live off, and give the amount that's in the account to the bratva with hopes they would then leave her alone.

"That sounds like a great plan, but there's no guarantee that we'll make money trading, especially in today's market," Tatiana pointed out.

"I agree. Then you'll just have to continue running but if the plan works, we can get them off your back."

Tony walked Tatiana back to the Marriott and then headed back to his hotel. The plan was to meet up in a couple of hours. Tatiana couldn't believe her luck meeting Tony. It was the first time since this all started that there looked like there might be an end in sight. She put a call into Malcolm and instructed him to wire the funds from the Warburg account to the Caymans.

Two hours later Tony was back, and they were hatching a plan. He was armed with charts explaining a strategy he thought would work in this market, shorting. Tatiana heard of shorting before but didn't know how it worked in practice. Tony explained the mechanics of it, you pick a stock that you expect to go down in value and borrow those shares. When it goes down to the point you expect you buy the shares to cover the ones you borrowed keeping the difference between the amount of the loaned shares and the purchased shares.

"So, if IBM is trading at $100 you borrow a share at $100. When it goes down to $80 you buy the share and use it to cover the loaned one, netting $20," Tatiana summed up.

"Exactly, you keep the $20 minus any loan and commission costs," Tony added. "But keep in mind if IBM goes up to $125 you would lose $25, if $130 the loss would be $30. You have to put in some safeguards."

"Okay, I like it. When do we get started?"

"There's other ways to play a falling market, buying put options."

Tatiana knew a little about options. You buy calls when bullish and buy puts when bearish, but she had never made such trades. She was glad to have Tony showing her the ropes.

"Step one we set up an account and fund it, then we do our homework. How much do you want to start with?"

"I'll tell you soon. Tony don't take it personally. I'm going to have someone check you out first. Do you have a problem with that?"

"Olga, you're a smart woman. Check away, I'll write down all my information. I don't want you worrying."

With Tony's information in hand, Tatiana asked him if he'd like to meet for dinner. When he left, she called Malcolm at home and told him of the plan.

"I'll have him checked out. Give me a day, with everything he's provided it won't take long."

Olga and Tony met in the Marriott lobby. Tony was worried about Olga and didn't want her wandering New York alone. Dinner led to drinks and a few hours later they were back at the Marriott.

"Olga, I need to return home to Alexandria tomorrow."

"What time we're you planning to leave?"

"After lunch."

"Meet me for lunch."

"How can I refuse lunch with you?" Tony, put his hands around Olga's waist and gave her a long passionate kiss. "I'll pick you up here at noon."

It didn't take long for Pavel to find the recording device on Mikheil's phone line. The question was who put it there, was it the FSB or the bratva. It was Litskevich who tipped off Katerina about Tatiana's whereabouts, if they were tapping Mikheil's phone why would he do that. Pavel concluded that it was likely the bratva. Mikheil wasn't going to like it, but it was time for him to move again.

Naturally, the next stop was Olena's, and as expected the exact same device was found on her phone line. Mikheil, Olena, and Jacques were reunited at the Ritz under the watch of the security team. Frustration with them was obvious, how long were they going to have to live like this.

Friday, December 20, 1996

For the first time in days Tatiana got a solid night's sleep. She lay in bed thinking about everything that transpired over the past week; it had been nuts. This constant running had to stop. One bad move and she would end up like Lev. The thought of that made her worry about Tony. She told him about Lev and the people she was up against, he just seemed naïve about it all. She would do everything she could to keep him in the background, out of their reach.

Tatiana found herself singing in the shower as she was getting ready for her lunch date. The last time she felt this way was with Matthew. Based on everything that happened she was glad things hadn't gone further. Should she do the same with Tony. She would reiterate the risks involved in being associated with her at lunch.

"You look great," Tony said as Olga stepped out of the elevator.

"You're not so bad yourself," she said taking his hand and admiring the suit jacket.

"I know this great place for lunch, it's nothing fancy. They have massive deli sandwiches that are the best in the city."

"It will be my treat," Tatiana insisted.

They walked a few blocks and ended up at the bustling Carnegie Deli. The sandwiches were massive, and the place smelled like heaven. It reminded Tatiana of a place from home that was one of her favorites.

Between bites, Tony explained he needed to get back home. He had trades to monitor, and it was difficult to do without being on the computer. Tatiana, putting her hand on Tony's, asked him to stay another day. We can explore the city together and go out partying tonight. It didn't take much arm twisting, looking into Olga's beautiful blue eyes he said, "okay."

"There is something I need to do; you can come with me. I'll stop at the library, tend to my trades and show you a few things on the computer."

"That will be great."

On the way to the library, Tatiana stopped back at her hotel room. While Tony waited in the lobby, she called Malcolm.

"Tatiana, how are you?"

"Much better now, Malcolm. Did everything go okay with the fund transfer?"

"Yes, you are all set to access the funds from the Caymans. If you need to move those funds anywhere else let me know."

"That's great, thank you. Were you able to complete that background check for me?"

"Yes, you have nothing to worry about with this guy. He's had his own trading firm for five years, he graduated from the University of Buffalo with a finance degree, no criminal record just a bunch of speeding tickets, and he's owned his house in Virginia for three years. He seems solid."

When Malcolm mentioned the University of Buffalo Tatiana thought of her friend Cindy from scuba class. "Malcolm, thank you so much. I have to run but I'll call soon with an update on everything."

"It's been my pleasure. Stay safe."

Tatiana returned to the lobby taking Tony's arm. "Let's go to the library."

On the walk over Tatiana told Tony that she was talking to an advisor, and the check she ran on him came back clean. She apologized for doing it, but she couldn't take any chances. Tony understood, "you'd be a fool not to do what you did," he said.

"Tony, there's one other thing."

"What's that?"

"My name isn't Olga, it's Tatiana."

"It's so nice to meet you, Tatiana," Tony said stopping and planting a kiss on her lips.

As they were leaving the library Tatiana's purse started buzzing. At first, she didn't notice it, it was Tony that pointed it out. Tatiana froze and fumbled for the buzzing phone. It was the one marked OST.

"Shit."

"What is it?"

Tatiana held up a finger. "Hello."

"Hello, comrade."

"What do you want?"

"You know. We are not going to stop until we get the money, all of it."

Tatiana hung up the phone. "It was them. They want the money."

"They have no idea where you are, right?" Tony asked with a worried look.

"No." Tatiana explained to Tony what she did to see where they were getting their information from. "We're safe for now but I don't know for how long."

"It sounds like they are trying to scare you and get you running."

"I think you're right."

"Let's stick with the plan."

"Let's make the next plan a drink," Tatiana said.

"I have the perfect place." Tony took Tatiana's hand, and they walked for about 20 minutes to the Museum of Modern Art. The wind was starting to pick up and it was nice to get in out of the cold. "We'll go up to the café, have a drink, and then check out the art." It was the perfect afternoon on a chilly day.

As they left the museum Tony asked if she had dinner plans. "Yes, as a matter of fact, I do," Tatiana replied. She could see the disappointed look on Tony's face and squeezed his hand. It's called room service. They made their way back to Tatiana's room, but food wasn't on their minds. Within seconds of entering the room, Tony pulled Tatiana close to him kissing her gently on the lips. Tatiana slid her tongue between Tony's lips and clothes started falling to the floor. Tatiana fell backward on the bed now wearing nothing, and soon after Tony was on top thrusting into her. Moans and hot breath hit Tony's ear as he drove into Tatiana over and over again. Minutes later there were simultaneous orgasms, and Tony collapsed on top of her. The only sound heard for the next few minutes was breathing and a few minutes later Tatiana's voice, "let's do it again."

Saturday, December 21, 1996

Armen received word from the guys surveilling Mikheil and Olena that they hadn't been seen in over a day. He realized they were discovered, both had been quickly moved; there was no point continuing to watch for them. A lightbulb went off in his head.

"Sasha, both parties have left their homes and haven't been seen in more than a day. It confirms my suspicion we've been made. They must have discovered our bugs and sent us on a wild geese chase."

"You mean goose chase."

"No, there's two of them. It makes them geeses."

"Fuck you! What now?"

"I'll call Raffael and see if he's come up with anything."

Raffael's orders were clear, "stay there. I might have something."

Tatiana and Tony's morning started with an hour-long love-making session, room service, and then more marathon sex. Tatiana was thoroughly impressed with Tony's stamina; he was an animal but after a room service lunch a break was necessary. They lay naked in bed propped up by pillows and watched The Bridges of Madison County. Tatiana appreciated that Tony didn't complain and call it sappy, she saw a real romantic side to him. After the movie ended the pair were at it again and started laughing when they looked outside. It was dark.

"Let's jump in the shower, head out and get some dinner," Tatiana said slapping Tony's bare ass.

"Good idea. If we stay in here, you're going to kill me."

They jumped in a taxi making their way to a seafood restaurant overlooking the Hudson. Tatiana immediately took control of the evening ordering a bottle of champagne and a seafood platter that was three tiers high. It had dozens of oysters, clams, shrimp, crab claws, and lobster tails. Halfway through the seafood feast, Tatiana ordered another bottle of champagne, they continued devouring the tiers of seafood. Now drinking coffee and Grand Marnier Tony asked Tatiana how much money they were going to be working with.

"Ninety million dollars," Tatiana casually replied.

Tony choked on his Grand Marnier. "Ninety million dollars?"

"Yep. Can I get some cheesecake?" Tatiana said to their waiter who was walking by.

"No wonder those guys are after you. We have some work to do."

"Does that scare you?"

"No."

"If it does, I understand. I won't blame you for walking away. It is crazy."

"I'm in, but we need to put a plan together."

"Tomorrow," Tatiana said.

"Okay. Let's go to my place tomorrow, we'll take the train."

"I would love to see where you live," Tatiana held her snifter up and they toasted.

"Nostrovia."

Sunday, December 22, 1996

Raffael, despite a dislike for his old boss, had to admire Voshkolup. What would he do in this situation. He'd reach out for help even knowing there would be a price to pay for such a move. Raffael picked up the phone and made the dreaded call.

"Nico, it's Mohammed Raffael."

"Who?"

You fuck went through his mind. "Raffael, Boris Voshkolup's guy."

"I'm sorry about Boris. What can I do for you?"

"I need help finding someone."

"Come and see me, we'll discuss it." Nico Yadin wasn't stupid, he wasn't about to talk business over an easily tapped phone line.

"I'm in Moscow but two of my guys are close by."

"Have them meet with Louie at the Tatiana in Brooklyn tomorrow."

Coincidence, the *Tatiana* Raffael thought as he hung up.

"Make yourself at home," Tony said as he opened the front door of his historic townhouse.

Tatiana put her bag down in the hall peeking into the living room where there were a few piles of books and papers. She was impressed by his sense of style; it was contemporary and comfortable. The kitchen was on the small side, but she could envision herself cooking up some of her signature dishes there.

"I'll bring your suitcase upstairs," Tony said as he lugged the pairs luggage to the bedroom.

"This is so nice," Tatiana called up to Tony.

Tony came into the kitchen asking Tatiana what she would like to drink, and they settled on water. Tony gave the grand tour that consisted of the basement that had a big couch and large screen TV. It opened to a small nicely landscaped private English garden. Upstairs was a guest room, his office next to it. The office had two bookshelves, one filled with thriller and historic fiction novels, the other with investing, finance, and business books. A large desk, that Tony made, took up a good portion of the room. It had two monitors on it and a computer tucked underneath. The last room he showed her had a king-size bed that was immediately put to use.

A couple of hours later Tony placed an order for Chinese food. They spent the rest of the evening chilling and watching movies. Curled up in his arms Tatiana felt things couldn't be better. She had never been this content before. There was a lot about Tony that reminded her of Matthew; he was tall, and athletic but didn't play any sports as he did.

His hair was short and dark brown whereas Matthew's was longer and blonde. Their personalities were very similar, the difference though was Tony's calmness and confidence. He seemed like someone that couldn't be easily rattled.

"We should call it a night," Tony said as the credits rolled after the second movie. "We're going to have a busy day tomorrow." Upstairs their clothes fell to the floor, Tatiana was relieved to find Tony was just as exhausted as she. They crawled naked under the covers, curled together enjoying each other's scent, and fell asleep.

14

"Tatiana, it's time to get up."

"Let's fuck first."

Tony wasn't about to argue. Breakfast wasn't the most important meal of the day. It was a great start to a day that was going to be filled with some challenges.

"Okay, one more cup of coffee and then we need to get moving on this stuff. First off, we need to get your account set up." Tony got his contact, Rob, at the brokerage firm on the phone, told him his friend Olga needed an account set up, and put Tatiana on the phone with him. The account was set up under LD Travel, the funds would be arriving shortly from the Cayman Islands.

"How much will you be funding the account with?" Rob asked.

"Ninety million dollars," Tatiana said.

"To confirm, you said ninety million dollars," Rob repeated keeping a level tone.

"Yes."

"You will be able to trade on that account immediately when the wire is received, however, you will not be able to withdraw those funds for five days."

"That's fine. So, we're all set?" Tatiana asked surprised at the ease of the process.

"Yes, I'll call you when we receive the funds."

Tatiana called Malcolm, who happened to be in a meeting but excused himself for Tatiana's call. "Tatiana I'll contact the bank now and have the funds transferred. You should be ready to go within the hour."

While waiting for the wire confirmation Tony went to work pulling up a chart of the S&P 500. The pair marveled at how it had risen steadily for the past 10 years with a sharp uptick in the last two years and now a leveling off. He then ran charts for the various sectors for the past year. None of this was foreign to Tatiana, her work at the bank exposed her to this data on a regular basis but what Tony showed her next was where the learning started. Tatiana was used to finance on a macro level, they were about to get into the micro end of things, individual stocks. Tony felt the tech sector was becoming overvalued and a correction was near. The uptick and leveling in the charts indicated this, the price-to-earnings ratios were pointing to that also. Tony's phone rang.

"The funds are in," Rob said.

"I'll tell her."

"The funds are in?"

"Yes," Tony confirmed, his blood pressure rising as he answered her.

"Let's do some trading," Tatiana said playfully.

"Let's go slow." Tony was an experienced trader and had made trades involving tens of thousands of dollars, but this was at a level that created a little discomfort.

The market was open for an hour when Tatiana logged into her new account. She was so glad to have Tony there, if she had tried to navigate the trading platform by herself, she would have given up. It took Tony a half hour to get the platform to his liking on the one monitor. The other monitor had a combination of quotes and charts that were in constant motion in green and red.

"Before we place an actual trade let's do a couple of practice ones first," Tony suggested. "I have been watching this company Neon Lights

345

Software, it's been down for two days." Tony typed in the symbol NNLL and a bid and ask price came up on the monitor, the prices changing every second or so. NNLL was trading for about $58.25 a share, Tony then pulled up the $60 put option contract expiring the third week of January. The bid price was $3.25 and the ask $3.35.

"If we did a buy order, I'd enter it at $3.30 and it would likely go off, it would cost you $330 plus commission for one contract because options are sold in units of a hundred." They watched the price of NNLL bounce around, moving in a range of $.40 over the next 10 minutes. The option price moved up slightly with the mid-price plus or minus 10 cents.

"If we timed it right over this past 10 minutes, we could have made $10?" Tatiana asked.

"Exactly. The volatility is low today because there isn't that much going on in the market. A lot of people are off with Christmas a couple of days away," Tony explained. "It's a good time to learn this stuff."

Tatiana watched Tony enter a trade for his account, now she had something real to work with. She was surprised to see him exit the trade two and a half minutes later.

"Why did you get out of that so quickly?"

"I just made $320 in less than three minutes on a $1,200 trade, not bad."

"That's great. That happens all the time?"

"No, sometimes I lose $320 in an hour. What I do is scalping, most of the trades I hold for less than an hour. We're going to watch the market today, and see if there's something for you." Tony opened Tatiana's account and they watched LPAL which was at a high for the day at $41.60. He pulled up the $40 January put, it was trading for $1.45, he bought 100 puts, total cost $14,500 plus a $150 commission.

"Does that worry you?" he asked Tatiana.

"Not at all."

Immediately, Tony entered a sell order, for all 100 put contracts at $1.60. They watched the LPAL put option price go up, the LP Algorithms stock price was going down. After two minutes the option was at $1.50, after five minutes $1.60, and the limit order was triggered.

"You just made $1,500 minus $300 in commissions."

"That's great!" Tatiana said excitedly. "I can live with $1,200 for five minutes of work."

"Don't get too giddy," Tony cautioned. "It doesn't always go that well."

The pair remained huddled over the computer with Tony pointing out various trend lines and moving averages. He wasn't liking what he was seeing and told Tatiana, "sometimes the best trade is the one you don't make." After a few hours, they called it a day, it was a lot to take in for Tatiana.

"Let's take a nap," Tatiana said grabbing Tony's hand.

Armen and Sasha met with Louie after a thorough pat down at the Tatiana Restaurant in Brooklyn. Louie wore a long-sleeved shirt that didn't hide all the tattoos that ran down his arms and up his neck. He asked a few questions confirming their identity before bringing them to a back room in the restaurant. There sat Nico who was flanked by a large man on either side of him.

"Gentlemen, how was your trip? Please have a seat."

"Good," Armen and Sasha both said.

"What can I do for you gentlemen today?"

"We need some help finding someone."

"Who?"

"Tatiana Belov."

"Why do you want to find Tatiana Belov?"

"She has disappeared with some of our money."

"How much?"

"I don't know."

"Fuck off then. Come back when you know."

Armen and Sasha stood on the boardwalk outside the Tatiana. "That didn't go well," Sasha said.

"I'll call Raffael," Armen said.

Tuesday, December 24, 1996

Tatiana and Tony already started a morning routine that kept them in bed until a half hour before the opening bell. While Tatiana made coffee Tony fired up the computer and did a quick market analysis with CNBC on the TV in the background.

"How's it looking?" Tatiana asked walking into the room with a mug in each hand and wearing one of Tony's shirts.

"Flat. The market will close at 1:00 today because of the holiday, so it will be a slow day."

"I'm fine with that. I have a few phone calls and errands to do."

"Me too. Let's put in a couple of hours this morning and then we'll do our stuff."

Tony closed out a position of his but didn't see anything that caught his eye. Tatiana watched and Tony pointed out some of the things he was watching explaining why he wasn't doing anything. Tatiana was perfectly fine with it; her mind was in other places.

"Tony, would you mind if we called it a day?"

"Not at all. Let's shower, grab some breakfast and do our errands."

Tatiana strolled King Street in Old Town Alexandria, Christmas lights were everywhere, and a dusting of snow had just fallen adding to the festive atmosphere. She wanted to buy something special for Tony, a very nice watch was something she considered but that wasn't his style. King Street was loaded with boutique stores, but nothing was catching her eye, finally, she hailed a taxi. Please take me to a computer store, for a nice tip the driver waited, and Tatiana returned with two store clerks in tow. The clerks each with a loaded cart assisted the driver in loading the cab with the computer gear. With the trunk and the back seat full Tatiana rode back to Tony's in the front seat of the cab.

Tony wasn't home, so the surprise wasn't ruined. Tatiana brought all the boxes to the basement. Wrapping paper, I'm going to need a lot of it. She put a sign on the closed basement door *Do Not Enter – Christmas Surprise*. Back out to King Street she ran returning to a still empty house and wrapped up the gear.

It was a surprise Tatiana didn't run into Tony. His first stop had been a local jewelry store that was buzzing with activity. When the store clerk made it to him, he had already picked out the diamond tennis bracelet. It was just a matter of a final inspection and payment before it was wrapped up in metallic gold paper with a small silver bow. Tony's other stops included the gourmet market, liquor store, and bakery. He was going to attempt cooking duck a l'orange. He wanted Tatiana to have the best Christmas ever, he had fallen for her.

Armen and Sasha were back at Tatiana's, the restaurant, and this time were enjoying some Russian hospitality. Raffael had spoken with Nico telling him there were millions of dollars out there and he would receive a generous cut if Belov was found. Naturally, Yadin's interest spiked. Raffael made it clear that these funds were well hidden and only he had the treasure map, cutting him out would leave a lot of money on the table. Yadin gave Raffael his word that he wouldn't go around him and wanted a guarantee of at least a million dollars if they found her.

The party started after lunch. The restaurant was closed to the public, but it seemed half of the neighborhood was there. A twenty-meter-long buffet of food lined one wall, and the bar employed two bartenders in constant motion pouring shots of vodka and various other concoctions. Music was blasting out from the DJ booth overlooking the dance floor which was beginning to fill up. Armen and Sasha sat at a table with several beautiful women, all curious about life in Moscow. It was a much warmer atmosphere than the previous day. They looked over at the table next to them, there was Louie, he was having a good time, also surrounded by beautiful women and with a dusting of white powder under his nose. He waved them over; the party went to the next level.

Wednesday, December 25, 1996

Tatiana was woken up by Tony whispering, "Merry Christmas" in her ear. She smelled the coffee next to her head on the nightstand and saw the small slender gold-wrapped box.

"Merry Christmas," she responded giving Tony a slow gentle kiss.

"I have something for you," he said nodding to the nightstand.

"I see," Tatiana said picking up the mug and smiling.

"Not that, next to it."

"For me?" Tatiana playfully said putting the coffee down. She removed the silver bow and carefully unwrapped it. "This is beautiful!"

"You really like it?" Tony asked attaching it to her wrist.

"Yes!" she said putting her arms around Tony's neck kissing him. "I have something for you," she said jumping out of bed naked.

"I see."

"Not that, at least not right now. Come on," Tatiana said descending the stairs leading Tony to the basement.

Tony, thoroughly enjoying the view followed like a greyhound after a bunny. "What is all this?" he asked as he reached the bottom of the basement stairs.

"Open them!"

He first unwrapped the computer.

"It's the best and the fastest out there," Tatiana said.

Next Tony unwrapped a monitor. "There's three of them," Tatiana added.

"This is fantastic, baby!"

"There's more," she handed him the box with the laser printer.

"I love it. Thank you."

"I know it's not the most romantic gift, but I have something along those lines in store. You'll just have to wait a bit."

"Baby, all this stuff is fantastic. I'll get it all hooked up today."

"There's another present," Tatiana announced as she darted up the stairs. Tony had an inkling and darted up the stairs after her.

When they finally emerged from the bedroom Tatiana sat on the couch and made Christmas calls to Lily, Anna, and her mother. All of them were doing well and enjoying the holiday season, especially her mama. She had never heard her mother so alive before, it was like talking to a new person. She was making new friends, doing day trips to the French countryside, and discovering new restaurants, there had even been a couple of dates with French gentlemen.

"Make sure you use protection, mama," she joked.

"Tati, please!" Valentina said giggling.

The only calls she couldn't make were to Mikheil and Olena, it would be far too risky for everyone involved. After her calls she went into the kitchen to see what Tony was up to; she heard some clanking of pots and pans and the occasional swear word. Tony was basting a duck and had a couple of pots on the stove cooking up something.

"Wow, I'm impressed. Not only can you cook in bed but in the kitchen too."

Tony put down the baster pulled Tatiana towards him and kissed her neck. "It'll be ready in an hour and then the best part, dessert."

At that moment her purse started buzzing, and both of their hearts sank.

"Merry Christmas, Tatiana Belov. We'll be seeing you before the year is over." The call on the OST phone ended.

The perfect day now had a dark cloud hanging over it. Tony, who listened in on the call tried to make light of it, but it was even difficult for him not to show concern. "Tatiana, you're safe here, let's enjoy the day and we'll work on our plan tomorrow." Tony put on some music and danced around the kitchen, Tatiana kissed him and helped finish preparing the meal. They both knew their plan had to work or things would never be normal.

Thursday, December 26 – Sunday, December 29, 1996

The Christmas Day call changed things. Instead of their morning romp, Tony got out of bed early and finished setting up his Christmas present. The only thing to do now was a couple of trading software downloads and they'd be up and running. Tatiana brought Tony his second cup of coffee and some toast.

"How's it going?"

"Good. We'll be ready to go in 15 minutes."

"I see by the futures the market looks flat again today."

"Yes, I was expecting there might be a Santa Claus rally but so far, it's not looking that way," Tony said while munching on his toast. "Okay, we're all set. I have everything configured. I don't have the third screen set up yet, but I'll work on that after the market closes."

Tatiana noticed that everything on the new setup looked like the old one, but Tony said the larger monitors would make things easier to see and they'd have things processing faster. The bell sounded; the markets were now open.

"I don't have any open positions so we can concentrate on your account today."

"Are you feeling bullish or bearish today?" Tatiana asked.

"So far, it's looking like the markets might be up today, at least according to these charts," Tony said pointing to a monitor.

Within a minute of the market open, Tony pointed out that Analog Digital had taken a sharp dip down while the overall market was moving up. He clicked on the January 105 call for ANDG; it was selling at $4.60. An order was placed to buy 1000 calls at $4.50, and a minute and a half later it went off. "On a scale of 1 to 10, how aggressive do you want to be?"

"A seven," Tatiana replied watching Tony click and type away.

Tony entered a sell order at 4.85, and they sat back and watched. "The market is still going up and it looks like we got ANDG at a low," Tony said to an agreeing Tatiana who had her eyes glued to the monitor.

Analog Digital calls were inching up now with the rest of the market and now at $4.70. "Looking good," Tony said.

The market was starting to level off and Analog Digital wasn't going up as quickly as it had been. "Let's get out now," Tatiana said.

Tony lowered the sell price to $4.80, and three seconds later the order was executed. In the first 20 minutes, they were up $30,000 and by lunchtime $57,000.

"So far so good, but I don't want you to think it's always going to be this easy," Tony cautioned. His words of wisdom were confirmed on the next trade that cost them $34,000. The day ended with them up $23,000.

It was Friday the last trading day of the week and one of the last trading days for the year. Tony was anticipating a busy one in the bullish direction. At market open he and Tatiana were huddled, eyes glued to the monitors. It wasn't long before Tony was typing and clicking away. By lunchtime, they were up $19,600 and another $6,000 after that giving them more than $25,000 on the day. Tatiana was pleased with how the day went but Tony was a little disappointed, with the market action he was hoping for a better day.

"It was a good day, honey. Don't be so tough on yourself."

"Any day we're in the black is a good day but with the money we're putting to work I was hoping we'd do better."

"There's always tomorrow," Tatiana said rubbing his shoulders. "Let's have a drink before dinner."

Tony and Tatiana had a nice weekend with Tony taking charge and being the tour guide. They jumped on the Metro and got off by the mall near the Capitol building walking to the Washington Monument. Tony pulled out a camera and wanted to take pictures of Tatiana, but she wasn't going to allow it. "Another time," she said.

They continued their walk and were soon ascending the steps of the Lincoln Memorial. These were all places Tatiana had seen in pictures and were now right in front of her. Even with the gray overcast sky, it was all so beautiful she thought. It was time for something to eat and a refreshing beverage, Tony knew just the spot, The Old Ebbitt Grill. Tatiana sat at the historic bar staring up at the mounts, an antelope and walrus among them. Tony introduced Tatiana as Olga to one of the bartenders he knew there, Andrea. She was bubbly and very chatty but not revealing to Olga any of Tony's drunken exploits there. The pair ended the day with an after-dinner drink at the Round Robin bar in the nearby Willard hotel. This place was straight out of a time capsule Tatiana thought.

"This place is fantastic."

"Many presidents have had drinks here."

"Imagine if these walls could talk," said Tatiana.

15

Tatiana's purse was buzzing but she was still sleeping.

"Tatiana, your purse," Tony said squeezing her shoulder.

Tatiana's heart was pounding as she pulled the OST phone from her purse. "What?" she yelled into the receiver.

"We're coming for our money, we know about the accounts," Armen said and hung up.

Tatiana and Tony lay in bed looking at each other. "We're going to stick with the plan. We'll give them the money once we hit 10 million dollars, that should put an end to it."

"It's going to take a while to make 10 million," Tatiana fretted.

"We can do it," Tony said confidently. "It's just going to take some time."

"Tony, don't get mad at me, but there's more money."

"What are you talking about?"

"There's another account with 60 million dollars in it."

"You're shitting me."

"No. I'll make a call today and have it transferred. We're going to have to be more aggressive or I'm afraid we'll, I'll run out of time."

"You're just full of surprises. I did some research on Abramov and he was worth billions. It shouldn't be a surprise he had 90 million here and 60 million there."

"There were also a few offshore businesses, but I haven't had a chance to look into those. I don't think they are anything significant."

"We'll do some research on them today."

Tatiana put a call into Malcolm, he was surprised to hear from her so quickly. Tatiana explained the plan to him, and Malcolm agreed it was a sound one.

"I had another client that had a run-in with the Russian mafia and it didn't end well," Malcolm said and immediately regretted it.

"Thanks, Malcolm," Tatiana said sarcastically.

"I'm sorry, I'm just worried about you. I'll transfer 30 million into each company from the Credit Suisse account over the next few days. I want to try to avoid attracting attention."

"Thank you, Malcolm."

"Stay safe, Tatiana."

It was still very early; the markets wouldn't open for another three hours. Tony and Tatiana had breakfast and spent a couple of hours studying data and charts on the computer. It was the last full day of trading for the year, they were prepared for a busy morning when the bell finally sounded.

Tatiana wasn't kidding when she told Tony they'd have to get aggressive, as Tony entered 5,000 calls for a new startup IQrideshare, Tatiana said, "make it 10,000."

Tony typed in 8,000. "If it goes down a little, we'll pick up 2,000 more."

"Sounds like a plan," Tatiana responded.

There were many stretches of the morning that seemed like they were moving in slow motion, but the afternoon moved along at an even slower clip. By the time the closing bell sounded the pair had made

$207,000. They sat there afterward looking at the pad of paper that Tatiana had been keeping track of their profits on and exhaled. Their adrenaline was still pumping. They read each other's minds and ran to the bedroom.

Tuesday, December 31 – Friday, January 3, 1997

New Year's Eve half day of trading was low key with really nothing really happening, the gains totaled about $4,000.

Tatiana and Tony were tired and a bit stressed; a romantic evening at home was in store. This time Tatiana cooked up a roast beef dinner complete with roasted potatoes and a Yorkshire pudding that Lily had taught her to make. She offered to make a borsch, but Tony's wrinkled-up nose made it a pass. Frigid weather had encapsulated the entire mid and northeast making New Year's Day a good one to stay in watch movies and play board games like Monopoly, Risk, and Scrabble.

It was also a time for them to get to know each other more and what made them tick. Tony recounted a summer when he was nine and he and a friend started a scrap metal business using a rebuilt discarded old wagon. They scoured the neighborhood for old washers or dryers, car parts, and anything that would fetch them a penny a pound. A car battery was worth a dollar, it was a jackpot item. It was a profitable summer with each of them pulling in almost $40.

Tatiana, along with Lev, made money as kids picking strawberries and doing chores at local farms. Money for either of them was never taken for granted. The stock market wasn't part of any conversation. It was a mini vacation before their work started again on Thursday.

Thursday arrived in a flash and Tatiana and Tony were huddled at the computer. Tony explained that January was usually a bullish month, but he was growing weary. That day was a crazy one with about fifteen trades executed, almost all on the bullish side. It was also, their most profitable one too, netting them a whopping $335,000. When the bell closed out the trading session Tatiana was dancing around the office waving her hands in the air. Tony sat there staring at the screen, days like this were good but he wasn't going to relax until they accomplished their goal.

Friday the trading wasn't going so well and during the middle of the trading session, one of Tatiana's phones rang. She was relieved it wasn't the OST phone but surprised to hear Mikheil's voice.

"Happy New Year, Tatiana!"

"Mikheil, Happy New Year! How are you? Are you safe?"

"Yes, all is well here. I won't go into any details but Olena and myself are well."

"How is Jacques?"

"Olena is spoiling the hell out of him, he is great."

"Good, I miss him and you guys so much."

"I snuck away to make this call and don't want to take any more chances, but I was dying wondering how you were doing."

"I am good and safe and so glad to hear you and Olena are."

"I'm going to go but will try and call again fairly soon."

"Thank you for calling, give Jacques and Olena a hug for me."

Tears started streaming from Tatiana's eyes. Tony got up from the computer and hugged her. He knew she was missing her friends and home despite the fact she never talked about it. Tony sat back down, closing out the third trade of the day for another loss. It was their worst day ever, by the close they were down $195,000.

Saturday, January 4 – Sunday, January 5, 1997

The weekend, for the most part, was uneventful. Tatiana and Tony managed to get out and walk around Old Town a couple of times in the still frigid weather. Both of them were more low-key than usual and they noticed it in each other. Tatiana was feeling pangs of guilt for bringing Tony into her mess, but he never once complained and seemed to enjoy the challenge of the situation. Even if the ten-million-dollar goal was met she would never be able to live with herself if Tony was ever harmed. There were sleepless nights thinking about keeping him, them, safe from unrelenting predators.

16

Monday morning Tony excitedly pointed out on a couple of charts why he thought it would be a good day to go short, adding that upcoming economic data could drive the market sharply lower.

"But the futures are up today," Tatiana commented.

"Ya, I see that, but too much good news might signal time for a pullback," he insisted.

That Monday the market opened higher on positive data; Tony started to buy puts on several companies. By 11:30 they had 3 million dollars of open put contracts. Tatiana just sat back silently watching Tony do his thing. Both of their nerves were frayed to the point lunch was skipped and then at 2:00 word from the Fed chief came out that there could be a need for tightening. The S&P dropped 65 points in a minute and continued falling for the next half hour. Tony started typing and clicking furiously while Tatiana quietly looked on. By 3:15 all of the put contracts were closed and they sat up 1.17 million dollars on the day. They both sat there with Tatiana holding Tony's hand in silence. There wasn't any dancing just two nervous smiles.

With a million-dollar reward, Nico was quite busy too. He ascertained that the Belov woman had flown into New York, staying at the Marriott by Times Square. He also had been provided security footage of her with a tall handsome guy, someone according to the footage she was fond of.

"Armen, what is the phone number you have for the Belov woman?" he asked at their dinner meeting.

"Do you know where she is?"

"We're getting close. She flew into New York last week and was staying at the Marriott."

"How did you find that out?"

"Are you writing a fucking book? What is the number you have for her?"

Armen reluctantly read it to Nico who grabbed the piece of paper from his hand. He pulled a burner phone from his pocket and called it.

"Hello, Tatiana," Tatiana and Tony were both listening at the dinner table, he had called during their evening meal.

"Who is this?" Tatiana said into the OST phone, not recognizing the voice.

"I could be cliché and say your worst fucking nightmare but instead you can call me Phil."

"What do you want Phil?"

"The money, I know you have it, and it doesn't belong to you. I'm the one that will be collecting it, all of it."

"What makes you think I have it?" Tatiana said trying to stop her voice from quivering.

"Cut the shit. I know you were staying at the Marriott in New York and were there with that tall friend of yours. It's just a matter of time until I hunt you down. Trust me you'll be much better off if you sit down with me and make arrangements for an amicable transfer of the funds."

"I'll think about it."

"Think fast, I'm giving you 72 hours before all hell breaks loose." The phone went dead.

Tuesday, January 7 – Thursday, January 9, 1997

The pressure on Tatiana and Tony was now becoming unbearable, it looked like the goal set wouldn't be possible. It was the middle of the trading week and they quietly sat in front of the computer. Based on his early morning research Tony still felt bearish, the overall sentiment of the market had changed, and sellers outnumbered buyers. The S&P futures were down 38 points when the market opened.

Tony went in aggressively buying puts mainly on companies in the tech sector. He was repeating a strategy that had worked well for him the day before. In the first half hour, they were up $95,000, Tony had a rhythm going bouncing between one stock and another. By 10:30 they were up $160,000 and at lunchtime $215,000 with most of the puts bought that day still held. At 2:20 the market took a dip lower, Tony did his thing, and by 3:00 all the positions were closed, and they were up $615,000. To date, Tatiana's account was up about 2 million dollars after commissions.

"Tony, I think we should call it quits. We're up a couple of million, I can live with that."

"We can stop now but we're doing so well. I think I can get us to the 10 million."

"Tony, I'm sure you can but time isn't on our side."

"We have a couple of days, no matter what I'm not going to let anything happen to you."

That evening watching a movie Tatiana's mind was drifting. The action movie, with a lot of elaborate stunts, had her thinking. She needed to come up with a plan if these thugs kept coming for her. That night she tossed and turned, her mind was racing and wouldn't turn off. It wasn't until it started getting light outside that she finally fell asleep. An hour later Tony was waking her with a cup of coffee in his hand.

"Tony, I didn't get much sleep, please wake me just before the market opens."

A couple of hours later they were drinking coffee and waiting for the opening bell. Tatiana was going to be the one entering trades today, but she wasn't feeling up to it and left Tony in the driver's seat. As they expected the market dropped at the open and a few profitable trades were made but 25 minutes into the session, a couple of Fed governors made dovish comments that sent the S&P up half a percent. Tony scrambled to close the few open positions, but the damage had been done, they had lost $430,000. Tony believed the market had overreacted and an hour later bought a large number of puts on three different companies. Within ten minutes of the market close they were down another $355,000.

"We should hold them until tomorrow," Tatiana suggested.

"I really think we should close them now and take the loss, it could be worse tomorrow."

Tatiana reluctantly agreed and the loss was realized. It was a terrible day, total loss $785,000. It was a quiet dinner.

The next day, after a pep talk from Tony, the pair were at it again, trading. The market was down, and Tatiana's hold strategy would have significantly cut their losses from the day before. There was no crystal ball for this stuff she told Tony. Tony felt bad about the decision but had stuck with his trading plan and today it was paying off. By lunch, they were up $290,000 and finished the day in the black, plus $445,000.

Over dinner that evening the OST phone started buzzing, Tony and Tatiana dreaded that sound but weren't surprised by it. Tatiana answered and the call was brief.

"I want the money tomorrow, no excuses."

"I can't have it for you tomorrow," Tatiana said. This response surprised Tony.

"You and your friend will be dead within 48 hours then."

"Go fuck yourself," Tatiana calmly said, really surprising Tony whose jaw dropped.

"You have no idea who you're talking to."

"I will have the money for you, but you'll have to wait."

"Wait, what the fuck for?" Nico inquired.

"The money is spread out all over the place. I need time to pull it together."

"How much time?"

"Five days."

"You have four." The phone went dead.

"Fuck," Tony said exhaling.

"We have some work to do."

By the look in Tatiana's eyes, Tony wasn't about to challenge her. "Let's do it," he said.

Tatiana disappeared into the basement after dinner and called Malcolm who was about to climb into bed. "I need you to wire the balance of funds from the SGW account to the Caymans and arrange something for me without any questions."

"I'll get on it first thing in the morning, Tatiana."

Friday, January 10 – Sunday, January 12, 1997

The closing bell sounded on Friday and Tatiana and Tony hugged, their hearts pounding from trades that were closed just minutes earlier.

"I'll get the champagne," Tatiana announced darting from the office. Tony just sat there waiting for the adrenaline to dissipate from his body. Tatiana was back with a cold bottle of Veuve Clicquot and handed it to Tony. "You do the honors."

While Tony popped the bottle open Tatiana danced around the office clinking the glasses together singing, "we made 3 million dollars, we made 3 million dollars."

Tony filled their glasses and made a toast. "To a long and happy life for my love." Tatiana gave Tony a long passionate kiss and they took a big swig of champagne. It was a fantastic day, but a gray cloud was still hanging over them. Over dinner, they had a conversation that at one point got a little heated. Tatiana was happy being up about four and a half million dollars and was insisting they should quit while they were ahead. Tony was adamant that while they weren't likely to reach their 10-million-dollar goal he could get them to 6 or 7 million.

I'll think about it, we'll talk about it more over the weekend. I don't want to fight; I want to ride you.

Tony had no quarrel with that.

On Saturday the final leg of their trading plan was put in place. They would trade for an hour on Monday morning, transfer all the funds to one Cayman account, then take the train to New York and meet with "Phil" aka Nico. All the funds minus their trading gains would be wired to him and they would live happily ever after. Tatiana knew in the back of her mind that was unlikely. She loved that Tony was so trusting but from her experiences, these people they were dealing with were ruthless animals that would kill someone over $10,000. To them, she was a golden goose that would keep laying prized eggs. It wasn't going to end there. With Malcolm's help, she was putting a backup plan in place.

Feeling that the heat was temporarily off, Tony and Tatiana enjoyed a nice dinner Saturday night at a steakhouse overlooking the Potomac. It was a beautiful night with the beams of a full moon bouncing off the water. They walked back to Tony's house through Old Town's quiet tree-lined historic streets. They held hands each deep in thought about the upcoming days.

Once home Tony took Tatiana's hand and led her upstairs. After two hours of passionate lovemaking, they fell asleep. Several hours later Tatiana awoke; it's time she thought. While Tony soundly slept Tatiana crept around the bedroom throwing some clothes and toiletries into a carry-on bag and slipped out. Before leaving she jotted a note for Tony and left it on the kitchen counter.

Sunday morning Tony woke up alone in bed and figured Tatiana was already up, he went downstairs and saw the note. His only word was "fuck." He immediately called Tatiana's cellphone, and as expected no answer. He left a message, "baby, don't do this. Call me, please."

Tatiana was halfway to New York when the call came in. She felt terrible about her middle-of-the-night departure but knew what had to be done. A couple of hours later Tatiana was exiting Penn Station walking south and checking into the first decent hotel she came across. She had just put her bag on the bed, and her phone buzzed. With a couple of seconds of hesitation, she answered.

"Hi, Tony."

"Tatiana, where are you?"

"Tony, I'm okay. I don't want you to worry."

"Baby, of course, I'm worried."

"Please let me take care of this. I'll call you in the morning."

"Please tell me where you are, I'll come right away."

"No, Tony. I'm safe, I'll call you in the morning. I love you." Before Tony could say another thing Tatiana hung up.

Tatiana was tired from her trip and crawled into bed putting the TV on. She found herself starting to nod off when her purse started buzzing. "Stop Tony," she said, but it wasn't Tony. It was the OST phone.

"Tatiana, I hope you have my money."

"I will have it tomorrow."

"Your life and Tony's depend on it. You will meet me tomorrow at noon. I will call you with the location."

Fuck, he knows about Tony, she thought. "I need until 4:00, the money will be wired to you."

"You will be here for that."

"We can't handle it over the phone?"

"We can but if something goes wrong Mr. Tony London of Alexandria, Virginia will disappear off the face of the earth."

"I will meet you."

Immediately Tatiana started dialing Tony's number but stopped. If they know his name and where he lives, they're probably watching him. For all she knew, they could be outside this Hyatt. She checked to make sure the door was locked and hunkered down for a sleepless night. What had she done pulling poor Tony into this she thought over and over.

"You're in New York, aren't you?"

"Tony, I'm safe that's all you need to know."

"Tatiana, you have me worried sick; I didn't sleep all night."

"I'm going to get this settled. If you want to trade this morning, go ahead just don't lose more than we made. I don't know if they know exactly what was in the accounts, but I don't want to take any chances."

"You're not going to meet with them?"

"Tony, I have this under control. No later than 1:00 wire the amount we started with to the Cayman account, I'll handle the wire from there."

"You're just going to wire them the money?"

"Yes. Tony, I have to go. Call me when the wire transfer is complete. I love you."

"I love you, Tatiana."

Raffael hadn't been able to get ahold of Nico and was getting really pissed off. He had done his homework, got the balance of one of the Swiss bank accounts, and was stunned to find out it was more than 90 million dollars. Those funds had been recently transferred. He also knew another account at another bank that had a large balance was recently closed. He had no idea about the third account but knew there was a lot of money out there. If Nico fucked him there would be a war of epic proportions. Armen told him that he and Sasha were watching the Tatiana Restaurant hoping the Belov woman would turn up there. They took turns, one in the car watching the street entrance and one on a bench watching the boardwalk entrance. Their surveillance started a half hour before the restaurant opened, they would be there all night if need be.

Tony, out of habit, found himself sitting in front of his computer 45 minutes before the market opened for the week. He was feeling frazzled and missing his sidekick but noticed signs that the market was due for a drop. Another Fed governor was making hawkish comments adding to an already pessimistic climate and the charts in front of him confirmed it.

He felt sure that despite the futures being slightly lower the market was about to be pummeled. Keeping Tatiana's orders in mind he entered 4 million dollars of market orders for puts on six different companies, they would all go off at the opening bell. It was a risky move that removed any control he'd have with limit orders, but he had to trust his gut on this.

As the opening bell sounded confirmation pings emanated from the computer seconds later, he now had most of their profits on the line. Five minutes in the market steadily inched up and Tony was feeling ill. His plan would have him exit by 10:00, 10:15 at the latest no matter where the market was.

The normally cool, calm and collected Tony was standing in front of the computer monitor yelling at it. "Come on you motherfucker," as the market was still slowly inching upwards, he was down over a million dollars in the first 10 minutes. By 9:45 the market was starting to lose the gains of the previous 15 minutes and was soon dropping. It was dropping fast, and Tony was entering his sell orders. At 9:57 the first ping came from the computer; one position closed. Three minutes later half the positions were closed but now the market was bouncing upwards and at 10:11 was only down 15 points. With half the positions closed Tony decided to extend his timeline to 10:30 but that was it. He was glad he did because over the next 15 minutes, the market dropped to the lows of the session and Tony was out and up 1.65 million dollars on the day. He turned off the computer, went to the kitchen, and grabbed the Grand Marnier bottle. It was a double shot lighter when he put it back.

Tatiana had a lunch meeting at one of her favorite New York City restaurants, the Carnegie Deli. The man she was meeting was 6' 4" and full of muscle. He saw Tatiana enter and waved from a table in the back corner.

"Hi, you must be Tatiana."

"Yes, it's nice to meet you. Troy is it?"

"Yes, please have a seat. I took the liberty of ordering a couple of different sandwiches."

"They both look good," Tatiana said opting for the pastrami.

"Malcolm tells me you need my help."

"Yes, I have some nasty characters after me."

"I don't know what he told you but I'm not a bone breaker."

"No, no. Troy, I need your help with a couple of things. You're from California, right?"

The two of them ate their massive sandwiches and Tatiana laid out her plan. Troy's initial reaction was a firm, hard no. He changed his mind when the topic of compensation was brought up.

Tony was getting very antsy. He called Tatiana and left a message on her phone, the wire transfer had gone through without a problem, and all the funds were in the Cayman account.

"Tatiana, where have you been?"

"Sorry Tony, I was just grabbing some lunch and didn't hear the phone. Thank you for doing that, you're the best. Did you trade today?"

"Yes," Tony said, trying his best to sound coy.

"And?"

"I made a bit more money."

"Great," Tatiana said with an obvious sound of relief. "How much is a bit?"

"1.65 million dollars."

"No fucking way!" Tatiana screamed. "That is fantastic! That puts us up over 6 million."

"You, baby."

"No, us! We are a team."

"Take care of the wire and come home."

"I will. I'll see you tonight. Don't go anywhere, wait for me. I love you and will see you soon."

"I lo…" The phone went dead.

Tatiana was fixing her hair into a bun when the OST phone rang. "Be at the Tatiana Restaurant in Brooklyn at 4:00, don't be late or Tony will be minced meat." She didn't recognize the voice but that didn't surprise her.

"I'll be there." She abruptly hung up trying to give the impression she was in control. She had an hour to make sure she had the bank information, put on her disguise that consisted of sunglasses, and grabbed a cab. Just before she left her room, she made a call.

"The meeting is on for the Tatiana Restaurant in Brooklyn at 4:00, I'm leaving now."

"10-4," was the response back.

Tatiana got out of the taxi, entering the Tatiana from the street entrance. She didn't notice the eyes watching her from a car parked across the street. Sasha immediately saw her but wasn't positive it was the Belov woman. After the door closed behind her, he got out of the car and reported his sighting to Armen who was on the boardwalk bench.

Seconds after entering Tatiana was met by Louie. "May I help you?"

"I'm here to see Phil, I mean Nico. I'm Tatiana Belov," as she said this she fought a quiver in her voice.

"Your purse," Tatiana reluctantly handed it to the tattooed man who pawed through it. Another man appeared with a metal detector and wanded her. "Come with me."

She was led back to a man in his fifties with a receding hairline that reminded her of an uncle she hadn't seen since childhood. "Hello, I'm Nico," he said with a bellowing voice and remained seated. "Have a seat, Miss Belov. Would you care for anything to drink?"

"A glass of white wine, please."

"Louie," Nico said.

Louie called out, "a glass of white wine."

"I could have done that," Nico said rolling his eyes and shaking his head. "How was your trip from Alexandria?"

"Uneventful," Tatiana said trying to sound casual.

"You have something for me?"

"If you think 185 million dollars is something, then yes. We'll need a computer. Do you have one of those?"

Nico smiled. "Of course, follow me." Tatiana with the glass of wine in hand was led to an elaborate office at the top of a flight of dingy stairs.

"The wire will come from funds that are in the Caymans."

"What a coincidence that is where my account is too, they won't have to travel far."

With the computer in front of her Tatiana tapped away. They waited in silence with eyes hardly blinking waiting for the confirmation. Minutes later a message appeared on the screen – '*Transfer Complete*' followed by a sixteen-digit confirmation number. Tatiana stood up and said, "I take it this will conclude our business, and Tony and I will have no further worries."

"You're good as gold Miss Belov. Would you like to stay for a nice Russian dinner?"

"No thank you," Tatiana descended the stairs heading briskly to the exit.

The taxi that dropped her off pulled up seconds later now facing the opposite direction and she sped off.

Armen and Sasha did a quick U-turn following the taxi, Troy was following Armen and Sasha.

Tatiana's phone rang. "You called it, you are being followed."

"Thank you. Stay on them and we'll proceed with the plan."

Back at the hotel Tatiana called Tony and told him everything went without a hitch, she would try and make it home that evening but could be delayed, she would explain later. "Please stay put and I'll see you later tonight or early in the morning."

"Are you sure everything is all right?"

"Yes, it's all good. Stay put, I'll see you very soon."

Tony was relieved. He could tell from Tatiana's voice it had gone well but why the delay he wondered.

Tatiana emerged from the Hyatt at 11:10 to a surprised Armen who almost missed her. She was wearing jeans and a heavy, puffy red coat, her blonde hair was whipped about by a strong breeze as she climbed into a taxi in front of the hotel. "There she is," Armen said thumping a sleeping Sasha in the chest.

Sasha still half asleep asked, "are we going to grab her?"

"No, not yet. Raffael is waiting to hear from Nico first. He just wants her followed."

It had been half an hour and they were following the taxi along Harlem River Drive. "Where the fuck are they going?" Armen said to a shrugging Sasha.

Finally, the taxi stopped, Tatiana paid and exited the cab at McNally Plaza. She walked for several minutes and was now walking across the arched Washington Bridge. Armen and Sasha were on foot following her and realized it couldn't be more obvious what they were doing with no one else in sight.

"What the fuck is she doing?" Sasha asked.

Tatiana stopped and stood in the middle of the bridge looking down at the Harlem River below. It looked like she was then tying the laces on her boot. She straightened and turned to Armen and Sasha who were trying to look like sightseers giving them the finger. Tatiana threw her legs over the bridge railing and just sat there. Four and a half seconds later her body crashed into the river.

"What the fuck just happened?" Armen yelled at Sasha who was standing with his mouth wide open pulling on his hair. "Let's go!" Armen yelled. "Let's go!" Sasha finally started moving.

It was early morning when Raffael's phone woke him up.

"Mo, you're not going to fucking believe this, but we were following the Belov woman like you told us and she jumped off a fucking bridge."

"No fucking way."

"Yes. We both saw it."

"She's dead?"

"Yes. There's no way she could have survived it. She knew we were following her, and she flipped us off before going over the railing."

"Stay until it's confirmed it's her."

"I'm sure it was but we'll make sure."

Tony had fallen asleep on the couch after watching Letterman, the TV still on. There was a knock at the door, and he looked out of the living room window to see a cop car in front. He opened the front door to a male and female officer.

"Are you Tony London?" the guy cop asked.

"Yes."

"Can we please come in?"

"Yes, what's wrong?"

"Have a seat." The three of them sat in the living room and Tony turned off the TV.

"Do you know a Tatiana Belov?"

"Yes. Has something happened to her?"

"Does she live here?"

"Yes, she's been staying with me. What's wrong?"

"Do you know why she'd be in the New York City area?"

"She had some business up there," Tony said not wanting to give anything away.

"What kind of business?"

"She is in banking, she's on a work assignment. What's this all about?" Tony said starting to get irritated.

"I'm sorry to tell you this but it appears she's taken her life."

"This must be a mistake. You're telling me she killed herself?"

"Mr. London, she left a suicide note to you on the bridge," the female officer gently added.

"No, no!" Tony yelled out, tears streaming down his face.

"The police in New York have it. They'll want to talk to you. I'm so sorry for your loss."

Tony sat in silence for a couple of hours before crawling into bed and crying himself to sleep.

Tony woke to the phone ringing next to his head.

"Is this Mr. Tony London?"

"Yes, it is." There was a hopeful lilt in his answer.

"I'm Detective Williams," New York City was oozing from his accent. "Were you contacted by your local police department?"

"Yes, late last night."

"So, you know why I'm calling?"

"Yes, I'm hoping you have good news."

"I'm sorry Mr. London, I don't. The only thing I can tell you is Miss Belov's body hasn't been recovered. They are still searching but nothing yet. It's unfortunate but for various reasons, it can take some time before a recovery is made. At this point, I don't want to give you false hope. It's not looking good."

Tony choked up but fought back tears. He had a number of questions about Tatiana's final moments but before they were answered Detective Williams was firing away with his. There was an element of routine to his questions that made them feel cold and unfeeling, an unemotional efficiency about them. The status of their relationship, her state of mind, medical history, drug/alcohol use, why she was in New York, where she was staying, who her employer was, and lastly next of kin.

Shit, Tony thought. I need to tell her mother, but what. Tony's mind was spinning out of control with all the questions he was being asked, all the questions he had, and with everything that needed to be done. Fortunately, the detective abruptly ended the call with a "sorry, I need to run. I'll be in touch later." This did nothing for Tony's spinning head except act as a circuit breaker. None of his questions had been answered which created more questions. He put on his coat and went for a walk along the river.

When Tony returned a little windswept and with ice-cold ears, he fired up the kettle and fixed himself a cup of coffee. He needed to organize his thoughts, or he would go crazy. Just as he sat down on the couch with a pad and paper in hand the phone rang, it was the Hyatt in Manhattan. Tatiana had paid for a night and her things were still there. Tony asked the front desk clerk to hold them, and he'd pick them up or make other arrangements. As soon as he hung the phone up, he called back and told him he would stop by that evening. If nothing else the drive would be a good distraction and he needed items from her purse to try and reach her mother. There would also be the chance to meet with Detective Williams face-to-face. Tony finished his coffee, packed an overnight bag, and was off.

It had been dark for about an hour and a half as two well-built men dressed in black scaled over the brick wall that surrounded Tony's backyard. The lights were out and there wasn't any visible activity.

"He can't be sleeping, it's only 7:00."

"He's had a rough 24 hours, maybe."

The key under the ceramic planter worked and the rear door opened with a slight squeak. The men entered the basement listening for any signs of life. Nothing. The dark living room was empty and after a very slow one step every few seconds the upstairs revealed the same results. No one was home. In the dark, a call was made to relay their findings.

"It can't be," was the response on the other end. "Wait for another couple of hours, maybe he went out for something to eat."

An hour passed and the key was put back, the wall scaled, and the men returned to their car. They sat in the cold for another hour watching the front of the house, but Tony didn't come home.

"This fucks things up," was the response to the update. "Come back, we have to leave. We'll have to come up with a Plan B."

Wednesday, January 15, 1997

Tony woke at the Hyatt and was soon heading to the 44th precinct in the Bronx to meet with Detective Williams. The gloomy day matched his mood as he drove up Harlem River Drive. He had time to gather his thoughts and put together a list of questions he wanted answered. After finally finding parking Tony entered the block-shaped brown-bricked building and informed the officer behind the bulletproof glass that he was there to see Detective Williams. Ten minutes later he appeared and escorted Tony into the guts of the building to a cluttered cubicle.

"How was the drive up?" the detective asked, attempting to be chatty and lighten the mood.

"Okay"

"Unfortunately, I don't have anything new to tell you. We had divers in the river early this morning, but they didn't find her. Mr. London,"

"Please, Tony."

"Tony, based on what you told me yesterday I'm at a loss. When people take their lives there's usually something that sticks out as a factor. Depression, drug use, the loss of a significant other. Nothing like that was going on?"

"No. That's what's got me so confused." Tony made up his mind he wasn't going to tell them about the Russian mafia. He concluded it wouldn't bring her back or change the outcome in any way.

"How long had you been seeing Tatiana?"

"Only about a month, but we've become very close. You know, she's the one. You know what I'm saying?"

"I do. My wife and I dated for only a few months before we tied the knot. You just know."

Detective Williams reached into his desk and gave Tony the suicide note that had been taped on the bridge, asked questions about it, and asked the same questions he'd asked the previous day making some notes. Tony read the note and immediately teared up. As Tony left the station with Detective Williams' hand on his shoulder, he felt that an effort was being made to figure this all out.

Tony got in his car and read the note again.

My Dearest Tony,
It's become unbearable, I can't go on living like this. I know you don't understand but with time things will become clearer. I love you and know we'll be together one day in heaven.
Tatiana

After checking out of the Hyatt with Tatiana's purse and carry-on bag Tony was now cruising through the Lincoln Tunnel on his way home. The drive back with the radio off was a long one. There had been a hope that this was all a mistake and Tatiana would be in the passenger seat for the return trip. Tony was in a fog on the way back and it concluded with the realization Tatiana was gone.

"Tony, Tony. You can't do that here."

"What."

"Tony. You were asleep on the bar."

"No, I wasn't. I just closed my eyes for a minute."

"You were snoring. Time to call it a night."

"Sorry, Nick."

Tony paid his tab and made his way out of Chadwick's, one of his local haunts, and headed home. It was the fourth night of overindulging, and the pain wasn't lessening. He had called Mikheil and broke the upsetting news to him. He took it well, but he wondered how many drunken nights were in his future after he passed along the horrible news to Tatiana's mother.

Tony stumbled upstairs and crawled into bed; he had been out for a couple of hours when his arms were pulled behind his back and handcuffs tightened on his wrists.

"What the fuck?" he got out, then duct tape covered his mouth and everything got blacker when the hood went on. He was lifted out of the bed, one person lifting under his arms, another at his now tied feet. Tony struggled, fell to the floor, and was picked back up. Soon he was out in the chilly night air, put in the trunk of a car, a blanket thrown on him, the lid slammed and they were off. This is it Tony was thinking. First, they threw Tatiana off a bridge and now they're going to kill me.

An hour later the trunk popped open, Tony could tell it was just starting to get light outside. There was a familiar smell in the air, it took him a minute to figure out it was airplane fuel. He was being put into the back of a small plane. Where the fuck are they taking me? The plane fired up, the cabin began to get warm, and he felt a jab in his ass. He felt woozy, everything went dark.

"How is it here?" Tony said to Tatiana who was coming into focus and stroking his hair.

"You are going to love it."

"I missed you, baby."

"I missed you too."

"Is heaven everything you expected?"

"Do you think you're in heaven?" Tatiana asked Tony in his dreamlike state.

"It is, isn't it?"

"No, you are in Cozumel, silly."

"You're not dead?"

"Nope and neither are you."

With his eyes wide open now Tony asked, "what's going on?"

"Tony, it's all right. I didn't die."

"But the police were at my house. You jumped off the bridge."

"No, no. I'm so sorry to have put you through that. I didn't jump off the bridge, well technically I did but I didn't hit the water."

"What are you saying?"

"I faked my death. I had to make the bratva think I was dead; they were never going to leave me alone. I bungeed off the bridge and as I was going off Troy, my stunt coordinator friend threw a dummy of me into the water. He had the dummy attached to a line and he later fished it out. At least for now, it's a suicide without the body being recovered."

"Do you know what I went through, what your mother and Mikheil went through?"

"Tony, I'm sorry, I'm so sorry," Tatiana said hugging Tony and showering him with kisses. Jacques, who was now reunited with his mama, watched all of this from the foot of the bed. "I talked to Mikheil; he knew the plan before you called. How are you feeling?"

"Like I've been at a three-day rave. What is it like here?"

"It's like heaven."

The End

...for now.

Made in the USA
Middletown, DE
14 February 2023

24805166R00215